# CHEAT
# THE
# DEVIL

A Cat Austen Mystery

by
## Jane Rubino

A Write Way Publishing Book

Other Cat Austen mysteries by Jane Rubino:

*Death of a DJ*
*Fruitcake*

"This light and darkness in our chaos join'd,
What shall divide? The God within the mind.
Extremes in nature equal ends produce,
In man they join to some mysterious use;
Tho' each by turns the other's bound invade,
As, in some well-wrought picture, light and shade,
And oft so mix, the diff'rence is too nice
Where ends the virtue or begins the vice."

—Alexander Pope
*An Essay on Man*, Epistle II

For Ann Buccieri Rubino
and
Lois Rubino Sutton

## PROLOGUE

"To present fears."

Cat Austen murmured the toast aloud as the rims of their champagne glasses exchanged a crystalline kiss.

Victor raised his dark brows, and Cat blushed, offered an apologetic smile. "*Macbeth*. 'Present fears are less than horrible imaginings.'"

"Then here's to Shakespeare and to the dwindling ranks well-read enough to quote him." Victor replied. *Macbeth*. What was that line, *There's no art to find the mind's construction in the face?* Considerable art in concealing it, though; one that he had mastered. As deftly, it seemed, as Cat concealed the workings of her heart. He had persuaded himself that six relatively uneventful weeks separating the prospect of San Juan from a perilous Christmas would acclimate her to the shift in their relationship that a, well, honeymoon implied. But here it was, mid-February and she still conveyed no sentiment for their trip save for the quiet martyrdom of one enduring the present fears and shutting her mind to the horrible imaginings. Making him feel like a reprobate without saying a word; Marisol had had that talent, too. Perhaps all women did. Still, Cat never flat out asked him to call it off. She had a resolute streak that bound her to a promise, even to one granted in haste and desperately regretted.

Eye-to-eye across one of Carolina's dozen tables, Cat saw the candle flame reflected in his dark gaze, glowing vertical pupils, flickering like the eyes of some predatory cat. *He wants to own me,* she thought, suddenly. *Devour me.*

"What are you thinking, love?" *I'd like to know what you're thinking, Cat Austen. I'd like it very much.* He had said that to her on their first date, what? Three months ago? Meant it then, meant it now, and was no closer to discovering it. Further, perhaps.

"Oh, work," she hedged. "But for a change it's worrying about scheduling my assignments—that's assign*ments*, plural, mind you—rather than not having a single one."

"Nothing crucial's come up, has it?" Knowing it hadn't, but offering her an escape hatch, nonetheless.

Cat shook her head. "I've finished the piece on Jim's Coffee Shoppe—Nancy got a terrific exterior shot that I think Ritchie might use. And I promised Ritchie a couple travel pieces on Puerto Rico for the *Chronicle*. Then I'm supposed to meet up with that *CopWatch* writer next week and *CopWatch* itself should be good for five or six pieces at least. But nothing immediate. I'm all—" she broke off and looked at her menu. *Yours.*

Victor laid down his menu, put his hand over hers. Valentine's day. She was wearing the dress she had worn on their first date, a slim black velvet with a low neckline. *You don't know what it's like to get absorbed by someone else's life,* she had said to him. *You lost your wife. You never lost yourself.* Two months ago, at the onset of the Sterling business, a month after they had met. *Three short months,* he reflected. *Would it kill him to wait a little longer?*

Why wait, when he knew what he wanted?

*Because she doesn't. And you're trying to rush her into an intimacy she's not prepared to undertake, knowing she doesn't regard sex casually, knowing that once she's committed, she would never retreat. Why don't you trust her enough to let her choose freely?*

"Mats doesn't want us to go."

"I thought he was okay with it," Victor said, though he could not deny Mats' coolness on his last few visits.

Cat shook her head. "I've gone over it every day and we count out the days on the calendar, but I think he's probably remembering when I was in the hospital."

"Why don't I come by early tomorrow and talk to him?"

The waiter came to take their orders and Cat set aside her reply to methodically instruct him in the poaching of her salmon, the amount of salt to be added to the steamed spinach and to inform him that by no means was dried dill to be used in her puree of carrot soup. Victor smiled at the waiter's bobbing head, wondered if her high-school Spanish would be sufficient to hector the Puerto Rican waiters or if he would be enlisted to translate.

"Did I ever tell you," he remarked, when the man had retreated, "that one of the first crime scenes I ever came upon when I joined the force was in a restaurant? Vespasian's out on the Black Horse Pike. The killer was a restaurant critic. Said the chef had put the garlic into the blender when he pureed his pesto."

Cat took a tentative sip of the Dom Perignon Victor had brought. Carolina's was BYOB. "You're supposed to mince and sauté the garlic and put it in after you mix the pesto."

"That's what *he* said. It was the basis of his defense, in fact."

"FDA approved pestocide," Cat commented, gravely. "FDA stands for the Fortunati Dining Authority, incidentally."

It was the side of her personality he liked best, that ability to come up with the capricious underside to the commonplace or the sinister; knew that another day, some other facet would emerge and that would be his favorite.

He drew a long narrow box from his breast pocket. "Happy Valentine's Day."

Obviously not a ring, but still she hesitated. "Victor, please don't ..."

"If you don't like it, I can take it back."

"I'm sure I'll like it."

He pushed the box across the table and Cat's fingers picked at the grosgrain ribbon cautiously. It was a necklace, a garnet pendant in the shape of a heart, suspended from a gold chain. Cat lifted it from the velvet lining and fastened it around her throat, fumbling a little with the clasp. The diamond-cut chain was short, dropping the heart over the hollow of her throat. The faceted garnets pulsed against her pale flesh, candlelight reflected as blood-red fire.

Cat felt a sudden weight as though the necklace were a shackle. She didn't want to go to San Juan. She wished something would happen to intervene. Anything. Anything.

Short of murder, of course.

## CHAPTER ONE

Friday morning, Cat woke before dawn, her gaze sliding toward the digital clock on her night table. Four and a half hours until her—*their*—flight.

Cat hesitated. The lull that had followed the commotion last Christmas had almost convinced her that the Dudek killing, and the bizarre conspiracy involving the upper echelon at the Sterling casino, were freak storms in her tranquil sphere, gales that charged through a sheltered harbor, then dissipated without leaving a trace. She had told herself that it was only the dead cold of January that had ground down her stamina, reduced the five weekly runs to three, then two. The epiphany came one day as she battled an icy mist blown horizontally from the sea, cold air searing her trachea. Her throat had thickened with panic, frigid sweat iced over her heart and Cat had stumbled onto a bench, her gasps audible, and knew that it wasn't the weather pounding her into surrender. It was Victor. Would they have come together if Ron Spivak hadn't lost his nose and the Jerry Dudek interview, stranding Cat with Dudek when he'd been shot?

Dudek's violent death had brought both danger and love back into her life, when she had thought she was done with them for good. Cat was not indifferent to irony of it, nor to the conflicts it had kindled, nor to the periodic tremors of well-bred-Catholic-girl guilt.

She mounted Ocean City's boardwalk at the north end, broke into a tentative trot, shut her mind to anxiety. She actually liked running this time of year when Ocean City was free of the seasonal crowd, when she didn't have to dodge the bikers, the skateboarders, the walkers, the casual athletes who choked the boardwalk in the summer. She played Rorschach with the clouds, mentally drafted an interview with that television writer, estimated the number of stories she could eke out of the *CopWatch* shoot in the spring. She thought of everything but the flight to San Juan, leaving in less than four hours.

Cat bounded up the back stairs, unlocked the door. In the cramped passage, she pried off her running shoes and kicked them into the pantry, pulled off hat and gloves, padded into the kitchen. Ellice was sitting at the table, reading the morning paper. A wide headband pushed her short glossy hair away from her face; her dark sloe eyes peered from a white facial mask.

"Mats still asleep?" Cat asked. He had awakened in the night again, called out for his mother.

Ellice nodded. "I got up to grab the phone. Don't worry, Cat, Freddy and I will keep him so busy mucking around in the apartment, the weekend'll be over before he knows you're gone."

Ellice Watson was engaged to Cat's brother Freddy; they had proposed renovating the ground floor apartment of Cat's three-story house; after the wedding, Freddy would give up his efficiency and Ellice would move downstairs, a proposal that Cat gratefully accepted.

"Who called this early?" Cat checked the clock. Seven-thirty. She poured some coffee from the pot, cupped her hands around the mug.

"Ritchie Landis."

"What does he want? He knows I'm out of town for four days." Landis was the editor of *South Jersey* magazine; he'd recently acquired a collection of local weeklies, harnessed them under the common banner of *The Cape-Atlantic Chronicle* and prepared to launch the first edition in a week.

"Not according to him. What I could amend and adapt to conform to conventional speech seemed to suggest that something major is up and he's wagering your trip is off."

*Something has happened to Victor.* Cat felt a dead chill sneak over her ribs, close in on her heart.

"There's nothing in here," Ellice nodded to the papers on the table. "Maybe the *CopWatch* crew is coming to town ahead of schedule."

"No, I would have heard from that producer, Steinmetz. She's been trying to set me up with their writer." Cat picked up the phone, dialed Victor's number, got his machine.

Mats padded into the room, his brown eyes wide, mournful. He leaned against Cat's leg, wordlessly, laying his head against the damp cotton sweats. Cat hung up the receiver, reached down and tousled his hair, trying to shake off the sense of dread.

"Is it time for you to go yet?"

"Not yet." Cat set down her cup and lifted him into her arms. "Do you want me to make you some breakfast?"

"I'm not hungry." His thumb crept toward his mouth.

Cat looked over his head at Ellice, blinked hard.

"Don't you want to help Uncle Freddy and me paint?" Ellice tempted. "You get to use the roller all by yourself."

Mats clung to his mother's shoulders, looked at Ellice. "Did you paint on your face?"

"I'm tryin' white, whaddaya think?"

"I liked you brown how you was. I like it when things stay how they is."

"I'm going to take a shower." *And page Victor and call it off. If something hadn't already happened to call it off.*

"Can I come upstairs with you?"

"Okay, sweetie. You can watch my little TV."

Cat carried Mats upstairs and set him on the unmade bed. She crawled across the rumpled spread and reached for the phone, dialed Victor's number again, preparing the announcement in her head. *Victor—something's come up.* No. *Vic-*

*tor, I haven't had sex in two years, eight and a half months and it's not like riding a bike.* Lame. *Victor, my son needs me.*

"Victor, my son needs me," she whispered. The phone rang three times before his recorded, no-nonsense voice kicked in again. *He's in the shower. Gone out for a morning jog.* Cat hung up, her mind flashing back to that April Saturday, Carlo and Vinnie on the front porch, and she saw it in their eyes even before Carlo said, "Babe, he's gone."

The phone rang and Cat jumped, grabbed the receiver in mid-ring. "Cat! Cat!"

"What is it, Ritchie?"

"You can start unpackin' is what."

Cat swallowed. *Victor's been hurt.* "Why?"

"I don't know, which means something's up, big time."

"If you don't know something, it might also mean there's nothing to know," Cat suggested.

"Trust me, somethin's goin' down."

"'Thou shalt not go up and down as a talebearer among thy people,'" Cat quoted, settling onto the bed. Dom had said that, the last time she had gone to Mass and that was what—three years ago? It had been this time of year, Lent, and Chris had gone with her, a couple weeks before he died.

"Talebearer's what I do for a livin'. Listen up. Over Atlantic City? Cops got a block up New York Avenue roped off around some low-rent condos between Mediterranean an' Baltic. Cops shut down New York two blocks on each side."

Cat closed her eyes, brought Atlantic City's geography into focus. New York Avenue bisected Atlantic City. Between Mediterranean and Baltic would not be near the casinos, the Boardwalk, Gardiner's Basin, not near anything, really. Except, it was, Cat realized, about five blocks from St. Agnes Church and St. Agnes Primary School. Her brother Dominic was the parish priest.

"They got the crime scene unit over there and I heard there's a call in to the DA. This ain't no drive-by and my gut's tellin' me Loverboy's vaycay's bein' revoked even as we speak. I'm on the scanner, but I think maybe they're switchin' channels 'cause they don't wanna share. I'm gonna fiddle with it, I'll call you back."

"What if I'm not here?"

"You'll be there."

Cat hung up and plumped up the pillows on the bed, got Mats settled in front of an old *I Love Lucy* episode, tried Victor's number again, got his machine again. She went into the shower, stepping over the suitcases heaped with summer clothes. Something *had* happened; Ritchie was a gnat, but as with all insects, his instincts were acute. And his snitches were reliable. Probably, Cat theorized, raising her face to the hot spray, because he paid them better than he paid his writers. Victor hadn't had time off in over a year. He had waited until Stan Rice was back from medical leave, prepped his unit thoroughly for his four-day absence. What could come up that would require him to postpone? Something that hadn't made the papers. Something more than a simple murder. If murder was ever simple.

Cat stepped out of the shower and dried off, wrapped a towel around her hair and pulled on a threadbare terry cloth robe. She sat on the edge of the bed, reached for the phone once more. "What's Lucy up to?" she asked Mats.

"She's gotta wrap these candies an' it's goin' too fast and they're eatin' 'em."

Cat lifted the receiver on the phone, dialed Major Crimes, got a dispatcher, identified herself, which got her an immediate and courteous "Yes, Mrs. Austen, the lieutenant has been called out. Have you tried his car phone?" The courtesy was a tribute to her brother, Carlo. There wasn't a law enforcement officer in the state who would knowingly treat the sister of Carlo Fortunati, New Jersey's top cop (retired) with less than impeccable politeness.

"No."

"Well, he may have reached the scene by now. I could beep him for you if it's an emergency."

Which Cat decoded as she would beep him *only* if it was

an emergency. "No, it's not terribly urgent. Please don't bother him, but if he checks in, could you tell him I called?"

"Yes, Mrs. Austen."

Cat hung up. Her fingers were shaking as she ran them through Mats' hair. *Victor isn't hurt.* "Baby, guess what?"

"What?"

"Mommy's not going to Puerto Rico after all."

The unconcealed joy in his expression broke her heart. How could she have been so selfish to think of leaving him him for four whole days?

Mats looked up at her. "Will Victor be mad at me?" Blaming himself for the alteration in plans.

"Don't be silly, baby. It's Victor's idea."

Victor had been locked into a dream when the phone rang before seven. The dream co-starred him, Cat; the content carried a borderline NC-17. Padre Vargas would have rebuked him for impure thoughts, nailed him with nine, ten Hail Marys on the low end for what had been going through Victor's mind.

The ringing phone touched off an equivocal sense that the dream would not materialize; he knew it for sure when he heard Jean Adane's quiet, "I'm sorry, sir."

"What and where?"

Adane recited the address. Victor scanned his mental layout of Atlantic City's precarious geography. In the years between the move from San Juan and his father's murder, the town had remained comfortably, seedily stable, was well into decline when he returned to join the force. Now it was like some restive volcanic isle, morphing, shifting, every week something being bought up, boarded up, built or burned. An obliterated this was replaced by a bigger that, condensing some pockets of decay, renovating others, erasing still others entirely. "Meet me there," he ordered and heard the note of surprise in her "Yes, sir."

The address Adane had named was one of the areas where

a respectable façade had been slapped onto a neighborhood on the downslide. Mediterranean and Baltic (the two cheapest properties on the game board, Victor reflected, cynically) cut off New York Avenue at the midsection. The barricade was a block below Baltic, at the intersection of New York and Arctic. Victor parked his car next to a ramshackle grocery—*Grocery* painted onto the board covering the sole window—and showed his badge to the cop.

"I can let you drive up, Lieutenant."

"That's all right, I'll walk." Victor saw, a half block down, a pair of black and whites; a half dozen uniforms; a black sedan, Kurt Raab standing beside it; a white crime lab van; Adane talking to a female in uniform; a young woman weeping into a crumpled tissue.

They were huddled in front of a tan block of apartments, side-by-side units with brown railings, brown shutters, narrow concrete paths leading up to a concrete step in front of the recessed front doors. Mail slots, though here and there a tenant had affixed a cheap mailbox under the low-wattage light; square patches on either side of the narrow walks filled in with gravel.

It was the only structure on the block; the rear view beyond a small deck or patio was thirty feet of jagged earth that extended all the way to Tennessee Avenue. Across Tennessee was what appeared to be a long-defunct commercial bakery, a charity clinic housed in a low, single-story building, and a fairly new high-rise on the corner of Tennessee and Baltic.

Victor completed his cursory survey of the area, approached Adane and her companion. The female cop looked up; she was black, with a plump, compact figure and suspicious eyes, Sergeant's stripes. Kurt Raab, his coat buttoned, a muffler drawn up to his ears, intercepted Victor. "I'm sorry. I'm sorry about this. I need you to get a look at this."

"The woman a witness?" Victor nodded to the weeping girl.

"Friend of the deceased. She says she and the vic—victim's name is Oliva, Carmen Oliva—work for the same temp agency, place called Business Briefs. They find out they live a couple blocks from each other, go to the same church, they started hanging out. Last time she saw the victim was Tuesday, some church dinner."

"Three days ago."

"Yeah. The vic's temping at some bank all this week. Thursday the friend, DeLuca"—Raab jerked his head toward the girl—"she calls over the bank, they tell her the past two days Oliva never came in, never called. The friend calls here, gets the machine, figures maybe Oliva's sick or something. She comes by this morning 'cause they're supposed to go to a friend's funeral, she says. She sees a couple days' mail stuffed in the box, tries the door, you know, like how you just turn the knob without thinking? Not locked. DeLuca goes in, finds the Oliva woman, runs out, calls nine-one-one from a pay phone down the block. They tell her to wait at the scene. First officer"—he nodded to one of the men standing on the graveled lawn area—"checks it out, the woman's obviously dead. Been dead a day at least."

"The door wasn't locked?" Victor ran his thumb through his mustache, pensively. "Are there other doors?"

"Back door off the kitchen, sliding patio door off the bedroom."

"Were they locked?"

"Yeah. So're the windows." Raab tugged up his muffler. "I don't wanna say anything more, I just want to let you take a look inside, then you tell me if, God help us, you're thinking what I'm thinking."

## CHAPTER TWO

Victor took the clipboard from the first officer, scribbled his name on the sign-in sheet, looked at the names above his, turned to the female sergeant. "Sergeant Moore?"

"That's right."

"Ernestine and I went through the Academy together, sir," Adane offered. She hung back, not sure of her status, her face pale against the upturned collar of her blue coat.

"You've been inside?"

"He went in," she nodded to the officer holding the clipboard. "Mr. Raab told the rest of us to hold off. I took a peek. There's a small entry, then right into the living room. She's on the floor. Looks to be a kitchen on the right, bedroom's in back."

"You checked the body?" He was speaking to the first officer, but his eyes were scanning the crowd forming at the barricade down the block.

"Yes, sir."

"Look around the house?"

"Only to see if there was someone else inside."

"Touch the body?"

"No, sir. She's ... she was obviously dead."

"Touch anything else?"

"No, Lieutenant."

Victor looked at the man's hands, ungloved.

"They won't pull my prints off anything. Sir."

"Excellent. Was the porch light on when you got here?"

"No."

"Did you touch it to see whether it was warm?"

Raab cleared his throat.

"I said I didn't touch anything."

"I just meant that if it was still warm, it might have been turned off or burned out recently. Where's her car?"

Adane spoke up. "Her girlfriend, Miss DeLuca, says the victim didn't own a car. There isn't any off-street parking here. Miss DeLuca says Miss Oliva usually used the jitneys or walked to get to her jobs."

Victor nodded. "Ask the crime lab if they could spare some gloves and something to cover our shoes. For Sergeant Moore here, too."

Moore looked surprised, suspicious, as though Victor had announced a pop quiz. Adane handed them each a pair of Latex gloves, woven paper booties. Victor donned them and opened the door, allowed the ladies to pass through ahead of him.

The three of them stood on a small square of linoleum. The apartment appeared to have been shut up for a couple days, the heat set around seventy. The heavy, rotting metal scent of blood hung in the air with the pungency of decay lurking, poised to overpower.

The foyer opened into a small living area. Victor glanced right to the dining area and kitchenette. An archway that cut through the living room wall exposed an abbreviated corridor that led to the single bedroom and bath. There were a pair of shoes in the foyer, lying over a floor vent, an umbrella propped against the wall.

Carmen Oliva lay in the living room behind a love seat, but it was not the pair of slender calves, stockinged, slippered feet that seized their attention, it was the blood. Everywhere. Walls, archway, love seat, carpet, all washed in blood, blood that had mingled with the mottled earth tones of the love seats, lacquered the walls, glazed the glass-topped table with a translucent crust.

Victor stepped onto the carpeted living area, moved a few paces into the room, looked over his shoulder. His covered shoe left no imprint on the low nap of the cheap carpet. Weak early sun penetrated the sheer curtains covering the front window and illuminated the irregular red-brown splashes on the opposite wall, the dark patches crusting on the pale rug.

Victor moved toward the love seat, stood over the victim. Carmen Oliva lay on her side. She wore a navy skirt, a white blouse, navy cardigan sweater. Her dark hair was primly braided down her back. Her skin had settled to a colorless paste. She was too small, it seemed, to generate that massive an amount of blood, but Victor detected the wound, barely an inch in diameter, the carotid expertly severed, and he knew that all the blood had come from her.

*Evidence*, Victor reminded himself, part of his silent mantra when approaching a particularly grim crime scene. *Their pain is over with, they're nothing but evidence now. You have to treat her like a piece of a puzzle.* He wondered what the face had looked like when it was animated, saw an arched eyebrow, a delicate cleft in the chin, full-lipped mouth, remnants of beauty. He squatted a couple feet from the corpse.

"There was mail in the box, you say?"

"Looked to be two, three days' worth," Moore said. "Ads mostly, a bill or two. It's been bagged."

"The witness said they were together Tuesday night?"

"Yeah, they go to church a couple blocks from here. Some kinda pot luck, pancake dinner, Tuesday night."

"The friend called her Wednesday?"

"Thursday." Nettled, knew she was being tested.

Victor backed up to the phone on a small table next to an upholstered chair. He saw a digital 4 on the answering machine, pushed the PLAY button with his gloved finger.

The first message was a woman from the victim's agency,

asking why Carmen hadn't reported for work. The second message was the same, irritated, asking the girl to please call in. The third was Miss DeLuca: "Carmen, it's me, Donna. What's up, girlfriend? They tell me you been outta work two days. Gimme a call, I can give you a ride to the funeral Friday."

The fourth was a man's voice, tremulous, frail. "I guess you're out ... I just wanted to thank you for the ... well, for everything." There was a pause, as though he had thought about saying more, decided against it.

The tape ended.

"Oliva ..." Sergeant Moore muttered. She padded onto the living room carpet, looked down at the corpse, swallowed. "Carmen Oliva."

"You know her?" Victor asked.

"I think when I was with vice she got busted once. Carmen Oliva. Yeah. I remember now, because it was Jimmy Easter who bailed her. Must've been a year or more."

"She was one of Easter's women?" Victor asked. James Easter operated a pair of successful enterprises, an escort service that attracted high income clientele and a lingerie boutique where customers could request live modeling of the scanty and provocative attire. Regarding Easter's proper designation, opinions varied; some said entrepreneur, some said pimp.

"I don't know if she was one of his; I only know he bailed her."

"But it doesn't appear she's with him now."

"Guess not."

Victor sensed Adane's ripple of alarm, but Victor's automatic "Don't guess, Sergeant," was calmly polite. "What is it, Printemps?"

"That's the escort service. It's French for spring. Like 'spring chickens.'"

"Underage?"

Moore shook her head. "Just damn young. The undie shop's called Nothing Sacred. You think she went in business for herself? Guy on the phone could be a john."

"Perhaps. Sergeant, I'd like you to make note of everything I do, anything I might touch or remove, understood?"

"Yeah. We get it at least once a month now in muster. Messin' with the crime scene, no contact without contamination, penalties for evidence plantin', all of it."

Victor nodded. "How are you doing, Adane?"

"I'm fine, sir."

"Tell me what you've concluded, please."

"According to Miss DeLuca, the victim was alive Tuesday night. At a social function, so we should be able to get confirmation. Miss DeLuca states that she gave the victim a ride home, dropped her off between eight-thirty and nine. It appears that Miss Oliva was alive at least through Wednesday morning."

"How so?"

"Her shoes." Adane pointed to the shoes over the vent. "There was no precipitation Tuesday evening, but it began to sleet after midnight; by Wednesday daylight it changed over to rain. Those shoes? There are water stains on the leather, and a little mud. That and the umbrella suggest she had gone out in the rain, came back, took off her shoes and placed them over the vent to dry. Most likely because she was going to wear them again when she went out to work. Her clothing appears to be conventional office attire."

"Very sound, Adane. Where did she go Wednesday morning?"

"Coulda been anywhere," Moore offered. "Out for a paper, cup of coffee."

"I don't think so," Adane said, hesitantly. "I think for a paper or a cup of coffee, she would have put on any old shoes, not one of her better pairs."

Victor nodded, motioned for the women to move around the love seat, face the body from his angle. He removed a pen from his pocket, slipped it under the victim's dark bangs, exposed the forehead. Even on the dead flesh, the trace of a black smudge was evident.

"Ashes," said Moore, heavily. "She went to church."

Victor nodded. "Wednesday was Ash Wednesday. The closest church in the area is St. Agnes. If her idea of an evening out with a friend was what was probably a Shrove Tuesday supper, it's likely she was enough of a churchgoer to receive her ashes Wednesday morning." He had run over to St. Bernadette's in Northfield to receive his own on the way to work. "Perhaps attend an early Mass. She came back home for breakfast, was killed shortly after she arrived."

"Walked in on a B and E?" Moore hypothesized.

Victor glanced around the room. "No sign of forced entry. Nothing appears disturbed. We'll check her bedroom, but the place doesn't look as if it's been ransacked. Her TV and VCR are untouched. And she had time to take off her coat, change into bedroom slippers, so it doesn't appear that she was surprised when she entered her home."

There was a single small bedroom. Pine furniture camouflaged with maple stain, a towel and robe tossed across the bed. Sliding glass doors overlooked an eight-by-ten concrete patio. The doors were locked, the curtains drawn. Victor lifted the lid of a carved wooden jewelry box with his pen. A few pairs of gold earrings, several chains, 14K and silver, a pearl stickpin and a pair of enamel combs. He let the lid fall, backed out of the room, cut across the living room into the dining area, the kitchenette.

The kitchen door was locked, the deadbolt in place. A small square table was wedged into a corner, a single wooden chair beside it. A purse was slung over the back of the chair. Victor opened it, prodded at the contents with his pen, lifted out the wallet. A Visa card, thirty-two dollars and change. Victor showed it to the women, replaced the wallet in the purse, glanced around. A calendar was tacked to the wall, the sort run off by a local printer for fund-raisers, this one from St. Agnes Church. Victor noticed the words "PSL 8:45-4:45" with a line that went through the week. "PSL?"

"Pacific Savings and Loan, maybe," Moore offered. "I'll

call the temp agency—Business Briefs? See if they scheduled her to work there this week."

Victor noticed a notation on the Tuesday square: "Dinner w/Donna, St. A's 6 PM." "The friend, Donna? How long have they known each other?"

"I think she said they met when Oliva signed up with Business Briefs, some time last summer."

Victor turned his attention to the sink, drainboard, counters: clean. The room's single window was over the sink, bracketed by shelves, a fragile blue-and-white teapot on the sill. On one side, the shelves held a couple cheap knicknacks, on the other a white porcelain teapot, sugar bowl, creamer. The top shelf was empty.

Victor stared at the arrangement for a moment. Then, reaching over the sink, he lifted the blue-and-white teapot with one index finger through the handle, one under the spout, examined the ledge. He set it back on the sill, braced his hands on the counter and bounded, landing on his knees on the countertop, which put him eye level with the uppermost shelf. His expression revealed nothing as he hopped down.

"I want you to look at the top shelf, Adane," he said. "I'll give you a boost."

Adane looked a bit startled, as if Cardenas had breached his characteristic decorum, but as Victor put his hands on her waist, she gave an obedient hop and landed in a kneeling position, straining to peer at the surface of the shelf. Victor kept one hand on her elbow, asked. "You see it?"

Adane's blue eyes widened and a faint smile crept over her placid features.

"What's the deal?" Moore asked.

Victor lifted Adane down. "The teapot—" He nodded to the one on the ledge over the sink. "She kept it on the top shelf. It's the good one, the one she didn't use often. Didn't dust the upper shelves, either, because there's a clean circle about the diameter of the bottom of that blue-and-white pot— smaller than the bottom of the plain one there. She would have had to make an effort to get at it."

"Usin' the company china," Moore interpreted.

"Correct."

Victor opened the cabinet under the sink, pulled out a plastic-lined trash container, one-third full. He shook it, frowning, put it back into place and took out a penlight, clicked it on and flashed it into the garbage disposal. He pushed his gloved fingers into the disposal, then drew his hand out slowly. "This—" He held out his index finger. "Loose tea?"

Moore and Adane examined the brown shreds on his gloved fingertips. "Or tobacco," Moore said.

Victor tore a sheet from the roll of paper towels under a cabinet, rubbed his fingertips onto it. "Have the crime lab bag and analyze this. Tobacco rarely winds up down a garbage disposal, Sergeant," he suggested.

"I don't get it. You sayin' she invites the doer over for tea?"

"Or he drops in," Victor replied. "Forming a provisional hypothesis is a good mental exercise, as long as it conforms to the facts and as long as you're flexible enough to adapt it if new facts come your way. Carmen Oliva may or may not have been one of Jimmy Easter's, but it doesn't look like she's living the life now. Works for a temp agency, possibly with a week's assignment at Pacific Savings and Loan." He looked at Adane. "Check to see who supplied her references. She goes out Tuesday night, Wednesday morning she goes to church, gets her ashes, comes home. She's got some time before she's going out again, so she takes off her good shoes, puts on house slippers. Someone drops by, someone she knows well enough to invite in and likes enough to get down the good teapot. They have their tea, she has to get to work, she cleans up. No," Victor paused, his face a mask of concentration. "He cleans up. Maybe while she's getting ready for work. She's showing him to the door, they're talking. She does not feel threatened." Victor paused. "He, on the other hand—I'll say he for the sake of simplicity—he knows what he's come for. He's come to kill her. She never sees it coming and he does it quickly. I didn't see any defensive wounds on her hands. A cut like that? Sever the carotid? It's very quick."

He had led them back to the living room. "They stood here"—he put a hand under Adane's elbow as he spoke—"like this. Talking. Maybe he's saying goodbye, walks around like he's headed for the door." Victor walked around Adane, slipping the penlight out of his pocket as he spoke. "No tension, she's perfectly relaxed, unsuspecting. Then—" Victor cupped his hand under Adane's jaw, arched her neck back, brought up his right hand and flicked the penlight across the side of her throat.

He heard Moore hyperventilating. "Jesus. That was fast, Lieutenant."

"She would be immobilized immediately. Arterial spray—" He released Adane, directed his pen light at the opposite wall. "He lets her drop, bleed out and he walks out the door. Neighborhood's not well populated, early morning, bad weather, no one's out. He has no trouble getting away undetected."

"Why didn't he lock it?" Moore asked.

"I don't know. But since he's made no effort to alter or hide the body, or disguise what he's done, we can conclude he doesn't care that she'll be found eventually. I'd be more interested to know why he bothered to clean up the tea things, cups and so forth."

"Why do you think he did it, sir?" Adane asked.

"There's nothing left out, nothing's even left on the drainboard. Which means, someone put things away, but didn't know where everything went."

"You think he cleaned up after he did her?" Moore asked.

Victor shrugged. "Or 'you get ready for work, I'll clean up.'"

"Lull her into a sense of security?" Moore suggested.

"Why would she feel insecure?" Adane countered. "She invited him in, she offered him tea."

Someone knocked "shave-and-a-haircut" on the door. The ME poked his head in. "How ya' doin', Cardenas? Ladies." He dropped his medical bag on the floor inside the front door, pulled on a pair of paper booties, Latex gloves. "This is how I like 'em, before breakfast. Get called away from dessert, that's when I get cranky." He pointed to the wall. "Someone's done an Old Faithful, huh? What is it, carotid?"

"So it appears."

"Mary Louise wannid to take this one, she's always tellin' me how only on TV does the ME show up on the scene, how I oughta just hole up in the cooler, send out my flunkies. Last time I didn't show was that suicide over Arctic and Miss? Guy's anatomy's a little shaky, the shot goes in but it doesn't exit, kinda takes a detour, winds up stuck in the vic's Eustachian tube and they're lifting him onto the sheet and ping, it drops out his ear and Keith, he don't know what to do, so he grabs the slug and"—the ME pointed his index finger at his left ear, made a corkscrew motion—"jams it back in."

He padded over to the body, knelt down, examined the small incision on the throat. "Nice job. This one musta aced his anatomy, ya gotta respect a guy takes time to do his homework. Forty-eight hours is my best guess until I get her over Decedent Ops. This neighborhood? You can lay around weeks before anyone comes by picks up the scent. What's this on the forehead? Ashes? She Cath'lic? Maybe someone oughtta call a priest, you think?"

Victor had an uncomfortable sensation, as the facts hooked up. A priest. Calendar from St. Agnes. She went to St. Agnes Church. Dominic Fortunati was a priest there. Cat's brother. Then, Cat! What time was it?

Victor checked his watch. He hadn't talked to Cat. Under three hours to their flight. He had to get to a phone.

"I got it! I got it!" the ME cried.

"Doctor?" Victor asked.

"Back December. There were two of 'em together, remember? Immigrant gal and another one. Both like this one, young, dark-haired gals. Same MO, single cut to the carotid. You know what I'm talking about, Cardenas, remember? File's gotta still be open, 'cause you guys never made an arrest."

"Yes, I remember," Victor said and then he knew what Raab had been thinking and realized that it didn't matter what time it was, because he wasn't going anywhere.

## CHAPTER THREE

Victor emerged from the house, peeling off the Latex gloves. He glanced down New York, saw a cluster of vehicles at the barricade, NewsLine90's van parallel-parked on Arctic, a reporter twirling her hand mike impatiently, the cameraman tap dancing off the chill.

Raab approached, keeping his back to the lens. "So you see what I'm thinking, Victor? I'm sorry—"

Victor shook his head. "It's all right. My plans can be postponed. Long's been working with ACPD on the two women, the file's open on them."

"The media, it's a 'no comment.' I don't want it released that we have—may have—three related murders and the killer's at large. That jerk Landis over *South Jersey* mag, he bought up those seasonal weeklies were goin' down the tubes, callin' 'em the *Cape Atlantic Chronicle*. He gets ahold of this, I'm lookin' at *Seaside Slasher Strikes Three.*" Raab halted, checked for eavesdroppers.

"Understood."

"I'll give the word to the ME, the crime-lab people, of course, but some of those characters in criminalistics—"

"I'm sure they understand the need for discretion," Victor said, his eyes roaming the crowd. "I'll have Adane interview the DeLuca woman, keep the press from getting to her right away. Does Oliva have next of kin?"

"Not that I'm aware."

"There's something else."

"'Something else' as in 'get out the Maalox'?"

"There was a call on the answering machine. A man, thanking Oliva for something. Jogged Sergeant Moore's memory. She says Oliva may have worked for one of James Easter's operations, got picked up for soliciting sometime back, Easter bailed her out."

"The vic's a pro?" Raab said, incredulously. "I'm not buyin' that. Easter's women live better than this. Unless she went solo, runnin' an out-call from here."

"Moore suggested the same thing."

"It wouldn't be a first."

Victor shook his head. "Working a nine-to-five, a church-goer? She had ashes on her forehead, looks like she went to church Wednesday morning."

"What, you didn't see *Never On Sunday*?"

Victor frowned. "Not a lot of traffic this far off Atlantic. The entrances face New York; it's unlikely someone in those high-rises in back saw anything. I'll need enough people to start canvassing at least a two-block radius, all the tenants here."

Raab grunted, "What we need's a shut-in with a picture window and cable on the fritz. I want the state lab to review the autopsies from December. What were their names, Montgomery ..."

"And Murillo."

"Either of them have a connection to Easter?"

"Montgomery was some sort of *au pair*. Murillo'd been working off the books when she was killed. Residential cleaning service, I believe."

Adane approached, hesitating to interrupt until Victor gestured for her to speak. "Miss DeLuca says Carmen Oliva didn't have any family, and never mentioned Jimmy Easter."

"What about—?"

"The funeral today? St. Agnes Church. The wife of the church custodian. The service is this morning."

"And—?"

"The Tuesday night supper was at St. Agnes, too."

"All right. Inform Sergeant Rice he's got the post mortem. Call Long and have him pull the files on the two women from December. Tomorrow, eleven a.m., the autopsy should be complete, everyone in my office. Get Miss DeLuca home and try to keep her away from the press."

"Yes, sir."

"St. A's," Raab muttered. "Mary Grace Keller? She's got a sister's a nun over there, and her brother's like an assistant priest, whaddayacallit? A deacon? She's the next at bat, but maybe I should put someone else on this one."

Victor said nothing. Mary Grace Keller was an assistant DA. He had met Maggie and Kevin Keller at Cat's Christmas Eve dinner.

Then Raab realized that Victor, too, had a connection. "I, uh, you wanna send someone over there, have a word with the, uh, priest?"

"I'll do it. Unless you'd rather send someone else."

Raab hesitated, realized that his hesitation could be construed as distrust. "No, no, you go."

Victor walked toward Arctic; the knot of reporters surged, but there was something in his eye that made them shrink back, part, not trail him to his car.

Interviewing a potential witness, nothing more, but this time the mantra did not soothe because the subject of interrogation would be Father Dominic Fortunati, Cat's brother. Cat. Victor began to punch buttons on his cellular.

Cat was drying her hair when the phone rang.

"Cat, love, I'm afraid I have some bad news."

She could hear the whiff of static; he was in his car. "We're not going."

"Why do you say that?"

"I heard it in your voice, Victor." She felt a rush—relief, then guilt. Then more relief: whatever had happened had released her from liability for the cancellation. Then more guilt:

nothing short of murder would have canceled their vacation. Someone had died. Still, she was off the hook and the jab of the hook was replaced by a prickle of curiosity; she did some fishing of her own. "I thought you'd cleared your desk."

"So did I."

And as late as last evening, which meant that whatever had come up had been recent and big. Ritchie was right. Cat reached for the radio, snapped it on to local talk, five minutes to the half-hour news update. "Someone important must have gotten"—she glanced at Mats—"k-i-l-l-e-d."

"No c-o-m-m-e-n-t."

No, it couldn't have been someone important. Ritchie had said New York near Baltic; not the high-roller/penthouse zone. "Shall I call the hotel and the airport?" she offered.

"I'll take care of it. I'm afraid I'll be tied up most of today, but I should have a little time before I have to go in tomorrow morning. Why don't I come by and take you and the kids out to breakfast?"

"All right." *You phony,* Cat chastised herself. *Sounding disappointed when you were going to call him and cancel.*

"Eight-thirty or so, would that be too early?"

"No, it's fine."

"I'll try to call you later. And I am sorry, *querida.*"

"Don't be. I understand, really."

Cat sat for a moment hugging the receiver to her breast. Okay, things *do* come up. It had happened with Chris dozens of times, all those something's-come-up cancellations, remember? Still ... intuition animated her fingertips, walked them along the Major Crimes number on the phone, connecting her once more with the dispatcher.

"Yes, the lieutenant just called in, Mrs. Austen. Haven't you spoken with him?"

"It's just— It's really important that I tell him something. I'm sorry to bother you again. Did he leave a number where he could be reached?"

"I believe so, just a moment." There was a pause and then

the dispatcher read an Atlantic City number that sent a ripple of recognition through Cat's brain. She dialed as her brain cells homed on the site. A kindly voice said, "Good Morning, St. Agnes Parish." Cat hung up.

She kissed Mats on the head, absently. "Go put on your clothes, baby. Put on a sweater."

Mats slid off the bed and skipped off, his spirits lightened by the fact that his mother was not going away. Cat dressed slowly, pulling on her jeans and a navy sweatshirt, retired running shoes. She looked at the silk peignoir Victor had given her for Christmas, lying in soft folds on top of the open suitcase.

There was a knock on the door. "Come in."

Ellice entered wearing faded jeans, an old State Police academy sweatshirt of Freddy's. "What's this Mats said about you not going?"

Cat flopped on the bed. "We're not going. Sorry if you and Freddy were planning a couple days of *la dolce vita*."

"*La dolce vita*? Wrong show. The word got out we're working on the apartment and all of a sudden, it's like Cecil B. DeMille's shooting *This Old House*."

Cat moaned. "I forgot about that." *Famiglia* Fortunati had volunteered to help Freddy with some renovations over the weekend. And it was President's Day weekend, which meant four days of extended family. "Spies. Lorraine wants them to find out how much rent I'm charging you."

"Not as much as she's gonna wanna know why the honeymoon's off. How much rent are you charging us?"

"Zero. Would you mind letting Mats and Jane hang with you if I took a drive into Atlantic City?"

"No way. The rent, I mean. You don't have to leave town. You can hole up here, I won't tell."

"All the work you and Freddy are doing upgrading the apartment, is more tha—"

"Cat, we're doing good, financially."

"I'm nearly solvent myself. And once the *Chronicle* takes off, I'll be getting more work from Ritchie. But I can't hole up here, Jane will rat me out. Besides, I do have an errand to do in AC. How about rent free for six months, then we renegotiate?"

"I'll run it by Freddy. Incidentally, Annie said to ask if *CopWatch* is hiring a local tech advisor. Carlo's lookin' for something to do and they all think you have an in."

"They're not buffing their résumés, are they?" Cat groaned.

"Uh-huh. They had Nancy do head shots, too."

"Dear Lord." Cat had a mental image of her brothers queued up for an open call, giggled. "That line producer person is supposed to call me about meeting with whoever's doing the teleplay. Apparently there's some confusion over what rights they have to use some of the material in the *South Jersey* piece, so I think they've decided it's cheaper to hire me than to hire lawyers to tell them who's got the rights to what. She gave me a list of exteriors the location unit is looking for, wanted me to fax them photos if I turn anything up. Imagine. Me, hobnobbing with TV folk, faxing. I've got some time on my hands, maybe I'll start embroidering my résumé and air brushing my glossies, too."

"So what happened to the trip? You chicken out?"

Cat shook her head. "Victor beat me to it. Something came up and he has to work."

"I thought he got off work so something could come up."

Cat pitched a pillow at her and Ellice caught it, chuckling. "So Landis was right?"

"It's killing me to admit it, but so it seems."

"And whatever's up is in AC?"

"I thought I'd return the travel guides Monsignor Greg loaned me," Cat said, innocently.

"As cover stories go, that one needs a rewrite."

The phone rang. "I'll work on it," Cat said, and reached for the receiver. Ellice mouthed "I'll dress Mats" and left, closing the door.

"Hello?"

"So, not on your way to the airport?" Ritchie gloated.

"All right, you told me so. So what's the deal?"

"Some gal got whacked inside her apartment over New York Avenue. PR guy with ACPD is sayin' it's bein' investigated as a possible B and E."

"There isn't much worth stealing in that neighborhood." And Victor wouldn't have canceled for a botched B and E.

"Who was the girl?"

"Name's Carmen Oliva. Office temp. Young, single. Cherry's called over the ME's office, all they'll say's the autopsy's scheduled for tomorrow morning."

"Why not today? I know they're not backed up over there and if this such a big deal that they have to keep it hush-hush, why isn't it big enough to push to the head of the line? What are they waiting for?"

"Don't know. But I know one thing they're hushing up."

"What?"

"I ran Oliva's name through my molehills, up pops a prior from a year, year and a half back. Solicitation. Only that one arrest, guess she either got careful or got out."

*Not careful enough.* "Don't guess," Cat murmured. A hooker? That didn't fit New York and Baltic, either. Too far off the stroll, if her geography was up to date. And if this woman was an ex-hooker killed in what the cops were calling a B and E, what was Victor doing over at St. Agnes?

"So whaddaya say, Austen, you think you can dig me up anything I can use for the *Chronicle*? The first issue's due out next week, and I'd like to launch with a bang."

"I'm supposed to meet with that *CopWatch* writer next week."

"So you do 'em both. Taggin' after some TV hack don't take much brainpower."

"Well, I'll concede that you're probably the expert in whatever doesn't take much brainpower."

"Very funny. Look, just 'cause your vaycay got canned don't mean you and Loverboy can't still hop between the sheets, swap a little pillow talk. Any time between now and the *Chronicle*'s deadline would be good for me."

# CHAPTER FOUR

Cat went into the bathroom, began brushing her teeth, saw the release of adrenaline reflected in the vibrant light in her eye, the color shading her cheek. She made a microphone of her toothbrush, intoned, "January was quiet. Too quiet. Dead quiet. Just ... really darned quiet." So much for a career in pulp fiction.

She gathered up the books from her carry-on bag, travel guides and maps she'd borrowed from Monsignor Gregorio, who had been Father Gregorio when Cat was a little girl, and who was currently dividing his time between St. Agnes and St. Nick's, with Dominic and Kevin Keller managing St. Agnes day-to-day.

Cat called a goodbye to Ellice and Freddy, who were taping the baseboards and window frames, preparing to paint the apartment's two bedrooms. She reassured Mats that she was only going into Atlantic City and would be back before lunch, repressed a smile at Jane's baleful gaze, her demand to know *why* her mother wasn't going away after all, having looked forward to four days of indulgence under the lenient guardianship of Freddy and Ellice.

Cat drove into Atlantic City. She had grown up there, but she was just a guest now, often felt like a stranger. Cat's marriage to Chris had set off the transition and the sale and demolition of Fortunati's Restaurant on Pacific Avenue had sealed it. Aunt Cat's premature death had left Cat and Chris possessors of her Morningside Drive house on the quiet island of Ocean City and when infant Jane was brought to St. Agnes to be christened, Cat felt like a visitor in the very parish where she had grown up.

Renegade transformations had stripped away landmarks, striking randomly; familiar zones could erode slowly or vanish in a week, with neighborhoods fragmenting into disconnected islands of struggling humanity. *Things fall apart*, Cat thought, not for the first time. *The center cannot hold.*

Cat drove Atlantic Avenue past the turnoff to the new bus terminal, past the new (only) supermarket, the new CVS, turned left on New York, which took her away from the Boardwalk casinos and anything new. Many of the interior sections of the city, removed from the Boardwalk, the casinos, the waterfront, the action, looked like any blue-collar neighborhood, the color fading, the fabric frayed.

She saw a police car parked laterally across the intersection of Arctic and New York, and made a casual left on Baltic, saw a couple uniforms at the doorstep of a ramshackle house, talking to a woman with curlers in her mathematically partitioned hair. A block up, a pair of men, too well-dressed for the neighborhood, walked away from a house, one of them hitching up his overcoat to tuck a note pad in his back pocket. Detectives. Cat thought she recognized one of them. She worked her way through the network of one-way streets, to St. Agnes.

The parish commanded one long block bounded by states and seas: Kentucky and New York intersected by Caspian and Barents. St. Agnes Primary School took up the entire Caspian Avenue side; a windowed corridor, like the bar of a letter H, bisected the block down the center and connected the school to the complex that took up one side of Barents Avenue: rectory, the offices and meeting rooms, and on the corner of Barents and Kentucky, the church. Across Barents were a couple modest houses; the one on the corner served as the convent. The school was the newest of the buildings, under forty years old, a flat-roofed, two-story structure of tan brick. It made an odd appendage to the turn-of-the century gray stone church and the sixty-year-old house that had been converted to a rectory. At the time the school had been built, the bid allowed for the passage linking church to school, the two-story wing annexing the rectory to the church, where the church office, kitchen and a couple conference rooms could be added at minimal expense.

Economy had annulled artistic integrity. The church, the annex, the rectory, ran along Barents in one unbroken and incongruous structure, looking like the site of some bizarre architectural combat, with no side willing to concede. The church building, a towering edifice of ornamental stonework, remained the most beautiful segment of the complex. For a few brief years, its steeple had made St. Agnes the tallest building in the city, but it had been eclipsed well before the advent of the casinos. Inside, late-day sun would penetrate the stained-glass windows on the southwest side, coloring the interior with jeweled light, which had made afternoon the preferred hour for weddings. Cruising along Barents, Cat could see how badly the weather had flayed the exterior of the bell tower, how one of the stained-glass windows was boarded up, the plywood sprayed with graffiti.

There was a small church parking lot on Kentucky Avenue set into the space between the church and the south wing of the school, and a corresponding recess on the other side of the building that had been paved, a couple pieces of play equipment installed behind chain link. Cat saw that Victor's black Jag was in the lot; she rounded the block, parked along Barents, out of the sightlines of the church lot and front windows of the rectory.

Cat grabbed Monsignor Greg's books, and armed with this thin alibi, ascended the worn slate steps to the church entrance.

A small marquee proclaimed: Welcome to Saint Agnes Roman Catholic Church. Msr. Gregorio Dominguez, Father Dominic Fortunati. Fri, Feb 15, Testa Mass. Sunday, February 17: "In Whom Shall I Place My Trust?" A schedule of confessions and daily Masses, below. The door was unlocked. Dominic and Kevin both thought it was wrong to lock the door of a church, though Monsignor Gregorio, who had served in Atlantic City for twenty-five years, had persuaded them to concede that at least it ought to be locked at night. Cat entered the vestibule, eased the door closed. On the opposite side of the entry, she saw the small, arched door that led to the bell tower, observed the fresh coat of inexpensive paint, the new padlock. Vandals must have taken advantage of that open door, she concluded.

Cat could still decode the separate silences of a church, heard the hush of receding ceremony. She stepped into the back of the nave, passed the pair of confessionals, headed toward the open passage that led to the church offices, meeting rooms, stairwell and an inner entrance to the rectory. Cat wondered if that was where Victor was. A tall, dark figure loomed up behind her and she jumped.

"Cat, it's me," he whispered.

Cat pressed her palm to her heart. "Kevin. You startled me."

Kevin Keller was a school chum who'd hung around with Cat and Freddy Fortunati. Cat and Freddy were ten months apart in age; all three had been in the same grade, same Catechism class, received First Communion, Confirmation, graduated high school together. The Kellers had demonstrated their devotion to the Church by boosting the parish census with nine children to the Fortunatis' seven. The Fortunatis had retaliated by turning out a priest. The Kellers attempted to match that and up the stakes by aiming their daughters at the convent, but came up short: Kevin was ordained a deacon only, headed off for overseas missionary service and of the five Keller daughters, only Margaret Mary took the veil. (The neighborhood snickered that Maggie had taken one look at her folks' marriage and decided that poverty, chastity and obedience had holy matrimony beat.) Moreover, the Fortunatis never forgot where home was, while the Kellers couldn't flee fast or far enough. Only Mary Grace, who was an assistant DA and Sister Maggie, who was the housekeeping sister at St. Agnes, remained in the county. The previous fall, Kevin wandered back, deciding perhaps that he couldn't save the world or that Atlantic City offered as much iniquity and pestilence as any he had witnessed on foreign soil. The rest returned only for their parents' funerals, decamped once more.

"Sorry. I just got back from the cemetery. Shouldn't you be on a plane right about now?" Kevin kept his voice reverently low.

Cat did likewise. "There was a change of plans."

Kevin's eyes softened. "Well, I'm glad to see you came to your senses, Cat."

Kevin had heard about the trip, and Cat knew he had not approved. "Kevin, you say that like I'm Mary of Magdalen coming back to the faith. Or the fold. And the truth is, I'm only coming back to return Monsignor Greg's books." *Liar, that's only a fraction of the truth.* "Victor got called in unexpectedly; he had to cancel."

"I'll take them. I think Greg's got a visitor." He tucked the books under his arm, as he had when he walked Cat home from school in the old days. "Look, Cat, it's none of my business. I just think, what with children and all, you have to think about the consequences of getting involved with a man who's not your husband."

Cat nipped a smile. She had always felt that "Black Irish" ought to mean something beyond the sable hair, clear blue eyes, bloodless complexions of the Keller tribe, should imply a certain devil-may-care that none of them possessed. Cat and Freddy had often wondered how Kevin's paper-white flesh fared under the equatorial sun, chuckled reminiscently over long-ago forays to the beach when the Kellers would arrive in long-sleeved T-shirts, wide-brimmed hats, zinc-smeared noses, horrified by the heedless Fortunatis who made do with a splash of Coppertone on exposed flesh that got browner and browner. Still, Kevin's letters home, communicated via Maggie, were filled with such tales of peril and privation that they stopped thinking of him as thin-skinned. "I do think about them, Kevin. And if I didn't, I've got six brothers more than willing to play conscience."

"Okay," Kevin conceded. "Sermon's over."

"Is Dominic around?"

"He drove Isadore home from the cemetery."

"Oh, dear, I'd forgotten about that. Mama told me the funeral was today." Isadore Testa had been the church custodian for more than thirty years. His wife had died earlier that week.

"Poor man's at the end of his rope."

"Dominic or Mr. Testa?"

Kevin blinked. "Well, I meant Isadore, of course. His wife had been ill for so long. Jennie must have told you about it."

Cat nodded. Jennie Fortunati, Cat's mother, was devoted to St. Agnes. When the parish secretary had retired at the end of last year, she and a few members of the Holy Rosary Society volunteered to fill the vacancy so that St. Agnes wouldn't be put to the expense of hiring a replacement.

"I'm on my way over to the rectory. Come say hello to Maggie."

"I'd like to hang around here a little." *Mustn't run into Victor.* "I'll come over in a few minutes." Mark time until he took off, then find out exactly what he had been doing there. "I haven't been inside ..." She let the words trail off.

"You're welcome any Sunday, Cat. Isn't it time you thought about First Communion classes for your daughter?"

"Kevin, do you ever give up?"

"Redemption's—what is it the cops say? 'Twenty-four seven'?"

"I'm unsalvageable. "

"No one is. You just have to catch them at the right time."

Cat shook her head, smiling. "Mama says, *'Passanu iorna e volanu l'anni.'* I think it means something like 'Time flies.' Sometimes, I think she makes these sayings up."

"Your mother's been a godsend to this parish."

Jennie Fortunati had taken pity on the pallid Keller clan. There had always been a place at her table when one of them wandered in, always a hug or a word of praise to alleviate the harsh discipline that alternated only with apathy in the Keller household. "I don't know what we'd do without her," he added.

Cat detected a note of melancholy. "Is something the matter, Kevin?"

"Dominic ever talk about the church?"

"Only that he was glad to be transferred out of Philly. He liked being closer to the family again."

"You know there's talk about closing it down?"

"Closing ... St. Agnes?" Cat blushed. Dismay seemed so hypocritical. She wasn't a churchgoer, anymore. But she had been married here, after all, her children christened here.

Kevin's frown was wistful. He had grown up in St. Agnes, too. "The school would stay open. Enrollment's been pretty good, even increased a bit in the past year or two."

"But it's not spilling over into church attendance."

"Well, you know, a lot of the parents aren't Catholics."

"Just a lot of Protestants looking to get their kids out of the public schools, those heathens."

"Don't let on to Dom I said anything. Look, I have some paperwork to do. Come on over to the rectory before you leave, Maggie'll make you a cup of tea."

Cat retreated to the back of the nave, allowed her gaze to take in the carved wooden doors of the confessionals, their red velvet insets, the dark oak pews, faithfully polished by hands that had grown wearier and less nimble each year, the diligence unable to camouflage the gashes ands scars of vandals. The carpet, worn when Cat had walked the aisle as a bride had eroded in several places. Statues of the Madonna and St. Agnes, shrouded in purple for the Lenten season, bracketed the alter.

The bells had been removed from the tower the year before her wedding. Aunt Caterina had played the wedding march on the church's old black Steinway the day Cat and Chris were married. The alter's brass railing had the patina of gold satin, rigorous buffing fighting off the corrosion of salt air. Cat imagined she could pick out the very spot along that railing where Chris had stood, perfectly calm, as Cat walked to him on her father's arm. Her father had leaned down and whispered, "He's not a Cath'lic, but I guess you know, I think your mama will come around," his voice shuddering as he surrendered at last his only daughter.

"You'll always be the number one man in my life, Papa, you know that," Cat had whispered back and through the mist of white organza saw tears in her father's eyes for the first time.

"God *dammi'*!"

Cat started. She had thought she was alone, realized there was a figure kneeling beneath the statue of St. Agnes, holding a taper to the bank of red, green, gold votive candles. The woman hissed again, prodded at the obstinate wick until it caught, the votive cup glowing green around the flame. She bowed her head and crossed herself, tugged a large green crucifix from her bosom, pressed it to her lips.

Cat moved down the aisle to get a better look. The woman was small. There were about two inches of snug black skirt visible under a coat of dark fake fur. Spike heels and black-seamed stockings. The narrow back straightened and she turned, yanking the hem into place, looked up. "Jesus, lady! You startl' me, creepin' aroun' like that."

She had an oval face framed with dark spiraling curls that fell to her waist, large eyes heavily mascaraed, a small, full-lipped mouth drawn into a skeptical pucker.

"I'm sorry," Cat apologized. "I was just looking around. I haven't been in here for a while."

"You an' me both. Looks like there's been some funeral or somethin'." The crucifix, malachite, hung from a black cord from her neck. She crossed herself and pressed the object to her lips, once more, rose.

"Did you know Mrs. Testa?"

"Who?"

"The woman whose funeral was held this morning."

"I don' know no one name' Testa. I jus' wanted to say a prayer for Carmen." She tucked the crucifix into her snug bodice, tugged her coat collar close to her throat. "I heard she goes to church here, I figure I'll stop in, light a candle. What could it hurt, you get me? What about you, you go here?"

"My brother's the priest." *Carmen?*

"The fat one or the ballet dancer?"

Cat smiled. The fat one was Monsignor Greg. "The dancer." Then, casually, "Carmen's what? A friend of yours?"

"Yeah. I knew her from back in the day, you know? Back in the life. Word on the street is she got cut up."

"That's terrible," Cat murmured, heard, *You think you can dig me up anything I can use for* The Chronicle?

The girl tugged a sheer white scarf from her pocket, arranged it over her hair. "Yeah, well. Walks out on Jimmy, hooks up with Jesus." She knotted the scarf under her chin. "An' was he ticked. Jimmy, that is. Lotta good religion did her. Lotta good it did Tammy or Renay, for that matter, either."

"Tammy and Renay?"

"You really that priest's sister, or like a cop or something?"

"I'm really his sister. Was Jimmy Carmen's, um, man from when she was in the, uh, life?"

"He's *the* man. Don' tell me you never heard of Jimmy Easter?"

No, she wouldn't tell her because even Cat, in her narrow universe, knew who Jimmy Easter was. Joey had said that the escort service, Printemps, was an out-call operation, the lingerie shop was the training ground. "I've heard of him." She paused. "I saw New York's blocked off a couple streets down. Was that where Carmen lived?"

"Yeah. They blocked it off all the way over to my place. How come you ask so many questions, you're not a cop?"

"I'm sort of a writer," Cat said. "I've been working on something for *CopWatch*, but you know how it is, I have to pick up work where I can find it, I try to keep my ear to the ground."

"I hear that." The girl's eyes were glittering now. "They really comin' here for a shoot? *CopWatch?*"

Cat nodded, tried to sound West Coast; failed actually, but the girl was too ignorant to detect the deception. "Oh, yeah, there's an open call next week to look for extras. You've got some pictures you should stop by. The Marinea Towers, that residence hotel all the way down Pacific? The middle of next week." Cat dug in her purse for one of her cards. She had never thought of having business cards, but lately, people had been asking for them. White with a simple border. She weighed her given name (too cumbersome) against Cat (too frivolous), decided on the latter because that was her *nom de plume*. Or *nom de PC*, if she ever got proficient with the thing. She offered the card to the girl. "Look, if you should hear anything else about your friend, I'd appreciate it if you would call me. You know, *CopWatch* is always looking for good material."

The girl took the card. 'Cat'? What kinda name is that?"

"Sort of a nickname."

"You got nine lives?"

"I don't know. But I seem to land on my feet more often than not."

The girl snorted. "In my line a work, that don' bring in dime one, you get me?"

"I believe so. What's you're name?"

"Luz. Molina. Me, I'm in the book." They had strolled toward the vestibule. "When you freelance, you gotta be easy to locate, you get me?" The girl had yanked on the door handle. Cat peered past her, saw Victor thirty feet away on the sidewalk, talking to Monsignor Gregorio, their backs toward the church entrance.

Cat stepped away from the door.

"Guy's a cop," Luz said knowingly. "You comin'?"

"I'm waiting for someone. Why do you say he's a cop?"

"He's got the look. My business, you don' know the look, it gets pretty 'spensive, you get me? An' I don' got Jimmy Easter to make my bail, like Carmen did." She pulled a pair of sunglasses out of her pocket, shoved them over her eyes. "So maybe I'll give you a call, Cat Lady, who knows?"

The girl walked out. Cat let the door fall into place, stopped it an inch before it shut, peered through the crack. She saw Victor turn, saw his implacable profile as he looked over Luz Molina registering, in the space of three seconds, the face, the lively saunter, the incongruity of such a woman emerging from a church.

Wind plucked her card from the girl's fingers. Cat jammed her fist to her mouth to keep from gasping aloud, saw Victor move to retrieve it. Luz Molina beat him to it, snatching the card from the sidewalk, shoving it into her coat pocket. The movement caused the pendant to spill from her bosom, caused the hemline to ascend. Monsignor made a show of averting his gaze from the display of cleavage and thigh, though Cat suspected he was peeking. Molina said something to Victor, thank-you perhaps, and put a little spice into her saunter as she walked away.

Cat allowed the door to close and leaned against it, kept her mouth securely muffled until she was certain she wasn't going to laugh aloud. Not polite to laugh in church. She tiptoed toward the main corridor, passed the church office, the two small conference rooms, the stairwell to the second-floor kitchen and dining hall with a custodial closet tucked underneath. There was a door at the end of the corridor that,

Cat knew, opened into the rectory's kitchen by way of the pantry. She pushed the bell and heard a brusque "Come in!" She stepped into a long rectangular room, ceiling-high shelves over a pair of clanking radiators. Cat did not check to see if the cans of Campbell's soup were arranged alphabetically. ("Cross my heart, Cat," Dominic had told her. "Alphabet, Bean with Bacon, Chicken Noodle, Cream of Mushroom— You want a good story, follow a housekeeping sister around for a day.") Cat was actually considering it for something to do after *CopWatch* was out of the way.

Cat wiped her feet on the rush mat Maggie had placed at the edge of the pantry, thwarting the grime that attempted to elude her by circumventing the back door. "Hi, Maggie."

Margaret Mary Keller—aka Maggie Keller, aka Sister Maggie—was taller and more muscular than her brothers. A rumor had circulated through the old neighborhood that what had gotten old man Keller to finally lay off beating the younger kids was when fifteen-year-old Maggie knocked him flat. There had been some suspicion that she and Dominic might pair up, considerable relief on the part of both families when each had opted for the church.

"Kevin said you were around," Maggie said.

"I came to return some books Monsignor loaned me. I thought I'd stop by and say hi to Dom since I'm here."

"I don't think he's back yet. Would you like some tea?"

"No, thanks. Could I go wait in his office?" Cat felt uncomfortable in the painfully immaculate kitchen. Maggie had not yielded entirely to secular garb, wore a wimple, a black calf-length dress covered with a spotless bib apron, black stockings, all as impeccable as her kitchen. If cleanliness was next to godliness, Cat thought idly, Maggie was home free.

"Sure, go ahead. I don't know why he isn't back yet."

"Kevin said he might have driven Mr. Testa home."

Maggie shrugged. "It's a blessing she finally went, caring for her was killing him, and don't you tell your brother I said so."

"Not a word," Cat promised. She walked down a narrow hallway to a front room that had been a library, when the residence had been a house. The parlor on the other side of the staircase was Monsignor Greg's office, where counseling and pre-marital classes were held. Cat and Chris had sat through their share of them. Monsignor Greg had been Father Greg then; he counseled them about the challenges in a "mixed" marriage, diplomatically inquired whether Chris might consider conversion.

Dominic's office was cluttered. Not unkempt, simply too small for the amount of material objects it contained. Ceiling-high bookshelves were crammed with religious texts, magazines, a few books on dance, stacks of folders, a week's worth of newspapers. A portable barre was shoved catty-corner behind a chair, the chair pushed against the desk to accommodate a metal file cabinet beside the door. Cat saw a picture of their parents on the desk, the same one she had on her mantle, Mom and Pop standing under the awning of Fortunatis Restaurant.

Cat peeked at a stack of mail on the desk, checked the three-ring-binder calendar, saw "Testa Mass, 8:30 AM." She began to turn back through the pages idly, checked her watch, saw notations for the Testa woman's viewing; notations of schedule changes in the Masses for the previous weeks; meetings; it seemed every page had a notation, some very detailed, others a word or two.

As in the one written three weeks before that said: C. Oliva, 3 PM.

"Hey, there."

Cat jumped, knocking the small binder to the floor. "I'm sorry ... clumsy ..."

"It's all right. I know it's a mess in here." Dominic shrugged off his black coat, threw it over the desk onto the chair, took Cat by the shoulders and kissed her on the cheek. "Why aren't you airborne?"

Dominic Fortunati was the fourth down the line. Carlo, Vinnie, Marco, Dominic, Joey, Freddy. All cops, except for Dom, who had thrown his rough-and-tumble brothers a curve when at age ten he had announced his intention to take ballet classes, stunned them again when at eighteen, he proclaimed that he would not be going into law enforcement, but had decided to enter the priesthood. Now in his mid-forties, he did not have the bulk of the three oldest; the dance training, which he continued to pursue, had honed his figure to a supple leanness; his eyes had a hint of merriment, as did Freddy's, Cat's.

Cat returned the hug. "There was a change of plans."

"Oh?" He walked around the desk, sat. "Sit down, Cat." Dominic leaned back in his chair, his hands laced behind his head. "So, is it: A, Victor couldn't get away? B, you got cold feet? C, the two of you had a fight? I'm putting my money on A. I think you'd be too stubborn to back out even if you wanted to and Victor doesn't seem to be the sort of person who allows himself to be goaded into quarrels too easily."

"They say Latins are hot-tempered."

"They say the same about Italians."

"But we *are*. And Victor doesn't even raise his voice."

"I like him, Cat."

"I like him, too."

"I hope that you more than like him."

Cat lifted her brows. "Because I was ready to run off to San Juan with him, you mean? A man I'm not married to."

"Now, Cat, you have to admit, I've been admirably restrained."

"Granted. You've shown remarkable self-control for a priest and a brother. Even Kevin's taken to lecturing me. He probably thinks our change in plans was the intervention of a righteous God. And Vinnie's been giving us the stare, like this—" She lowered her brows, squinted balefully.

"Well, you're the baby sister, Cat. So, Victor got called in for something?"

Hadn't he been told that Victor had been here? "Yes."

"So maybe you weren't meant to run off together at this point in your relationship. The intervention of a righteous God, after all."

"Victor's a homicide cop, Dominic," Cat reminded him, gently. "If he got called in, it means someone's been killed."

"Sorry. The besetting sin of the Fortunatis. Misplaced levity. Sort of a survival mechanism, I suspect." He paused. "I really shouldn't have said that. God doesn't bring about a woman's death to harry us into righteousness. Any more than he stranded that girl on the roadside in order to lure Chris to her aid."

*And to his murder. But He didn't prevent it, either, did He?*

Cat rose. "I'd better go, I promised Mats I'd take him to lunch."

"Cat, look, I've kept my mouth shut, but you are here, so let me do my number. If you're not free, here"—he laid his hand over his heart—"entering into a new relationship, an intimate relationship, is a lie."

"Victor was married, too."

"And his wife died, I know. But I think Victor's forgiven God. Which is really saying he's forgiven himself, because God doesn't require our forgiveness. Maybe it's time for you to forgive yourself, too."

"Forgive myself for what?"

"For 'I should have done this,' 'I should have done that,' 'I should have made him pot roast,' 'I should have kissed him twice on Sundays.' You did fine."

"I should have had time to do better."

"We don't get to determine that. We do the best we can with the time God gives us. Stop hounding yourself." He winked. "God gave you six brothers, that's our job."

Cat wiped her eyes. "You've been working overtime."

There was a rap on the door behind her and Cat turned. Monsignor Greg was standing in the doorway. He was tall, with a girth that was the result of the hospitality of two parishes, his face pleasantly jowled, though now it was set in a somber expression. "Alley Cat, your young man was just here."

"Victor? Really?" *Liar, liar.*

"Am I interrupting?"

"No, no," Dominic said. "Is something wrong?"

"One of our parishioners was found murdered this morning. A woman named Carmen Oliva, you know who I mean?"

Dominic nodded, slowly, slipped his thumb and index finger under the rim of his glasses, rubbed his eyes. "God help us. Did she have family, do you know?"

"I don't know. The lieutenant will probably call you, he asked where you were, if you'd heard about it. I said I didn't think so."

Dominic shook his head. "No, not a word. I drove Isadore home from the cemetery. He wanted to talk awhile."

Not a word? *God doesn't bring about a woman's death to harry us into righteousness.* But, Cat thought, I didn't say it was a woman's death that had interrupted our plans ... did I?

## CHAPTER FIVE

When Cat cruised into her driveway, she saw the door to the ground-level apartment open, caught a whiff of paint thinner and raucous male laughter. She crept toward the front steps, decided she was not going to sneak around in her own home, and stepped into the apartment doorway. Vinnie's three boys were mixing paint on a newspaper-covered tarp on the living room floor. She heard a couple of her brothers bickering jovially somewhere in the back of the house.

"Everyone out here now!" she shouted.

Carlo and Vinnie emerged, dressed in worn jeans, paint-smeared sweatshirts, Freddy trailing with Mats, who was decked out in one of his uncle's sweatshirts that reached to his knees, a painter's cap, the brim turned upward.

Carlo opened his mouth and Cat said, "Don't say anything." She ticked off the items on her fingers as she spoke. "One: I am not going to Puerto Rico. Two: there will be no questions. Three: Anyone who does ask a question is liable to get a shot in the mouth for his answer. Four: I am not in the mood. And, five, six and seven, I'm going upstairs to work on an article, in a little while I'm taking the kids over McDonald's to lunch, and you will clean up after yourselves without tracking paint through my house. Got it?"

"So what happened to the trip?" Carlo asked. "Victor have to cover that New York Avenue business, or what?"

Mats looked up at his Uncle Carlo in alarm. "Mom, are you gonna shoot Uncle Carlo in the mouth?"

"When he least expects it." Cat turned on her heel and headed up the porch steps to the front door, heard someone calling her name, saw Miss Althea Nixon hustling across the street, a magazine rolled into her gloved fist. The Misses Nixon were the daughters of one of Ocean City's first police chiefs; one of them had been a recent chapter president of the NRA. They had a chamber in their hearts reserved for all police officers and they had thought the world of Chris.

"Hello, Miss Nixon." Cat had become quite fond of the ladies. Other than the Ufflanders, whom Cat had never seen at close range, the Nixon sisters were the only other year-round residents on Morningside Drive.

Miss Nixon opened the magazine. "My sister and I just thought you would like to see this, Cat, dear. We've been featured in a magazine article."

Cat got a glimpse of the cover—a recent issue of *Guns and Ammo*—and was shown a black-and-white photo of Miss Althea wearing a flowered print dress with a lace collar, cradling a shotgun in white-gloved hands. Miss Althea drew up the spectacles that hung from a beaded cord around her neck, placed them over her eyes, read aloud. "'While the twenty-two cannot be considered a brawl-buster, Miss Althea Nixon declares, I believe it is a mistake to rule it out for home defense. A trained shooter aiming for the center of the face, the base of the throat or the forehead, should cause sufficient hesitation in the intruder for the shooter to position her follow-up shot.' Would you like to look it over?"

"Thank you, Miss Nixon. I'll get it back to you today."

"Oh, no, dear, you keep it. You might need it."

Cat repressed a sigh, smiled.

"Those television people never seem to get their weapons quite right," Miss Althea lamented, "and none of those actors know how to execute a proper combat stance. So I thought, if they should need some advice or some coaching, my sister and I would be happy to offer our services."

"I'll be sure to mention it, Miss Nixon."

Cat tossed her coat over the arm of a living room chair, pushed the PLAY button on her answering machine. Call-mebacks from her mother, Ritchie Landis, Victor. She grabbed a Pepsi and headed for her bedroom, threw the magazine on the bed, reached for the receiver and dialed *The Chronicle*.

"What do you know about James Easter?" Cat asked, when Ritchie came on the line.

"He's a pimp."

Cat took a swig of Pepsi. "You said the Oliva woman had a prior, and she got bailed out? What would you say if I told you Easter bailed her?"

"Why should he? You're sayin' she was one of his?"

"I'm not saying anything, I'm asking you a question."

"C'mon, Austen, who's your source on this?"

"You're not the only one with gophers."

"Moles. And mine are comin' up empty. Don't diddle with me. The vic was owned by Easter?"

"I heard she worked for Easter and quit and that he wasn't happy about it."

"Cops got this yet?"

Cat hesitated. Victor had gone directly from the scene to St. Agnes, not to Easter's home. "I don't know."

"So where'd you pick up the goods on Easter?"

"At church."

"Quit kiddin' around, Austen. What else you got?"

"You mean besides the fact that the victim may have been a prostitute and there was animosity between her and the guy who may have been her pimp? What're you going to be paying for front page at the *Chronicle*?"

"Unless you can come up with some backstory, this ain't enough for front page. Pimps and hookers on the outs, even with a little bloodshed, that's so-what."

"You ever read Sherlock Holmes, Ritchie?"

"Quick Watson the needle, yeah, yeah."

"He never said that. Anyway, his most famous conclusion is the dog in the night-time. The watchdog doesn't bark at an intruder, which meant the intruder wasn't a stranger. It's the absence of the dog's bark that was significant."

"So what watchdog's not barkin' here?"

"The police. It's one thing to 'no comment.' But a total media lock-out? When was the last time moles came up empty?"

"So whaddaya thinkin'?"

"I'm thinking of a very interesting run-in I had with a friend of the victim's. One who isn't very likely to go to the cops."

Ritchie's voice went soprano with excitement. "The vic was connected? The mob? Drugs, is it drugs? Some kinda sex ring, is that it, it's sex, isn't it? Sex?" He was hyperventilating.

"Good things come to those who remunerate." Cat hung up, took the phone off the hook so he could not hit call-back and continue haranguing her until she figured out exactly what it was that she knew.

She flung herself back on the bed, frowning. Tammy and Renay. No surnames. Uttered by a hooker she ran into at church. What a terrifically solid lead. Stop expecting it to be dropped in your lap, Cat chided herself. Just because with the Dudek interview and the Sterling feature, you were lucky enough or stupid enough to have a corpse dropped at your feet, doesn't mean you can sit back and expect dead bodies to just be handed to you on a ... bier.

Cat put the receiver back on the cradle and the phone rang almost immediately. She snatched it and said, "No conversation without compensation!" was about to hang up again when a throaty female voice said, "I thought we agreed on the dollar figure. This is Cat Austen, isn't it?"

"Yes."

"April Steinmetz. I'm producing your *CopWatch*, remember?"

"Oh. Sorry, I thought you were someone else."

"Come across any good murders lately?"

"Well, they don't exactly hand them to you on a bier," Cat replied.

"A what?"

"A platter."

"Oh." Steinmetz was something called a line producer. She and Cat had spoken a few times after Ritchie had sent Steinmetz the proofs of Cat's piece on the Jerry Dudek murder. "Look, I faxed Teddy the proofs of your *South Jersey* piece and he's crazy about the writing. He'd really like to be able to put that, that *thing* you've got going in your writing, that, you know *tone*, the way you put stuff, you know that ... that—?"

"Mode of expression?" Cat suggested.

"Yeah. Anyway, Teddy—he's writing the DJ episode, he'd really like to hook up with you. I know you said something about being away a couple days—"

"That got called off."

"Terrif. Well, let me fill you in. We got S and M Casting over in Atlantic City to pick up our extras, they'll be holding open call a couple days next week. We're gettin' stonewalled by the homicide cops and the DA's office. What gives?"

"Maybe they're a worried that if the show airs before the trial, you may adulterate the jury pool."

"Look, it's not our fault the wheels of justice drag butt. I'm not gonna hold up a sweeps contender while the DA wades through a year of pre-trial garbage. We already got the principals locked in, except for someone to play your friend Ellice and someone to play Dudek's sister. I told S and M to peel back their lids."

Cat was surprised that they were writing Ellice into the cast; she hadn't really been pivotal to the Dudek drama.

"Maybe not, but the thing is, she's African-American and black females are hot. These days, you go multi-cult with your casting if you want the numbers. So far we got a pretty good mix. We locked in Tommi Ann Butler to play Kate Auletta and Red Melendez is gonna direct and play the cop and we've got a verbal handshake from Bigg Phat P.I.G."

Cat wondered if Steinmetz was spelling because there was a small child in the room, realized that the silence indicated it was her turn to say something. Perhaps "big fat pig" was some sort of Hollywood jargon. It occurred to Cat that she might squeeze a short humor piece out of West Coast lingo. She needed something to replace the travel pieces she'd had to forfeit. She asked for a translation.

"It's not a what, he's a who," April explained, patiently. "You know, Bigg with two g's and Phat with a p, h, and p-i-g—"

"With a p, i, g."

"You got it. You hadda heard of *Booty-Duty? Killadilla? Yo' Mama?*"

"The cellist," Cat hazarded, groping for terra firma.

"Not YoYo Ma, *Yo' Mama.* Music. All broke into the top ten. Anyway, he's trying to get into film and his handlers say we can have him for scale. His real name's Gary Biggs. He says the P.I.G. stands for Peace In Justice."

"With all due respect to Mr. P.I., um, G., I think justice starts with a J."

"Not the way he spells it. We're getting the bargain rate on Red, too, onaccounta what happened with his career."

"Didn't he used to star in *The Advocates?*"

"Yeah, but out here? 'Used to's' how you begin your eulogy. Past couple years, he's been lucky to get a PSA."

"And who's Kate Auletta?"

"That's you, hon. Teddy came up with that. Red said we oughtta go with something more gal sleuth and your number one gal sleuth handle is Kate."

Cat winced.

"So we're gonna be looking to pick up maybe two hundred people for the nightclub, the parking lot and the church scenes. The club's gonna let us shoot inside and we'll know if we got the permits to shoot on the parking lot after next city council meet. You turn up a church with a real feel for the area, fax me some interiors, I'll get them to Red."

"Church?"

"Yeah. For the jock's funeral scene."

"Jerry's service was in a funeral home."

"Red thinks church'll give it more zip."

Kate Auletta. Churches with zip. "I thought *CopWatch* was more like a documentary."

"Documentary, schlocumentary."

Cat said nothing.

"Teddy's from NJ, you know. He did the *CopWatch* book came out last spring, *CopWatch: Life on the Reel Streets*, you read it?"

She hadn't. "I'm thinking that would be reel, r-e-e-l?"

"Right."

"Is that why he got the assignment?" Cat asked. "Because he knows New Jersey?" Maybe she could get a local-writer-hits-the-big-time piece.

"No, he and Red go way back. Red and Ted. Hellraisers is what I heard. Anyway, Ted's got a leave from the college, he's been in and outta Atlantic City since the fall, soaking up the ambience, he's ready to rock and roll."

"Considering the ambience in question, I imagine he's ready for a shower as well," Cat muttered.

"Like I said, he loved your piece, so I gave him your number. He's at the Marinea Towers. He's been havin' a tough time hooking up with Calderone, maybe you could grease it so's they could log some face time."

Cat's brain scraped together a fair translation, except for "Calderone?"

"The homicide cop. We're changing it from Cardenas to Calderone. Nobody knows how to pronounce Cardenas, an' anyway, Calderone's got more *huevos*. Namewise."

Cat's brain shifted from the standard to the colloquial glossary. "More, um, male sleuth."

"Right, and we wanted to hang onto a Latino name—"

"Because of the multi-cult factor."

"Right."

"I'm a quick study."

"Anyway, you got full access while the casting goes on and even during the shoot, but when we're rollin' you're gonna wanna be like the incredible shrinking woman, 'cause you know what they think of writers on the set."

"I didn't know they thought of writers at all unless they're looking for someone to blame when something goes wrong or trying to forget whom they neglected to pay."

"You got that right. I useta write until I got smart and saw production's where it's at."

"The personal satisfaction," Cat interpreted, politely.

"Honey, personal satisfaction I can rent on Hollywood Boulevard. It's where the money's at. You give Ted a buzz."

Cat said goodbye, hung up and took the phone off the hook again, rolled off the bed and slid into the chair in front of the PC her brothers had given her for Christmas. She had installed it on a long library table in front of a large bedroom window and lost no time in advancing from apparent ignorance to near total ignorance of its operation.

"On the other hand," she said—she had taken to talking to the thing, hoping conversation would lure it into a spirit of cooperation—"Kate Auletta, gal sleuth, probably has MENSA-caliber computer skills. So listen, I'm going to dial into my online thing and I don't want to get a busy signal and I don't want your hard drive to start grating and griping and then tell me you've developed a general protection fault and we need to close ourselves down. I mean, if I just upped and closed down my system every time my sense of general protection defaulted on me, I never would have gotten up the hard drive to follow up on the Dudek story, and *you'd* probably still be sitting in some warehouse in Minnesota." She tapped a few keys, respectfully, coaxed, "Help me out here and I'll get you on *CopWatch*. I've got an in with the producer."

"Aunt Cat, are you talking to your computer again?"

Cat turned. Jason, the second of Vinnie's and Lorraine's three sons, was standing in the doorway. At sixteen, he had his father's height, lean jawline and wariness of expression. He knew his mother was ticked because Aunt Cat had gotten herself into some pretty hairy situations lately, but he liked the way Aunt Cat stood up to his dad. It wasn't easy being a cop's kid, having to walk the straight and narrow all the time.

"Of course I'm talking to it. How is it going to know who's boss around here?"

"Ellice says they're gonna order subs, want anything?"

"I'm taking Mats and Jane to McDonald's."

Jason crossed the room and sat on the corner of her bed. "What are you trying to do?"

"Dial onto the online thing."

"That's 'logging on,' Aunt Cat. Go ahead, I won't look while you put in your password."

"I don't care if you know. You're not going to sneak up here and downshift pornography, are you?" Cat typed in L-o-n-g-b-o-u-r-n.

"That's 'download,' Aunt Cat. No, Dad would kill me if I did that. What's that word mean?"

"Longbourn? It's where the Bennet family lived in *Pride and Prejudice*. You ever read it?"

He shook his head. "Sounds like chick shi— stuff."

"Good writing transcends gender, young man. Can you show me how to get the web pages for the local papers?"

"Can you get my head shots to the callback pile at the casting call next week?"

"Your father would let you be on *CopWatch*?"

"*Mom's* going. Don't tell her I told you."

"Get me to the web pages, and leave your head shots."

She scooted her chair aside and Jason leaned into the keyboard. He began manipulating the mouse, clicking rapidly. "Okay, I even bookmarked them for you. Just scroll down the categories, the stuff that's linked is in green."

"Like if I wanted to read the obits, I'd click under 'obituaries.'"

"Gross, Aunt Cat. You can use their engine, if they've got one, just type in the key words. Usually the most recent stuff will be first."

"I think I've got it. Tell your Uncle Freddy to get Mats cleaned up for me, will you?"

"Yell if you need help."

"Oh, Jason? Does *Yo' Mama* mean anything to you?"

"Bigg Phat P.I.G? Like who does *Booty Duty?*"

Cat sighed. "Thanks." She began plodding down the screen, backed up and typed Obituaries+January in the Search within a Search bar. A couple post-holiday suicides, a common law husband stabbed his wife, a few chronically ill who had hung on for Christmas and died after the first of the year. A drive-by.

Cat twisted the rings on her right hand, idly, pushed her hair behind her ear and tried to think like Kate Auletta. Obituaries+December yielded a New Year's Eve hit-and-run, two dead in a housefire. Earlene Adkins, December twenty-fifth, apparent homicide.*Apparent*, Cat frowned. Poor Earlene. Estrella Murillo, 24, homicide, Atlantic City. Born in Central America, survived by a mother and brother in Piedras Negras, Guatemala.

Something rang. If not a resounding chime, at least a distinct ping of recollection. Something Victor had mentioned before Christmas, when Cat was becoming immersed in the Sterling business. A young immigrant woman stabbed in her roominghouse somewhere off Pacific.

Cat logged the name in her brain and continued backing up, ran smack into Tamara Sue Montgomery, 20, Atlantic City, apparent homicide. Survived by her parents, Elsa and Thomas Montgomery and one brother, Thomas, Jr., in Vineland. The funeral had been at Sacred Heart Church, Vineland. But hadn't she been a drowning?

*Lotta good religion did her. Lotta good it did Tammy or Renay for that matter, either.*

Tammy. Tamara ...Tammy.

The web pages only recorded the two recent months, yielded Tammy—maybe—and someone named Murillo, who rang a bell for some reason, but no Renay. Cat decided that what Kate Auletta would do if her web pages fizzled out would be to hop into her charmingly littered two-seater with the leather interior, dash over to the public library and search the microfiche. She would not have to throw in a load of laundry first, or dry and put away the breakfast dishes and get her kids ready to go to McDonalds because Kate would drop her clothes off with the colorful multi-cult character who operated the laundry below her charmingly shabby flat, and she wouldn't have kids and when her big brother came out to ask, "You goin' out, or what?" she would tell him to mind his own damn business, not reply, "I promised to take the kids" (because Kate wouldn't have kids) "to McDonald's and then I'm going to the library."

"What's over the library?"

"Books. Want some?"

"Get outta here. Who's got time to read?"

Cat fed the kids and headed for the local library, settled them on a beanbag chair in the children's section with a book about tigers. Jane, convinced that she was left to mind Mats because her mother was going to do something fun that she didn't want Jane to see, plopped into the chair and informed Mats that tigers *ate* people.

Cat went upstairs and got a refresher course in microfiche from someone whose title had been Assistant Librarian, but who had taken his cue from the educational community and added syllables to his job designation while the job itself remained pretty much the same; he was now the Media Resources Technician and, Cat observed with dismay, not much older than her nephew Jason.

Cat located the Murillo woman and used her as a starting point from which to backtrack. Back to Tamara Montgomery, Craig Somebody, Khamillah Bolton whose accidental shooting had touched off a season of chaos for Stan Rice last December, a couple accidents, Noreen Dunn's suicide, old Mrs. Thurman whose death had inadvertently led to the death of Mrs. Bolton, Jerry Dudek ...

And there it was.

Cat had almost missed it because of the spelling. She had been looking for a 'Renee' or 'Rene,' but it was R-e-n-a-y, and Cat remembered hearing about it on the radio, the morning of Jerry Dudek's murder. Early twenties, homicide. Cat squinted at the glowing type. Atlantic City resident, no immediate survivors. Funeral arrangements by Morosco's Funeral Home, Atlantic City. Cat had gone to school with Trina Morosco, who had been anything but funereal. Requiem Mass to be celebrated at—

Cat blinked.

St. Agnes Church, Kentucky and Barents Avenue, Atlantic City.

Was it possible the death of this Renay was somehow linked to the death of Carmen Oliva? Was that why Victor had gone straight from Oliva's to St. Agnes? Then how did Tamara Montgomery, buried in Vineland, Estrella Murillo, buried in her native Guatemala, figure in? Was it possible that all of these women had been murdered by one killer? Was that why Victor had been called to Oliva's and abruptly canceled their trip? No, that didn't happen around here, not down the shore, things like that happened Someplace Else, where all those evil things occurred. But Jerry Dudek had happened here, and Earlene Adkins. And Chris.

Cat recalled her first date with Victor, the Rhinebeck killings had come up. Over dinner, of all things. Rhinebeck had chained several young people in the basement of his townhouse, fed on them. One survived. Cat recalled the news, recalled Rhinebeck being ushered into his arraignment, clean-shaven, nondescript, looking like anybody. The reporters had camped out on his parents' front lawn until Rhinebeck's white-haired mother emerged at last, looking like anybody's mother. ("I just don't understand. Growing up, he got everything he wanted and then some.")

Cat backtracked again, this time searching for any articles about the investigations of the deaths of Tammy and Renay, and the Murillo woman. A few brief paragraphs, investigation ongoing, the CrimeStoppers number, routine plea for potential witnesses to come forward, then nothing. The dog in the night-time. Cat shut the microfiche down, and returned to Jane and Mats. Jane had wedged herself next to her brother in his beanbag chair, was reading to him. "The *Bengal* tiger is the largest of the *great cats*. They will seize their prey with their *claws* and kill with a *crushing bite* to the throat. After a kill, the tiger will roam for days until hunger causes him to *kill again*." Mats looked up at his sister, worshipfully.

Cat felt a wellspring of love for the pair; the intensity of it terrified her. What a hostage it made you, to love like that, to love the way she loved her children, loved Chris. Loved ... Cat bit her lip. Hostage to the people who had killed Jerry Dudek and Mrs. Thurman and Earlene, Carmen and Tammy and Renay, hostage to people who drifted along in the current of society looking like anybody and everybody, getting anyone they wanted. And then some.

Jane looked up. "What's *wrong*?"

"Nothing, nothing." She leaned down, kissed Jane on the forehead, kissed Mats' unruly hair.

"What are you *kissing* us for? We didn't *do* anything."

"It's not for you, sweetie, it's for me," Cat smiled.

"What were you looking up?"

"Watchdogs," Cat murmured, leaning down to button Mats' coat. "The kind that don't bark when they should."

## CHAPTER SIX

Victor pulled up shortly before eight-thirty Saturday morning, saw that the door to the ground floor apartment had been propped open. There was a bay window overlooking the small slate patio, the tiny quadrangle of lawn. The window was uncurtained and Victor could spot a few overalled forms moving around inside.

He went up to the door and knocked, peered in. A couple young boys, two of Vinnie's sons, laying newspapers over a section of carpet beneath the window, said a polite hello to Victor. The living room was large and segued on the east side to a narrow sunroom. On the opposite side were a dining area with a kitchen in back that overlooked the fenced-in yard. The bedrooms faced back too, two of them, a bath and a half.

"Is your Aunt Cat around?"

"I think she's upstairs. Uncle Freddy and Mats are in the bedroom."

Victor followed a short corridor to the back of the unit, found Freddy and Mats in the master bedroom. Freddy had painted a large square near the bottom of the inside wall, let Mats fill in the space unsupervised.

"Yo, Victor, you don't mind I don't shake hands." Freddy held up his hands, splotched with dark-green paint. Victor nodded, squatted beside Mats.

"Are you ready to go out to breakfast?"

"I don't want to. And Mom's not gonna, either."

Victor heard the note of triumph, resentment. "I see."

"Jane says she'll go." *Traitor.*

Victor nodded. "That's a good job."

"I'm almos' five."

"Yes. Next month, isn't it?"

Mats eyed him. "How come you an' Mom didn't go away?"

"I had too much work to do and couldn't get away."

"Are you gonna go when your work's all done?"

Victor heard the tremor. He remembered how frightened his nephew Ernesto had been when Milly went to the hospital to have baby Victor. "I think what we'll do is wait and see. And if we want to go, we'll ask you if it's okay."

Mats studied Victor, his brown eyes owlish, disbelieving. "You mean I can say you can't go?"

"That's right."

"Aunt Sherrie's gonna come over with that new baby," Mats informed him, scrutinized Victor for his reaction to the news.

Victor did not appear particularly impressed. "I'll bet he doesn't know how to paint."

"He doesn't!" Mats concurred, gleefully, then offered, "You wanna paint a little?"

"Perhaps some other time. I'm not dressed for it. When I have time, you can show me how to paint properly, I'm out of practice."

"Okay."

Victor rose.

Freddy murmured. "Sorry about the trip."

"He really was concerned?"

Freddy looked at Mats, lowered his voice. "Cat didn't want to say anything because your plans were set. It's been awhile since any of us been four, we forget how it was."

"I'll try not to forget. What's Cat up to?" He had called last night from the office; she had sounded preoccupied.

"She spent most of yesterday at the computer, still tryin' to figure out how to use it, that's what she said. You want the dish, you're gonna have to feed the canary."

The canary was Jane, who was descending the front steps wearing her best jeans, a white sweater with satin appliqués, a heavy jacket thrown over her shoulders. "So, it's just the two of us, *linda*? A small and intimate?"

Jane nodded, blushed like her mother.

"Where is your mother?"

"In the kitchen."

"Let me go tell her we're leaving."

Cat was scanning the morning paper's cursory account of Carmen Oliva's murder, balancing a coffee mug in the palm of her hand.

"You're leaving your front door unlocked?" Victor bent down to give her a kiss, noticed that she closed and folded the paper hastily, shoved it aside.

"Freddy and the boys are right downstairs. They're going to be underfoot all weekend; if you'd like to try your hand at home renovation, you're more than welcome."

"I have to go in right after breakfast. Mats says you're not coming."

"I have work to do, too." Cat hesitated. "I would be remiss if I didn't observe that you had to cancel our trip and yet this morning you're perfectly free."

"I'm waiting for some paper, I don't expect it much before eleven."

"Related to that girl who turned up dead yesterday?"

"Cat."

Cat shuffled through the paper, held up the page with the headline, WOMAN SLAIN IN AC APARTMENT. "This is hardly cancel-the-reservations, this is the sort of thing your unit handles every day, and was ready to handle when you were away. What is it about a Region Section, page-three event that puts homicide on red alert?"

"No comment."

"Is that 'no comment' extended to the press at large or just to me?" She tapped the by-line. "Someone didn't give

Karen Friedlander a 'no comment.'" *Why are you riding him so? Because you were ready to cancel the trip before he beat you to it?* Guilt, making her bitchy.

"If Raab orders a lockdown, I have to respect it. I don't know who leaked to Friedlander. Don't let's make this a trust issue, Cat. It's work, that's all."

"Sooner or later, everything that's anything between two people comes down to trust, Victor. And people talk about work all the time. Didn't you talk about it with Marisol?" Cat bit her lip.

Victor looked at her, his dark eyes unreadable. "She knew when it was better not to ask."

"It wasn't her job to ask," Cat replied, quietly. "It is mine."

"And sometimes it's going to be mine to issue a 'no comment.' And I know you won't assume it means I don't trust you." He thought fleetingly of Carmen Oliva, who had trusted someone enough to let him into her house, someone who had killed her so swiftly she didn't even put up a fight.

"Well, can you tell me how she died, at least? The paper said she was 'apparently stabbed.' If someone's been stabbed, it would seem redundant to say that it's apparent. I can't think of any more apparent manner of death. To state it is like saying, 'She was apparently stabbed, but it's possible she took poison or maybe got hit by a truck.' Was she stabbed or not?"

"Apparently."

The restaurant was crowded; President's Day weekend with a lot of college kids using the time off to run down the shore and lock in a summer job. Jane picked up her menu, scanned it with her mother's critical scrutiny. Victor imagined Jane informing the waitress that "The oatmeal mustn't have *any salt*" and the "bacon has to be *crispy* but not *burnt*."

"Victor ..?"

"Yes?"

"Can you be my ethnic friend?"

Victor looked at her over his menu. "I beg your pardon?"

"Like, at school? We got Ethnic Heritage Week and then Diversity Day and on Diversity Day we can come in dressed like the country where our ancestors are from and we can sign up to bring in an ethnic friend and he tells what his job is and where he's from and stuff like that."

"Well, I'm from Atlantic City. That's not very different from here, except for the casinos and so forth."

"But you're *really* from Puerto Rico."

"Well, *linda*, if they teach you geography properly, you'll learn that Puerto Rico is part of the United States, not a separate country. Why don't you ask Ellice?"

"I *did*. But all she did was *laugh*, and when I tried to explain about Diversity Day, she just laughed *more*."

Victor tugged his mustache into a composed line. "I don't have to, what was it? Dress like where my ancestors are from, do I?"

"Uh-uh. You just come in and say what your background is and what you do for a job and stuff."

The waitress came to take their orders. Jane requested home fries, toast, bacon and chocolate milk, Victor a Spanish omelet and coffee.

When she departed, he leaned forward on his elbows. "Okay, what am I up against?"

"Ashley Kreisberg's next-door-neighbor owns Cardozo's Cakery."

"He bringing samples?"

"He's not *allowed*. Andy Chu's hyper*active*."

"I'll do it."

"Really?"

"On my honor."

The waitress brought their drinks. Jane plucked the paper from her straw, dropped it into an ashtray."How come you an' Mom aren't going to Puerto Rico?"

"At the last moment, I couldn't get away from work."

"Oh. I thought it was 'cause Mom maybe had to work."
She sipped her milk. "Did someone get killed or something?"

"Yes." He watched the expression in her dark eyes. She
knew what getting killed meant. She had been about seven
when her father had died.

"You gotta work Saturdays a lot?"

"Sometimes."

"Aunt Sherrie says she wishes Uncle Joey could stay home
more because the baby wears her out but Aunt Annie says
Aunt Sherrie doesn't know how good she's got it because she'd
rather have a little baby than a big one. She says since Uncle
Carlo retired, he's driving her crazy trying to fix things that
aren't even *broken*. She says that if she didn't have her job to
go to, they'd wind up *killing* each other. And they *all* want
Mom to get them on TV," she confided. "Don't you wish you
could be on TV?"

"Not particularly."

"Not even on *CopWatch*?"

*Especially* not *CopWatch*. Victor shook his head.

The waitress came with their food. Jane unfolded her paper
napkin, laid it on her lap. Cat's teaching, Victor concluded.

"Aunt Lorraine does. She's gonna get a job typing over
the hospital. She says it's just to put away college money for
Vinnie and Johnny and Jason? But Mom says, she just wants
to store up symptoms for her invatory."

"Inventory," Victor corrected, repressing a smile. Lorraine,
married to Vinnie, was a hypochondriac.

"She was *awful jealous* of Mom for getting shot."

"Your Aunt Lorraine was? I can't think it was a pleasant
experience for your mother." His mind flashed back to Cat
on the floor, blood pooling on the checkerboard linoleum.

Jane attempted to decipher the chill that froze out the
smile. "Did you ever get shot, Victor?"

Victor tapped his right shoulder, below his clavicle.

Jane's eyes widened, impressed. "Can I *see*?"

"Juanita," Victor said in a low voice. "What would those ladies staring at us think if I started to disrobe right here at the table?" Thinking he was a weekend father, which amused him a little.

Jane blushed. She peeled away the fat from a piece of bacon, popped the remaining splinter of meat into her mouth. "Victor ..."

"Yes?"

The large brown eyes scrutinized him. "Are you an' Mom gonna get married?"

Victor propped his elbows on the table, his fork dangling from his fingertips. "Why do you ask?"

"I was just wondering ..."

"Jane, I think you're old enough not to be kept wondering. Your mother is the sort of person I would want to marry. But I don't know if she's ready to think about getting married again."

"But if you *did*, what would *we* be? Me and Mats?"

"In that case, I would be your stepfather and you would be my stepchildren. Like your Uncle Joey is to Meryl."

Jane stripped the crust from a wedge of toast, studied the packets of jelly in a bowl. "What's currant taste like?"

"Grape."

She peeled off the lid, not looking at him. "I still love my real Dad."

"I hope so."

"In stories? The stepparents, like, don't give you enough to *eat* and make you do all the *work*."

"Is that the way it is with your cousin Meryl?"

Jane shook her head. "Uncle Joey wants to *adopt* her. They gotta, like, go to *court*? And the judge asks them stuff and then Uncle Joey could get made her real father and her real dad won't be *anything* anymore. He was, like, in *jail* or something. He *beat up* Aunt Sherrie. Meryl told me."

Cat had called Jane The Italicizer, but Victor had heard enough of Sherrie's history to know that Jane wasn't exaggerating. "If that's true, then her natural father is not fit to be with her or her mother. In that case, a judge can sometimes allow someone else to adopt her."

"Mom says Uncle Joey treats Aunt Sherrie like a queen. And I heard Mom tell Ellice that Uncle Freddy would treat her like a queen. And Nonna said once that Daddy treated Mom like a queen. So I asked Mom if all the girls in our family were the queens, were all the men the kings and she said no, they were just prince consorts."

Victor laughed. Jane felt a thrill of triumph; making Victor laugh was something of an accomplishment, though she wasn't sure what she had said that was so funny.

"Prince consort would suit me fine," Victor grinned. "So what's Mom up to, other than following the TV crew?"

"Trying to figure out how to do stuff on the computer."

"I meant, is she working on any other stories or anything?" Feeding the canary. Cat's brothers were not above it but he could not quite believe he had sunk to the same tactics. But Jane was Mata Hari reincarnate, and it would have been rude to slight such talent.

"I think maybe she's gonna write something about the church where Uncle Dominic works."

"Why do you think she would be working on something to do with St. Agnes?"

"'Cause she went over there yesterday."

"Oh, really? When yesterday?"

"In the morning. An' when she came back she took us to McDonalds for lunch, and then she had to look up something at the library and then she was at the computer all day."

"Oh?" Victor turned his attention to his omelet, feigning indifference.

"I think Jason was showing her how to get web pages."

"Oh? Which ones?" he inquired. Just so as not to seem rude.

\*\*\*

Cat decided she couldn't keep Ritchie hanging all weekend; so when Jane and Victor left, she made a pre-emptive
strike, called him at home.

"Austen, I could be with a woman here."

"Then since you've got your checkbook out, start making
one out to me. Or did your moles come through?"

"All day yesterday, all's I come up with is Oliva's PM's
early today and the powwow's scheduled for—"

"Later this morning, I know. Look, Ritchie, if I pass something along, you cannot hint, assume, imply, convey that I
got this from a police source."

"Did you?"

"No. Now, give me a nice round number preceded by a
dollar sign."

Ritchie aimed low.

"Try again."

This time he hit the mark.

Cat hesitated. *Sooner or later everything that means anything
comes down to trust, right?* "You remember around the third week
of December, they found this woman in a rooming house?
Guatemalan woman named Murillo? Dead a couple days?"

"Got her throat ... cut," Ritchie muttered.

The bell chimed again, clearer. "A few days before that, a
girl, Montgomery, was fished out of the inlet."

"She drowned—"

"Do you know that for certain?"

"How do I know anything?"

Cat paused. "Honest to God, Ritchie, do you want an
answer to that?"

"You sayin' she didn't drown?"

"The obit says 'apparent *homicide*' and the article said she
was pulled out of the bay, it never said she drowned. And
there was very little follow-up copy on either of these cases.
Check it out."

"So whaddaya sayin'?"

"I think Carmen Oliva, the Murillo woman and the Montgomery woman were all killed the same way." *Renay, too.* "Make a play for those autopsy reports? I'll bet their frozen."

"ME can't freeze 'em, they're public record."

"But the DA can, or he can get an order to do it. What you offered me just now? Would you like to go double or nothing that the DA's moved to seal the autopsy records?"

"Austen, you're right about this, you can have half interest in the *Chronicle.*"

"'May no fate willfully misunderstand me and half grant what I wish,'" Cat quoted. "Robert Frost. And cash on acceptance will be just fine."

Cat hung up. Why hadn't she told Ritchie about Renay? Maybe because holding back extended her hold over him a little longer. Ritchie was smart, and he'd been throwing assignments her way pretty consistently but he still thought of her primarily as his Entertainment Girl. Because she hadn't really initiated anything in the Dudek or Sterling matters, she'd merely had the dubious distinction of being the first one to trip over the corpse.

What she needed to do was to think like Kate Auletta, Ace Detective. Kate would go after a common link to more than one of the victims, Cat thought. Young women. *Big deal.* Race? *Two Hispanics, one white, one black. The multicult factor. Think.* That woman, Molina, had hinted that Easter had bailed out Carmen Oliva, that Renay had worked for him. That's two of the victims who had known, probably worked for, James Easter. What were the names of Easter's businesses? Joey had told her. Printemps Escorts and the lingerie shop, Nothing Sacred.

"Kate Auletta, Investigator Extraordinaire," Cat muttered as she dialed information, got the number for Nothing Sacred. "No task too daunting, no ... no assets worth flaunting." She stifled a giggle. "Misplaced levity," she whispered into the receiver. "The sin of the Fortunatis. Now *that* would be a great title for a book. One of those books where the girl on the cover does have assets worth flaunting."

"Nothing Sacred, Helena speaking, how may we help you?"

Helena sounded like a receptionist in a mortuary.

"I'd like to speak to Renay, please."

"I don't believe you have the right number, ma'am."

"I'm sure the salesgirl I spoke to was named Renay. She waited on me when I bought some, uh, Christmas gifts."

"I'm sorry, ma'am, I've been here for two years and we haven't had a personal service representative named Renay in that time." Helena told her to have a very nice day and hung up before Cat could ask for Tammy or Carmen.

Kate Auletta would have flat-out asked Helena if she knew any dead women named Renay. Cat got the number for Printemps, dialed.

"Thank you for calling Printemps. This is Gloria speaking, how may we help you?"

"I'm calling for my employer who will be in the city next week and he would like to"—*dear Lord, what on earth is the appropriate verb here?*—"engage"—*close enough*—"Renay? I believe they had a, uh, date last fall?"

Also, how to hire a hooker would have been in Kate Auletta's Lexicon of Street Savvy: "Hookers: Contracting Of."

There was a pause, longer than someone as schooled as Gloria was in the smooth response should have permitted. "Renay, you said?"

"R-e-n-a-y."

"May I have your employer's name?"

"He ... prefers to go by Ritchie. He says Renay will remember him."

The pause, shorter, was still too prolonged. "Would you hold a minute, please?"

On-hold music, but at least it was Cole Porter and a decent arrangement, not that loopy New Age she got when she called her online tech support in California. Gloria returned. "If you could hold, please, Mr. Easter would like to speak to you personally."

Kate Auletta would have called his bluff. Cat hung up.

There was a knock on her door and Cat turned to see Victor standing on the threshold. "I dropped Jane downstairs. You working?"

"How long have you been standing there?"

Victor leaned against the door frame, looked down at her. "'There was a sort of sulky defiance in her eyes which only goes with guilty knowledge,'" he quoted.

"Says who?"

"Sherlock Holmes, *querida. The Norwood Builder.*"

"And what was she guilty of?"

"Fraud, conspiracy, attempted murder."

"I haven't done one of those things this morning."

"Well, I might respond that if you haven't done one, I'd like to know which two you have committed." He stepped into the room, sat on the bed across from her. "Jane says you went into Atlantic City yesterday."

"I went to return Monsignor Greg's books."

"Dominic there?"

"Why?"

"I haven't seen him in awhile, I just wondered."

"No, you don't. Just wonder."

Victor looked at her, the dark eyes receding to a wary distance. *Sooner or later, everything that's anything between two people comes down to trust.* He leaned toward her, took her hand in his, looked down at the slender fingers, the pair of thin gold rings. "The woman they found yesterday? Apparently, she was a parishioner at St. Agnes. I was just wondering if Dominic mentioned it to you."

"No." She looked at Victor; his gaze was flat, unreadable. It was the truth, she told herself, stubbornly. Dominic *hadn't* mentioned it; it was Monsignor Greg who had divulged the news. "I know he had a funeral Mass yesterday. He probably read about the murder in the paper today like everyone else. How else would he know?"

"News travels in a neighborhood like that."

"Aren't your people canvassing the neighborhood?"

"My people? No." Which was the truth, of course, he had gone to St. Agnes himself, the local detectives were canvassing the area. Half truths. Worse than lies. He rose, her hand still between his. "I have to go."

The phone rang. Cat disengaged her hand, picked it up. A deep, melodious voice said, "This five-five-five, two-two-two-eight?"

"Who's calling?"

"You tell me. Your number came up on our caller ID."

"No it didn't, I'm unlisted and blocked," Cat replied. Printemps. Or the lingerie place. "You must have the wrong number." She hung up.

"Who was that?" Victor asked.

Cat looked at him. "Wrong number."

The phone rang again.

"I'll get rid of them," Victor said, reached for the receiver, but Cat snatched it first. "Hello?"

"What do you want askin' about Renay?"

"I'm sorry, you really do have the wrong number."

"But I didn't have a hard time gettin' it, what with all your phone block and unlisted, did I? Maybe you wanna think about that before you call here again, okay?" the voice suggested, pleasantly.

This time he hung up.

"Who was it, Cat?"

"Just someone fooling around."

## CHAPTER SEVEN

"What do you have for me?" Victor settled in the high-backed leather chair behind his desk. Detectives Phil Long and Jean Adane sat in the pair of burgundy leather chairs, Stan Rice perched against the makeshift bookcase. Adane spoke. "A reporter from the *Press* called, inquiring about Miss Oliva's investigation, whether we had any suspects. I referred him to Mr. Raab's office."

"Very good."

"Your sister called. Remedios."

Damn. He had promised Remy she could use his flat while he was out of town. "I'll get back to her, thank you."

Stan spoke up. "The city fielded us one. Last night woman finds her husband on the carpet, he's just layin' there, she says, 'You want me to call nine-one-one,' the husband, according to her, says, 'No,' so she goes off to bed, leaves him there, this morning, he's cold."

"What do they want us to do about it?"

"They wanna know if we're gonna investigate it as a possible manslaughter."

"Sergeant, what was the age of these people?"

"Guy's in his mid-nineties, the woman's eighty-nine."

Victor stroked his downturned mustache. "Would you tell the city department that I appreciate their desire to defer to us in what I am sure is a very interesting situation but that I trust to their discretion and ability to take the appropriate course of action?"

Stan tugged out his notebook, began to scribble, muttering, "Tell city boys to stuff it."

Victor sighed. "Anything else, Adane?"

"A Professor Ted Cusack called to ask when he might schedule his interview."

"What interview?"

"He's a television writer, working with a program called *CopWatch*. He's been in town conducting background interviews relating to the Dudek matter. He's staying at the Marinea Towers, here's his number—"

"Call him back. Tell the professor I'm not doing interviews."

Adane bit her lip.

"What's the matter?"

"Sir ... it seems that Cusack already contacted Captain Loeper and Captain Loeper told him you would cooperate."

Victor's expression remained composed, his voice neutral. "Anything else?"

"And Captain Loeper said to remind you about the retirement dinner for Captain Lombardi Friday night. The banquet room of the Marinea Towers. He'd like for all of us to attend."

"Didn't think Benny the Beak would ever retire," Stan Rice chuckled. "Can we bring a date?"

"Let's move on to Oliva, shall we?"

Long spoke up. "Already we been gettin' on the average of five, six calls an hour. Usual stuff, I seen this, I seen that. Keeps up, we're gonna need more manpower—'scuse me, Jeannie, personpower—just to handle the phones." He shook his head. "We gotta follow up on every call, we're lookin at a lotta overtime." Phil shook his head. "That or havin' Mr. Raab set aside a task force."

"Task force," Stan griped. "Couple guys from the Sheriff's

department, couple troopers, your rent-a-feds and a partridge in a pear tree. Pretty soon, it's a turf war, with everyone wantin' to be the star."

"I did call Pacific Savings and Loan," Adane offered. "Carmen Oliva was filling in for their receptionist this week. Since she'd only worked the two days, no one really knew her very well."

Victor nodded, looked at Stan. "Where's my autopsy report?"

"ME'll fax you a prelim, any time now."

"I was expecting more than a prelim."

"Basically, it looks to be cut and dried. No pun meant. Carmen Oliva died from massive blood loss, shock, severed carotid artery with the cut being only yea big—" Stan put an inch and a half of air between his right thumb and index finger. "Short, sharp blade, double-edged. But there's no bruises, no defensive wounds, no head trauma like she wasn't knocked out or anything. She wasn't a virgin, but there was no sexual assault."

"I repeat, if it's cut and dried, what's the hold-up?"

"ME's bringin' people down from the state lab to do the tox screen and review the tox work on the other two, Montgomery and Murillo."

"Why?"

Stan shrugged. "He said he'll tell us when he's got something to tell."

"And how long does he expect that to take?"

"Your guess is as good as mine."

"I don't guess."

Adane spoke up. "We decided to go ahead and look over the files. Phil gave me Montgomery's and I reviewed it last night. Tamara Montgomery, age twenty. She left home after high school and for the six months before her death had been living with a Mr. and Mrs. Howard Leeds at The Madison, high-rise condominium units out near the inlet."

Victor rubbed his thumb under his chin, pensively. "She was pulled out of the inlet around there, wasn't she?"

"Across the street. She was sort of an *au pair*, was given room and board and a small salary for caring for the Leeds' two children. Phil interviewed them last month. They said Miss Montgomery didn't go out much. Church on Sunday, which was her day off, and an occasional movie with a girl-friend. She didn't have a boyfriend. She had talked about taking some college courses in the spring, mentioned that she was going to spend Christmas with her family. Talked like she hadn't seen them for awhile. On the night of Thursday, December sixth, she went out, the Leeds family said they thought it was some holiday party, but they weren't sure. They had planned to leave the following morning, early, for a month-long skiing trip to Europe and Miss Montgomery was going to house-sit, except for the few days over Christmas she was planning to visit her parents in Vineland. The Leeds departed on Friday, December seventh, around five a.m. They assumed Miss Montgomery had come in and gone to bed. They returned from their trip January seventh."

"'S why I didn't get to interview 'em 'til last month," Phil added.

"So they *think* she went to some party, but weren't sure, and they don't so much as take a look in her bedroom to see if she got in all right before they leave?"

"That's right, sir. They said she had a key. They were anxious to make their flight. And I suppose ..."

"Please don't hesitate to speak up, Adane."

"I was going to say that people who surrender their young children to someone else's care six days a week, eight or ten hours a day, would probably not be motivated to keep track of someone else's daughter."

"That's an assumption, Adane."

"I prefer to call it a provisional hypothesis, sir." Adane clenched her fists, looked him in the eye. "And I believe it conforms to the facts. Of course, I would be willing to amend it if new facts come my way."

Victor cocked an eyebrow, his mouth curving in an appreciative smile. "How did they come to hire her?"

"They placed an ad, interviewed her."

"She provide references?"

"Two high school teachers and a couple from Vineland she babysat for during high school."

"She was twenty. Those references had to be two years old. This family doesn't do a background check?"

"They called her references and the people all said Miss Montgomery was a very nice girl," Adane replied.

"What about this party she attended?"

"Phil found out the party was an Advent dinner at St. Agnes Church. Apparently she attended Mass fairly regularly, at either St. Agnes or St. Nick's, she wasn't officially enrolled in either. It's likely she went to whichever suited her schedule. She stayed to help clean up and was seen leaving around nine. She didn't have a car. A young woman could have walked from the church to The Madison."

"But you wouldn't have done it," Victor interpreted.

Adane shook her head.

"I can pull the interviews if you wanna check them out," Phil volunteered.

Victor nodded slowly. He remembered escorting Montgomery's parents to the morgue, the stamp of grief on the faces of her father, her mother. "She was a good girl," the mother had said to him, almost pleading for him to concur. Comes of age, leaves home, two years later winds up in Atlantic City. Beautiful young woman, Victor remembered from the photograph her mother had pressed into his hand. What had she done in those two years? If she had gotten a job, why hadn't she used it as a reference? Why had her mother insisted so that her daughter had been a good girl? "And the ME's report, if I recall, said that she suffered massive blood loss, found no defensive wounds, no external injuries and that she had been sexually active, but there had been no sexual assault, no street drugs or alcohol."

"Except the drug screen? There was a trace of some kinda sedative," Phil tapped his pen against the folder on his lap. "I asked the Leedses if she was takin' sleeping pills or anything, they said not to their knowledge. They let me check their place out. Usual stuff, makeup, aspirin, vitamin C. Didn't find an address book or anything like that."

"Call the pharmacies?"

"The ones in the area. No prescriptions on file for Montgomery."

"Let's move on to Murillo." Victor propped his elbows on the arms of his chair, pressed his fingertips together.

Stan spoke up. "Phil was following her, too, brought me up to speed. Basically, she's Central American, no work visa. The story is she came to take care of a relative, uncle or something who was terminal, he died in the fall, she stuck around. Lived in a crummy place down St. James, sort of halfway between an apartment and a boarding house, tenants were mostly transients. People who work the summer trade, come the fall they head to Florida. By December, there's only Murillo and the building manager living in the building. Buildings on either side been boarded up, word is crackheads, homeless holed up in 'em, and there'd been some problems with break-ins at Murillo's place. Building manager, Ruiz, says she was quiet, paid her rent on time and in cash, kept to herself."

"Where'd she get her cash?"

"Workin' for an outfit called the Grime Reaper. Cleaning service does office and residential. Woman who runs it, Reba Grimes, lives out West AC. She said all she knew's Murillo wanted to take her pay in cash, which is fine with Grimes, keeps the paper to a minimum and Murillo gave notice after Thanksgiving."

"Why?"

"Grimes woman said Murillo was talkin' about how it wasn't right to take money under the table like she'd been doin'." Stan shrugged. "Like maybe her conscience was botherin' her or something? Grimes said a couple weeks before Murillo turned up dead was the last time she saw her." Stan shifted position, rubbed his rib in the area of the knife wound. "Last time Murillo was seen was December twelve. That was a Wednesday, some kinda holiday—"

"*El Virgin de Guadaloupe*," Victor murmured. His mother's mother was Mexican, had a zeal for that particular occasion as for no other.

"Yeah, I think that's it. Churches that have a lotta Hispanics go all out. Ruiz saw her that morning, said she'd probably go to church that night. He and his wife went up to spend the holiday with his wife's mother in Union, were gone overnight."

"Murillo's alone in the building, then?"

Stan nodded. "The ME puts her death right around the last time Ruiz saw her, December twelfth, thirteenth maybe. Ruiz says when he gets back, he's checkin' the place out, looks like a couple of the places been hit. There'd been break-ins in the neighborhood, he goes knocks on her door, lets himself in, she's on the floor, throat cut. ME's report says no external wounds, no defensive wounds, no sign of a struggle, no sexual assault. She was a virgin."

Phil spoke up. "This guy Ruiz, I talked to him three times, Stan here talked to him once, he's not the type puts a lot of trust in the cops. He didn't find the girl dead, I bet he wouldn't even have mentioned the break-ins."

"What about boyfriends, visitors?"

"Nope."

Victor's eyes were on his fingertips, pressed together as if in prayer. "The Murillo woman's apartment wasn't ransacked, correct? No valuables taken?"

"That's right," Long said. "Only thing outta whack was it looked like the doer went out the fire escape insteada the door. Crime lab found traces of her blood there."

"The building was vacant. Why would he go out the fire escape?" Victor scowled.

"Maybe he heard someone come in? I dunno. But there were a couple traces of her blood on the fire escape and the window was unlocked. I don't think Murillo looked the type to leave her doors and windows unlocked."

"The guy Ruiz, I could try him again," Stan offered. "Threaten to bring in INS, see if something more shakes loose, but I really don't think he knows anything, Lieutenant. And I ... I don't like to do that." The knife had missed Stan's infamous soft spot.

Raab knocked on the doorframe, entered and shut the door. "Whole crewa jerk reporters hangin' around outside synagogue, I hadda hole up in my rabbi's office while six members of Hadassah run a diversionary tactic an' Patsy zips the Plymouth outta the lot, they think it's me, right now she's shootin' up the Pike with six, seven newsmonkeys on her tail. Sit down, Long, I can stand, thanks. How's the side, Stan?"

"I'm good."

"I just got off with the guy came down from the state lab, he took samples from Oliva last night."

"Sedation?" Victor asked.

Raab stared. "How'd you know that?"

Adane said, "Montgomery's samples showed a trace of sedation. Now they're reviewing the work on her, Murillo."

"Lucky they didn't toss the samples like they did in the Arquette case, remember that one? Lab tech tosses the blood and panics and he thinks, 'Why not tap one of the other slabs?' And the guy he taps was HIV, so the ME reports it and his office, they're goin' nuts tryin' to locate all the contacts of the guy whose blood they *tossed* thinkin' *he's* the HIV positive. And one of that guy's contacts, not the real HIV, the other guy, tries to hang herself. Thank God someone got to her in time. Mary Grace did some fine footwork to keep the county outta a lawsuit with that one."

"So did Murillo's labwork show sedation?" Victor asked. Raab nodded, slowly.

Victor clasped his hands, reflectively. "A woman living like that keeps her paper trail to a minimum. She's not going to the doctor to ask for a prescription, she's having trouble sleeping, she'll buy over-the-counter and pay cash. And none of the women were users."

Long got up from his chair, turned, offered it to Raab. "I think maybe you better sit down."

"I'm fine."

"I think you're gonna wanna sit down."

Raab took Long's chair. "Tell me flat out, am *I* gonna want a sedative?"

"That or a good stiff drink. I think we got a little more of a problem," Long said. As he spoke, he slid the folder in his hand onto Victor's desk, spilled out a black-and-white photograph. "You remember this one, Lieutenant?"

A young, light-skinned black woman, a head shot taken at the morgue. The blood had been hosed away to reveal that a jagged gash had nearly severed her head from her body, that the body was decomposing.

"November ..." Victor said slowly. "Multiple stab wounds. Two children found her in some abandoned house." The kids had been ten years old, climbed into the window of a boarded-up tenement. Ten years old, Victor thought, a year older than Jane. *Dios me salve.*

"I don't get it," Stan said.

"Multiple stab wounds," Long said, "but technically the cause of death is the same. Severed carotid, massive blood loss. Lotta defensive wounds and the fatal wound wasn't as neat as it was with Oliva, but basically she died from the same cause."

"You're saying this one"—Victor flipped the picture over, read the name printed on the back—"Harris? You think she was the first? That he hadn't refined his technique?"

Long nodded. "She turned up November eight. ME put the date of death about a week before. Crack house they found her in was one the neighbors got together threw out the dopers, they're gonna tear down the place and renovate it, you know, like that group helps folks rehab a house an' move in? People around the neighborhood said she seemed like a real nice gal, goes to church, helps old ladies across the street; she was real interested in helpin' with the rehab, gettin' involved in the community."

"That doesn't tally with her record," Victor recalled.

"That's right. 'Cause you go back six months before she got knifed, she's on Jimmy Easter's payroll."

Victor nodded, thoughtfully. The case had been eclipsed by the Dudek murder; the investigation had cooled.

"An' I talked to Easter at the time. He had an airtight. Halloween night, he tells me he's takin' his kids trick or treatin'. The next day, he's playin' Mr. Mom while the missus works, because it was some kinda school holiday."

"He say why Harris quit him?"

"He said no. Said he was okay with it, though."

"Was he okay with it?" Victor asked.

Long shrugged. "Who knows? It was me, I'd be ticked."

"Why?"

"After she turns up dead, I make the rounds, go by Printemps. They got books there, like a directory, pictures, stats. Whaddaya like? Tall, redhead, Asian? They got it. You don't see it here ..." he tapped the picture on Victor's desk. "But Harris? She was a rainmaker. She walks, it's money out the door."

"How much money?" Victor asked.

"Back when I worked vice? Word was a Printemps date went for one-fifty an hour and that was just for your chit-chat and you spring for the Tattingers. A grand a night was not unheard of. Easter takes a two-thirds cut."

Stan took the Lord's name in vain, hastily said, "'Scuse me, Jeannie. Hey," he suggested, "maybe you wanna sting Printemps, have someone play the john? I'll volunteer."

"I'm not sure I could float a voucher for that," Raab said.

"I'll do it free."

"We decide to run a sting, I'll keep you in mind."

"As I recall, Harris was wearing a little jewelry, money left in her wallet," Victor said.

Long grunted. "Doper woulda lifted that."

"Oliva's jewelry was untouched, too," Victor mused. "Interesting that the killer doesn't think to disguise it as a robbery."

Raab was sitting with his elbows on his knees, his head in his hands. "So you're saying we got four women now, all likely killed by the same person?"

Victor looked at Long. "Harris' autopsy, there was no trace of sedation, was there?"

Long shook his head.

Raab looked up.

"He targets Harris," Victor explained, "but she fights him. It's messy. So he sedates them first. Which might explain," he added, turning his glance toward Adane, "the tea. She makes the tea, he slips her the sedation. He offers to clean up—"

"To give it time to take effect, make her lethargic," Adane concluded.

"Why not just slip 'em an overdose?" Long asked.

"Perhaps he doesn't have a sufficient amount of whatever's he using," Victor suggested.

"Doling it out so he's got enough to go around," Raab interpreted. "How far around?"

Adane spoke up, reluctantly. "I've, well, I've taken the liberty of contacting Missing Persons and asked for a print-out of their reported disappearances in the past year. Any young women in this age range."

They were silent for a moment, contemplating the horrible possibility that there were others lying somewhere, not yet found.

"We've got four women dead," Victor said, quietly. "Killed very efficiently by someone who is able to get into their homes or to lure them into an isolated place, with little or no resistance. That implies the killer was known to the victims. Or at least a person of trust."

"Rules out your used car salesmen," Stan muttered.

"Rules out my profession too," Raab replied, cynically. "But not yours. Folks see a cop, nobody blinks. Who else do people trust? Doctors, priests, teachers, who could all four of 'em known?"

"Well, two of them had a connection to Easter. Montgomery's unaccounted for since high school, but can't—or doesn't want to—come up with recent references."

"You think she worked for Easter?" Long asked.

"I'm saying I'd like you to check Easter's two businesses and see if anyone knew her." He looked at Raab. "Can we subpoena his employment files, IRS records?"

"That could take time. Might be better if you check with city vice, show their pictures around."

"Perhaps it might be possible to bring up Social Security or IRS files on the web and trace his list of employees that way," Adane suggested.

"Is that legal?" Raab asked.

The burst of laughter lessened the tension somewhat. Even Victor smiled when Adane replied, "Well, it can be done, sir."

"Pretty much sums up the state of the law today: can I get away with it," Raab muttered, ruefully.

"When the ME's finished with Oliva, where does she go?" Victor asked.

"Whaddaya mean?" Long asked.

"I mean she had no family. Neither did Harris. Who made the funeral arrangements?"

"Harris went to Moroscos, I'll see if Oliva's going there, too. Montgomery and Murillo went back to family."

Victor stroked his mustache with his thumb. "Murillo was sending a few dollars home to her family, wasn't she? Who paid to have her body shipped to Guatemala?"

"Follow the money, you mean?" Long interpreted.

"Please."

"Look," Raab said, "We're not close to an arrest, I can see that. I'm gonna have to screw my courage to the sticking place and give a statement. Do it during Oliva's funeral. It's what they call 'counter programming,' let the media figure out how to cover both. The other thing is money. I hate to bring this up, but the Hopper prosecution is gonna cost. Hopper, that sonofabitch, waived his right to speedy trial, and Marty Bevilacqua filed to postpone again. And the Amis thing is real iffy. Mary Grace says Cape May County's not gonna file 'cause neither Mrs. Austen nor Stan could give a positive ID on the assailant, and the weapon never turned up."

Stan ran his fingers through his hair. "I never saw the face, what with those Santa whiskers on. Deposition took the whole day, and I heard they put Cat through even worse."

Victor looked up. Cat had said nothing, wouldn't let Victor accompany her to the deposition.

"I think I got a lock on manslaughter and aggravated assault, but the big stuff, conspiracy, is shaky. I'm gonna take it to a grand jury, we go to trial it's another one's gonna cost." Raab continued, "So what I'm sayin' is there's not a lotta cash for extras. I can transfer a few uniforms over from AC, I can put in a call to the fibbies, ask them to look over our reports. You know a pro who'll work bono, gimme a name."

They were silent.

"Then if you don't mind, I'd like to have a word with the lieutenant alone."

Victor rose to his feet when Adane stood, waited until she had left before he sat again.

Raab fidgeted a few seconds, patted the yarmulke pinned over the balding spot on his crown. "I'm a little worried about these TV people supposed to hang around next week. That's a media magnet. Couple dozen newsmonkeys with too much time on their hands, lookin' for the big score."

"And Mrs. Austen is one of the newsmonkeys."

"Victor, look. I like Cat Austen. She's smart, she's a decent person and after what happened to her husband, I'm real glad to see her getting her life back on track. But, in case it hasn't occurred to you—"

"She has a knack for stumbling over corpses."

Raab cleared his throat. "That bug Landis actually calls me at my home last night. Patsy's just lightin' the candles and this jerk goes off on me about what's the deal with Carmen Oliva's arrest record."

"And you would like for me to tell you that I didn't leak Miss Oliva's record to Mrs. Austen."

"I just want us all to be careful. And one more thing. The Harris woman? I make my statement to the press, I'm holding her back. She was a good month before the two in December, got buried in all the brouhaha over the Dudek shooting. You're already getting your crank calls, I bet; we hold something back, we can use it to weed out the crackpots."

"I didn't mention Oliva's record to Mrs. Austen."

"C'mon, Victor, let's not make this a trust thing."

*Sooner or later, everything that's anything between two people comes down to trust.*

## CHAPTER EIGHT

*Thank God for Mom*, Cat decided. The musings over Rhinebeck's poor mom brought Jennie to mind, for Jennie who would like nothing better than an invitation to come over to Cat's and feed the crew that was overhauling the apartment below. The residue of gratitude settled in Cat's subconscious, while she and Jennie stood side-by-side at the kitchen counter.

Cat removed the rings from her right hand and began kneading the mix of ground beef, Romano cheese, minced capers, eggs and bread crumbs for *polpette de carne,* with Mats kneeling on a chair beside her, while Jennie quartered redskins for pan-roasted potatoes, a favorite of Carlo's.

"Carlo been here all day?"

"Mmmm. And Vinnie and the boys. Sherrie's coming by to drop off some wallpaper samples she thought Ellice might like. Joey has to work. You didn't have to bring all this, Mama. When I asked you to come by, I didn't mean for you to fuss. We could have sent out for pizza."

"Hah. You wanna know what's the matter with people today? Nobody wants to fuss. What kind of mother are you, don't wanna fuss a little? When I get too old, you put me in the home, I'll have plenty of time to sit around and not fuss."

"Nobody's putting you in the home, Mama." Cat reached

for one of the cast-iron skillets hanging by a peg on the wall, set it over a burner on the stove.

"So, maybe you could get Carlo on the television. He knows about cops, those TV people could find something for him to do. He's gettin' too much time on his hands. You know what happens, you got too much time on your hands?"

"You get in trouble," Cat recited from memory. "I'm not the producer, mama. I just get to sit in on the open call."

"You remember the Daughters of Sicily did *High Button Shoes* to buy that computer for the church, then it gets stolen? I played Mrs. Longstreet?" To refresh Cat's memory, Jennie sang a few bars of "Papa, Won't You Dance With Me?"

"Nanette Fabray couldn't hold a candle to you, Mama." Cat handed Mats a lump of ground beef, helped him roll it into a ball between his small hands.

"Is Victor coming over to eat?"

"I think he's going to be tied up all day." Cat took the meatball from Mats, made a discreet modification before she laid it on the waxed paper.

"I'm cookin', Nonna," Mats boasted.

"You're nonna's *bammin'*. Victor, he works too much. Work too much, he's gonna have a heart attack. You got any good olive oil?"

"I'll get it." Cat handed her mother a bottle of extra virgin. "It was that woman who got"—she nodded toward Mats—"k-i-l-l-e-d, Mama."

"What, you mean Carmen Oliva?"

Cat blinked. The fragment of gratitude dislodged from her subconscious, emerged in an image, Jennie sitting behind a desk in the little office at St. Agnes.

"Did you know her, Mama?"

"She'd been coming to church. She was helping Isadore with Mary. I'm gonna need another skillet to do all these potatoes. The insurance, they want him to put her some-where, but Isadore says why should she lie around in a nursing home? So some of us, we took turns going over the house so he could keep working, get to the grocery store, run his errands."

Cat tried to recall the particulars of Mary Testa's condition. "The kind of care she needed, wouldn't you have to have some kind of medical knowledge?"

"Well, Beth showed us what to do. Such a nice lady. I expect she'll put up for Carmen's funeral if there's no one to pay. That's the best thing about having family, Allegrezza, you die, there's plenty of people to put in for a nice funeral, you don't have to take charity. Trina Morosco told Dom that Carmen doesn't have family and somebody's gotta pay to lay her out. That wild girl workin' for a funeral home. I die, you don't let Trina fix me up, I'll look like some *puttan'* laid out."

Cat promised her mother that when she died, Trina Morosco would not get her hands on Jennie. Mats wanted to know what a *puttan'* was, and Cat told him it was a potato.

"And something nice, green, and that rosary you gave me Christmas before last."

Cat promised her mother she would be laid out in her green dress, not the crepe with the black collar, but the rayon with the bodice pleats and the long sleeves and that she would have the jade and silver rosary in her hands. "Who's Beth?"

"Beth Easter."

A meatball slipped from Cat's hand, plopped on the linoleum. *Not James Easter's wife?*

"Don't worry about it, we got plenty. She knows your friend Jackie. Annie, too, they all worked together. Married to that pimp, it makes you wonder what some people see in each other. And those two little girls of theirs, you think he wants his daughters prancing around in their underwear in front of strangers? I don't think so."

Why would James Easter's wife "put up" for Carmen Oliva's funeral? Cat's friend, Jackie Wing, was a nurse; so was Carlo's wife, Annie. So Beth Easter was a nurse, too.

Jennie plopped a cube of butter in each skillet, adjusted the heat. "How about a nice string bean salad, too?"

Ellice lumbered in, carrying three volumes of wallpaper samples, followed by Sherrie Fortunati, carrying baby Gio. "Gee, Cat, thanks for having us over. I was too tired to cook and Joey's working overtime. Victor, too?"

Cat nodded, saw that Mats was eyeing Gio skeptically. She gave Mats a hug.

"Can I nurse him in here?"

"Sure, go ahead."

Sherrie settled in the booth, tossed her long blonde braid over one shoulder.

"This home renovation by committee is not makin' it," Ellice commented. "I go out and come back an hour later and Freddy and Carlo are still paintin' the same damn spot on the wall, I keep thinkin' of that line from 'An Essay on Man': 'In human works, tho' labor'd on with pain, A thousand movements scarce one purpose gain.'"

"Pope?" Cat asked.

"The Pope, he's a smart man," Jennie declared. She got a small plastic trash bag, poured in about a cup of olive oil, a dollop of salt, shoveled in the pile of diced potatoes and began to shake the bag vigorously. Ellice looked over Jennie's head at Cat, bit back a laugh.

Jennie divided the potatoes between the two skillets, adjusted the heat. "What's Victor's number at work?" she asked Cat.

"Why?" Cat let Mats set the meatballs into her skillet. She began to sauté them.

"I'm gonna call him, tell him to come over and eat."

Cat told her the number, concentrated on browning the pan of meatballs, while Jennie said, "You tell him it's Jennie, he'll pick up the phone." Then, "Victor, did you eat dinner? ... Well, you come over Cat's, come by in an hour ... Well, you gotta eat ... You don't eat, you know what happens? ... That's right." She held out the receiver to Cat. "He wants to talk to you."

Cat stretched the cord as far as it would go so that she could continue cooking while she talked. "How's it going?"

"Cat, I appreciate the invitation, but I'm not sure I can get away."

"Don't you know what happens if you don't eat?"

"You get run down," Victor replied promptly.

"And if you work too hard?"

"You get a heart attack. I have a mother, too."

"Then it's not just a Sicilian thing."

"I don't believe so, no. Please give my apologies to your mother. Tell her to put something aside for me, I'll try to come by this evening, if Mats doesn't mind company. Is he there?"

"Yes."

"Put him on the phone."

Mats crawled into the booth with a scornful look at little Gio. *He* couldn't talk on the phone. "Hello."

"Your mother invited me over this evening. Is that okay with you?"

"Aunt Sherrie's here with the baby."

"I see. I expect everyone's making a fuss over him."

"Uh-huh."

"Well, people do that with babies."

"He don't have teeth yet and he can't talk or go potty by hisself or anything."

"Yes. It's a shame he doesn't have a big brother to help him out. Someone to look out for him and show him how to do things like that."

"Jason and Johnny are here."

"Yes, but I was thinking they might be too big. Someone about four years old or so would be just the right age. I know I always wished I had an older brother or cousin or someone to look after me."

"I'm four," Mats reminded him.

"So you are. Well, I hope that baby knows how lucky he is to have a cousin like you."

"Are you gonna come over to eat here?"

"I may come later, not for dinner."

"We're havin' meatballs and puttans for supper."

Ellice let out a whoop and Cat grabbed the phone from Mats.

"Did your son say what I think he just said?"

"I hate to disappoint you, but it's just Sicilian meatballs and pan roasted potatoes and salad. I'm sure we'll have plenty of leftovers. If you haven't eaten, I'll just nuke whatever's in the little dish. You know about the little dish?"

"As in 'Don't throw that out, put it in a little dish'?"

"Exactly."

Cat hung up and chucked baby Gio under the chin when Mats wasn't looking, told Mats she wasn't laughing at him, she was just smiling because he was such a good helper in the kitchen.

The phone rang and Cat picked it up. It was Ritchie, who began the conversation mid-sentence. "... so I figure I'll work the Jimmy Easter angle, I go over Nothing Sacred. They got like a shop downstairs, upstairs you pick something out, wanna see how it looks, they got gals'll model the skimpies for you. I hadda buy some stuff, make it look legit? Wanna lace buster?"

"*Bustier,*" Cat corrected. "B-u-s-t-i-e-r."

"I think the chick who modeled it, we're talkin' bustiest. Fifty bucks says she hasn't seen her knees in a decade. And I'm makin' chit-chat, and remember the gal you were tellin' me about this morning? One they fished out last December?"

"Montgomery?"

"That's her. Useta work there. Over a year, quit last summer. Gal told me Tammy—that was her name, Tammy?— she'd been on the outs with her folks, but they'd patched things up, she was havin' second thoughts about workin' for an outfit like Easter's. Quit to take a housesitting, babysitting job, something like that."

Cat frowned, thoughtfully. Babysitting couldn't pay better than lingerie modeling, so it wasn't the money. And that made three suspects now with a direct connection to Easter: Renay, Tammy and Carmen.

Ritchie expressed the sentiment, added, "That Hispanic chick's the wild card. You can link her to Easter, I'll pay a bonus."

"Oh, yeah? How much?"

Cat immediately converted the sum named to a new winter coat for Mats, a much-needed tune-up for her car and two month's worth of heating bills. "Where'd she live?"

Ritchie gave her the address. "The building manager there, I heard he was pretty close-mouthed with the cops, maybe he'll open up for you. Oh, and I figured out where she was workin' when she got whacked. There's this cleaning service, called The Grime Reaper. Get it? Grime Reaper? The woman runs it's named Grimes, Reba Grimes, she works outta her home in West AC, they do homes and offices. Cherry says they do the place she gets her hair done, the shampoo gal knew Murillo."

"What about the autopsy reports?"

"Yeah, you told me so. They're frozen. So I go over Nick's Subs, that kid Keith works there preps the stiffs for the ME? You know, he bags their gear, hoses them down? He prepped Oliva and Montgomery, said they were both drained like Dracula's dinner. Incision to the carotid."

Cat thought. "Incision? Not just cut? Incision implies medical knowledge."

"'S what Keith said. Maybe he picks up the lingo workin' there."

"He also works at Nick's Subs, but he didn't say slice and dice," Cat replied. Perhaps they had been killed by someone with medical knowledge, Cat thought. A doctor. Or a nurse. "What'd he say about the Murillo woman?"

"He wasn't workin' when she was brought in, but he said some guy from Newark came down to take fluid samples on Oliva and run some kinda tests and he was asked by the DA to look over the fluid samples on the other ones. Guy said he was glad they kept somma Murillo's fluid, onaccounta she was air-freighted back to Central America. So I call a couple air freight services, they said something like that could run around eight thou—"

"—sand dollars!"

"You got it."

"Who would have that kind of money to spend?" *James Easter. Or Easter's wife.*

"Not me. Call Moroscos, they packaged her for shipping. I hear they're doin' Oliva, too, when the ME cuts her loose. You said you knew 'em, right?"

"Yeah." She and Freddy had gone to school with Trina Morosco. Trina had been one of the "wild girls," though Cat suspected the reputation was largely myth. True, Sister Mary Frances Xavier had dragged Trina to the office and yanked a comb through "that rat's nest of hair," ripped out the hems in her kilts and gave her twenty-four hours to get them lengthened, sent her to the lavatory to scrub off that eye make-up, the carnelian lipstick. Still, it had been Trina who had gotten straight A's in science, took honors biochem when the rest of them were struggling along in basic biology, won the state science competition in her senior year for embalming a cat. Danny Furina, who took photographs for Journalism Club, snapped a good one of the departed feline, captioned it "Doesn't He Look Like Himself?", switched it with the photo of Trina and her trophy and got it into the school paper. "I guess I could give her a call."

"Plus, I hear Raab's callin' a press conference. He's gonna hold it way out Mays Landing, prob'ly do it same time as Oliva's funeral just to drive us all nuts tryin' to cover both. I want you to go over there."

"The funeral?"

"No, the press conference."

"Ritchie, I don't know ..." She could always hide in the back, not ask anything.

"You don't wanna do it, I hear Karen Freelancer's looking to pick up some work and she's a real go-getter."

"Then go get her."

"Aw, c'mon, Austen. Friedlander's always gettin' on my case about how she doesn't get her money on time and stuff."

"You mean when you give her an assignment and she turns it in and you run it, she wants to get paid? That bitch."

Jennie nodded sharply toward Mats, slapped Cat's hand.

"Look, you're always sayin' you want more than the concerts and the movie blurbs, so you want in or not?"

Kate Auletta wouldn't be afraid of a measly press conference. Kate Auletta would muscle herself down front, and if Victor Calderone was there, she would look him right in the eye. "Sure." Cat tried to put some Auletta in her voice. "I'm in."

Ritchie said Estrella Murillo had lived on St. James Place, a half block that extended from Pacific Avenue to the Boards. Cat insisted on driving Jennie home and figured since she was already in Atlantic City, why not just swing by and have a look at the place?

The place was not much to look at, the second of three buildings that no one had torn down yet because they weren't standing in the path of some cash-laden Sherman rousing the battle cry of Eminent Domain and razing a path to the Atlantic. Surveying the dilapidated structures, Cat decided that their time was indeed well past, though she suspected that the arbiters of eminent domain were, as Carlo had expressed it, "playing a little fast and loose, original intentwise." She even had a back-burner piece, a follow-up to the short feature she'd done on the eminent domain situation involving Jim's Coffee Shoppe, called it *Droit de Seigneur*, floated it past Ritchie, who said he'd run it but that title would have to go.

Cat parked her car a couple blocks away at the nearest proximity to Murillo's building where there would be the likelihood of her finding the Maxima intact. She noticed that the two buildings flanking the one where Murillo had lived were sealed, condemnation notices tacked to the boards covering the front entrances, saw that a couple of the boards had been pried loose on one of the buildings, suspected it had been colonized by vagrants, and dopers, people with questionable immigration status, neighbors who don't welcome trouble and don't call the cops when trouble drops in uninvited.

There was an entry with a dead bulb affixed overhead, a vertical row of buzzers next to the metal mailboxes imbedded in the wall. There was only one buzzer with a strip of tape pasted next to it, *Ruiz, Mgr* inked on the surface.

Cat pressed the buzzer. She heard it echo somewhere inside, pulled up the collar of her jacket and placed one hand on the glass door, preparing to be buzzed in. She looked over her shoulder at the deserted street. *And of course, ladies,* Marco had instructed in his Self-Defense For Women class, *there are places you do not go alone. We got some feminists in the group, this is not a sexist remark, this is survival. There's places your grizzly bear don't go unless he's got a grizzly buddy to watch his back, you know what I'm sayin'?*

Cat heard a shuffling sound, saw someone coming toward the grimy glass door, push the inside handle, poke his head out. He was short, with a few strands of black hair combed across a hairless crown, a protruding belly straining at the buttons of the faded plaid shirt.

"*Si?*"

Cat tapped into her high school Spanish. "*El dueno, señor?*" She hoped *dueno* was the word for landlord.

"*No vive aqui. Soy gerente.*"

*Gerente* = manager. She didn't trust her vocabulary to hold up to much small talk, got to the point. "*Conoció usted Estrella Murillo?*"

The shiny eyes narrowed and he edged back. "*Policia?*"

"*No, no, soy*"—what was the darn word?—"*periodista.*" Sort of. Apparently, reporter was a scant rung above cop, because the suspicion did not abate. Still, he hadn't slammed the door in her face.

"*Muerta.*"

Dead. "*Si,*" Cat agreed, shivering. "Murdered." What was the word for that? *Matado? Matada?*

"Las' December."

The shift to English startled her. Apparently, he employed the native tongue as a sort of gatekeeper.

"Is anyone living here now who knew her?" Cat asked.

The man shook his head. "Not in the building."

"Were you here the night she was killed?"

"No. We went up to my wife's family."

"Has her apartment been rented?"

"No. *Es maldito.*"

"Could I ..." Cat hesitated. "Could I go up and have a look at it?"

"*Es maldito.* Estrellita kept her doors locked, always. Only the devil could get through."

*Or she let him in, the devil in disguise.* Cat fumbled in her pocket for her wallet, wondered how much it would take to mitigate the curse. But the man shook his head vigorously, stepped back and allowed her to enter the hallway. "*No, se- nora, no quiero tu pan.*" He dug a key ring out of his pocket, held it up by a single key. "Bring it back to apartmen' one. It's number Five B."

Cat thanked him and walked the five flights, the sway- backed stairs showing the imprint of decades of weary tread. She imagined Estrella Murillo after a day of cleaning houses, making this dreary climb, again for each trip to the market, each trip to the laundromat.

The unit was a single large room with an alcove that was not large enough to be called a kitchenette, a tiny closet of a bathroom. The single bare window was high, uncurtained, a portion of Boardwalk and dark ocean visible, though the build- ing next door blocked most of the view. Cat saw a wrought- iron fire escape through the glass.

She snapped the switch on the wall; two of the five bulbs on the ceiling fixture illuminated walls freshly covered with bargain-priced paint. The expanse of fresh, flat white sent a shiver along Cat's ribs; had there been that much blood to conceal?

She walked over to the window, her shoes echoing hollow in the empty room, twisted the hasp on the window. It was difficult to lift, would have been impossible from the outside. Unlikely the assailant came in through the fire escape. She felt the draft of cold salt air and closed the window. December had been cold. She imagined Estrella Murillo sitting on her cheap furniture in this bleak place, not speaking much English, few friends, if any. Cold, and longing for the warmth of home, close to Christmas and longing for family, companionship. Lonely enough to let the devil in the door.

Pity no one was around who had known her. No, that wasn't exactly what the landlord had said; he had said "Not in the building." He hadn't said no one at all was around.

Cat locked the apartment door and brought the keys back to Mr. Ruiz, heard the *CopWatch* theme song drumming inside his apartment when she knocked on the door. Ruiz came to the door and Cat handed over the keys. "Who found Miss Murillo's body?"

"I did, *señora*. There have been robberies. You know how it is. This building will be the next to go."

"But her apartment wasn't robbed."

He shook his head. "So much blood ..." he murmured. "I did not think one person could hold so much blood ..."

Cat shuddered. "How long have those buildings next door been boarded up?"

"Many months."

"Then they were vacant when the murder occurred?"

The man shrugged. Like Jennie's, his shrugs were eloquent.

"Did you ever see people hanging around in those buildings?"

"People who would live in such a place do not like to be seen."

"I thought I saw a couple boards pulled loose."

Shrug. "Rats, perhaps. Rats always find their way back to a favorite hole."

"Why don't you call the city if you have a rat problem?"

"I call the city, I'm the one who gets bothered. The rats, they see the police, they run off, the police leave." He shrugged. "They come back. It's a cold world, *señora*."

"It was cold last December, too."

"*Sí*."

Cat wished him *Buenas noches* and stepped to the curb, one hand on the car keys in her pocket. *Ladies, it's dark, you're headed to your car, you got your keys in your hand.*

Well, she had the keys in her hand, but since she was already here, she could take one small peek at the building next door, the one with the boards pulled loose.

Cat approached the building, saw that a board covering the window was hanging by a single nail at the top corner. She reached up and gave it a push with her gloved palm; the board fell loose and Cat had to sidestep to keep from being bashed on the head. The window was shattered; she could hear wind sweeping through vacant space inside the building, but couldn't boost herself high enough to get a look inside.

She walked around back, saw the board that had been nailed to the rear door had been pried loose, propped up inside the doorway. There was a scattering of broken glass, a stack of yellowed newspapers, another condemned notice peeling away from the wood. Someone had scrawled an obscenity on it, misspelled it, Cat believed, but wasn't certain. Carlo would know.

Cat didn't know what to do. She tried to imagine what Kate Auletta, Queen of the Asphalt Jungle, would do, figured she'd want to see what's what. So Cat took one step back and kicked at the board with the flat of her shoe, a gal sleuth move if ever there was one, except Katie A. wouldn't have yelled "YeeOOOWWW!" and hopped up and down on the good foot. Or get herself knocked flat by the figure that burst from the back door and sped toward the alley.

## CHAPTER NINE

Cat lunged to her feet and took off in pursuit. She thought for a moment that she was hallucinating; her brain and muscles told her she was closing in, but the figure she was pursuing did not expand to an adult height, adult mass. Cat flung out both arms and grabbed a clump of sweatshirt material, yanked hard enough to send both of them tumbling on uneven, trash-strewn earth.

*A kid!*

Twelve, maybe. But wasted, thin, with dark, hostile eyes clouded over with desperation. A fist glanced off Cat's jaw; she feinted and hauled the figure to his feet, shoved him against a telephone pole.

At this point, it occurred to her that he might have had a gun or a knife.

"Whaddaya want, I ain't got no money."

"Young man," Cat gasped. "Do I look like a mugger?"

"You bet. Why, whadderyou, a cop or something?"

"Do I look like a cop?"

"I seen *CopWatch*, none of you look like cops."

"That's because they're actors."

"Yuhn-uh. They use the real cops."

"Look," Cat panted. "They use actors and then at the end, they use some of the real people who were involved. I'm going to be working with them when they come to Atlantic City."

The kid's eyes popped. "You're with *CopWatch?*"

Dear Lord. "Sort of."

"So whaddaya doin' around here?"

"I heard about a murder in that place next door, heard the cops're trying to sweep it under the rug."

"Yeah, well, I didn't see nothin'."

Not: "I don't know nothin'." Cat side-stepped the lie and took an intuitive leap. "The woman who got killed was alone in the building that night. Would've been an ideal time for a break-in, if one were so inclined."

"Says who?"

"That place you holed up? You can see who comes and goes. Transients, illegals. The sort of people who don't call the cops, even if they come home and find their place has been ransacked. And they're also the sort who tend to work under the table, and don't put a whole lot of faith in banks."

"All I found was a couple bucks in the downstairs apartment."

"You settled for a couple bucks? And stopped after one apartment? I don't think so. I think you planned to work the whole building, but something stopped you."

The kid gulped.

"Did you see his face?"

He got that stunned look Jane would get when she'd come downstairs on a school morning complaining of a headache and Cat would ask "What homework assignment did you forget to do?" Nothing nurtured ESP like motherhood.

"I didn't see nothin', I swear, I didn't see nothin'."

Lying again, but genuinely scared. "Yes, you did."

"Just his coat. I was on the landing, around the fourth floor and I seen the coat. Black. Shiny. Maybe satin or something. Guy's all black. Black pants. I see the pants, he's comin' down the stairs, I think he heard me, he stops and goes back up. I duck back into the apartment on the first floor, I wait. I don't hear nothin'. Couple days later, there's cops all over the place and I take off, find someplace else to crash, I hear some woman got killed. I'm thinkin', I go to the cops, they're gonna think it's me. Couple weeks, the heat starts to cool, I move back in."

Cat looked over her shoulder at the decaying tenement. "How old are you?"

"Fourteen."

"Where do you live?"

"There. Or wherever."

"I mean, where's your home?"

"Whaddayou care?"

Cat thought for a moment. "You're coming with me."

"Go to hell."

She did the Kate Auletta voice. "I said you're coming with me." She got a grip on his sleeve and started dragging him toward St. James. No one messed with Kate Auletta.

Cat unlocked the Maxima and told him to get in. St. James was a block from New York; she turned down New York and drove to St. Agnes, pulled into the parking lot, got out and opened the kid's door.

"Hey, what is this, a church or something?"

Cat kept a tight grip on his sleeve. There didn't look like much fight in him, but she held fast as she walked him up to the rectory's back door and rang the bell.

After a moment, a light came on upstairs, then the kitchen light. Cat saw a figure in black sweats shuffle toward the door. Dominic peered through the glass, opened the door.

"Cat! What's wrong?"

Cat shoved the kid into the kitchen and stood with her back to the door to cut off escape. "That 'whatever you do for the least of my brothers you do for me' deal, how exactly does that work?"

Dominic surveyed the kid, who stood shivering in the kitchen, staring around the room with a mixture of suspicion and awe. Cat suspected it had been some time since he had seen a place so utterly immaculate.

"Who's your friend?" Dom asked.

Cat looked at the kid. "What's your name?"

The kid eyed Dominic. "So what are you, like a priest or something? You like boys, and she's your pimp, is that the deal?"

Dominic took a fistful of the kid's sweatshirt, shoved him against the wall. "The deal is she's my sister, and if you're not the worst idea she's ever had, you're as close as it gets. Now go over to that table and sit down."

The kid crept over to a chair, sat. He floated his palms over the smooth wood as if reluctant to touch the surface.

Dominic turned to Cat, pressed his palms together. "First, let me say that you're my sister and I love you—"

"You don't have to remind me."

"I have to remind myself. I don't suppose he has anything as obsolete as parents?"

"I don't know. He was holed up in an abandoned house. He may have been a witness to a murder. You remember that women who was killed last December in her apartment, an immigrant named Murillo?"

"Yeah, I knew her." Dominic eyed the kid, lowered his voice. "You're saying he saw the killer?"

"I don't know. He saw something. But he's scared and he's got no place to go."

"I've got to notify the police and Social Services."

"I know. Just let me talk to Victor about him. You can give him a bed for the night, can't you?"

"How old is he?"

"Fourteen."

"Lord Jesus, grant me the forbearance to keep from wringing my sister's neck. Amen. Young man, what's your name?"

"Mark."

"No kidding. I got a brother named Mark." Dominic

picked up the receiver on the wall phone, dialed. "We have a little situation here, could you run over?"

Five minutes later, Sister Maggie arrived, wearing a dark coat over her black chenille robe, a wimple set over her hair. The kid was finishing the last crust of the sandwich, polishing off the milk Dominic had provided.

"Maggie, this young man needs someplace to stay the night. He'll be sleeping in my room. I'll bunk in my office. We're going to need you to chaperone me in case he attempts to jump my bones."

"Don't you leave those dirty dishes in my sink."

Dominic walked Cat to her car. They could hear Maggie issuing an injunction that concluded with "—get you out of those filthy clothes. And God help you if you have head lice."

Dominic opened her car door. "When I said you should come around more often? This isn't exactly what I was talking about."

"Don't be silly." Cat settled behind the wheel. "He can't be any more trouble to you than I was at that age."

"Point well taken."

## CHAPTER TEN

Cat realized as she approached Longport Bridge, which linked the island community of Ocean City to the southern part of Atlantic County, that the spare change had been cleaned out of her ashtray. Fumbling in her pockets for change to pay the toll, she saw that her hands were shaking. The kid had seen something. Maybe, even in his own mind, it didn't amount to anything, maybe he'd done his best to scuttle it in his unconscious, but Cat knew from personal experience that the first interview with a witness didn't always bear much fruit, that often it served only to kick memory into gear, set loose a chain of recollection.

She saw that Carlo's car was still in the front of her house, Victor's jag parked behind it. It was not until she had her key poised to slip into the lock that she realized her jeans and jacket were smeared with grime from her tussle with Mark, her hair was disheveled, one of her gloves was ripped. She heard laughter from inside the house, rubbed her sleeve over her face, finger-combed her hair into place, beat her hands against the jacket to shake free the dust. If the front door didn't stick, which it usually did, she might get in without the obligatory shove and make a dash for the stairs, clean herself up before she faced them. Cat slipped her key into the lock and suddenly felt a strong embrace circling her, pinning her arms to her sides. A deep baritone whispered in her ear, "'Dids't thou not hear a noise?'"

Cat's exhale vibrated with suppressed laughter and she had the wit to respond with, "'I heard the owl scream and the crickets cry.'"

"'Who lies i' the second chamber?'"

"Mats and Jane." Which rhymed, scanned so neatly with the actual line—"Donalbain"—that Cat began to giggle.

Victor turned her around, held her at arms' length under the porch light. His gaze traveled over the streaks of grime on her coat, he ran his thumb along a smudge on her cheekbone, intoned, "'This is a sorry sight.'"

Cat's laughter bubbled to the surface in spite of his grim expression. "I have never met a cop who could quote *Macbeth*. What are you doing sneaking around on my porch?"

"I'd just turned off my headlights when I saw you drive up. I might ask why you're sneaking around your own porch."

"I wasn't sneaking." Cat unlocked the door, shouldered it open, called out, "I'm home."

She shed her jacket, went to hang it in the stair closet. Freddy, Carlo and Ellice were playing Scrabble on the living room floor. Mats was lying on the couch, asleep, an afghan thrown over him. Cat sighed. "Jane in bed?"

"Yeah. We're playing a penny a point. You want in?" Ellice said.

"No thanks." Cat wedged past Carlo and lifted Mats.

"He wouldn't go up 'til you came back," Freddy said. "What happened to you?"

"I tripped."

Victor offered to carry Mats up for her, but Cat insisted on putting him to bed herself. She laid him under the covers and smoothed his hair. Mats eyes opened and a sleepy smile crept over his lips.

"You sleep now, Mommy's here," Cat whispered, waited until sleep settled in again.

She tiptoed into Jane's room. Jane was sound asleep. In repose, her childish features took on a maturity that hinted at the beauty to come. Cat knelt beside the bed, looked at her. She thought of the kid, Mark. Fourteen. In five years, Jane would be fourteen. Cat tried to imagine Jane hanging out in some crack house, trolling for handouts, drugs, sex. Never. Never. Never.

She went to her room, wriggled out of her jeans, threw off her sweater and retreated to the bathroom, faced her reflection over the double sinks. "'Whose horrid image does unfix my hair and make my seated heart knock at my ribs?'" she muttered. *Macbeth*. She washed her face and hands, brushed her hair and pulled on a long caftan of gray sweatshirt material.

Ellice knocked on the doorframe, poked her head in. "We're having cake and coffee, the game's on hold. Carlo's a trip, keeps makin' words like 'gomer' and 'scumbag.'"

"I'm sorry if he's been a third wheel."

"It's okay. He's kinda at loose ends, 'cause Annie's been workin' doubles. You had a couple calls. Ritchie Landis called a couple times and some writer from *CopWatch*." She dug into her jeans, yanked out a scrap of paper. "Ted. That's as in, please-call-me-Ted, in this absolutely gelatinous voice. Like Elvis, but with an advanced degree."

They headed down the stairs. Carlo and Freddy were laying cake plates on the dining room table.

"I had a college professor like that once," Cat frowned.

"Didn't we all. Except mine was Edmund."

"As in Spenser?"

"Trachtenberg."

"So what did please-call-me-Ted want?"

Cat went into the kitchen, got a tin of *pizzelle* from a cupboard. "Put these on the table," she told Carlo. She grabbed a container of cream from the refrigerator. "Victor, do you want some dinner?"

"No, thanks."

"There's plenty."

"You should eat," Carlo added.

"He wants to set up a meet some time next week, when they hold the casting call. Those were his words, incidentally, 'set up a meet.'"

"April Steinmetz called it 'logging some face time.'"

Cat set five mugs on the counter, poured from the electric pot. "Does this Ted have a last name?"

"It's not Cusack, is it?" Victor asked Ellice. "Someone from that show's been after me for an interview."

He heard Freddy cry out, "Cat! Jeez!" sprang toward the kitchen. Freddy had his arms around Cat, was easing her into the booth.

"Put your head down," Freddy was saying. "You're not gonna pass out, are you?"

"No ... I'm sorry. Don't hover, I hate that."

"She needs to eat something," Carlo insisted.

"I'm okay, just felt lightheaded for a minute. I'm fine." Cat raised her head. "Get me a Pepsi, will you Freddy? And let's go sit in the dining room."

Victor kept one hand on her elbow until she sat in a dining room chair.

Cat looked up. "Stop staring at me like I'm covered in chocolate or something." Victor heard the note of tension in her voice, couldn't figure out what had provoked it.

"How come it takes you almost two hours to drive Mom home and back?" Carlo asked.

"I stopped by to see Dominic, actually. A sisterly moral support kind of visit," Cat said, sipped her Pepsi, diverted the course of conversation. "Kevin said the diocese is thinking of closing St. Agnes."

Carlo grunted. "'S true. I don't think Mom's wise to it yet, so don't let on. Jeez, Annie and me, we were married in that church. Our kids, they made their First Communion there, got confirmed there."

"Sherrie's got Meryl in First Communion class, she says there's only nine kids," Freddy broke a pizzelle, handed half to Ellice. "Cat and me, we made our First Communion, there were fifty of us, remember? Us, Steve, Rose, Trina, Kevin." He began to chuckle. "Danny. He goes in to make his first confession, he's in there forty-five minutes; I thought Father Greg was gonna pass out by the time Danny's done with him. Jeez, those were great times. Million kids. Summer we'd be on the streets 'til ten, eleven at night. Hey, Cat, remember when we had that box turtle that died?"

Cat burst into a peel of reminiscent laughter.

"Honey, you forget, Victor and me here, we're not Sicilian," Ellice reminded her. "Dead pet humor's not part of our cultural heritage."

"You hadda be there," Freddy chuckled. "Kevin, he's already talkin' about bein' a priest, right? So we had this box turtle Pop picked up on the road. One day, all of a sudden he's not movin' anymore."

"Would that be Kevin, Pop or the turtle who's not moving?" Ellice asked.

"The turtle."

"And, point of information: how can something be not moving *all of a sudden?*"

"Like, he's moving, he's moving and then all of a sudden, boom, he's not," Freddy explained. "And a couple more days like that go by, we figure he's dead, right? 'Cause with a turtle, sometimes it takes a while to figure that out, they could be hibernating or something."

A hint of mischievous color livened Cat's pallor.

"And Kevin, he decides the bugger needs a funeral. He's like, what, eight, nine years old?"

"The turtle?" Ellice asked.

"No, honey, Kevin. Those turtles, they can live eighty, ninety years."

"Not this one," Cat trilled.

"So we get the shoe box and dig the hole in the back yard and Kevin puts on this black bathrobe he got from one of his brothers, and does the priest bit—"

Cat could barely speak for laughing as she intoned, in unison with Freddy, "In the name of the Father, and of the Son and *into the hole he goes!*"

The table erupted in laughter.

Cat wrapped a hunk of the cake for Carlo to take home to Annie and right after he left, Ellice chased Freddy out and went upstairs, leaving Cat and Victor alone.

Cat rinsed the dishes and mugs, left them in the sink.

"Come sit down, Cat."

"I'm okay."

Victor reached over the sink and shut off the tap, grabbed a dishtowel and dried her hands. "Come sit."

They settled on the couch. Cat wrapped the long folds of her caftan around her legs, shoved a cushion under her head.

"Why'd you really go over St. Agnes?" Victor asked.

"Can't I go visit my brother if I feel like it?"

"Why'd you feel like it tonight?"

Cat looked at him, her dark eyes watchful.

"Tell me straight out, is Landis goading you into an assignment you have no business getting involved with?"

"Ritchie doesn't determine what I involve myself with. It was Marcus Aurelius, if you must know."

"I beg your pardon?"

"Marcus Aurelius. He's a—"

"I know who he is."

"Ellice reads him a lot. And she was saying something about how he said when you're looking at a problem? The things that follow are always connected to what came before, you just have to find the rational connection."

Victor toyed with a strand of her hair. "Sherlock Holmes said much the same thing. That once a reasoner comprehends all aspects of a particular incident, he should be able to comprehend not only all the events that lead up to it, but also all the results that follow."

"How'd that work out for him?"

"Not well. In this particular story, there were multiple murders, Holmes' client was killed and he never did apprehend the guilty party."

"Oh." Cat pushed her hair behind her ears. "Does the reason the vacation got canceled have anything to do with a woman named Estrella Murillo?"

Victor dropped the strand of hair, hooked his finger under her chin, turned her face toward his. "Where did you come up with that name?"

"I was just thinking," Cat hedged. "This woman who died? It reminded me of something, and then I remembered this news story from before Christmas. A young Hispanic woman, stabbed in her apartment. Unmarried, lived alone, like the Oliva woman, you know? So I looked up the piece in the microfiche. They never found her killer."

He suspected she was holding something back, wasn't certain. There was so much she continued to withhold, doling out her trust in small portions, watching to see if he deserved more.

"No, we never found her killer."

"I may have found someone who saw him."

"What!"

"Shhh! The kids are asleep." She repeated her interview with Mr. Ruiz, her examination of the abandoned building, her tussle with Mark. "And then I've got him by his sweatshirt—"

"Cat, did it occur to you that this *kid* could have had a gun or a knife?"

"In an after-the-fact sort of way."

"*Dios me salve.* You have five brothers who are cops. What were you thinking?"

"I was thinking that I'm behind the times. When I think fourteen-year-old, I do not think of someone who might be, I believe the expression is, 'strapped.'"

"It might be a good time to start."

"Then again," Cat argued, "I had the element of surprise working in my favor. I mean, he had to be taken aback by having a middle-aged woman just pounce on him, don't you think?"

Victor scowled, thoughtfully. "Sherlock Holmes also said more than once that we should never theorize without data. In order for me to decide how emphatically aback one would be taken in the situation, I would have to be pounced upon. I'm quite willing to experiment, incidentally."

"Do you want to hear the rest of this or not?"

"Lay it on me."

Cat's lids lowered, balefully. "I meant, yes, I want to hear the rest of it."

Cat repeated the rest of the version of the night the kid broke into the apartment, the night Estrella Murillo had probably met her death. "The manager, Ruiz? Said the other rooms were vacant in December, Murillo was alone in the building. A woman like that alone? She'd be behind closed blinds and a half a dozen dead bolts." Her gaze softened, in dreamy introspection. "I think someone knew she was alone. And I think she let him in. So the killer would have to be someone she knew. Trusted. And who would a woman like that trust? Or who could be persuasive enough to get her to let him in?"

*Only the devil could walk through.*

"So where's this kid now?"

"At St. Agnes."

"Did it occur to you to tell the police?"

"I'm telling you now. You're the police." Cat sighed. "Victor, he's fourteen, scared, hungry, God only knows where his home is, I thought it was best to bring him someplace where he could get cleaned up, get something to eat, a good night's sleep. You know, like sanctuary."

Victor didn't say anything for a moment. He knew too well what it was to be fourteen and have the world shake you loose. He had been fourteen when he father had been killed, when a giant in uniform named Carlo Fortunati had stepped in to see his family through the investigation, the trial, started him thinking he might like to be a cop.

"Cat, you're not going to get involved in this."

"I'm sure you meant that to be interrogative rather than imperative."

"Cat, look, last Christmas, during all that craziness, I remember how you struggled to keep Jane and Mats from discovering how dangerous your situation was. Don't you understand that I worry about you for the same reason?"

"I'm not a child."

"No. But you protect the people you love."

"Whether they want protection or not?" Cat asked.

Victor nodded slowly. "Whether they want it or not, whether they require it or not, even whether they deserve it or not."

"Sometimes I wish you weren't a cop."

"If I hadn't been a cop, we wouldn't have met."

Cat shook her head, gently. "Do you believe that? Don't you think that something would have inevitably brought us together if we were supposed to be together?"

Victor's studied her face, the expression in her dark eyes, the slanting brows, the curve of her cheek, the shape of her mouth. He leaned over and pressed his mouth to hers, consciously, as if trying to commit the image of her mouth to memory with his lips. Cat slid her arms around his neck, and Victor drew her close, thinking that if Carmen Oliva had gone undiscovered one more day, he and Cat would be in San Juan now, would be—

The phone rang. Cat pushed Victor away, yanked her legs free from the folds of her gown and picked up the phone on the end table. "For you," she said. "Detective Adane."

"Sir, I spoke with one of the chemists who came down from Newark. She's reviewed the lab work on the previous victims and she says she'd like to re-test one more time, if the samples hold out. But she said there did appear to be a small amount of sedation, benzodiazepine, diazepam perhaps. That would be the generic term, of course. The lab wouldn't be able to give us the specific brand name. She suggested a half dozen we might consider as possible prescription drugs that would fit into this category."

"Was she able to detect this substance in the other"—he glanced toward Cat, who had settled back on the couch—"the others?"

"All three, yes, although as I said, she would like to repeat the tests. I took the liberty of phoning a psychiatrist for his opinion of what sort of condition would warrant such medication. He said that would be difficult unless I gave him the brand name and dosage, but generally he would suggest depression, general anxiety, perhaps insomnia."

"This is something that's prescribed in pill form?"

"Or administered intravenously in a physician's office. When I took my sister to have her wisdom teeth extracted, they gave her Valium intravenously and she became extremely compliant. Of course the ME didn't detect any needle marks, so ingestion is the most likely course."

"Could be crushed—"

"In a cup of tea, for example? Yes, sir. And that was tea in Miss Oliva's garbage disposal."

Victor thought of Oliva, making tea for her killer; Estrella Murillo opening her door to him.

"Phil's going to put the word out on the street. There's some traffic in more powerful sedations, rohypnol and so forth. The lab didn't seem to think that was what we're dealing with, but of course it doesn't hurt to check. But if it is prescription medication, either the person administering it is the user, or at least has enough medical knowledge to be familiar with its effects."

"See that Raab gets this information."

"Another thing. Miss Oliva's references when she made

an application to Business Briefs? James Easter's secretary and James Easter's wife."

"Interesting. Anything else?"

"No— Oh, yes," she added, reluctantly. "It's that Professor Cusack. He called twice more. He said he'd really like to conference with you. That's what he said, 'conference,' as if it was a verb all of a sudden. I had thought that was just restricted to the educational community, turning perfectly serviceable nouns into verbs. But I imagine television people do it, too. I gather that he's one of these people somewhat enamored with police work. Ernestine Moore told me he even signed up for a ridearound. It's just ... if he's around for Mr. Raab's press conference, discovers there are multiple murders, he might become even more of a nuisance. You know how writers can get."

Victor looked at Cat, her expression a bit too calculatedly indifferent. "I know how they get."

## CHAPTER ELEVEN

Victor figured that it served him right, the homily had to do with trust. Trusting in the love of a righteous God and submitting to that trust by loving each other as the Father loved us. Victor had a sense that the homily was addressed directly to him, as if Dominic could see how tenuous the bond of trust was between Victor and Cat. Dominic spoke Spanish fluently and with a conversational intimacy, straying from the pulpit to wander the aisle, make eye contact with the parishioners.

Fifty, perhaps, in the pews. Victor sat alone, patiently reciting the proper responses from memory. He did not go up to receive Communion.

He had called the rectory early that morning, got Sister Maggie. "Of course that boy's still here," she declared. "As soon as Dominic talked him into taking a shower, I dumped his clothes in the trash bin outside the school. He wants to prance around in twenty degrees in his long johns and a bedspread, that's his privilege."

"I'll be over this morning."

"He's still asleep. You let the boy sleep. You have some time on your hands, you can pick up some gloves and warm socks and a pullover or two. And if he's still not up, it wouldn't kill you to go to Mass."

"Yes, Sister."

"And a pair of jeans."

"I thought you were supposed to appeal for charity, Sister, not shake people down for it."

"Size sixteen slim," she told him, and hung up.

Victor hung back while the parishioners queued past Dominic, noticed that he called each by name, though he had only been with the parish since last fall. Kevin Keller helped some of them into the church van, a couple had cars, the rest headed home on foot.

Victor followed Dominic across the rear of the church, genuflecting at the center aisle. They passed the locked offices, entered the rectory kitchen, which was empty; spotless.

"I'll go see if he's up," Dominic offered. "Sit down, Victor."

He left and returned in a minute. "Still asleep. Can you give him a few more minutes? He's wiped out."

Victor checked his watch.

"How about a cup of tea, Victor? Maggie won't mind."

"All right." Victor sat at the long wooden table. Dominic filled an enamel kettle, set it on the stove, turned on the burner. "I don't think I've ever seen you at Mass before."

"Was that the last service today?"

Dominic nodded. "I do Saturday evening and two of the three on Sunday. Monsignor does the Saturday Mass at St. Nick's, Sunday he does one here and two there." Dominic reached into a cupboard, retrieved a tin of loose tea. "You missed Mom. She's first Mass, front and center."

"My mother's the same way." Victor paused. "I thought you might drop by Cat's last night for dinner."

"I was pretty wiped out. I got the regular stuff, and the premarital classes Friday night, Communion classes are starting up, and I have visitation at the hospital and the Rescue Mission." Dominic spooned black tea into a tea strainer, rinsed a china pot in hot tap water, suspended the strainer over the rim.

"Teabag's fine for me," Victor said.

"Maggie's got me used to this."

"Sounds like you've been working too hard."

"I'm gonna have a heart attack, right?" Dominic smiled; Victor noticed the stamp of weariness in the smile, the strength, or stubbornness that rose to replace it.

"Jennie must be glad to have you living back home."

"Yeah, well, none of us really strayed far from the nest, come to think of it. Freddy went to the State Police Academy and Cat went to college up north Jersey for awhile. Dropped out. Finished up around here after she married."

"She never mentioned that. College."

"Well, the two of you have only known each other, what? Three, four months? There's probably a lot you two don't know about each other."

Victor propped his elbows on the table, rested his chin on his clasped hands. "Did I mention how much I liked the homily? Not overly preachy, but the point was well made."

The kettle began to whistle. Dominic took cups and saucers from the pantry, his back to Victor. "You and Cat are grown-ups. And you didn't ask for my blessing." He poured steaming water slowly over the strainer. "She's my kid sister, Victor, what do you expect me to say?"

"I'd like you to make your point now."

Dominic laid the cups and saucers on the table, sat opposite Victor. "You and Cat gonna get married?"

Victor stroked his mustache. "Well, that's direct. Jane beat you to the punch, though."

Dominic smiled. His brown eyes sparkled and Victor saw the trace of a resemblance to Cat. "You should have seen Cat at that age."

"I wish I had." Victor paused. "Whether we marry ... I think that's going to be up to Cat."

"Have you discussed it with her yet?"

"No."

Dominic ran his hand over his thinning hair, raised his cup to his lips. The steam fogged his spectacles. He smiled and removed them. "We're a pretty traditional family, Victor. I don't know much about you. I know what happened to your wife, and I know a little about your reputation on the force." He paused. "I do premarital counseling. Some of them, they're so young it scares me. And I try to tell them what they're gonna need for the long haul, and how it takes time to really know someone and they all think I don't get it, why they have to get married right now. Like celibacy dulls the imagination."

"I should think it would have the opposite effect."

Dominic's laugh was hearty, unpriestlike. "In my younger days, maybe. I try to tell them there are worse fates than abstinence, they look at me like I'm nuts."

"I'll try very hard not to look at you like you're nuts."

"Thanks." Dominic stirred his tea. "Greg told me you were asking around about the Oliva woman."

Victor nodded. "Her obit was in this morning's paper. Said the funeral Mass was tomorrow. Said there was no immediate family. Requiem Mass, Moroscos handling the funeral arrangements? Someone's paying for that," Victor commented.

"Private party."

Victor set down his cup. "Come on, Dominic. I called Moroscos, they said you took care of it."

"A good Samaritan asks for anonymity, I give her my word. Don't ask me to go back on that, Victor."

Victor nodded. *Her* word? A woman? "What can you tell me about the Oliva woman?"

Dominic shrugged. "I think she'd only started coming to Mass a few months before I transferred here. I got the idea it was the old story, lapsed Catholic coming back to the fold. The last time I saw her was Tuesday night. The Holy Rosary Society had a Shrove Tuesday dinner, she and a friend came early to help set up, then helped clean up after."

"Monsignor Gregorio said she was at seven o'clock Mass Wednesday morning, received Communion."

Dominic shrugged. "Well, I'm betting there weren't twenty

people at seven a.m. Mass, so it's not unusual that he'd re-member. Twenty, you're lucky ten, fifteen of them come up to receive the sacrament."

"She was active in the church?"

"She seemed to be making an effort. As a matter of fact, we had a meeting scheduled, she wanted to ask about confir-mation for adults."

"You know if she had any particular friends? Boyfriend?"

"I don't know. It wouldn't surprise me, she was quite a beauty."

Victor cocked an eyebrow.

"I'm a priest, Victor, not a corpse."

He was about to say something else when there was a creak on the threshold. Victor looked up, saw Sister Maggie in the doorway, stood.

"I'll clean up after myself, I promise," Dominic kidded.

"I was going to start making lunch. Is the boy up yet?"

"No."

"Will you be staying, Lieutenant Cardenas?"

"No, thank you. Sister, may I ask you a few questions?"

"Mary Grace already called and interrogated Kevin and me. Yes, I knew who Carmen Oliva was."

"What did you think of her?"

"She certainly acted like she was turning her life around."

"Acted like?"

"I wasn't born yesterday, Lieutenant. Mary Grace told me Carmen Oliva had an arrest record."

"What?" Dominic said, surprised.

"Just the one offense," Victor said.

"Humph. Meaning she just got caught the one time."

"I don't recall nuns being such cynics, Sister."

Kevin stepped up to the back door, wiped his feet vigor-ously, entered. "Morning, Lieutenant."

Victor nodded, checked his watch. "I'd really like to speak to the boy now, if I could."

"Still upstairs asleep?" Kevin inquired.

"That's right, you weren't around last night to see what the Cat dragged in," Dominic chuckled. He bussed the teacups and saucers to the sink under Sister Maggie's watchful eye, unscrewed the tea strainer, knocked the ground into the garbage disposal.

Kevin removed his coat, stuffed his wool hat in a pocket, started to hang the coat over the back of a chair.

"Take those clothes up to him," Maggie ordered, nodding to the shopping bag Victor had brought. "And hang your coat in the closet on your way up. Tell that boy we don't sleep until noon around here."

Kevin said, "Yes, ma'am," grabbed the bag and the coat, headed for the stairs.

"I'll probably have to take him with me," Victor said.

"You'll let him stay long enough to get something to eat, won't you?"

Victor nodded, but couldn't keep from checking his watch again.

Kevin came down. "There were signs of life under the covers. I told him to get dressed, he said he'd be right down. What's he, a runaway?"

Victor said, soberly. "Possibly a witness."

"Witness to what?" Kevin asked.

Dominic looked troubled. "Where will he wind up?"

Victor shrugged. "I don't know. They'll try to contact the parents first, but if he has witnessed a capital crime, he may have to remain in custody."

"Not jail, Victor."

"I don't determine where he goes."

"Well, then I'm going to wrap some sandwiches just in case," Maggie said. "He's not going to say we let him be carted off without a bite to eat."

"Let me go see what's keeping him," Dominic offered.

Victor turned to Maggie and Kevin. "The Oliva woman's

funeral is tomorrow," he said, casually. "Either of you have any idea who's paying for it?"

Maggie looked at Kevin, began laying slices of bread on the counter. "I don't know. But I wouldn't be surprised if it was Elizabeth Easter."

"As in Mrs. James Easter?"

"That's right."

"Why would she pay Carmen Oliva's funeral expenses? Were they acquainted?"

"Not that I was aware. But it wouldn't be the first time Beth Easter came to the rescue, financially."

"So, she's a parishioner? What about him?"

"That pimp?"

"Maggie ..." Kevin said, mildly.

"What is it, a case of opposites attracting?" Victor asked.

Maggie got packages of lunchmeat, sliced cheese from the refrigerator. "He's not attracted to Mass, to answer your question. If they close the parish, that pimp won't lose a wink of sleep. And meanwhile, poor Dom's at the end of his rope."

"He doesn't let on."

"Hidden fires, indeed," Maggie commented, and when Victor raised an eyebrow, she added, "Mary Grace said you were a Sherlock Holmes fan. Cat's a reader, too." She said it grimly, as if the bookish crowd were akin to St. Agnes' flock, dwindling.

Dominic's agile step was heard on the stairs. He sprang into the room. "Victor, he took off!"

Victor ran past Dominic, bounded up the narrow staircase, pushed through the half open door of the first bedroom he saw. The single bed was unmade, the window open. He looked down. A six foot drop to the porch roof, another eight to the ground. "Damn it!" he hissed, his eyes scanning the streets below. "Damn."

Cat poured herself a second cup of coffee, checked over

the paper for something new on the crimes, found only Oliva's obit. Funeral arrangements by Moroscos Funeral Home.

Cat hunted up Morosco's number, dialed hesitantly, was amazed to hear Trina herself pick up and cry in her husky/ shrill voice, "*Alley* Cat! I've been *wanting* to give you a call! How *is* everything?"

Like Jane, Trina's commentary was liberally seasoned with italics. (Cat wondered if she applied the same conversational style to her profession, could exclaim, "Doesn't he look just like he did when he was *alive? Don't* you just expect him to get up and *walk?*")

"Everything's fine. I was—" Cat realized she had dialed before coming up with a cover story. "I was working ..." *on a story and your name came up?*

No.

*I've been thinking about you, too?*

Worse.

"I was talking to Danny Furina a while back and your name came up." Which wasn't exactly a lie.

"Is he too *much?*" Trina squealed as if they were back in the girl's locker and a wigged and kilted Danny had just been busted for attempting to infiltrate female territory. "I heard he's working for *Fawn Sterling* now, at the Phoenix. Security or something."

"So did I."

"Isn't it so *weird* how we all turned out? Remember graduation night, we all said what we were going to be?"

Yes, Cat remembered graduation night, how before Danny had turned it into a calamity, they had banded together, whispered their dreams for the future.

*I want to be a science professor, Trina had said.*

*I'm gonna outrank my brothers, Freddy had declared.*

*Clarence Darrow, Steve Delareto stated.*

*I want six kids. And the others had cried, Rose!*

*Always to remain in a state of grace. They had groaned again and* said, *That's not a career, Kevin,* and Danny had muttered, *It is to me,* made a face and declared his intention of becoming a billionaire.

Cat held back, then, after relentless prompting, ventured, *I'd like to be a writer.* It had sounded less likely than Danny becoming a billionaire.

"What was it you were going to call me about, Trina?"

"Is it true they're gonna shoot an episode of *CopWatch* here and that you're actually the *producer?*"

Cat wondered how far down the lane her tangential involvement had been whispered to turn her into a producer. "Well, I'm going to be working with them, yes. As a matter of fact, I'm supposed to meet with the casting people next week when they have the open call for extras. In fact, I was just talking to one of the production people about shooting Jerry's funeral scene around here. If they're looking for a local consultant, maybe I'll pass along your name." Baited.

And Trina bit. "I'd give *anything* to work on *CopWatch.*"

"That is," Cat added, "if I don't get hung up with the story my editor handed me this week. That woman who died last week, Oliva or something?"

"Carmen Oliva? Gee, I'm doin' her right now. Hell of a way to spend your Sunday, but the funeral's tomorrow and the medical examiner wouldn't let go until late last night."

"It's nice of you to take care of her funeral. I mean, since I heard she didn't have family or anything."

"Hey, I'm no good Samaritan. She's bought and paid for. You know, the guy that runs Printemps, Easter? His wife's footing the bill again, God bless her."

"Again?"

"Yeah. She picked up the tab for some woman died last year, some illegal didn't have a dime. Mrs. Easter puts out eight grand to have her sent back to God knows where. Central America, I think."

"No kidding?"

"Yeah. Oh, gee, Cat, don't print any of that. I think she

wanted it to stay hush-hush. I never even spoke to her, Dom played proxy. Look, I go over this casting call, what should I wear? I'm ten hours a day in a smock and scrubs, I don't even know what I got in my own closet. Dressin' the clientele, that's a snap, but it's like, for me? I can never make up my mind what goes with what, you know, and by the time I decide, it's too late to go out, I'd just rather veg out in front of the tube with Ben and Jerry."

"Maybe you should pretend you're a corpse," Cat suggested.

She bit her lip, afraid she might have offended Trina, but Trina replied with a thoughtful, "You might have something there," and thanked Cat for her help.

## CHAPTER TWELVE

Allegrezza Caterina Fortunati was to marry young, marry Catholic, marry Italian, settle in and produce a family. Not that wild Danny Furina, of course, or Trina Morosco's hoodlum brother or one of those good-for-nothing Colucci twins. Louie Cicciolini proved not to be, as his mother forlornly expressed it, "the marrying kind of boy," and Steve Delareto, whom the Fortunatis regarded as the most auspicious prospect, headed for college, then law school, and who knew what sort of girl might get her hooks into him before he got back to Jersey? Kevin Keller, always underfoot, was a good boy, but the Fortunatis winced at the thought of the feeble Keller blood diluting their hardier strain and chafed at the prospect of the senior Kellers getting their hands on Cat's children. The fact that Kevin was more interested in Dominic—not in the Louie Cicciolini sense, but in a hero-worship kind of way—alleviated their fears that Cat would wind up mated to him simply because he was all that was left of a dwindling field. It never occurred to them that Cat was nurturing ambitions of her own. Her mother's younger sister, Aunt Caterina—unmarried and as wild as Trina Morosco—promoted Cat's desire to go off to college. "If I was your age now, I'd have gone to college back when," she declared, and even offered to pay Cat's tuition, an offer which Cat's parents refused. If Allegrezza took it into her head to get more education than she needed, her own parents could well afford to support the whim without Aunt Cat's assistance.

When Cat came home abruptly in her junior year, the family allowed themselves to believe that it was concern for her father's failing health, nothing more. They were truly happy to have Cat back home, but not insensible to the change. Their Alley Cat, who had swung between quick-witted scrappiness and pensive detachment now seemed only detached. When Chris Austen strayed into a marital field gone barren, Cat's family decided, okay, Austen wasn't Italian, wasn't Catholic, but he was a decent enough young man and he made Cat laugh when they were beginning to think she had given up *allegrezza* altogether.

It had been Chris who nudged Cat into finishing up her degree; not even Aunt Cat had been able to accomplish that. When they moved into the Ocean City house Aunt Cat had left to her niece, it was Chris who emptied out the little pantry off the kitchen, put in a desk, a typewriter, a couple file cabinets and christened it "Cat's office." A feature here and half a column there; Chris had been the one who started a scrapbook, took over bragging rights when he decided Cat's brothers weren't doing their job.

After his death, no longer sustained by his praise and encouragement, Cat believed she would abandon for good her hope of doing anything with her writing. No one was more surprised than she with her tenacity when she collided with the Dudek investigation, no one more amazed when she hadn't backed away from the Sterling conspiracy. The opposition of her brothers, of Victor, even getting herself shot had not blunted her zeal. She had begun to believe that her future had kicked into gear once more, when the past threw an obstacle across her path.

She tried to reason it away. A stupid TV show, after all— Would the Professor Cusack she had known get involved?

*You did. Your own family's buffing their glossies. Miss Althea wants to be the firearms supervisor.*

But it couldn't be the same man, Cat told herself. Cusack

wasn't an uncommon name. She was just unnerved by the mystery of these four dead women, suffering some residual agitation from the disruption in her vacation plans and exhausted by her tussle with the kid. Mark.

The phone rang and Cat picked it up. Jennie. "You all right?"

Cat wondered who had ratted her out. "Why wouldn't I be all right, Mama?"

"You fainted last night."

"I did not. I just got a little lightheaded."

"You didn't get enough to eat last night. Why don't you bring the kids over for dinner this afternoon? Carlo's coming by and Marco and Nancy with the kids and I told Dominic and Kevin and Maggie to come, too."

"I think the kids just want to hang around today. Freddy's bringing a couple videos over for them. Is Dom coming over?" What had happened with Mark?

"He's gonna call me, he says it depends. Depends on what? You still gotta eat. You don't eat right, you know what happens? Your weight goes down, and you get sick, whaddaya gonna pull on?" Jennie, ninety-eight pounds from age fifteen to age seventy one, save for the seven pregnancies, nonetheless subscribed to the theory that excess poundage was essential to good health.

"I'll pull on my thighs. Maybe he has to prepare for the Oliva funeral tomorrow."

"He's still gotta eat. You don't wanna come over, have Freddy and Ellice bring the kids, you can get some rest."

"I'm fine. And the kids need a veg-out day."

"You're not getting enough rest."

"Mama, I don't know what Carlo told you, but I'm fine. I ate breakfast this morning, I got a good night's sleep, I did a lot of running around yesterday and got a little lightheaded and now I'm fine."

"You don't wanna talk about it, it's none of my business. You change your mind, there's gonna be plenty."

"Thank you, Mama." Cat said goodbye and hung up. Opened the paper, and then the portent of Jennie's call hit her. She picked up the phone and dialed her mother's number.

"I am not pregnant," she declared, indignantly.

"It's none of my business."

Cat decided to give Carlo that shot in the mouth, called his house and woke Annie.

"Oh, gosh, I'm sorry, I forgot you were working the late shift."

"You okay?" Annie yawned. "Carlo said you passed out."

"I didn't pass out. Is he there?"

"I don't think so. Maybe he went over Ma's. Poor baby, I've been working doubles, he's really been at loose ends. I'll leave a message you called."

"Thanks."

"Cat ..."

"Yeah?"

"Look, I don't like to ask, but I heard you've got an in with that TV crew and I heard they use local people. Local cops, when they shoot on location? And, I mean—"

"I'll pass along Carlo's name."

"You're a doll."

Cat hung up and went up to her room, looked over her folders on the *CopWatch* stories, the murders. She should do some prep on the *CopWatch* stuff, try to come up with one halfway decent question to ask at the press conference. She wondered what had come of Victor's interview with Mark, wondered if they had put Mark in foster care somewhere.

Cat checked her watch. After noon, the last Mass was over. Cat dialed St. Agnes Rectory, got Maggie on the phone.

"No, Dominic and Kevin are scouring the neighborhood for that stray you dragged in last night."

"He didn't run away!" Cat exclaimed.

"Oh, didn't he? With the clothes the lieutenant brought over for him, Kevin's winter jacket and a bottle of Dom's prescription medication. Thank heaven there were only a couple pills left, though the Lord knows what the street value of something like that would be."

"I didn't know Dominic had been sick."

"Oh, I think it was something for aches and pains. Pulled a muscle in dance class, I think that's what he said. He's a fine man, I can't fault him as a priest, but when we were coming up, you wouldn't have heard of something like that. I mean, can you imagine Monsignor Greg prancing around in a pair of tights when we were kids?"

Cat's no was immediate and emphatic, almost devout.

"I still have a program from last season's *Nutcracker*. Gypsies from some casino revue, kids from the local tap and toe and Father Dominic Fortunati as the Rat King."

Which had no effect on Cat other than the realization that she had a perfectly good semi-humorous human interest piece right here in her family, and she had overlooked it. "Tell the Rat King to call me if he finds Mark."

She hung up and got out a fresh legal pad, wrote "Ballet Dancing Priest," wondered if it was something that could cover the cost of a new bike for Mats' birthday next month, threw it on the back burner and spent the rest of the day fooling around with the kids, heating up leftovers when they got hungry, playing several rounds of CandyLand, and not wondering until well after she had put the kids to bed why simple over-the-counter hadn't been good enough for Dom's aches and pains.

Monday dawned flat cold with a wisp of snow settling on the lawns, reflecting off the asphalt like crushed glass. Cat ran her six miles, recalling that Carmen Oliva's funeral was that morning at St. Agnes. And Ritchie had been right, called late Sunday night to gloat: Kurt Raab had announced a press conference to be held Monday morning, out in Mays Landing. There was no way the media would be able to cover both.

Cat took a shower and stood before her closet, deliberating. Generally, comfort, speed and denim ruled, but Cat felt a nudge of self-consciousness, a sense that, going into a press conference that might be televised, broadcast, she had to dress, well, like Kate Auletta. Gal Sleuth. Documentary schlocumentary.

Of course, Kate probably *would* have gone denim, but Cat chose tailored brown slacks, low-heeled brown suede boots, an off-white sweater and Chris's old bomber jacket, which Kate would have chosen because she could tuck her necessities—gun, ammo and so forth—in its dozen pockets and not have to carry a purse. Kate Auletta never carried a purse, too *femme.*

Cat dropped the kids at her mother's; Jennie had called and invited them over to bake cookies, but Cat knew her mother wanted to get a look at her, would insist Cat stick around for lunch, so that Jennie could see her eat something. Cat explained that the press conference might run through the lunch hour.

"It'll save."

"I can pick up some take-out on the way back."

"All this pick up and take out. You eat like that all the time, you know what happens?"

"You get run down, you get a heart attack and you don't have anything to pull on," Cat replied promptly.

"That's right."

"Mama," Cat sighed, with a quick glance at Mats and Jane. "There's no reason I need to eat more."

"It's none of my business."

"'It's none of my business.' Write that down, make six copies, get the guys to sign it and have it notarized." Cat kissed Mats and Jane, checked her watch. She had more than an hour before she had to go over to Mays Landing. Maybe she could run over to St. Agnes, see if Mark had turned up. She parked on the curb in front of the main entrance, saw "Oliva Funeral, 11 AM" on the sign in front. She stepped inside, heard the whoosh of wind reverberating in the bell tower, saw the padlocked door shuddering against the hinges. The alter had been prepared for Requiem Mass. The sight of the alter, the purple-garbed statues, the whine of the wind that crept through the crevices of the doors, and set the votive candles flickering in the dim light, gave the place an eerie, almost pagan allure. Yeah, she thought suddenly. This *would* make a great set for *CopWatch*. And if Jerry Dudek had his say, he'd much rather be eulogized here than in that impersonal parlor at Wiley's Funeral Home.

She saw a flutter of black out of the corner of her eye and noticed a small figure slipping mimeographed programs inside the pews. He was a small man, neatly dressed in a jacket and tie, a black all-weather coat over that; he had a wisp of lifeless hair sprouting from his scalp, dead tired eyes.

Cat felt a rush of recognition, realized it was Isadore Testa. She had seen him around church since she was a kid, knew that his wife had been stricken with a debilitating illness; her funeral had been the day Carmen Oliva's body had been found, the day Cat and Victor were to go to San Juan.

The man looked up, startled.

"It's me, Mr. Testa. Cat Austen? I'm Jennie's daughter, remember?" She noted that he wasn't dressed in work clothes, wondered if he were attending Carmen Oliva's funeral as a mourner.

"Father Dom's sister." Testa tried a smile; it half-formed, faded.

The wind whoooooed down the shaft of the bell tower and Testa's half-smile evaporated. "I'm gonna have to stick some paper in that door, cut down on that racket. The floor up in the tower, it's all torn up; the wind cuts through it like a tunnel."

"The church looks just like I remember it when I was a kid," Cat said.

"No, it's changed. Things change. We gotta keep the tower locked up, 'cause it's not safe and the carpet oughtta be replaced, but there's no point in doing that if they're gonna close the place up."

"I hope they don't," Cat said. "I was married here."

"So was I."

Cat looked at him, realizing that there were ties to the church firmer and more far-reaching than hers. What do you turn an old church into? Cat thought again of *CopWatch*. If they shot a few scenes on location, they wouldn't expect to get the site for free, would they? April Steinmetz had talked about site fees. Cat evaluated the structure with a theatrical eye, wondered if *CopWatch* would replace the boarded-up stained-glass window, wondered if they could restore the bell tower, spring for the new carpet. "Mr. Testa, could I run up and have a look at the bell tower?"

"Oh, no, Cat, it's a death trap up there."

"Just for a minute. It's sort of for a piece I'm working on. I'll be careful."

Testa's pale forehead creased and he ran his hands over his threads of hair. But he fished a large keyring out of his trousers pocket. "The stairs are all right, but the tower room, the floor's gone except around the edge." Then, in a last attempt to discourage her. "I don't *think* there are any bats up there."

Cat patted her hair, nervously, wished she had brought a head scarf. The days were gone when it would have been sin to enter church without at least donning a chapel veil.

She unlocked the padlock and propped the door open. The corkscrew stairwell was constructed of masonry walls, worn granite steps. The wind spiraled from the open arches in the tower. The degree of the curve was so acute that Cat could see no more than three steps ahead as she wound upward, zipping her jacket to the throat. At the top of the landing an arched wooden door was ajar, its hinges rusted and powdery. Cat shouldered it and it creaked inward to a drafty chamber sixteen feet in diameter. A vicious bay breeze drove through the trio of open arches cut into the outer wall. Cat remembered the first time she had come up here, with her Catechism class. Seven or eight years old, and not knowing what the bay was or the land beyond, had thought, gazing at the Beach Thorofare in high tide, she was looking clear across to Europe. Thinking that the whole world was within the scope of her vision.

Metal rungs implanted in the masonry across the room had allowed access to the bells and catwalk, but both had been removed many years before, and the rungs ascended into darkness above her. The room was octagonal, the only sound floor on the two-foot perimeter of newer lumber bordering open space; the center of the floor was a shaft, dropping into a blackness that appeared infinite, though Cat estimated it was fifty or sixty feet down to the crawlspace beneath the church. The open space was criss-crossed with a few foot-wide planks. Several feet ahead, Cat saw that a few wooden pegs had been driven into the wall; a cracked raincoat of black rubber hung from one of them, an extension cord looped over another, a length of rusting chain coiled underneath.

She pulled her collar close around her throat, walked along the perimeter, her eyes scanning a well-remembered spot. She pushed aside the raincoat, lifted it several inches and smiled. Still there: DF, AF, AF, RC, SD, KK, TM. Danny Furina, Cat (Allegrezza) Fortunati, Freddy (Alfredo) Fortunati, Rose Cicciolini, Steve Delareto, Kevin Keller, Trina Morosco, their initials carved deeply into the wall with Danny Furina's pen knife, how many years ago? Nineteen? Cat whispered the names, reminiscently, smiled as she recalled the graduation night prank that had ended in calamity.

"What are you doing up here?"

Cat stifled a shriek, grabbed a fistful of the coat to keep from stumbling into the pit at the center of the floor, regained her balance. "Kevin, I didn't hear you. Good Lord, you priestly types know how to creep around. Sure you didn't take ballet lessons, like Dom? He can just about walk through walls."

"I've been places in the world where you move silently or

you get eaten." Kevin smiled his solemn, funeral service smile. "I heard a noise, I thought it might be the boy."

"He hasn't turned up yet?"

Kevin shook his head. "The lieutenant said he was a witness to something. I hope he doesn't get desperate, do something rash."

"You don't think he'd harm himself?"

"Who knows? It's not exactly the same as it was when we were that age. He didn't tell you where he might go, did he?"

"No. He said he lived 'wherever.'"

"What are you doing up here, Cat?"

"I was feeling nostalgic." She edged along the perimeter. Kevin extended his hand, took her elbow. "Remember how we carved our initials there?"

"We? That was Danny's idea. Of course, we followed along, so I suppose we were equally guilty." Kevin allowed Cat to pass in front of him.

She headed down the spiral stairway. "I was really checking the place out to see if it has any dramatic potential. I'm thinking I could sell this place as a location for part of the *CopWatch* shoot."

"St. Agnes?" Kevin was shocked.

"They shoot movies on location all the time."

"It's sacrilegious, Cat."

Cat looked back at him. "Kevin, how can you say that? People shoot videos of their weddings, First Communion. And they don't pay you." She stepped into the vestibule, took the keys out of her pocket. Kevin took them from her and padlocked the door.

"A church is supposed to be a church," Kevin insisted, stubbornly. "Not a meeting hall for AA or where you hold the Christmas bazaar or a movie set."

"Kevin, for God's sake—"

"Cat."

"For *heaven's* sake! You're getting to be as bad as Monsignor Greg when he wanted to lock the doors."

"I'm not locking anyone out, Cat; I just don't think the house of God should be used as the backdrop for a TV show."

"Well, I'm going to bring this up to Dominic. Everyone's been telling me how the church is going down financially, and yet when you have a chance to bring in some money, you want to turn it away. In the name of the Father and of the Son and into the hole you go? Without a fight?"

Kevin's smile was brief, rueful. "You have to pick your fights, Cat, accept what's lost and save what you can."

Cat sighed. She was never going to win a theological dispute with Kevin. "Look, I have to run over to the DA's press conference. Is there someplace I could wash my hands?"

"The restrooms should be unlocked and there's a sink in Isadore's closet. Can you find it?"

"Yeah. Don't hang around for my sake. I know there's a funeral here later this morning."

Kevin nodded, solemnly, and they parted in the corridor outside the church office. Cat poked her head into the large custodial closet under the stairs. There were shelves of cleaning materials, a mop and bucket, a sink splotched with old paint stains. Cat rinsed the dust and rust from her hands, grabbed a paper towel and rubbed the ruddy streaks from the bowl of the sink, grabbed another to dry her hands, checked her reflection in the square foot of mirror suspended from a nail over the sink.

When she came out, she saw Testa directing a couple people arranging baskets of flowers at the alter. Too many and too expensive for Carmen Oliva's blue-collar girlfriends. Trina had said Easter's wife was paying for the funeral, and it struck Cat again, looking at all those costly arrangements, how odd it was. If Chris had been in the business of maintaining women like Carmen Oliva, Cat did not believe she would be feeling magnanimous enough to spend a couple thousand dollars on the girl's funeral. Then again, maybe it wasn't a display of generosity, but one of satisfaction, glad that Carmen—and Tammy and Renay—were out of her husband's orbit. Or maybe guilt.

Cat tiptoed to the church office, went straight to the Rollodex on the desk, hunted up the Easter's home number. This way, if the number came up on Easter's caller ID, it would be the church.

The phone rang three times and then a gentle, cultivated voice said, "Hello?"

Cat thought it was the maid, asked to speak to Mrs. Easter, and was surprised when the voice said, "This is Mrs. Easter speaking."

Again, she hadn't prepared a cover story, began babbling. "Mrs. Easter, my name is Cat Austen. I'm a writer working on a piece for *South Jersey* magazine. It's about St. Agnes parish. Sort of a monument-in-decline, neighborhood-church-facing-termination kind of piece. I think I was given the story because my brother is Father Dominic."

"You're Father Fortunati's sister?"

"Yes." At least that part wasn't a lie.

"Did he tell you to call me?"

"Everyone at St. Agnes speaks highly of you, Mrs. Easter."

"Mrs ... Austen? I have to go out in a few minutes. A friend's funeral ..."

"I'm sorry. Maybe we could talk more at some other time. I was just wondering about ... well, your commitment to the parish when there's been a particular need, like a financial need? Like contributing toward funeral expenses when there's been no next of kin, helping the custodian with his wife's medical care ..."

"Did your brother tell you all this, Mrs. Austen?"

"No, just talking to different people at the church ..."

"I really will have to discuss this at another time. Why don't you leave your number and I'll call you back?"

Cat's hesitated, saw no alternative. "Five-five-five, two-two-two-eight."

Mrs. Easter repeated it and wished Cat a good morning.

Cat tucked the phone number into her pocket and left, closing the door. She slipped across the back of the nave, saw

Kevin at the alter, speaking in a low voice to a couple alter boys, the boys looking up at him with that reverential awe, the way Kevin had looked at Dom when Dom attained the priesthood.

Outside, the wind had picked up. An appropriately bleak day for a funeral. Chris' funeral had been in April, the sun had been shining. Cat could still recall the scent of freshly mown grass at the gravesite. She never visited on the anniversary of his death, she would go later this month, on Chris' birthday. He would have been thirty-nine, kidding around at getting close to the big four-o.

Cat drove out to Mays Landing, fighting back the memory of that day, her fingertips stained with Easter egg dye when she had yanked open the door, saw Carlo and Vinnie on the threshhold. She looked now at her fingertips, saw ruddy streaks along her nails that had not washed off, shuddered. She pulled into a service station and went into the ladies room, scrubbed her hands again with soap. It's just rust, she told herself, realized she was hyperventilating. From that junk in the bell tower. Eroding. Soon the decay would filter down to the sanctuary, the corridors, the rectory, and St. Agnes would disintegrate, scatter.

Cat shook off the thought, headed toward the compound where the prosecutor's offices were located. It was off the main drag, set in a thickly wooded area, well back from the road. The tall structure of reflective glass had "Get Lost" written all over it, and the only people who came by on a regular basis were the kids looking to take their behind-the-wheel at the DMV testing station situated behind the office buildings.

Cat had not believed she was going to need a press pass, though Ritchie swore she would and left one at the door. She did need it, and a copy of her driver's license, photo ID and a once-over of her handbag. Kurt Raab wasn't making this easy.

When Cat made it to the conference room she felt like she

had gone to black-tie in jeans and a sweater. Every other women was in identical garb, attire that, Cat realized with chagrin, Kate Auletta would have pulled out of her closet without a moment's misgiving: black, thick-soled shoes, jeans, white shirts, black blazers.

*I am out of my league.* Cat glanced around the room for an empty chair. A tightening sensation migrated from her duodenum to her larynx as she counted out forty-seven reporters, not including the camera crews from NewsLine90 and New Jersey Public Television and one of the Philadelphia stations. There was Morgan (male) Connolly from NJTV and Morgan (female) Wyszybyk (known as "the gal with no vowel") from Philly 5 Live!; Karen Go-Getter Friedlander, who had managed to go get herself a seat down front and on the aisle, brought her own tape recorder and mike; Ron Spivak scribbling something onto a notepad, one finger tapping unconsciously along the bridge of his latest prosthetic nose; Deanna Halprin from KRZI, who had lately been promoted from weatherperson to roving newsperson, and who was the only other woman not in Auletta regalia, having opted for a pantsuit of dark red crepe, matching shoes.

There was a desk in front, a bank of mikes, a pitcher of icewater, a portable podium. Kurt Raab emerged from the door at the back of the room without ceremony, so as not to give the cameras a head start. He gave the lone chair at the table a longing glance, as though he would have loved to sit, decided to stand. Probably, Cat thought wickedly, because it would be easier to make a dash for the door from a standing posture. He took a prepared statement from his pocket, adjusted his glasses, and began to read.

"On the morning of Friday, February fifteenth, the body of Carmen Oliva, age twenty-four, was discovered in her apartment on New York Avenue in Atlantic City. The cause of death was massive blood loss due to a single knife wound to the throat, which severed the carotid artery. It appears that Miss

Oliva had been dead approximately two days at the time of discovery. It is the opinion of this office, our investigators, the medical examiner and the forensic lab, that the crime has pronounced similarities to the deaths, last December, of Tamara Montgomery, age twenty, and Estrella Murillo, age twenty-three, and that there is a strong indication that these three murders were committed by the same perpetrator. While my office will make every effort to keep the community apprised of any new evidence, it must be recognized that it would not be in the best interests of the community for any details to be disclosed which would compromise the investigators' ability to make an arrest or inhibit the ability of this office to obtain a conviction."

He folded the paper, drew off his glasses and put both in his breast pocket. "I'll take a few questions at this time."

Cat felt the palpable thrill, the pulsation of shocked silence that follows a collision. Quickdraw Karen Freidlander was on her feet, her black-sleeved arm in the air. "Mr. Raab, what specific indications are there that these crimes may have been committed by the same person?"

"There are similarities in the manner of death as well as some of the toxicology results, certain factors relating to the condition of the deceased," Raab stammered. "My office will not release anything more specific than that at this time."

"Do you have any suspects?"

"Not at this time."

"Are you working with any federal agencies?"

"If any federal agencies would like to volunteer their assistance, we wouldn't refuse it. Someone else?"

Morgan Connolly spoke up. "Did these women know each other? Did they have any acquaintances in common?"

"We have no information that they were acquainted. To the second half of your question, I'll have to give a 'no comment.'"

That brought half the room to its feet and the gal with no vowel cried out, "If there's a serial killer at large in the Atlantic county area, don't you think it's imperative for your office to release as much information as possible?"

A sheen had emerged on Raab's forehead. "Not if it would impede the progress of the investigation."

Ron Spivak: "Did any of the victims have criminal records?"

"We know that Miss Oliva had a prior arrest for solicitation."

One of the Philadelphia reporters spoke up. "There were two murders in December, you say? When the second occurred, did you realize it was related to the prior one?"

"The possibility had been discussed. However, there was insufficient data for us to alert the media or alarm the public at that time."

Cat recalled the hectic Christmas, the corpse in the Sterling casino, the flood of copy after the arrest of Cookie Amis.

"But," Friedlander shoved herself to the forefront once more. "Don't you think that if you *had* alerted the public, there's a chance that Carmen Oliva might be alive today?"

Raab's temper flared. "The operative word is 'might.' It's possible she might be, and equally possible it would have made no difference. One more question, someone who hasn't asked one yet?"

Cat realized that her hand was in the air, saw Raab's eyes settle on her with a look of relief. That nettled her. Looking to the neophyte for a soft question after he'd been pummeled by Friedlander and the Morgans.

Cat stood. The door behind Raab opened and Victor slipped quietly into the room, leaned against the rear wall, his arms crossed over his chest. His eyes settled on her with quiet indifference, as though she were just a reporter, nothing more.

"Mrs. Austen?" Raab prodded.

Cat swallowed. "I, uh, have two questions."

Raab smiled, indulgently. "Go ahead."

"Isn't it true that at least two of the women have links to a local escort service and lingerie showroom operated by a Mr. James Easter?"

Raab blinked. "No comment."

"And isn't it true that another woman with ties to the same employer was killed in a similar manner last November?" Her voice echoed hollow in her ears; she realized that it was the hush of the room that made her voice resonate so; she looked down and saw that the notebook in her hand was shaking. "Discovered November eighth ..." she continued, her eyes settling on the wavering page; it was blank, she was faking, but she couldn't allow her gaze to risk a chance encounter with Victor's. "A Miss Renay Harris, whose body was discovered in an abandoned house. I believe the news report mentioned that there were multiple wounds, but the fatal wound was a severed carotid artery. And, isn't it true that not only did Miss Harris and Miss Montgomery and Miss Oliva work for businesses owned by James Easter, but that they all quit shortly before their murders?"

Cat lifted her eyes then; Victor's gaze was black and impersonal except for the faintest spark of something that she hoped wasn't fury, wasn't sure.

Every reporter was standing now, arms raised, shouting toward the podium. Karen Friedlander shot a "Nice-going-kid," over her shoulder. Cat hoped that what she returned was a "Kid, nothing," but she wasn't sure, so preoccupied was she with ducking behind the bounding forms and scuttling toward the exit.

## CHAPTER THIRTEEN

Six uniforms hustled Victor and Raab upstairs to Raab's office. Raab said, "Lizette, if you've got an ounce of mercy in your heart, no calls," and shut the door, sank into the chair behind his desk. Victor knew what was coming, expected it; still, he felt a ripple of irritation when Raab asked, "Look Victor, I gotta know. Did she find out about the Harris woman from you?"

"No."

Raab sighed. "You wanna know how much I hate asking this?"

Victor's expression relaxed a bit. "I believe you."

"How in the name of God does she turn up this stuff? The Dudek business buried the Harris story. And, I know she and Oliva worked for Printemps, what's the deal with Montgomery?"

"Rice turned it up yesterday. Said she'd been employed at the lingerie store, Nothing Sacred."

"I am never going to underestimate that woman again."

Victor hesitated, spoke. "I think it would be a mistake to underestimate Mrs. Austen, or to assume that because she hasn't been handed this caliber of story in the past, she's incapable of handling it." Victor knew exactly why Raab had called on Cat.

"Yeah. You know what I'm thinking, Victor? I'm thinking maybe it's time we had a little chat with Jimmy Easter." Victor shrugged. "It's going to be difficult if he doesn't want to talk to us. But he usually spends some time commuting between his businesses in the middle of the day, and I've heard his driver's racked up some moving violations." "Let's see if we can't catch him in mid-flight."

Cat made a dash for the elevators, concentrating on getting to the ground floor, out of the building, into her car. She saw the blur materialize behind her reflection in the dull metal of the elevator door, made a lateral move that it shadowed, intercepted. The elevator door opened; he blocked her retreat, edged her into the cubicle. *In tight quarters, you never wanna give the enemy your back*, Marco had instructed. Actually, he hadn't said enemy, he'd said dickhead. The door closed and Cat turned, realized she was eye level with a nubbly pale blue silk tie, hoisted her gaze a good twelve inches to the face.

"Don't do nothin' dumb, Mrs. Austen. Elevator door opens, we're gonna walk side-by-side to the exit."

*Scream. Push the emergency button.*

He stood with his back to the panel, grinning up at the security camera.

*Scream.*

The elevator door opened. Nobody in the lobby except one uniform at the desk. A massive hand closed over her elbow, guided her toward the door. "Make some small talk, Mrs. Austen, like everything's hunky dory."

"Everything isn't hunky dory."

"Let's just pretend."

"How about those Eagles?" Cat offered, lamely.

"It's basketball season."

"How about those Knicks?"

"Sixers."

"The Sixers stink this season." Joey had told her so.

Cat felt a cold slap of air and realized she was outside in the parking lot, heard a rumble that might have been repressed laughter, the more distinct hum of an engine and a limousine materialized, glided in front of them.

*Run.*

The limo's back door opened.

*Three things you ladies gotta remember,* Marco had instructed his Self Defense For Women class. *One: You don't get in the car; two: you don't EVER get in the car; three: YOU DON'T EVER GET IN THE FUCKING CAR!*

"Get in the car, Mrs. Austen."

"You don't get in the car," Cat informed him.

"Say what?"

Cat opened her mouth to scream.

"Aw, c'mon, Mrs. Austen," crooned a deep voice from within the limo. "You're not gonna scream, are you?"

Cat, lungs fully distended and ready, nodded.

A trousered leg emerged, another. A shaved pate appeared, righted itself and Cat's gaze fixed on a pair of shrewd brown eyes as the head rose, rose, rose. She looked up at the heavy, arched brows, the black mustache that cut a horizontal gash from mid-cheek to mid-cheek, the teeth white save for the incisors that flashed gold. A slick comma of scar tissue ran from below the right nostril to the lip, snagging his mouth in a permanent grimace. She realized that it hurt her neck to look up so.

"Mrs. Austen, I'm James Easter."

Cat didn't think she would ever see anyone close up who was near to Carlo in height, mass. "You're the second biggest human being I've ever seen," she blurted.

The gold fangs flashed. "I guess you met Ma."

Cat laughed, couldn't help it. It was something Carlo would have said. He offered his hand to help her into the limo and Cat hesitated, not out of fear, but because she was loath to step onto that plush white carpet before wiping her feet.

Her escort, named Jojo, got behind the wheel. Cat settled onto a seat that was more comfortable than her den furniture. Easter sat opposite, stretched out his long legs. He pushed an intercom button, said "Let's cruise."

The car took off, the acceleration so smooth that Cat was barely aware that they were moving at all.

"How 'bout something to drink, Mrs. Austen?"

"I don't suppose you've got a Pepsi?"

"Diet, Regular, what's your pleasure?"

"Diet, thanks."

He opened the mini-fridge. It was stocked with soft drinks, seltzer, mixer. There was a silver ice bucket, crystal glasses. Cat noticed the mini-TV/VCR, the fax, the phone, wondered if the long back seat expanded to a bed. "My brother's apartment is smaller than this," she murmured.

He handed her the drink. "Me, I don't like pants on a woman. You need to get rid of that jacket, go a little more snug on the sweater, nice skirt, show yourself off a little more. Call me a chauvenist."

"You're a chauvinist."

The smile flashed. "That's what Mrs. Easter tells me. I tell her I'm workin' on it. I hear you gave Mrs. Easter a call." He crossed one leg over the other, nodded to the mini-TV. "I saw the press conference. And I know it was you callin' Printemps, askin' about Renay. You put Renay Harris into the mix real quick. I like a woman with a quick mind. What you think, you think the cops put it together and were holdin' back or you think they didn't connect to Renay?"

"I think they know."

He was looking at the tinted window. Cat studied his profile. It was strong, compelling; might even have been noble on a nobler man.

"So, you think I did away with those women, that it? What about that Hispanic chick got killed?"

"Who cleans your offices?"

"What? You wanna know who's my cleanin' lady?"

"Pretend I'm doing a human interest profile. A day in the life and I'm following you around and I ask 'Who does your office cleaning' and you say ..?"

"Who cleans the agency, Jojo?"

"Grime Reaper."

"And do you have a housecleaning service, too?"

"Grime Reaper," Jojo called over his shoulder, steering with two fingertips.

Cat wondered if she had the guts to leap from a moving car. "Estrella Murillo worked for Grime Reaper. That links all four victims to you, Mr. Easter. Or to someone close to you."

"Like who?" The two syllables had a lethal undertone.

Cat took a deep breath, figured, *If I'm going to die, at least I'm not going to die ignorant.* "Did you know that your wife paid the funeral expenses for Renay Harris, Carmen Oliva and Estrella Murillo? The bill to have Murillo's body shipped back to Guatemala was eight thousand dollars. That's a lot to put out for a stranger."

Easter nodded slowly. "Y'ever think she mighta done it outta the goodness of her heart?"

"'There is some soul of goodness in things evil,'" Cat quoted. "Shakespeare."

"Shakespeare's gonna have to come up with something better in the way of a motive." There was an undercurrent of anger, well-controlled, but enough to make her wonder what this man would be like in a rage.

But not enough to keep her from coming back with, "You don't need to be the bard to figure out why a woman might not like seeing her husband surrounded by young, beautiful women. That doesn't take much imagination."

"Sees her wolf in the fold, you mean? Decides to lead his lambs to the slaughter?"

"Well, not exactly Shakespeare, but yes, that's what I was thinking."

Easter surveyed her coolly; she thought there was a shade

of something very much like pity in his gaze. "Tell me something, Mrs. Austen. Whaddaya think I picked you up for?"

"Well, I'm guessing this isn't job recruitment, looking to supply an unanticipated employee deficit."

He flashed the smile again. "Don't count yourself out, Mrs. Austen, some men like 'em spunky, even if they got a little mileage on 'em."

"You want me to shut up about Renay Harris."

"That press conference was on TV, everybody's on to Harris now; what would be the point in shuttin' you up?"

Cat shook her head, shrugged. "I give up."

"Look, you stick by your own. I feel the same way. Got no use for a woman with no loyalty. But I didn't kill those four gals. Mrs. Easter didn't do 'em. That means there's someone else out there able to get close to all four. So the only question left, Mrs. Austen, is this: You got the guts to take this one all the way home?"

"Yes," Cat said, but it was Kate Auletta talking, because Cat hadn't the foggiest notion what he meant.

"So, just for argument's sake, let's take me outta the picture. Where would you start then?"

Cat thought a moment. "Did you keep profiles of your clients? Maybe the victims had a, well, customer in common. Or maybe they were doing business on the side, cut you out of the action. Picked up someone, his name got passed around."

Easter shook his head. "My ladies don't do off the books. They want out, they can quit any time."

"What about men who work for you? Jojo there for example."

"Yo, Jojo! You been killin' my ladies?"

"No, boss."

"There. Ain't Jojo."

"I was thinking of a little something more in the way of an investigation."

"Investigation takes two things, Mrs. Austen: the brain and the balls."

"I think that's three things."

Easter laughed aloud; the laugh was warm, infectious. "Let's say, brains and courage. Courage enough to go where you don't wanna go."

"'Courage is the price that life exacts for granting peace,'" Cat quoted, hollowly. Amelia Earhart had said that; Cat had called it to mind when she had needed to renew her own mettle during the Dudek investigation.

Easter nodded, thoughtfully. "I don't believe that. Sometimes, courage makes you do something takes away the last little bit of peace you got left. I just want you to think about that, Mrs. Austen, before you start something you don't got the guts to finish."

"Such as what?"

Easter paused as if considering how to frame his reply when there was a rap on the security glass. "Boss, we got the blues."

Cat looked up, saw a flashing bar of lights through the rear window.

"Jojo, were you over the limit again?"

"Not by much, boss."

"Aw, shoot, pull over an' put a call into my lawyer, will you? Damn tinted windows, they prob'ly think we been partyin' in here, they're lookin' to score a bust."

The limo came to a halt. Cat heard a megaphoned voice call out "Everyone step out of the car."

Great. First make a spectacle of herself at the press conference, then take off with a pimp in a speeding limo.

"Routine," Easter assured her. "I had a nickel for every time I been pulled over, I could retire. Comes to it, I'll bail you, don't worry about the money." He opened the rear door, stepped out, reached in to give Cat a hand.

But it was not Easter's hand that gripped hers, pulled her roughly from the car, spun her around. Cat found herself staring at Easter across the trunk of the limo. He winked.

Cat felt her legs kicked apart; a hand begin to prod at her ankles, calves, knees. Male hands.

"Aren't you supposed to call a female officer?" Cat demanded.

The cop said nothing; his hands ascended. Cat had had enough. She whirled around, and neatly blocked the cop's hand, took the defensive stance Marco had taught her. She was astonished to see that he looked no older than twenty-five. When did cops get so young all of a sudden?

"Hey, lady—"

"Lady? *Lady?* Whatever happened to 'Ma'am'?" Cat realized that the finger shaking in his face was her own. "Those hands of yours go any higher, young man, you'd better be carrying an arrest warrant or an engagement ring!"

No way Kate Auletta could have topped that, Cat thought, smugly.

Easter was chuckling. "Mrs. Austen, mileage or no milage, I'll put you on the payroll you're interested."

The young officer gulped. "Mrs ... Austen?"

Then a familiar voice yelled out "Whoa, whoa, whoa!" and Cat saw the uniformed cop back off, saw Stan Rice hustle up from an unmarked car. "It's okay, I know her. It's okay." He took Cat's arm, began leading her toward his car. Cat saw that the uniform was shaking. No cop wanted to be accused of disrespecting Carlo Fortunati's sister.

"I'm sorry, ma'am. I beg your pardon, Mrs. Austen."

"You can call me Kate," she said.

Stan was pacing in the corridor, outside the dayroom, ready to intercept Victor as he approached the bureau.

"You got Easter?" Victor asked.

"Yeah." Stan danced in front of the entry, blocking Victor's way. "Uh, Lieutenant, there's something you gotta know right off. We got him heading down Tilton Road, the guy's goin' sixty, like you said."

"You read him his rights?"

"Yeah, by the book, everything. Thing is, he wasn't alone. He sort of had a woman with him."

"His wife?"

"No."

"One of his women?"

"Uh, no ..."

"Sergeant."

Stan winced, stepped away from the double doors, pushed one open. Victor saw Cat sitting in a chair outside his office. A silence settled over the people in the day room, a hush of avid curiosity to see how this would play out.

"Thank you, Sergeant." Victor's voice was calmly polite. "Please notify me when Mr. Easter's attorney arrives."

He walked over to Cat, took her wrist, drew her to her feet, into his office and closed the door. Just a bit more emphatically than was his custom.

"Sit."

"I beg your pardon?"

"*Por favor.*"

Cat sat in one of the weathered burgundy chairs across from his desk, noted that the office seemed more cramped with the addition of a large marker board propped onto the makeshift bookcase logging the names, probable dates the victims had died. Their photos were taped to the border, photos taken when they were alive, thank Heaven.

Victor sat behind his desk, leaned back in his chair, his hands folded on his knee. "Is there anything you'd like to tell me?"

"Aren't you going to ask me if I need a lawyer?"

"Haven't you been read your rights?"

"No, I was not. The officer just tried to frisk me."

Victor tugged at his mustache.

"Don't you dare laugh."

"It's not ridicule, *querida*. It's envy." He paused. "Who told you about Renay Harris, Cat?"

"Her murder did make the papers. Only this much copy"—she indicated about two inches with her thumb and forefinger—"because she was found the night Jerry Dudek was killed, remember?"

"How could I not?" It was the night they had met. "How did you come to dig up those two inches of copy?"

"When I went over to St. Agnes."

"Friday."

"Yes. I was looking around the church and ran into this girl. She was lighting a candle for Carmen Oliva, who was a friend of hers, so she told me."

"Friday morning? How'd she hear about Oliva's death so soon?"

"Word on the street, she said. She made some remark about not wanting to wind up like Tammy or Renay. So I started backtracking and came up with Tamara Montgomery—*she* nearly got buried, too, by the Sterling thing—and then I just kept slogging back through the microfiche until I bumped into Renay Harris' obit."

"Nice work."

"Thanks."

"She have a name, this woman you met in church?"

"Luz Molina. I don't know where she lives, and I suspect she's not a parishioner."

Victor scowled, reflectively. "Small woman. Long, dark hair? Fake fur coat? Wore a big green crucifix around her neck?"

Cat nodded.

"And the business of riding around with Easter?"

"He picked up the press conference. Wanted to know just what you're asking. How I came up with Renay Harris, and so forth. Is he under arrest?"

"No comment."

"But picking him up for speeding was pure subterfuge."

"He *was* speeding, then?"

"*He* wasn't driving."

Victor shook his head. "I cut you loose, you gonna stay out of trouble?"

"Define 'trouble.'"

"Anything to do with this investigation."

"Define 'anything.'"

"Cat—"

There was a rumble, the reverberation of approaching thunder that was part heavy tread, part sonorous vocalization.

"Did you call him?" Cat demanded.

"Define 'call.'"

Carlo Fortunati plowed into the room. "What the fuck is my sister doin' runnin' around with some pimp!" he demanded, slamming the door. The windows shook and the marker board toppled forward. Victor reached out and caught it with one hand, shoved it back into place.

Cat rose, took her brother's beefy hand, pressed it into a fist, knocked the knuckles against the door frame. "This is what we do before we enter a room."

"How much trouble is she in?"

"Define 'trouble,'" said Victor.

"Trouble is my sister cruisin' in the pimpmobile with Jimmy Easter."

"It was a job interview," Cat told him.

"You're not Printemps material."

"Some men like them spunky," Cat replied, solemnly.

"Where you holdin' Easter?" Carlo addressed Victor. "I wanna have a talk with him, set him straight."

Cat would have liked to see that, Carlo pitted against Easter. She could tell by the glint of humor in Victor's eye that he was thinking the same thing.

"I'm afraid if I allowed that, Easter would wind up anything but straight and I'm going to need for him to be intact when I interview him," Victor said. "Why don't you take Cat back to wherever her car is parked, and we'll finish our discussion later."

"There's nothing to discuss," Cat protested. "And Stan drove me to my car; I followed him here. And do I need to add that I'm of age, I'm perfectly capable of forming my own associations and"—she paused, reached up and put three fingers over Carlo's mouth, with her other hand put a finger to her lips, then raised her voice—"and the only reason I didn't have a stitch on when we were pulled over was because ..." She stepped beside the door, closed her hand over the knob and gave it a quick turn, yank.

Stan Rice, two uniforms and one of the guys from Narcotics tumbled over the threshold. They scrambled to their feet, fled.

Cat's laughter bubbled over. "'Now I think I shall fall like a bright exhalation in the evening, and no man'"—she poked Carlo in the chest—"'will see me more.'" Cat walked out.

"What was that, some quote or something?" Carlo demanded.

"*Henry the Eighth*, Shakespeare." Victor resumed his chair. "Sit down, Carlo."

The chair groaned under his weight. "That's the problem," he grumbled. "Reads to damn much."

Victor could not look at him without remembering how Carlo's hat had brushed the doorframe of his parents' bodega the day Victor's father had been gunned down, how his sisters had wept and trembled at the sight of this giant, how Carlo had hunkered down to eye level, his bellow sinking into a croon. He wondered if Carlo recalled it as well, or if it had dissolved into some collage, bits and pieces of a thousand crime scenes, hundreds of thousands of kin merged into one mosaic of despair.

"I saw the press conference," Carlo said. "Raab said he won't turn down a professional opinion. I'm offering."

Victor hesitated, saw the glimmer of desperate interest, the hunger for the game that a good cop never surrendered. "You talk to Raab?"

Carlo shook his head. "I'm talkin' to you first. Because Cat's my sister and I bet you already got people wondering if there's gonna be a conflict of interest problem."

"My only interest is getting this guy off the street. I have no conflict as far as that's concerned."

"You got the three women linked to Easter. What's the deal with the fourth?"

Victor hesitated. "You heard about that kid Cat brought over to St. Agnes Saturday night?"

"Dom said he took off."

"Your sister managed to get something out of him. He said he saw a black man, or a man all in black, coming out of the Murillo woman's apartment around the time she was killed."

"Shaky witness."

"Yeah," Victor agreed. "But sometimes an unreliable witness will see something critical." He leaned back in his chair, wondered how Raab would regard his confiding in Cat's brother. Wondered how he ought to regard it himself. The lines had always been very clear. He should know; he had drawn them. Any woman with even a marginal connection to a case had been on the other side. Now Cat had crossed that line, or he had. "I went to a lecture once, when I spent some time at Quantico. A forensic psychologist. He called it 'decoding the fantasy,' what you have to do to figure out what the doer's getting out of it. Because until you know that, you're stumbling around in the dark."

"I dunno if I buy that. I figure, a guy like that, inside his head's the last place I wanna be. You got what you got and you work with that. You got four dead women. Women, he may just be doin' them because they're an easier kill. They let this guy get next to them. They trusted him. So, me, I play who do I trust and I figure off the top, it's family, cops, friends, doctor, nurse, priest, teacher."

"None of them had family close by," Victor said. "Few friends. Doctors rarely make housecalls, though a visiting nurse might. Cops?" Victor shrugged.

"Boyfriends," Carlo offered. "That or a common john."

"There's something else," Victor added. "They were all Catholics."

"Someone they're runnin' into at church?" Carlo shifted in his chair, and the chair grunted in protest. "Easter's wife's Catholic. I don't mean your Good Friday, Christmas, confession twice a year, I mean every Sunday and sometimes in between."

"But not Easter."

Carlo snorted. "Don't bet. You been married, Victor, you know the drill. You find yourself a nice girl, you go out, you're havin' a good time, you're goin' to the movies, meet the folks, you put that ring on her finger, you're goin' to church, like it or not. Especially after the kids come down the pike."

Victor smiled. Marisol would not even have sex on Sundays, departed for Mass with such an expression of mournful reproof that Victor decided it was better to accompany her than to suffer his Sundays in the reproach of those beautiful eyes.

"I'm thinkin' it's not a boyfriend. I mean, I heard of it, guy datin' two three women the same time, even a guy married four women, kept it up two and a half years before he got caught or wore himself out." Carlo chuckled, grimly. "Me, I only got energy for one woman."

"It doesn't look like any of them had steady boyfriends."

"Only problem I got with Easter as the perp is this guy looks to be low-profile, and Easter's not exactly what you call inconspicuous. This guy's no publicity hound, either, don't leave notes, does he?"

Victor shook his head.

"Don't write 'Satan Rules' on the walls in their blood, none of your showy stuff. Kinda guy can make his kill, then blend into the woodwork. Or gal. You don't often see women doin' this kinda work, but you can't rule it out. Another thing against Easter, I'm bettin' this guy doesn't have family, or the wife, husband works long hours."

Victor nodded. He had thought the same thing. "Because of the timing of the murders."

Carlo nodded. "You got Murillo killed at night; Harris, the papers said afternoon, evening. Oliva, Joey says they're sayin' she was done in the morning. Guy's on his flex time."

Victor's phone rang. He picked it up, listened briefly, said, "Okay, I'm on my way over." He hung up. "You want to talk to Raab, stick around."

Carlo shrugged, rose. "I'll hook up with him later; I figure it's gonna take some time to get anything outta Easter." He walked to the door, stopped with his hand on the knob. "So, Victor, you don't mind my askin', you and Cat gonna get married, or what?"

Victor cocked an eyebrow. "Don't be coy, Carlo, say what's on your mind."

"It's none of my business."

"Force yourself."

"Look, you know, she's done a couple nutty things. Saturday night, she practically passes out, Freddy says she didn't do much but lay around yesterday, said she had to think." He paused. "You know how it is, Victor, you got sisters."

Victor thought of Remy. "It doesn't mean I understand them."

"It's just, if you're gonna get married, maybe it would be a good idea before, you know ... if she's ... you know ..."

"I beg your pardon?"

"You notice Cat seems like lately she's been all over the map, emotionally?"

"Carlo," Victor said. "You've known Cat all her life. Has it ever occurred to you that what she was when she was mourning her husband was the aberration, and the way she is now is the way she'd always been?"

Carlo thought about that, his broad face creased in concentration. "You know, you might have something. She was a kid, she was a pistol. A little down when she quit school, but Pop'd been sick, then." He shook his head. "What, this is the way she's gonna be from now on?"

Victor walked around his desk, clapped Carlo on the shoulder. "C'mon, I'll walk you out. And Carlo, I'll say, although I hope I don't have to say it again, I have a very profound respect for your sister."

Carlo nodded. "I didn't mean to butt in."

"Yes, you did. My sisters are in their thirties and I still do it."

"I was just thinkin', she gets married again, maybe that would keep her outta trouble."

"I'm afraid keeping her out of trouble would take more ingenuity than I possess. More energy, too."

Carlo surveyed Victor's sober expression, assessed the reflective tone. His laughter vibrated the blinds on the window, the glass, and the cops in the day room looked, remembered the old days.

## CHAPTER FOURTEEN

Victor and Adane approached the room where Easter was installed. Raab was pacing in the hall, looked up at Adane with a frown. "She gonna be in there? Easter's language could get a little ripe."

"It's all right," Adane assured Raab, gravely. "I've been showing Phil how to link through to the law enforcement web pages and he's been helping me compile a glossary of street vernacular. We've almost finished the R's. I don't think Mr. Easter can say anything that might shock me so long as it falls within the first two thirds of the alphabet."

"Rocking horse."

"An underage courier who delivers crack cocaine. Noun."

"Belly bag."

"To ingest packets of drugs in order to transport them by air. Verb."

"Not bad, Adane. Uh-oh." A staccato click of high heels echoed through the halls. "I know that sound."

Victor opened the door to the interrogation cell, allowed Adane to enter. There was a long table, several chairs, the shutters raised on the two-way glass. Victor held a chair for Adane; she sat and began to set up the tape recorder.

"This is Detective Adane," Victor said to Easter. "She will be sitting in on the questioning. I expect you to remember that she's a lady as well as a police officer."

Adane ducked her head to hide her chagrin. As long as the lieutenant continued to be that finicky in matters of courtesy, she would never feel like a real cop.

"I don't need you to be tellin' me how to treat a lady," Easter purred. His voice had dropped to a seductive register. "You oughta fix yourself up a little, some makeup around those pretty eyes, do something with your hair."

There was a rap on the door. Victor opened it and Lauren Robinson stepped into the room, followed by Raab. Raab shot Victor a look over her shoulders, rolled his eyes.

"Don't be givin' the lieutenant that eye, Kurt."

"It's simple admiration, Lauren. You're looking lovely, as always."

"Cut the crap." Lauren wore a navy suit with screw-you shoulder pads, a white silk blouse, a cashmere coat thrown over her shoulders, navy Etienne Aigner pumps with gold metal clips at the heels. Pearl earrings glowed cream white against her coffee skin, and the ebony hair was slicked back in a chignon. "Now I know that if my client has been arrested, someone's going to produce a copy of the warrant for me right about now, aren't they?"

"Your client is just wanted for questioning."

"Don't sweat it, Lauren, they're just ticked off cause the Austen feline blew them away at the press conference."

"James—" Lauren began.

Victor leaned forward, bracing his hands on the table, his face a foot from Easter's. "For the sake of clarity, we'll use proper names." His tone was barely audible, not at all agitated; he even smiled, but it was not a smile that was comfortable to see. "For example, if the person you're referring to is Mrs. Austen, you'll say 'Mrs. Austen.' Understood?"

In the vacuum, Raab's swallow was audible.

Easter's Adam's apple plummeted, rebounded. "Understood," he muttered.

"Excellent." Victor turned to Lauren. "Your client has

been read his rights. If he chooses not to speak, that's his prerogative."

Lauren sat, smoothed her skirt. "Why don't you tell us what's on your mind, Lieutenant, and we'll see what we can do for you."

Raab excused himself. Victor knew he was going to retreat to the adjoining room, observe through the glass. "A woman named Renay Harris was employed by Mr. Easter for six years. From the time she was eighteen—"

"Eighteen's of age," Easter said. "There's a market for your tadpoles, but I don't handle it."

"Commendable."

"I don't think we need to indulge in value judgments, Lieutenant," Lauren said.

"I don't think the phrase 'value judgments' is necessarily pejorative, counselor. When did Harris leave your employ?"

"Last year."

"Hard feelings?"

"Hard feelings aren't relevant," Lauren examined her manicured fingertips. "Hard evidence is all that matters. I don't think you need to have your memory refreshed concerning when it needs to be hard and when it doesn't, do you, Lieutenant?"

Adane could barely conceal her astonishment but Victor replied, evenly, "I think I can keep it straight."

"Well, thank heaven for favors, great or small."

Victor repressed a smile. "Why did she quit?"

Easter shrugged his massive shoulders. "She'd been sick the winter before, pneumonia or some such. She comes back to work, but it was like, she wasn't with the program, she tells me she wants to get into some other line of work."

"Had she been hospitalized?"

"Day or two, I think."

"Were you surprised?"

"That she quit? Yeah. She did good with Printemps."

"You continued to see her?"

"Not relevant," Lauren drawled.

"How'd you find out about her death?"

"Wasn't from the papers, that's for sure; they buried it. Some cop came by to question me."

"Did you go to her funeral?"

"No."

"But Mrs. Easter did."

The dark eyes spat. "Hey, I thought we were gonna keep the ladies outta this."

"I just meant that Miss Harris began attending the same church your wife attends. While that alone doesn't necessarily imply a friendship, people don't usually go to the funeral of a total stranger."

"Don't tell me what people don't do. You'd be surprised what people do."

"Not any more." Victor stroked his chin, thoughtfully. "Tamara Montgomery," he said.

Lauren lifted her straight brows, yellow alert flashing in the amber eyes.

"What about her?"

"She was employed at Nothing Sacred, as a lingerie model."

"She was eighteen, she had the stuff. She tells Helena she wants to quit, I figure she'd just been puttin' away money for school. Lotta my women do it to put money away for their education."

"And, again, the parting was amicable?"

"I'm an amicable guy."

"What about Carmen Oliva?"

"Same story. Worked for me, wants out, leaves."

"Mr. Easter, don't you find this unusual, that three of your employees decide to quit and within a relatively short period after they leave your employ, they're killed?"

"I don't believe it's my client's job to come to any conclusions on that score." Lauren ran her fingertips along the rope of pearls that hung from her neck.

"I'd be interested in hearing his opinion."

Easter rubbed his hand over his gleaming pate. "I don't know ... they were all of them makin' good money, and my policy is my women don't gotta do anything they don't wanna do. The rough trade, that's not my style. They left me for more cash, I could dig that, but bailin' out for nine to five and church on Sundays? I don't get it."

"You go to church, Mr. Easter?"

"I'm not what you call a regular. My girls go to Catholic school, Mrs. Easter wanted that."

Victor's pacing was slow, rhythmic, his voice hypnotically low. "Is Mrs. Easter familiar with the operation of your businesses?"

"No."

"So, she wouldn't have run into the victims at your office?"

"No."

"Not friendly with your employees?"

"No."

"Yet she gave Carmen Oliva a job reference. As did your secretary. They consult you about that?"

Easter chuckled. "I like women know their own minds. I like 'em to work for me, and I like bein' married to one."

"When these women asked your permission to leave your employ—"

"Quit, Lieutenant. I don't believe they required Mr. Easter's permission to leave their jobs."

"There was no contractual arrangement?" Victor asked.

"Even if there was, they wanna leave, I'm okay with it," Easter declared. "There's plenty of fine women looking to make some decent money. I don't have to put a knife to anyone's throat get 'em to work for me."

"What about when they want to leave, would you be inclined to put a knife to their throats then?"

"Outta line, Victor," Lauren snapped.

"Did they have clients in common?" Victor detoured.

"Mrs. Austen asked me the same, like I didn't already think of that. We got our regulars and then we got our day-trippers. Our regulars we keep on file—"

"Which are confidential business records, that will not be easily obtained," Lauren said to the two-way glass.

"Most of them pay cash. They gotta come with a referral, but a lotta them don't exactly give the name momma put on the birth certificate."

"And consequently many of your johns are Smiths."

Easter grinned, the gold incisors flashing. "Plus, a guy goes to Nothing Sacred, he doesn't gotta sign in."

"Did you have a personal relationship with any of these women?"

Easter's looked honestly offended. "Look here, I'm a married man, Lieutenant. I do not step out on Mrs. Easter."

Victor shifted topics again. "Mr. Easter, where were you last year, the night of October thirty-first, the morning of November first?"

"Now Victor, my client doesn't have to answer that."

"Hey, it's okay. 'Sides, I already been asked that an' I told the detective I was trick-or-treatin' with my girls. We come home, I gotta check the candy 'cause there's a lotta damn fruitcakes out there. Next day, I stayed home with them doin' Mr. Mom while Mrs. Easter went to work. Girls didn't have school 'cause it was one of those holy days. Cath'lic schools, they work it different."

November first, All Souls Day. Victor nodded. "What about December twelfth, thirteenth?"

"I don't know, man. That's a couple weeks before Christmas, Nothing Sacred picks up."

"What about last Wednesday?"

"Went into work. Late, I remember, 'cause I hadda wait for my wife to come back from church, it was whaddayacallit, Ash Wednesday. I got the girls their breakfast, got em dressed for school. Twins," he grinned with a paternal pride that surprised Victor.

"What time did Mrs. Easter leave for Mass?"

"Early ..." the smile evaporated. "What are you drivin' at, man?"

"Mrs. Easter is a registered nurse, is that right?"

"What about it?"

"You said Renay Harris had been ill, hospitalized. Is it possible your wife became acquainted with her when she was a patient?"

"I don't know."

There was a knock on the door and Philip Long poked his head in. "Excuse me, Lieutenant, can I interrupt you for a minute?"

"Hey, man, I know you from someplace?" Easter asked.

"I believe Detective Long spoke with you last fall after Miss Harris' death."

"I guess." Easter squinted. "You got a sister? Pretty gal, little on the skinny side, name o' Phyllis?"

Long looked stricken. It had been a couple years now since he and Joey Fortunati had run their stings, Joey as a suave pimp, Phil as his number one lady, Phyllis. That was before the transfer to Major Crimes, before the mustache, the dapper suits, back when Phil had looked fine in a little silver sheath, stiletto heels that had wrought havoc with his instep. Easter had heard about this pair that threatened to cut into his high-roller clientele, got a peek at Phyllis and scoffed, "You mean to tell me she makes him any decent money with those knob knees and that skinny butt?"

Lauren Robinson, who had known Phil in his previous incarnation, was smiling wickedly.

Victor gestured for Phil to step into the hall.

Long tugged a linen handkerchief from his pocket, mopped his forehead. "I got your pro and I got your con," he said, when Victor had closed the door behind them.

"Con."

"Judge Harkness won't sign a search warrant for Printemps.

Jeannie wrote out this affidavit, I mean it was Shakespeare, man. It was poetry. But Harkness, she says the women were not in the employ of Printemps and Nothing Sacred at the time of their murders, and onaccounta that, we don't have sufficient cause for a search. Plus, I hadda listen to that Fourth Amendment speech of hers all over again. That woman does love her Constitution."

"And the good news?"

"I got a link between the Guatemalan woman and Easter. It's thin, but it's something. Grime Reaper? The cleaning service?"

"Murillo worked for them."

Long nodded. "One of Grime Reaper's regular gigs is Twenty-five New York Ave, office building with a coffee shop, street-level parking."

"That's Printemps address."

"Right. Grime Reaper cut back on their help a couple weeks after Labor Day, but they kept Murillo on. Woman like her's a hard worker, needs the bucks and don't complain. Every employer's dream, right? I tried explainin' this to Harkness and she says she hopes we got a better connection to Easter than that and she says to me, 'Detective, let me hear you explain to me what you think constitutes probable cause,' an' I'm startin' to sweat, it's like when you were in school and the toughest subject, you're holdin' on by your fingernails and they give you a pop quiz? I wish to hell someone would nominate her for the Supreme Court, get her outta our hair."

"So, simply put, we have nothing to hold Easter?"

Long shrugged. "Well, we got that speeding ticket. We could maybe talk ACPD into helping us out with a loose tail for a couple days."

Victor shook his head. "I don't think it would do any good. If he's our man, he's going to be extremely cautious."

"There's one more thing. Oliva's funeral, dozen people, maybe. I took Kenny, the photographer works for the ME?

He's a pretty good shooter, he says he'll have some stuff on your desk tomorrow morning, but he lets me use his lens as a scope. She was there, Easter's wife."

"At Oliva's funeral service?"

"Uh-huh."

"Good work, detective."

Victor stepped back into the room.

"A few more questions, Mr. Easter."

"My client does have a job to get to," Lauren reminded him.

"Estrella Murillo, you know the name?"

"She's the other vic. I saw the press conference."

Victor saw wariness shade Easter's dark eyes. "Detective Adane, do you have pictures of the victims?"

"Yes, sir." Adane produced a manila envelope.

"Show Mr. Easter the picture of Murillo, please."

Adane drew out a black-and-white photo of Estrella Murillo taken at the morgue. Victor took it from her, slid it onto the table in front of Easter. "Ever see this woman?"

"No."

"You're certain?"

"You got a no, Lieutenant. That means my client is certain."

"She worked for a business called the Grime Reaper, they clean offices."

"An' now you're gonna tell me how they clean my businesses. Austen—Mrs. Austen—beat you to that one, too, Lieutenant. Maybe you oughtta put her on the payroll."

*Might be one way to keep an eye on her.* "Who might have seen her? Someone has to let them in, pay them, correct?"

"My office manager, Gloria, she writes the checks. They do the offices after hours, the security guy at the building's gonna have to let them in."

"What about Mrs. Easter, she ever see Miss Murillo?"

"I doubt it."

"Why?"

"I said, Mrs. Easter doesn't come to the office—"

"Not when you're there. But, as you said, your cleaning people work after hours," Victor persisted.

"When Mrs. Easter isn't working nights, she's home with the family."

"Or at church."

Easter grunted, ruefully. "Or at church."

"Perhaps she met Miss Murillo there. Miss Murillo was Central American; most of them are Roman Catholics."

"World's crawlin' with Roman Catholics."

"Your wife paid eight thousand dollars to ship the Murillo woman's body back to her family in Guatemala."

"Mrs. Easter doesn't have to account to me for how she spends her money."

"Is your wife a jealous woman, Mr. Easter?"

Easter laughed, scornfully. "What's she got to be jealous about?"

"Victor, dear, I'm afraid I'm going to have to ask you if you plan to charge my client with anything."

"Is you client going to answer my question?"

"I think my client has been a model of cooperation," Lauren rose. "James, please tell Jojo I'll expect him to observe the speed limits when he drives you back to town."

Victor helped Lauren on with her coat, held the door for her. Easter gave Adane a wink, strolled down the hall, his tall figure gliding down the shabby corridor with renegade grace. Raab intercepted Lauren in the hall. "So what is it with you?" he asked her. "Justice for all, the right to a defense, constitutional crusade, what?"

"None of the above, Kurt." Robinson patted his cheek. "It's the money. Give my love to Patrice."

## CHAPTER FIFTEEN

When Cat Austen reflected on her recent life, she was convinced it could be summed up in the sucker's refrain "I never saw it coming." She hadn't seen Chris coming, hadn't anticipated his death, ran smack into the Dudek murder, into Victor, into the Sterling conspiracy, into the *CopWatch* deal. Everyone marveled over her intuition, her cleverness; Kurt Raab still talked up her astute unraveling of the Sterling/Amis scheme, but Cat was convinced that an intuitive person wouldn't have stumbled into one calamity after another; a truly clever person would have had the skill to avoid disaster.

Perhaps, though, her gift wasn't in the anticipation, but in the follow-through; not in the scope of forethought but in the vigor of her response.

She stood, working the pepper mill over her bubbling *puttanesca*, checked the pot, grabbed a fistful of vermicelli, eased it into the boiling water.

What had Easter meant, what could he possibly have meant, all that talk about how he understood her loyalty, as if *she* possessed some special insight to the case? What could she possibly know that might give her an advantage, other than the fact that a couple of the victims had gone to her brother's church?

Who could she possibly come up with that might disclose

some relevant information they would be reluctant to give to the police? No one except Ruiz, and she had already spoken to him. No one but Mark, and he had disappeared.

Cat put a colander in the sink, gave a strand of vermicelli the pinch test. What about those people Tamara Montgomery lived with? Unlikely. They were probably lying low, scared Tammy's family might file some sort of civil suit for negligence.

Cat dumped the vermicelli into the colander, gave it a shake. She poured some of the *puttanesca* into a large glass bowl, dumped the pasta in and tossed it, adding a little more of the sauce. Jane didn't like too much sauce.

Ellice came in and began to set the table. "You wanna eat in front of the television? I think the NewsLine90 at Six is runnin' tape of the press conference."

"N-O." She had taken the phone off the hook an hour ago. She didn't even want to hear the machine.

"Victor mad?"

Cat rolled her eyes, began to slice a loaf of Italian bread; she held up a two-inch slice. "James Easter has carpeting in his limo this deep."

Mats came in and informed his mother that he was hungry. Cat buttered the slice of bread, handed it to him.

"Now there's a crime," Ellice griped, pouring out milk for Mats and Jane. "Freddy and I can't even afford that for the apartment. We're replacing the carpet, incidentally. 'Course, at least we got carpet, which is more than I had over Connecticut Avenue."

Ellice had been living there when she and Cat had met, fleeing a brutal lover, working her way toward invisibility.

Jane came in and slid into the booth. Cat put the food on the table.

"Oh, that guy called while you were out. Please-call-me-Ted? He says he'll be out tonight, but over the Towers tomorrow for the open call, he wants to hook up with you."

Cat forked-tossed the pasta, forked some onto a plate, set it before Mats. She realized she was deliberately tensing her wrists to harness her shaking hands. "You working tomorrow?"

Ellice shook her head. "February's a light month for subs. I guess teachers figure only twenty-eight days, plus your four-day weekend, plus there's usually a snow day or two, taking a personal day's pushing it."

"Wanna come into Atlantic City with me tomorrow? It might be fun."

"Why can't I go?" Jane wailed.

"You have school."

"Jason says you're gonna help get *him* on TV."

"Way I figure it," Ellice said, "they could cast this whole show on the Fortunati friends and family plan."

"Are you taking *Mats?*" Jane demanded.

Cat placed three more plates on the table. "I am not taking Mats. He's going to visit with Nonna at the church office in the morning." She sat next to Mats and put his napkin on his lap. "I can't wait until this *CopWatch* thing is over."

The conversation drifted. Cat and Jane washed dishes, chatted about what had happened in school ("Andy Chu's big brother stole the Pea Pod Pal from Mrs. Paganelli's desk and he's gonna hold it for ransom."), sorted laundry, let Mats take a bath in her sunken tub while she wrote a draft of the press conference. It would be all over the dailies tomorrow, old news by the time Ritchie put out the first edition of the *Cape-Atlantic Chronicle* on Thursday, but maybe she'd come up with something to give it a little spin before the Wednesday deadline, and she may as well get it written now, since she'd have to write up the casting call feature tomorrow night.

Reading time, and Cat decided to pass on the juvie lit that was all the kids read in school anyway, in what had been called Literature when she was in school, but was now labeled Communication Arts and Technology.

She got out a battered paperback copy of *The Old Curiosity Shop*, tucked Mats in bed and perched at the foot with Jane beside her and began to read with an energy that overcame the children's skepticism regarding the lack of pictures. "'She put her hand in mine as confidently as if she had known me from the cradle, and we trudged away together: the little creature accommodating her pace to mine and rather seeming to lead and take care of me than I to be protecting her. I observed that every now and then she stole a curious look at my face as if to make quite sure that I was not deceiving, and that these glances (very sharp and keen they were, too) seemed to increase her confidence at every repetition.'"

Jane was absolutely compelled to interrupt here. "She shouldn't go off with some *stranger*. He could be a *pervert*."

A sentiment Mats endorsed. "Teacher says we shoulent go with strangers even if they says they know us. What's a pervert?"

Cat would not to Dickens sink without a struggle. She continued reading, got as far as the line where the narrator said he "avoided the most frequented ways and took the most intricate" when Jane interrupted with, "What's 'intricate'?"

"It means out of the way."

"That's how they *do* it if they're *serial killers*."

"No, I think this is someone she's probably seen around," Cat offered as a feeble defense.

"That's how they *get* you. They hang around where the kids are," Jane argued, knowingly. "Uncle Marco says."

"Well, this man is very old and frail," Cat protested.

"He could still have a *knife*."

Cat decided to skip a couple paragraphs, got to the grandfather's house, whereupon Jane demanded why she couldn't have been named Nell instead of Jane, which was a dumb name, and Cat tried once more to explain how Jane bore the name of the most gifted writer in the English language, but Jane wasn't buying. Cat capitulated. Mats had fallen asleep, anyway.

Cat put Jane to bed and knocked on Ellice's door.

Ellice was perched on her bed, reading Marcus Aurelius. "Freddy coming over?"

Ellice shook her head. "How'd it go?"

Cat groaned. "You ever try to get the kids in your classes to read Dickens?"

"Honey, I got a dickens of a time gettin' my kids to read, period." Ellice tossed her book aside. "I caught the press conference on *NewsLine90*. I thought Kurt Raab was gonna spew like Vesuvius."

"I didn't stick around for the finale. I don't know why I let Ritchie talk me into that one. I mean, I've got *CopWatch*, I'm the only reporter in the area who's got an 'in' with the production, a television gig, and I'm nudging it aside for another murder."

"Who was it, Dillinger, Baby Face Nelson, robs banks and they ask him why and he says 'cause that's where the money is? I think it's also 'cause that's what he was good at. I didn't see In-Your-Face Friedlander comin' up with the Harris woman."

"I am—I mean I've sort of gotten lucky with this sort of thing lately."

"Cat, honey. Repeat after me: 'I'm good at it.'"

"I think I may have a certain knack for it, how's that? The getting myself in trouble part? I'm certainly good at that. Toil and trouble," Cat muttered. "That's what my life has come down to."

She took another peek at the kids, threw the clothes in the dryer and went to her room, put the phone back on the hook, bet herself a pack of Raisinettes that it would ring within three minutes. Two minutes and ten seconds later, the phone rang.

It was Maggie Keller. "Dominic's not back yet. He made his hospital visits and then decided to cruise around a little, see if he could catch sight of that boy. He asked me to call, see if you'd heard from him."

"No. Haven't the police heard anything?"

"No. They dug up his clothes. They said I shouldn't have thrown them out."

"Well, I guess there might have been trace evidence or something that you might have contaminated."

"He did a good enough job at contaminating those rags without my help," Maggie grumbled. "If you hear anything about the boy, would you give us a call? Dom, Kevin, Monsignor, they're all worried."

"He has to turn up," Cat assured her, not believing it. The kid had managed to hole up for weeks at a time without surfacing. "He can't hide out very long on the dollar's worth of change he stole from my car."

"Dom's worried he might be trying to sell his meds on the street."

"Something for aches and pains couldn't have much street value, could it?"

Maggie dismissed Cat's naiveté with a gruff laugh. "They'd sell chalk dust on the street if they could con someone into thinking it was cocaine. Remember how one of the Coluccis snorted alum on a bet?" She sighed. "Fourteen? God forgive me for saying it, but by fourteen, these kids are just about gone. Don't tell Kevin or Dom I said so."

Cat promised not to rat her out, promised to call if she heard any news about Mark, even promised to drop by Mass sometime, hung up and went down to the kitchen and got herself the last pack of Raisinettes.

Victor ran a check on Elizabeth Easter. She was a registered nurse, had worked with the critically ill. He sent Adane and Rice into the hospitals, the hospices where she had worked and they came back with reports that were better than exemplary; they glowed, illuminated with the radiance of good will and good character that cast an odd light on her unconventional marriage. She was one of the most faithful, most generous parishioners at St. Agnes and was an active volunteer at St. Agnes School. Victor rubbed his forehead, wearily, pushed aside the mug of coffee that had long since cooled. And with ties to all four women. Did women kill like this? He'd read about a coed who stabbed her roommate fifty-three times, over someone reading someone else's e-mail. But to kill again and again?

And the toxicology report, what to make of that? The pharmacies balked at identifying all their diazepam users without a warrant, though they agreed to confirm a prescription if the police gave them a name. None of the victims had been prescribed diazepam, generic or brand name.

Victor checked his watch, picked up the phone, dialed Cat's number. The line was busy.

He signed out, noticing that only Adane was left in the darkened dayroom, fixed on the computer screen. "Go home, Adane," he said, and she replied with an obedient "Yes, sir," but he suspected she'd finish whatever was occupying her unless he dragged her out of the building and put her in her car. Somewhere down the corridor, in one of the other bureaus, the tape of the press conference was running. Victor heard Cat's recorded voice, heard laughter.

He headed home, reached for his car phone to try Cat again, the phone trilled. It was Long. "Lieutenant, I got a line on that Molina chick. She's a freelancer. The girls on the street, they're pretty tight. All's they'd tell me is she's been off the stroll, looks to be taking reservations, but they don't know who's booking her, or they're not telling. She's not with Printemps. I tailed her from her place, she looks to be hookin' up. Got as far as Bud-n-Lou's but I don't know if I should go in. I mean, after today, I gotta wonder if she's gonna recognize me from, you know, back in the day."

"Thanks. I'll check it out."

Heads turned when Victor walked into Bud-n-Lou's. He had few friends on the local force; his detachment, the rumors regarding his prolonged and dangerous undercover assignment, his surprising relationship with King Carlo Fortunati's sister gave him the aura of some complex and puzzling beast. An excellent cop, but not exactly one of the fraternity; no one recalled ever seeing him at Bud-n-Lou's.

Bud-n-Lou's was a cops' hangout on Baltic, a low brick building with a green-black asphalt roof, mullioned windows, within walking distance of The Temple, the epithet for the old police headquarters. It produced the best cheesesteak east of Philadelphia, but when *Philadelphia* Magazine attempted to honor Lou in its "Best of the Shore" issue, Lou turned them down flat, said he didn't want every tourist running down to suck up his local color. Between "every" and "tourist" there had been five or six modifiers that the magazine was loth to print, and which eliminated any misgiving the editor might have had regarding Lou's sincerity or the possibility that he might simply have been disguising his tender soul with a curmudgeonly persona.

Victor sat in a corner of the bar, watched the action at the far end of the counter where Lou, seventy years old, his shock of white hair glowing above the mist of cigarette smoke, was taking on an off-duty patrol cop forty years his junior. Lou had been a cop, his son was a cop, his son's son was headed for the Academy. The bullet that had put Lou out of commission was in a glass cube behind the bar; the rumor was that the head of the punk who had fired the bullet was mounted on the wall of Lou's den.

"How 'bout a little sex on the beach to get you started?"

Sex on the Beach, Orgasms, French Ticklers, drinks that had migrated from the Jersey shore to South Florida, the Caribbean, who took credit for their origin.

The voice sent a thread of adrenaline through Victor's blood and he looked up.

She looked the same, the mass of fiery hair, the spray of russet freckles along the exposed collarbone, the tensile thinness, hazel green eyes giving the come-on, but cautioning them not to cross the line. "Long time, no *te veo*."

"Sheila."

"What can I getcha, sugar?"

Victor's gaze took in the shirtwaist unbuttoned to the top

of a lacy bra, the snug black skirt, the spark of a diamond on her left hand. He nodded toward it. "Is that what I think it is?"

"It is. What, you never expected me to settle down?"

"Do I know him?"

"Lover, you introduced us. Gino Forschetti."

*Gino?* Squat, simian Gino with a woman like Sheila?

"Hey, don't look so surprised."

"I'm not aware that I looked surprised."

"You don't really. You never give it away. Lover, you ever quit the force, play poker, you got the face for it. But, hey, everyone's surprised. I know Gino's not exactly a prince in the looks department, but he treats me real good."

"He's a good person." *He saved my life*, Victor did not add, wondered if Gino had told Sheila about that episode.

"Gino says you're with the King's little sister. I thought Stan told me she'd sworn off cops." Sheila crossed her arms, leaned on the counter. "We had the press conference on the TV." She jerked the auburn mass toward the small television perched on a shelf over the bar. "She really nailed Raab to the cross."

"Yes, she did."

"So, is it serious?"

"She's been married before. I'm not sure she's ready to get serious."

"What's the point of waiting until you're ready?"

"We're not all as resilient as you, Sheila."

"Loose, you mean?"

"I didn't say that."

"Yeah, well, I like men. Liked. That's history. I'm down to one guy, and it's for keeps."

"So when's the wedding?"

"April. Gown, veil, walk down the aisle," she shimmied her shoulders. "Premarital counseling and let no man put asunder, the whole bit."

"Tell Gino I said he's a lucky man."

"Tell him yourself. I'm getting off in fifteen minutes; he's supposed to pick me up, if he isn't late again. I still live over Ocean near Caspian, I could walk it, but Gino's antsy because of these women who got killed."

"Gino's right. Give me whatever you've got on tap."

Sheila sashayed over to the tap; Lou's opponent lost his concentration and Lou took him down, sent him off the stool onto the floor. A round of laughter filled the room and the guy on the floor shouted "Thanks a lot, Sheila!"

"Sugar, your wife told me you like to be the one on the bottom," she shot back, provoking another roar. She set a mug in front of Victor.

He thanked her, let his glance slide around the room, the slow pan of a seasoned cop. He saw a familiar form, gave the image a moment to hook into memory, turned back to Sheila. "The young woman in the back booth, she a regular?"

Sheila shrugged. "I think I've seen her somewhere. Now, you're gonna behave yourself, aren't you?"

Victor blotted his mustache on a cocktail napkin. "I always behave myself. Excuse me."

He rose and walked over to the booth. She looked up, dark oval eyes sparkling slyly, an insouciant chin raised.

"Miss Molina?"

The smile stiffened, warily. "I know you?"

"I'm not your date, if that's what you mean. May I sit down?"

"Hey look, my guy comes in sees me sitting with a cop—"

"Did I say I was a cop?"

"Everybody in here's a cop."

Victor slid into the booth across from her. She had positioned herself so that she could see the door. "Isn't this an unusual place to be waiting for your date?"

She shrugged. "I think he's some kinda cop junkie, you get me? I guess it gives him some kinda rush. He sees you hangin' around, he might make a rush for the door."

"A minute or two of your time and I'm gone."

"Hey, my time, it's worth something, you get me?"

"Yes, but I'm going to pretend I don't get you and spare you the inconvenience of postponing your date."

The slender form shifted, tensely. "So what do you want?"

"Carmen Oliva."

"What about her?"

"You knew her."

"So? Us girls, we hang out. Swap the down and dirty, what john likes what. Carmen, she was a good kid."

"You know why she quit on Easter?"

She shook her head. "But hey, I'd take her place, he'd have me. Jimmy, he takes his cut, but he plays fair and he never lays a hand on his girls."

"Renay Harris."

"She and Carmen hung out. I got the idea she was the one talked Carmen into quitting the life."

"Tamara Montgomery."

"Tammy was modelin' for Nothing Sacred. I can't get that gig, either; I'm too short."

"She quit Easter, too."

Luz shrugged, tossed her head. A crucifix, dark, swirling malachite, hung from her neck, but the faint trace of color ringing her throat was not the indentation of its silken cord. Luz followed the direction of his gaze, slid her hand over her throat. Victor drew her fingers away. "Who's roughing you up, Luz?"

"What do you care?" She yanked her hand free.

*What do you care?* Remy had been eighteen the year after his wedding, the three of them in a standoff in his mother's kitchen, Remy bruised but defiant, screaming at her mother and Victor. *What do you care?*

*You tell me who put his hands on you!* His words thundered throughout the small house; he had not yet learned the power of silence. He could see in his mother's eyes that she knew and would not tell, afraid Victor would kill him.

Luz gave him a crooked smile, patted his hand. "Hey, look, a couple years I'll be too old for the life, maybe I'll take up typing, too, go to church."

"He use anything on you other than his hands?"

Luz snorted. "He better if he wants to get his money's worth, you get me?"

Victor repressed a smile. "I meant a knife. He ever try to cut you?"

"No."

"What about your girlfriends? Any of them mention a guy who likes to cut?"

"Sometimes their man, not a customer."

"You don't have a man, you don't work for Easter, how do you connect?"

The sly smile returned. "We're talkin', what do they call it, hypothetical, right?"

"Of course."

"I got a kind of pipeline thing goin'. People who're connected give me, like, referrals. Guy wants something, one of their girls don' do that, they turn him on to me, you get me?" She looked past Victor. "Look, this one likes his thrills, but like I said, he sees me talking to a badge, he could bail out."

"Let him."

"Hey, I don' need a big brother."

Victor took his business card out of his breast pocket, pushed it across the table. "You think of anything you want to tell me, you get in a jam, you give me a call."

"Sure, 'mano. An' there's anything you wanna get into, you call me."

Victor excused himself and left her, his gaze traveling the bar, looking for some cop junkie, waiting in the shadows for him to depart. Nothing but cops. Cop junkie, meeting his pickup at Bud-n-Lou's. Victor nodded Lou aside, paid for his beer. "That one?" he flicked his eyes toward Luz Molina. "You recognize the guy who picks her up, give me a call."

He found Sheila standing outside on the corner of Baltic, her coat turned up to her throat, pacing irritably. "Cops," she muttered. "Think the whole world runs on their clock." She checked her watch again. "You wouldn't wanna give me a lift, would you?"

"What would Gino think?"

"Gino would think he's late and one of his buddies was enough of a gentleman to give me a ride home."

Victor took her elbow, guided her to his car, held the door for her. He was struck with the chivalry of it. Sheila had usually come to his place from work; sometimes he would go to hers for dinner. No movies, no concerts, no restaurants. And then the sex, always sex; Sheila had deserved better. She had deserved a gentleman back then.

Victor glanced at the entrance tucked under a stone arch, the dimness of the lighting. "I'll walk you up."

"I'll be okay, just watch me 'til I get inside."

"No." Victor got out of his car, helped her out.

"It's four flights."

"I remember."

Sheila's heels clicked against the worn granite stairs. "I'll be outta here soon. Gino and I are getting one of those places on New Hampshire. It's getting kinda nice over there, a little sterile, but I like being near the water." She stopped at her door. "I'm okay now." She slipped the key in the lock, bit her lip. "Okay, maybe you can come in and look around. I'm not paranoid or anything, but there's something about this creep, you know? How he gets so close to all these women? You just don't know who to trust anymore."

## CHAPTER SIXTEEN

Victor got to the office early Tuesday morning, set his takeout coffee on his desk, threw his coat on the beat-up coat rack in the corner. He ran through the notes Adane had laid on his desk, knocked on the glass and waved his unit in.

Long slid a manila envelope on his desk. "The pix from the Oliva woman's funeral, Lieutenant."

"Thank you. Sit down. What's going on?"

"Mrs. Finkle called, sir ..." Adane began, hesitantly.

This time Victor finished a sentence of Adane's. "And she knows her husband is dead, she just knows it."

Mrs. Finkle's husband had died of natural causes six years before; she frequently forgot that his ashes were kept beside her bed.

"Call Social Services again, please."

Stan and Jean looked at each other, uncomfortably.

"Is there something else?"

"She asked if her husband might have been killed by the, um ..."

Stan unrolled the newspaper in his hand to reveal the headline, *Seaside Slasher Claims Four Victims*.

Victor sat, rubbed his eyelids with his thumb and forefinger. "And whom do we thank for disseminating that bit of hyperbole?"

"What I heard's Raab said it off-the-cuff, someone from the press picked it up and ran with it," Stan said.

"I would be grateful if we could refrain from using that particular epithet here." Victor spilled the photos onto his desk, arranged them in two rows. He pointed to one of a prim, light-skinned black woman, clutching a Bible to her coat.

"That's her. That's Easter's wife."

Victor studied the face. The contours were soft with a resolute curve to the lips, a sweet patience in the eye. Not the look of a killer, Victor thought. But then, she didn't look like a woman who would be married to Easter, either.

"Pallbearers are from Moroscos, they couldn't find six guys admit they knew her to carry her out. There's the girl-friend, DeLuca," Stan nodded. "Those two a couple more from Business Briefs, the temp agency. The Molina chick."

Victor's gaze moved on to a photo of an older man, wisps of thinning hair upswept in the wind, thick, dark-rimmed glasses. There was a second shot of him beside Kevin Keller at the gravesite, Dominic in the foreground. "This one looks familiar."

"Custodian over St. Agnes. Name's Testa. Just buried his own wife last week, same day they found Oliva."

"Does the church custodian ordinarily attend a parishioner's funeral?"

"I don't know."

Victor's brows shot up.

"I'll find out."

Victor sat back, resting his elbows on the arms of his chair. "What did the wife die of?"

Long scratched his head. "I heard it was some degenerative something; she was paralyzed. He kept her at home. Wasn't suspicious death, if that's what you're thinking, Lieutenant."

"I was thinking that the tape we recovered from Miss Oliva's apartment contained a message from an elderly man, thanking her for something."

"You think," Stan theorized, "I mean ... your wife's vegged out, it's gonna kinda put a crimp in your conjugal interaction. Maybe he's been lookin' for companionship, worked out a little something on the side with Oliva."

Victor thought of Marisol, lying in the hospital bed, nothing left but the waning voice, the restless heartbreak in her dying gaze. The despair that settled into his bones, hardened into hatred for the healthy, the hopeful. No lust could have penetrated that armor. But Marisol had lasted only weeks. What would he have become if she had survived months? Years?

Victor looked up, saw them staring, mesmerized and a little alarmed by the expression on his face. But when he spoke, the words emerged in his normal monotone. "The tape from Oliva's answering machine? Would it be possible to sign it out? I think I'd like to listen to it again."

Cat was not going to be out-Kated again, dressed for the visit to the casting call in good jeans, black ankle boots, a white collarless shirt, black wool double-breasted jacket.

She had a pang of guilt as she buckled Mats' seat belt, got behind the wheel next to Ellice. She should have said something to Ellice, some hint of what she suspected, not dragged her along as some sort of bodyguard. Ellice had trusted her with the confidences about Ira; she, Cat, should reciprocate, shouldn't she? But then, seventeen years was a long time, it probably wasn't even the same Ted Cusack. Why dredge up the past?

Jennie was sorting files in St. Agnes church office, dressed smartly in a crisp white blouse with a lace collar, tailored navy slacks. Pearl earrings.

Cat took one look at the outfit. "Mama," she said.

"Who needs a whole hour for lunch? Besides, I hang around here, Maggie's gonna want me to come in and eat and you know I can't eat what she cooks."

Cat helped Mats off with his coat. "Nice try. Is there anyone in my family who's not trying to get on *CopWatch?*"

"Look," Jennie reasoned. "They're gonna need some old lady to play your mother, right?"

"But they're not going to get my own *mother* to play my mother. They'll get some actress to play the part."

"Why pay all that money to some actress doesn't even know you, when they can get your own mother a lot cheaper?" Jennie countered. "You wanna see my head shots? Nancy took them real nice."

"You were always a beauty, Mama. You want to get in good with *CopWatch*? They're thinking of shooting a couple scenes in St. Agnes; tell Kevin not to put a damper on it."

Jennie's dark eyes narrowed, shrewdly. "How much they pay for something like that?" She straightened her petite form. "Maybe I'll put in a call to the bishop."

The Marinea Towers had started out as a time share, but no one wanted to pay those inflated prices for what was essentially a renovated hotel room. Plan B was conversion to an all-suite hotel, but located on Pacific, close to, but not quite on the Inlet and a long, unsightly block to the Boardwalk, with no gaming license and no prospect of getting one, it did not present an attractive prospect for those who actually stayed overnight in the city. Plan C, the last option before a flat-out declaration of bankruptcy, was a residence hotel that pitched extended-stay accommodations to mid-level casino executives relocating to Atlantic City (the CEO candidates stayed in the casinos, penthouse) and the occasional film crews that came to exploit the city's unique synthesis of seediness and ersatz glamour (director and stars stayed in the casinos, penthouse).

Disastrously located, but it wasn't downright awful, Cat had to admit. The entrance was AC Renaissance, glass upon gloss. The floor of the long lobby was diamond-shaped marble, the row of tiered chandeliers reflected on the polished surface. Ferns and fronds in wicker baskets, wicker chairs with blue velvet cushions were arranged in small clusters; mood music drifted unobtrusively through the air.

Past the front desk, a long corridor led to the rear wing of the ground floor, a coat check, a newsstand, the bar/coffee shop, then made a sharp left at the pair of elevators, continued past a gym and sauna, corporate offices, restrooms, a couple of modest-sized meeting rooms and finally to a large conference/banquet room. Along this stretch of corridor were the hopefuls, queued two deep on the right side, primarily women, dressed in bright nylon jogging suits or their dress sweats, the cotton knit pullovers garnished with colored beads or glitterglue script. Cat ran her eyes along the row to see if she recognized anyone: She saw three teachers, a woman she had seen behind the counter at McDonald's, Deanna Halprin from KRZI and her sister-in-law, Lorraine.

Using Ellice as a shield, she whisked past them to the desk outside the conference room, where a woman sat, motioning two at a time into the room. The woman at the desk wore jeans, dark shoes, white shirt, black blazer. Cat wondered when this had become femme chic, wondered if there was a short piece in the observation, wondered if this was what restaurants meant when she would be writing up a review, called to double-check on the dress policy and would be told it was smart/casual.

Cat fired up her journalistic neurons: "Chimera of Celebrity Hales Hollywood Hopefuls," she murmured.

"Uh-uh," Ellice looked over the crowd. "Honey, this is the tackiest crew I ever saw, and I been to South of the Border. Editor like Landis? He'd red-flag chimera. Small Screen Summons Seaside Citizenry."

A woman near the front of the line was puzzling over the form in her hand, muttering to a companion "When they got, like, address? Do they want, like, where I'm livin' right now?"

Cat didn't trust herself to look at Ellice. The woman at the table glanced up. She wore a laminated ID around her neck that said, *Hello, I'm,* then **Raine** in marker, followed by S & M CASTING.

"I'm Cat Austen," Cat said.

"Oh, marvelous! Marvelous piece they're running in *New Jersey* magazine."

"*South Jersey.*"

"Right you are." She looked up at Ellice. "Marvelous. You bring pictures?"

"She's with me," Cat said.

"'Cause they're gonna be casting for the friend, you know, the black girlfriend?"

"No kidding," said Ellice.

"It's still open, that part and the nutty DJ's sister. You dance any?"

"Like Pavlova," Ellice vowed, straight-faced. "But I'm just here as Mrs. Austen's gal Friday. Is this a typical S and M crowd?"

Cat grabbed Ellice's sleeve and dragged her into the conference room, tugged her notebook out of her totebag and wrote "Lining up for S and M," began scribbling descriptions of the crowd.

Another line of people stood against the wall in the conference room, waiting to be called before two women who took their applications and looked over their pictures. Some were dismissed immediately, others were directed to a table at the opposite side of the room where they posed in front of a sheet tacked to the wall, a couple Polaroids snapped and they were given a sixty second interview, confirming their availability.

"'What's fame?'" Ellice murmured, looking around the room. "'A fancied life in other's breath.'"

"'A thing beyond us, ev'n before our death,'" concluded a mellifluous voice.

Cat's spine iced over; she pulled the muscles of her face into a composed mask. *Think of everything you've gone through in the past couple months. You've been shot. You can get through this.*

Ellice turned, smiled. "I was ready to bet good money nobody in this room read Pope."

"I used to teach him when I taught full time. Ted Cusack."
He extended his hand, broadened his smile to include Cat.
"And you must be my Kate," he purred.

*He doesn't recognize me.* Cat felt a warm, nauseating rush,
realized only by the composure reflected in the faces confronting her that she looked perfectly normal. Her own face hurt.

"So when can we get together, my dear? I was thinking of
dinner sometime this week?"

"I, uh." *He doesn't know me.* "My schedule—I mean, I have
children in school."

"I understand. I heard you lost your husband."

"He died," Cat correctly, flatly. She hated it when people
said she had lost Chris. Like she'd misplaced him somewhere,
like there was still a chance he'd turn up.

"I'll watch the kids," Ellice offered.

Cat decided to kill her. She'd find new friends. Not as good
as Ellice, of course, but they'd do. She looked away and saw
Jackie Wing in jeans so snug it looked as if she'd spray-painted
her legs with denim. "Excuse me, I see someone I need to talk
to," Cat mumbled, couldn't tell, through the pounding in her
ears, whether her words had even been audible, lucid.

Jackie was standing before the women at the table, answering a couple questions about her application, shaving a year
or two off her age. She was told to go get a snapshot. Cat
introduced herself to the women. "Oh, you're Kate!" one of
them exclaimed. "We're S and M Casting."

"Cat," Cat replied, felt less discomfiture by this announcement when she saw by their badges that S was Sunny and M
was Misti. "I'm going to just walk around and, uh, record a
few observations."

"Teddy says you've got free rein."

Teddy. Cat thanked them and came up behind Jackie,
murmured, "I didn't know you were younger than I was."

Jackie's tilted eyes crinkled as she laughed. "I wanted Stan
to come with me, but he says the Lieutenant is dead set against

it." She tugged at her spiked bangs. "Says anyway it's twenty-four seven, whatever that means, until they find out who's been killing those girls in Atlantic City. You wanna know the creepiest thing? I think I knew that last one, the one they found last week? When they put her picture in the paper, she looked familiar."

"You knew Carmen Oliva?"

"Not knew her, but saw her around."

"Around where?"

"ICU. You think these jeans make me look fat?"

"Those jeans make me want to kill you. Was she a patient?" Cat asked.

"No, friend of one, or family, maybe. Elderly woman who'd been bedridden, came in with respiratory problems. I saw the Oliva girl waiting around with the husband."

"You remember their name?"

"An Italian name, I forget."

"Testa?" Cat asked, startled.

"That might have been it. She was Beth Easter's patient. I saw Beth talking to them a few times, she'd probably know. Gee, maybe I should mention this to Stan, you think?"

"I ... guess."

"You guys goin' to that dinner Friday night?"

"What? Oh, the retirement dinner?"

"Stan says the unit got the word they all have to show up. Is that really how it is with cops?"

Cat nodded, mutely.

A woman summoned Jackie before the camera.

Jackie posed in front of the sheet, smoothing her ribbed sweater over her tiny form.

Cat swallowed. Old Mr. Testa? Did he have some sort of personal relationship with Carmen Oliva? Was that why he had attended her funeral? Cat recalled the image of Testa, a nondescript figure wrapped in a thin, black coat. Mark had said he saw someone black, or wearing black, leaving Estrella Murillo's apartment.

Cat looked up, saw Ellice shooting her the "I'm at the end of my chit-chat" glare. Cat raised her chin with determination. *I've been through worse than this. I can be as strong as I need to be to wring a couple features out of him, get through the* CopWatch *shoot and then he can go straight to hell.*

"When would you like for us to get together, Mrs. Austen?"

*Have I changed that much?* He looked almost the same. The pale brown hair had gone silver at the temples and crows' feet formed smug smiles at the corners of his eyes.

"Why not right now?" she suggested. "The three of us could go into the coffee shop."

Cusack checked his watch. "Sorry, I have an appointment I can't put off. What about this evening?"

"I have family coming over this evening," Cat lied.

"April mentioned some locations she wanted me to look into. Said you suggested a local church? I don't know what they're paying for site fees these days, but I believe they'd go as high as ten thousand if it's available and got the look they're after. Perhaps tomorrow we could have a bite of lunch, then take a ride over there."

Ten thousand dollars would mean the world to St. Agnes. Could she forget what it had felt like to have this man grab her, shove her down on his desk, try to rape her for ten thousand dollars, plus the seventy-five hundred dollar consulting fee she would be getting from *CopWatch*?

"Mrs. Austen?"

Kevin or Dominic would be around, someone would be in the church office, school would be in session. She wouldn't be alone with him. She wasn't strong enough for that. "Tomorrow should be all right."

"When and where shall I pick you up?"

"I'll have to get back to you."

"I'm staying here, room Two-Thirteen. I'll be expecting to hear from you. Miss Watson," he turned to her, "'If we do meet again, why, we shall smile.'"

"'If not, why then, this parting is well made,'" Ellice countered, smiled as he walked off, then turned on Cat and hissed, "You wanna tell me what that was all about?"

"I can't talk about it."

"Try charades."

"Look, Ellice. I used to know him, that's all. It was a long time ago, and it's obvious he doesn't even recognize me, doesn't connect Cat Austen with Allegrezza Fortunati. Can we talk about it later, please? Let me just try to act like a writer on assignment."

Ellice seemed about to say something, reconsidered. "Okay. Take your notes. Describe that lady over there in the lavender sweats with the silver glitter. Dear God, I ever put on something like that, you shoot me."

"You have my word. Let's go in the ladies' room. Everyone who's getting held over for a picture's running in there to check their hair and makeup; that's where all the good eavesdropping's gonna be."

Cat and Ellice wedged themselves into the ladies' room. There were a couple love seats where a few women sat smoking, comparing glossies. In the lavatory, they were hip-to-hip in front of the mirrors. Young, trim, elevating teased hair, outlining pursed lips. Cat looked at her reflection and decided to leave well enough alone.

"Hey, Cat Lady?"

The voice plucked a chord of recent memory. She glanced two mirrors down and saw Luz Molina, the woman who had been praying at St. Agnes the day her friend Carmen turned up dead.

"You here checkin' out the open call?" Luz asked. She was wearing a snug black skirt barely south of groin level, a wraparound top of green Spandex that squeezed up cleavage. The green crucifix swung below the neckline; dangling earrings chimed when she tossed her head. "She's the one was on TV, ladies, she writes for the papers," Luz announced to the company at large, dabbed a flat sponge into a flesh-toned compact, blotted at her neck. Cat saw a reddish bruise, like a thin, scarlet necklace circling her throat. Luz saw the target of Cat's glance. "Rough nights. You think this is gonna show up on Polaroid?"

"Do you expect to get a callback?"

"Honey, I always get a callback." She gave Ellice a rival's once-over. "You oughta be a model or somethin'. Jimmy saw you, he'd snap you up like bait. You got a man, or you work solo?"

"I got a man. They call him Ready Freddy."

"I think I met him."

"Is Jimmy looking for girls?" Cat asked, in a I-really-don't-give-a-darn voice. "I mean, what with so many of them leaving him."

"So many of them dead, you mean."

Cat nodded. "What about his wife, you know her?"

Luz snorted. "Jimmy's wife? You mean, Miss Priss?" She yanked the long sleeves over her wrists; Cat saw that the wrists were braceleted with thin weals, nodded toward Luz's throat. "It still shows."

Luz groaned, leaned into the mirror, squinted critically. "Hey, Gloria," she called to a girl three mirrors down. "You got any foundation, olive beige? Mine's not doin' the trick."

Gloria's hips rotated impudently as she walked. Cat resolved to practice that strut when she got home. "You're not doin' the trick, I'll book him elsewhere." Gloria handed over a bottle of tawny liquid. "Don' forget where it came from."

Luz went to work on the camouflage.

Expertly, too. Cat shuddered. She knew how to cover her wounds. "Why do you let men hurt you like that?" she blurted, regretting the words immediately.

The dark eyes reflected in the glass flicked up toward Cat; she flicked her thumb across her four fingers. "Green. My favorite color. Some women, they stick with a guy works them over, gives them zip an' she comes back for more. How come no one asks a woman like that why she stays?"

"Good question," Ellice muttered.

"Damn good question. Me, someone wants to take his shot, it's cash in advance," Luz replied, coldly. "Carmen, an' Tammy an' Renay? Outta the life and into church and what does it get them?" She threw her head up, looked at the camouflaged throat with satisfaction. "You see, not a scratch. Drop dead gorgeous."

Cat interviewed Sunny and Misti, who had actually built up a thriving little enterprise supplying actors and models for local trade shows, commercials and radio voice-overs, and discovered that the amusement generated by their company name was not wholly unpremeditated. She linked up with the photographer Ritchie sent over and managed to get a picture of several of the extras, generously pulled her sister-in-law Lorraine into one of the shots; Lorraine reciprocated the kindness by offering a nearly polite "Hello" to Ellice. Cat looked around for Luz Molina, whose short skirt and insouciant prettiness would have made a fetching front page photo for the *Chronicle*'s debut, but Luz had vanished. Cat dug up Luz's résumé (under Occupation, she had written Entertainment Industry), her snapshot. Cat made a note of her address, wondered how many women in the Entertainment Industry had made the cut. She thought of her own designation with *South Jersey* magazine, Entertainment Girl. Sisters under the skin. Except Luz got paid in advance and Cat had to put out well before Ritchie came across with the cash.

Mats was sitting at Jennie's desk, coloring in the image of St. Agnes on an old church bulletin. "So," Jennie demanded, "they have a lotta people there? What did the old ladies look like?"

Cat kissed her mother's bright auburn hair. "You're a shoo-in."

"Hah."

There was a brief knock on the door and Kevin Keller

entered. "Jennie, here's the information for the printer on the confession schedule. Hi, Cat. Ellice." He ruffled Mats' hair. "Maggie's getting ready to make lunch; I'm sure she'd love it if you stayed."

"Thanks, but I have to get home and start working. Any word on Mark?" Cat asked in a low voice, glancing at Jenny, who was getting into her coat.

Kevin shook his head.

"How's my hair look?" Jennie asked.

"Mama, you're beautiful."

"I gotta go run a comb through this hair." She dug a comb out of her purse and went into the restroom across the hall.

There was a sharp rap on the door and Cat backed up so that Sister Maggie could enter. Her mannish face had softened with concern and she was clasping and unclasping her large hands. "Kevin, a detective was just here, talking to Isadore and he asked Isadore to go somewhere with him. Dom got in the middle of it and went along. Is something wrong?"

"What detective?" Cat asked.

"I think his name was Long."

"Maybe it was something about Mark," Cat suggested.

Maggie continued chafing her hands absently; they were raw from unrelenting housekeeping. "I don't think so. I don't like it. I was thinking that maybe I should give Steven Delareto a call?"

Delareto was one of the pack that had included Cat, Kevin, Freddy. He was a successful attorney.

"I don't know ..." Kevin said. He looked to Cat for guidance. "What do you think?"

"He didn't a-r-r-e-s-t anyone, did he?" Cat asked.

Maggie shrugged, palms up.

"I'll call Steve," Kevin offered. "What's his number, Cat?"

Cat told him the number and Kevin began to dial.

"Isadore and the Oliva woman," Maggie murmured in Cat's ear. "You know they were friendly ..."

## CHAPTER SEVENTEEN

Victor stared soberly at the street. Thirty years he had lived in New Jersey, had adjusted his chromosomes to the rhythm of the seasons, but there was something in the post-holiday bleakness that stimulated a craving for warmth and sun, for something tropical and sweet. That first winter, they had run out without their coats, stunned to see the colorless sky shedding white flakes. Milly had screamed as though confronting Armageddon, while Remy had thrown her head back, arms flung wide, and spun like a dervish, catching snowflakes on her tongue.

The landscape was bleak, partially obscured by the grime coating the one window of the interrogation cell. The pale green walls and scarred linoleum floor were reminiscent of schoolrooms. Victor didn't think anyone brought there was deceived.

Easter, Elizabeth Easter, now Testa. None of them fit the profile of a killer. It would have been simple if the act left its stamp somewhere, if all they had to hunt up was the portrait of Dorian Gray that exposed the infected heart and polluted soul. Instead, they scraped for evidence, interviewed over and again, and—though never admitting it—prayed for luck. Victor wondered if heaven held some hidden likeness of them all, if his own was branded with the anger inflamed by his father's murder, the bitterness that sprang from Marisol's

premature death, the violent abandon of those years undercover, while all the time he gave a Spartan face to the world.

Adane's hesitant knock dispelled the reverie. "Come."

The man's form was less substantial than the photograph,
as if the picture had fixed a spirit in place that had already
begun to separate itself from the flesh. Victor was surprised to
see Dominic Fortunati follow the man into the room.

Adane had begun to set up the tape recorder.

Victor nodded to Dominic. "Thank you for coming down,
Mr. Testa. Do you have an attorney?"

The man shook his head.

"Father, would you mind waiting outside?"

*Father.*

"This man is a parishioner, an employee of the church
and a friend of mine," Dominic replied. "Is there really a
problem if I sit in, Lieutenant?"

*Lieutenant.* Well, they had marked their turf. Cat's brother.
He and Cat the only two of the family who hadn't gone into
law enforcement, but he knew the drill well enough to know
that Testa was in trouble. *Why does he really want to sit in?*

"It's all right, Father Dom." The man put a fragile hand
on Dominic's arm. "I got nothing to hide. I can help them
find who killed those girls, I'm happy to do it."

"Isadore, I'm sure the lieutenant will be the first one to
tell you how many people there are whose last words as free
men were 'I got nothing to hide.'"

Adane pushed the PLAY button.

Victor stated the date, time, people present for the tape
recorder, then said to Testa, "Did Detective Long explain your
rights to you, Mr. Testa? You can ask for an attorney, that
you don't have to speak to me, and that if you did speak to
me and change your mind, you could end the interview?"

Testa looked from Victor to Dominic. "Yeah, he told me
all that, pretty much."

Pretty much. A savvy defense attorney could detonate
that "pretty much" and blast apart the man's testimony.

There was a sharp rap on the door and Long poked his head in. "Hey, Lieutenant, there's a Mr. Delareto here, says he's Mr. Testa's attorney."

Adane pushed the STOP button.

Victor's expression remained impassive. *Who the hell called Delareto?* "Send him in." *Damn it.*

Testa looked baffled. "I didn't call no attorney. I can't afford ..."

"Someone from the church must have called," Dominic said. "Steve's an old friend of my sister's."

Not "of the family," Victor observed. "Of my sister's." *Nice shot, Padre.*

Steve Delareto stepped in, a charcoal-gray coat thrown over his dark suit. He offered his hand to Dom. "Wanna fill me in?" He nodded to the lieutenant, his dark eyes sizing up the situation, deciding that he and Victor were rivals once again. "How are you, Adane, isn't it? Think any more about coming to work for me?"

"Thank you, sir. No, I haven't."

"Steve, I don't know if you've ever met Isadore Testa?" Dom offered. "He's the sexton at St. Agnes."

Delareto offered his hand.

"Who called you?" Victor asked.

"Kevin Keller. Maggie saw the two of you leave. What's the deal?"

"I would like to question Mr. Testa regarding a matter under investigation."

"Tell him he didn't have to talk to you?" Delareto threw his coat over the back of a chair, slipped his briefcase onto the table.

"Of course."

"He gave a verbal consent."

"Verbal gerbil," was Delareto's lawyerly reply. "Make me some paper."

Adane produced a consent form. Delareto pulled his chair

close to Testa, who looked a little baffled by Delareto's bra-
zenness. "How do you feel about this, Mr. Testa? You don't
have to talk to him."

"I know I didn't do anything."

"Why don't we sit down?" Victor suggested. "Can I get
you something, Mr. Testa? Coffee, a glass of water?"

"How 'bout you get me a nice double cap, no cream and
hold the cinnamon," Delareto suggested. "Then we can get
down to biz."

Victor put a hand on Adane's sleeve; she had actually
begun to rise, scurry out to hunt up the requested cappuccino.
"Let's start the tape," Victor said. He stated that Delareto had
been added to the group. "Mr.Testa, were you acquainted with
a woman named Carmen Oliva?"

"Ye—"

"Carmen Oliva?" Delareto made a "gimme" gesture. He
wore a class ring on his right hand, a watch that had been
more expensive than it looked.

"She was a parishioner," Dominic answered. "The young
woman who was found murdered in her apartment last week."

"Why would you think my client would know her?"

"She was a parishioner at St. Agnes. He works there."

"I drop in St. Agnes once in a while, that mean I'm a
suspect?"

"What if I told you they had been seen together?"

"What if I asked to see your fishing license, Lieutenant?"

"And that he was in the habit of calling her at her home?"

Delareto flicked his wrist, checked his watch.

Victor nodded to Adane. She produced an evidence envelope with the tape from Carmen Oliva's answering machine.
She switched tapes and played it, exchanged tapes again.

"Is that your voice, Mr. Testa?"

"Don't answer that," Delareto ordered.

"I could send it to the state voice lab and have them
compare it with the tape we've got. But budget constraints

being what they are, I'm sure Mr. Raab would be happier if we were spared the expense. Is you client willing to answer the question, or shall I move on?"

"Move on."

"No," Testa interrupted, meekly. "I don't gotta lie about it. I called Carmen last week."

Delareto shook his head. "Lieutenant, I'd like to have a word with my client alone."

"Certainly—"

"No," Testa objected. "There's other people knew she was helping me out."

"Helping you out how?"

"I was ... my wife? She was bedridden."

"Mrs. Testa died last week after a prolonged illness," Dominic interjected. "Mr. Testa cared for her at home with the help of a professional nurse and some women from the church. I believe Miss Oliva was one of them."

"Jennie, she kept me fed." The man smiled at Dominic. "Beth Easter, Donna DeLuca, Dottie Cicciolini and her boy, Louie, they all helped me out."

Victor nodded, gravely. "You know Carmen Oliva before she started coming to St. Agnes?"

Testa shook his head.

"That's a negative response," Victor remarked for the tape. "How did she come to know that you were in need of some help at home?"

"Well, Father Dom made an announcement, but I think— I'm not sure, but I think Beth Easter talked to her. She talked to a few of the young girls who were new to the church, looking to maybe get more involved."

"Was Tamara Montgomery one of them?"

Delareto's gaze shot up, but Testa had already echoed, "Tammy ..."

Victor's eyes met Delareto's. "That's right. Estrella Murillo? Renay Harris?"

"What's your point, Lieutenant?" Delareto demanded.

"They're all dead."

"So's my grammom."

Victor tapped his lip with a crooked finger. "I'm sorry to hear that. I hope that if she was sedated and murdered, you had the crime investigated."

"She was ninety-seven and she died in her sleep."

Victor stared through the grimy window. He hated this. He knew cops who relished it, to whom the thrill of cornering a witness was almost sexual. An old man. He reminded himself what Tammy Montgomery had looked like, lying on the slab, twenty years old. She never had her chance to get old. He took an envelope that Adane had brought into the room, removed a glossy of Tamara Montgomery, slipped it onto the table. "This is Tamara Montgomery. She was twenty years old. Her parents gave me that picture. I have pictures of Estrella Murillo and Renay Harris, too, but they were taken at the morgue and they're not very pretty."

"Bag it, Lieutenant," Delareto snapped. "You pull this *CopWatch* crap and we're outta here."

Victor looked at Adane. *This was how they staged interrogation scenes on* CopWatch? He put the envelope aside. "So your relationship with Miss Oliva was just that of one parishioner helping another?" he resumed.

"She was just a nice girl helping out an old man."

"Tuesday night, the twelfth. Shrove Tuesday. Did you see Miss Oliva at church?"

Testa shook his head. "Tuesday, my wife passed. I didn't go in to church at all."

"What about Wednesday morning?"

"I ... let me see ... they took Mary Tuesday night. Then the next morning, Deacon Keller came by; Father Dom stopped by after Mass. The woman from Moroscos came by to talk over the funeral arrangements, you know."

"Later that week you called Carmen Oliva. Why?"

"My client didn't admit to calling Carmen Oliva," Delareto reminded him.

"How did you learn of her death?"

"Deacon Keller told me when I got back from Mary's funeral. He didn't want me to see it in the paper."

"Tammy Montgomery. When was the last time you saw her?"

"December, I think. She told me she wouldn't be able to help me out a couple days over Christmas because she was going to visit her parents."

"When did she tell you this?"

Testa scratched his head. "I think there was an Advent Mass and a little gathering at the church for the young people. She offered to stay after to help clean up, so that I could get back home to my wife."

Victor and Adane exchanged a glance. "You remember the date?"

"I can look it up," Dominic offered. "I'll check one of our old church bulletins, if they haven't all been recycled."

Victor's thoughts took off at a sprint; he struggled to rein them in. "Advent. That would be, what, a few weeks before Christmas?" Tammy Montgomery's disappearance had been around three weeks before Christmas, her body fished up a week later. "Did you see her at this function?"

Testa nodded, mutely, his eyes turning toward Delareto. "What about you, Father?"

Dominic looked up, startled. "Why, yes, I believe I did."

"You know how she got there?"

Dominic looked confused.

"What I mean is, she didn't own a car. She had been allowed to drive the Leeds' car on occasion, but she didn't have it that night. I'd like to know how she got to the church, and how she got home."

"I don't know if Kevin ran the van pool that night; it's mostly used for senior citizens on Sunday. A lot of the young people give each other lifts."

"Let's talk about a woman named Renay Harris."

There was a knock on the door, and Phil Long poked his head in. He passed a folded paper to Victor, whispered something in his ear. Victor nodded, closed the door. "Mr. Testa, did you know any of these women—Carmen Oliva, Tamara Montgomery, Estrella Murillo, Renay Harris—before they started coming to Mass at St. Agnes?"

Testa blinked. "No."

"Mr. Testa, were you arrested for soliciting the services of a prostitute two years ago?"

"My client doesn't have to answer that!" Delareto cried. "Mr. Testa, you don't have to answer that."

The old man was stricken, muttered, "It was just the one time ..." He appealed to Dom. "I went to confession ..."

"Did you have a sexual relationship with Carmen Oliva, Tamara Montgomery, Estrella Murillo or Renay Harris?"

"Victor, for the love of God," Dominic pleaded.

Testa shook his head; he pushed his glasses onto his forehead, wiped his eyes. "I don't think I want to say any more."

"My client's got nothing more to say," Delareto declared. "Are you charging him?"

Victor hesitated. "Not at this time."

Dominic rose, slipped a hand under Testa's elbow. "You don't have to say any more," he assured the man. He looked up at Victor. "It's been a week since the death of Isadore's wife. Maybe it would be better if I took him home." Quiet, reasonable, the way he would have explained to a penitent the error of his ways. "He's not going anywhere."

*Neither was the killer; he's been damned territorial*, Victor thought. "One more question."

"Make it short," Delareto snapped, whipping on his coat.

"Mr. Testa, do you take any medication?"

"Something for nerves. What with my wife ill, I haven't been sleeping well."

"What do you take?"

"Sorry, you got your one question," Delareto said. "We're outta here."

Dominic helped Testa on with his coat, then, looking a little ashamed of his coldness, offered his hand to Victor. *For Cat's sake,* Victor concluded, and for Cat's sake he shook it. Delareto was less generous, simply nodded, said, "Nice to see you again, Lieutenant."

*I doubt it.* "Detective Long will show you out."

Adane was rewinding the tape. Victor turned to her. "You think I terminated the interview too soon, Adane?"

"It's not for me to offer an opinion, sir."

"It's your job to offer an opinion. What about him?"

"Mr. Testa? He would have access to the entire church property, the offices, the files. Addresses of the parishioners. He admitted to knowing Miss Montgomery. That was valuable; we hadn't confirmed her whereabouts at the time of her disappearance."

Victor crossed his arms over his chest. "But?"

"Well, sir, all this talk about thinking like the killer? I'm sure it's helpful, but sometimes one ought to put oneself in the mind of the victim. In this case, the least likely victim, who I think is Murillo. To a killer, she might seem the most vulnerable. But her consciousness of her vulnerability would, I believe, make her the most cautious. She would worry about crime in general, worry about the INS. And she doesn't speak much English, which would restrict her circle of acquaintance, and I don't think she would open her door to a stranger."

Victor nodded. Cat had thought the same. "So you would ask yourself, 'If I were Estrella Murillo, who would I let in?'"

Adane nodded. "I can think of reasons she might have buzzed someone into the building. Perhaps the manager was expecting a package, asked her to buzz in UPS. Perhaps she really was expecting company that night when the killer came to her door. But whoever knocks on her door, whether that person is expected or not, she's going to look through the peephole. Maybe she lets him in right away, but if she hesitates, he's going to have to overcome that hesitation. He would have to say something, something that reassures her. And in order to communicate that to her, it would be easier if he were fluent in Spanish. It's just a thought."

"It's an excellent thought."

"So I probably would have asked Mr. Testa if he spoke Spanish, that's all."

Cat and Ellice stopped by the grocery store to shop for dinner; Cat thought the eggplant looked particularly inviting. She bought three, drove home, made Mats' lunch and peeled and halved the eggplant, sliced the halves lengthwise, arranged them in a colander and salted them. The three eggplants made a substantial mound and Cat realized she would have to put on a pot of pasta too, because Jane would not eat eggplant and that would mean there would be a pile of leftovers. Which was no problem, *melanzane alla Allegrezza* was good cold, so was pasta, but still, Dominic absolutely loved *melanzane alla Allegrezza* and since there would be so much, why not give him a call and ask if he and Kevin and Maggie would like to come over to eat? And if the fact that Mr. Testa had been called into Victor's office that day and Dominic had gone with him and nudged her toward the produce aisle, so what?

After lunch, while the eggplant drained, Cat went to her room and wrote a short piece on the casting-call crowd, sketched out a first draft of her interview with S(unny) and M(isti) Casting, finished up her piece on the press conference, omitting her interview with Easter, but, after some hesitation, throwing in the bonus, that the police had questioned the employee of a local church that day. She re-read the article, deleted that last portion, reinstalled it, brought up her fax program, attempted to fax it to Ritchie, failed twice, finally e-mailed it to him, then called Cherry and told her to bring up *her* e-mail and told her to tell Ritchie she didn't want to name the employee in question, and if he wanted it he'd have to call Major Crimes for confirmation.

She returned to the kitchen, mopped up the juice under the colander, pressed out the eggplant slices between paper towels and re-salted them. Ellice escorted Jane from the bus stop. Jane flung her bookbag on the table. "I am *not* eating eggplant."

"How was school, sweetie?"

Jane yanked open the refrigerator door. "Andy Chu says if Victor comes on Diversity Day, is he gonna bring his *gun*." She grabbed a bunch of grapes, washed them at the sink.

"Isn't there a ban on weapons at school?"

"Only with the law enforcement," Ellice commented. "As far as the kids go, it's accessorization."

"Do you have homework?"

Jane gave her a pointed look which could mean either: A: Yes, I have homework, but I got it done in school, or B: You know they don't give us any homework anymore because half the kids won't do it. "You *know* they don't give us homework when we have an assembly."

"What was the assembly about?"

"Ethnic pride."

"Can I use ethnic pride as an excuse when I don't have time to do all my work?"

"Mo*mmmmm*."

"Take some paper towels if you're going up to your room with those grapes."

Ellice groaned. "Every time I consider going back to teaching full time, I hear a little voice reminding me why I've been putting it off. And speaking of putting things off, you gonna tell me how come I got enlisted for baby-sitting duty today?"

"Baby-sitting?"

"Catsitting."

Cat got a Pepsi from the refrigerator. "I guess it was pretty obvious."

"That you didn't want to meet this guy Cusack alone? Yeah, pretty much."

Cat fortified herself with a swig of Pepsi. "My family ... they're pretty traditional."

"No kiddin'."

"It's not that they didn't want me to go to college, it's just that they wouldn't have minded if I didn't."

"Because you were gonna get married and have kids and all that education would go to waste," Ellice concluded.

"Mama got married at eighteen."

"Freddy told me."

"And I really hadn't been anywhere. The restaurant tied Pop down so much, we never traveled much or anything. College was another country. I didn't run into him until I was in my junior year."

"We talkin' about Cusack now?"

"I'm not saying this right." Cat peeked through the kitchen archway to make sure there was no danger of Mats or Jane interrupting. "He was one of my professors, and I'd heard talk, like he hit on a couple of the coeds and so on. He was very attentive and I was flattered. It all started out as 'Maybe we could continue this discussion—'"

"Over coffee! Oh, God, I *know* him! And don't you just think you're the most grown-up person in the universe?"

Cat nodded. "I was taking one of his classes and he asked me to stop by his office one evening and, stupid me, I went." Cat laughed, wearily. "Before I went off to school? All the boys took me aside and gave me these pointers on how I was to handle it if any of those college boys got fresh."

"But it wasn't the college boys who got fresh, it was the prof."

Cat nodded. "If I'd kept my mouth shut, it would've been okay, I guess. But I reported it. And the school was going to take the position that it was my word against that of a tenured professor and I went to his office voluntarily and he

was going to play it like I came on to him and was rebuffed."
Cat swallowed back a sob. "So I backed down. I quit. They all
thought I was concerned about Pop's health; his heart had
been giving him trouble around that time. I let them think
that's why I came home. And then Freddy brought Chris
around and we started going out and got married."

"So why'd you agree to meet him tomorrow?"

"Look, I've got to be professional about this. And why
should I be the one to back down again because of Please-call-
me-Ted Cusack? I'm not letting him turn me into a quitter a
second time. He'll be dropping in and out of AC until the
shoot, then he's here for ten or twelve days, then I don't ever
have to see him again."

"You're not a quitter, Cat."

"I'm trying not to be."


The trick with the eggplant was to slice it wafer thin,
dredge the slices in a batter of flour, baking powder, club
soda and a sprinkling of parmesan, then deep fry them until
they crackled like tempura. Cat boiled some penne, tossed it
with some leftover *puttanesca* sauce.

Dominic devoured a small mound, muttered, "Maggie
doesn't know what she's missing," and Kevin said, "Cat, if I
realized you had this much talent as a chef, I would have
reconsidered the religious life."

Cat laughed. "You could have married. Married men can
be ordained as deacons, isn't that right?"

Kevin nodded. "But the life I lived, it wouldn't have been
fair to ask a woman to make that kind of sacrifice."

Cat smiled. "I think you came closest to living the life
you set out to, remember? You wanted to, what? Stay in a state
of grace, or something? Danny wanted to be a billionaire,
Trina wanted to be a scientist."

"You wanted to be a writer, and you are."

"Scraping around for a feature here and there isn't really
writing," Cat sighed.

"It's close enough," Kevin smiled. "And if it doesn't work out, you can always go into the restaurant business. I didn't get food like this in central Africa."

"What *did* you eat?" Jane asked.

Kevin pursed his lips. "I have recollections of a sort of broth made with grass and the parts of a goat that nobody else wanted."

"Uncle *Kevin*. That's *yuck*."

After dinner, Cat recruited Dominic to help with the cleanup; Kevin offered, but Cat gave Ellice the eye, and Ellice enlisted him in team Scrabble, her and Mats against Kevin and Jane.

Dominic rolled up his sleeves. "Okay, so let's get down to the real reason I rated an invite."

"Don't be silly."

"I'm rarely silly. Okay, maybe I *look* silly in tights but I think I'm otherwise rational."

"Fully aware that you're a priest and I'm your sister, I'd like to say that you look great in tights."

"Yeah, well, lately? South of the equator, gravity's been testing my faith."

Cat giggled. "Join *my* congregation." She rounded up a dishtowel. "Anybody heard anything from Mark?"

Dominic shook his head. "But I talked to Vinnie and Marco, he turns up in AC, they'll give me a call. And I know people in the ERs, too." He started tackling the dishes. "And Kevin makes the rounds at the shelter and the Underwood, he'll get the word if the kid shows up." The Underwood was the euphemism for the area beneath the boards staked out by the homeless; locals called it the Underwood Motel.

Cat shifted topics. "I wanted to talk to you without Kevin around. *CopWatch* is going to shoot a funeral scene in a church and they asked if I knew of any picturesque available locations. I heard they might pay around ten thousand for a site fee."

Dominic exhaled, impressed. "I won't say we couldn't use the money. I'd have to float it by the bishop."

"I think I should tell you that I mentioned this to Kevin and he's dead set against it."

Dominic rinsed a plate, set it on the drainboard. "I won't say I don't see Kevin's point. He's even opposed to Bingo." He looked at Cat and they both began to laugh.

"What's so *funny* in there!" Jane called out.

"Nothing."

Dominic tried to sober himself. "I do get his point. A church is a house of worship. God's house, we're just custodians. You get to where you're using it as a drug rehab or a cafeteria or a movie set, you can start to lose sight of your purpose, which is to spread the word of Jesus Christ, to restore people, like Kevin said, to a state of grace, preach the gospel."

"People in rehab and in the movies need God, too. Kevin just doesn't know how to mingle."

"Kevin's mingled plenty," Dominic said. "I think of the kind of service he undertook, I feel guilty about worrying whether one small parish will make it."

"But you are worried?"

Dominic shrugged. "There are a lot of people attached to St. Agnes. I guess some of them could transfer to St. Nick's, but I worry about the ones that will drift away altogether, the ones who haven't, I don't know, forged enough of a commitment to stand the change. And I'm afraid our most faithful are also the oldest."

"And dying off? Like Mrs. Testa?"

Dominic nodded.

"How is he? Mr. Testa."

"Cat."

"I'm just *asking*."

"Look, Victor's doing his job, I can respect that. I just wish he went about it a bit more ..."

"More what?"

"I don't know. Compassionately. Isadore's had a hard time the past few years. Victor started asking about his acquaintance with Carmen Oliva, if he knew those other women who died. Personal questions that I thought were a little out of line."

"What kind of personal questions?"

Dominic started to work on the silverware. "I'd rather not say."

"But he was friendly with Carmen Oliva. Maggie said so and Jackie told me she saw Carmen Oliva going to the hospital with him when Mary was in ICU."

Dominic nodded. "She was nice enough to give him a hand when he needed it. So were a lot of people in the church."

"Dominic ... can I ask you something?"

"You can ask me anything, Cat."

"Last Friday, when I dropped by church? We were talking about how my trip got canceled because someone had gotten killed. And you said that God didn't bring about a woman's death to keep us from, you know, sin? But you said you hadn't heard about Carmen Oliva's death yet. How did you know it was a woman who had been killed?"

"You're quite as good as the police, you know that?" He hesitated. "I wasn't talking about Carmen."

No, he had just come from bringing Isadore Testa home from the cemetery. "Were you talking about Mr. Testa?"

Dominic shrugged. "There are things I can't discuss. You know how it is, Cat. I'm sure there are things Victor can't talk about with you."

Cat nodded, ruefully. "You're not the only one under the seal of confidentiality, that's for sure."

"I don't mean to be hard on him, Cat. It's not easy, keeping secrets. Sometimes you would give anything to be able to share your secrets with someone else."

Cat thought about Cusack, all the years she had said nothing, not even to Chris. Thought about that kid, Mark, who had kept whatever he had seen to himself.

Dominic grabbed a paper towel. "Look, I hate to eat and run but Kevin and I wanted to drop in on a couple of the shut-ins. And on Isadore. Plus, I've got to do a rewrite on Sunday's homily."

"Let me know if you need an edit."

"I'd prefer an audience. You come by for the service, you'll be among family."

"I'll be there for the christening. I don't know about Mass."

"Come for Mass."

Cat shrugged. "We'll see. Remember how Mama always used to say that when we asked for something we really wanted? 'We'll see.'"

"We always got it," Dominic reminded her.

Cat walked them to the door and went back to the kitchen. The phone rang.

"Austen's Italian Take-Out."

"What are tonight's specials?" Victor asked.

"What are you in the mood for?"

"Something fresh—"

"Got that."

"Nothing fancy."

"You've definitely called the right place."

"Well seasoned."

"Ouch."

"Will there be much of a wait?"

"How fast do you want it?"

Victor chuckled, "'Haste is less important than taste.'"

Cat searched her memory. "'... the sweetest honey is loathsome in its own deliciousness, And in the taste confounds the appetite.'"

"'Therefore love moderately, long love doth so,'" Victor concluded, promptly. "'Too swift arrives as tardy as too slow.'"

"Don't tell me you played Friar Laurence?"

"No, the drama teacher thought I didn't look priestly. I was Mercutio."

Cat laughed. "Kurt Raab told me he once played Shylock. I never would have thought the prosecutor's office was a den of frustrated Shakespeareans."

"How was the *CopWatch* meet? I suspect there weren't many frustrated Shakespeareans there."

"Not so you would notice."

"I heard you were over St. Agnes."

"I left Mats with Mama when I went over to the casting call."

"So whom do I thank for throwing Delareto into the mix this afternoon?"

"I'm sure out of a sense of compassion you would have wanted a bereaved old man to have legal counsel when you're browbeating him."

"No one was browbeaten. Did Delareto say that?"

"I haven't talked to Steve. What do you want with Mr. Testa, anyway? You can't think he murdered four women."

"Cat, it's very natural you'd feel protective of St. Agnes, but I have to check into anyone linked to Carmen Oliva."

"Victor, an old man?"

"Cat, love, let's not fight."

"We're not fighting. I'm asking a simple question. Do you think there's a link between these four murders and someone at my brother's parish? Don't they have enough grief just trying to stay afloat?"

"Love, you know the drill. This early in an investigation, with so little to go on, you don't rule anything out."

"Well, how far is this going to go, Victor, before you do? What's next, you're going to interrogate Dominic, Monsignor Greg, the Daughters of Sicily?"

"I've been persuaded to eliminate the Daughters of Sicily, though under protest. I've heard they're a pretty volatile bunch."

Cat hung up, gave it a good slam.

The phone rang almost immediately. Cat lifted up the receiver, prepared to slam it down once more when she heard Ritchie's squeal, "Cat! Cat! I gotcher e-mail. Who over St. Aggie's they pull in?"

Cat put the receiver up to her ear. "I don't know if I want to say."

"Guy named Testa, right? Was it a guy named Testa?"

"Why do you say that?"

"'Member what I said, how the cops been checkin' to see if any of the vics were takin' sedatives?"

"Uh-huh."

"One of the moles tells me the cops been asking were they takin' dizapeme, diazepam, I forget, but none of the vics pops up on the computer. But when they run this guy's name past, up it comes."

"Isadore Testa?"

"Yup. He's takin' prescription something or other."

"So?"

"So he goes to the doc, he says, I need something, I can't sleep, I'm feelin' panicky. I mean an old guy's gonna off some young girls, not gonna be easy to overpower 'em unless maybe they're too zoned out to put up a fight."

"So what was he taking?" Cat asked. "Sleeping pills?"

"That, or jeez, we could even be talking about something for aches and pains. Somma that prescription stuff'll knock you silly. An' I figure, an' old guy's joints are gonna be shaky. Get something for the rheumatiz, slip it to some young gal in the coffee, all those self-defense classes she been takin' at the Y don't amount to squat, she's goin' out. Don't tell me I don't know what I'm talkin' about."

Cat didn't.

## CHAPTER EIGHTEEN

Anxiety tainted her sleep and dreaming was neither an intact scenario, nor blessed nothingness, but vignettes whose common theme was separation, falling away from everything secure and familiar into a void. She rose, dressed for her run with a sense of sickening apprehension that she could not decode.

The first explosion of frosty air shocked her brain into clarity, comprehension. Victor's investigation was turning toward her St. Agnes, and consequently toward her brother, her family and she dabbled with an awful conjecture: What would happen to her relationship with Victor if one of his investigations involved her family? The possibility of professional conflict had always cast Cat, the novice reporter, as the intruder in a criminal investigation, never Victor as the disrupter of family ties.

Cat tried to shake off the supposition, couldn't. The fact that the murder had many links to St. Agnes could not be denied, but, she insisted, it could be explained. Explained in a way that did not link the four dead women to her brother's church.

*Think.* What could the killer possibly be getting out of the murders? Did he have a grudge against these women? Or a grudge against St. Agnes? Or did he kill simply because he was in a killing mood and the women were there? Chris had been killed like that. Someone firing a gun, not caring who was hit. But to kill four times, there has to be something more in it for the killer than just the act of killing. What would Easter be getting out of it? Killing off his quitters might keep the other girls in line. Mrs. Easter? Hated her husband's business, putting a scare into him? Testa? Or some anonymous stranger, trolling, tracking, luring, killing. Trolling ...

Cat shook her head, blanked out her mind and concentrated on the mechanics of her run, pacing, breathing, pushing herself into oxygen deficit, shoving the ugly speculations from her thoughts. She didn't cut back to a walk when she descended the boardwalk ramp, sprinted all the way to her house, up the back stairs, met Ellice on the way down, carrying a batch of paint samples, held one up. "Whaddaya think? It's called Brandon beige."

"I'd eliminate Brandon as a marital prospect. That's pink."

"That's what I said. I'm gonna tape it up to the living room wall and have a look."

Cat opened the back door, yanked off her gloves and hat. She heard Ellice's step on the back stairs, turned.

Ellice came in the back door, shut it, leaned against it. "Cat, you better call the cops. I think someone broke into the apartment. It didn't look right, and the window over the sink in the kitchen? It was open."

"Freddy didn't leave it open to air out the paint fumes?"

"I don't think Freddy would be that careless."

Cat heard Jane rummaging through her drawers; Mats was still asleep. "Call the police," she told Ellice.

Cat went upstairs and got the key out of her jewelry box, drew a flat, locked case from her night table, went downstairs and set it on the kitchen table, unlocked it and took out the nine millimeter, examined it, reached into a high cabinet for the canister where she kept her ammo. She began to load.

"Cat, you're not going down there!"

"It's probably nothing. Just don't let the kids go outside."

Cat worked open the front door, crept down the stairs, the firearm at her side, aimed low. *Low, ladies, is right here.*

Marco had slapped his outer thigh, demonstrated for the Firearms for Females course. *You do not point it out, and you do not turn it toward your groinal area. As you make your approach, your support hand will come under your grip, and your support will be firm but not tensed up. Hands together, steady, and only then do you begin to raise your weapon.*

Except that Ellice had locked the door after her, and taken the key upstairs. Okay, even Kate Auletta could forget a key once in a while; she'd figure, what the hell, kick it in. Except it might cost a few hundred dollars Cat didn't have to replace the door. Besides, the last time she'd kicked in a door she'd almost broken her foot. Cat tiptoed around the side of the house, checked the sliding glass doors; locked. She crept around back, checked the back door, which was also locked, continued her circuit to the kitchen window on the west side of the property. It was about five feet off the ground, and pushed up about ten inches, the screen torn away from the frame.

She heard the screech of tires in the street, the heavy tread on her side lawn.

"Mrs. Austen?"

"Back here!"

Excellent response time, but the sister of King Carlo Fortunati deserved no less.

"You wanna keep that weapon down, ma'am." They knew she had a permit, knew she'd been trained by Marco Fortunati.

Cat showed them the window. While the cops examined all points of entry, Cat ran upstairs to get the apartment key, ran down and unlocked the front door. Disorder made it difficult to determine if the place had indeed been ransacked. There was a litter of painting gear, wallpaper and carpet samples, cans of paint lying on newspaper, smocks and over-alls tossed on the floor. Cat checked the kitchen, the refrigerator, found an empty juice container, plastic cheese wrappers. Maybe the remnants of lunch, maybe not.

She eyed the window sill, saw black grooves imbedded in the ledge, dirt in the sink, a few blades of dried grass.

"He got in through the window. Anything missing?"

"There's nothing much here. It's being renovated. It looks like he just wanted a place to stay and whatever was in the refrigerator."

*I mean, where do you live?*

*There. Or wherever.*

"Any high school kids live in the area?"

Cat shook her head.

"We can dust the place if you want, but if there's been a lot of people through here, it might not be worth it. Better double-check to make sure the doors and windows are locked when the workers leave. How many houses on this block are year-round, you have any idea?"

"The Nixon ladies and the people on the corner. Ufflander."

"We're gonna cruise around, check the other vacated places in the area. You have any idea where he mighta holed up?"

"Wherever."

"Cat, I called Freddy. Look, there's so many of us running in and outta there, if I forgot to lock it—"

"No, he broke in. Probably some runaway looking for a place to hole up." She saw Jane come down the stairs, her eyes wide, wary. "Sweetie, everything's okay, but we had a little problem. Someone broke into the apartment downstairs."

Jane's eyes moved toward the gun in her mother's hand. She knew Mom had a gun, but had never seen it in Cat's possession. "Did you *shoot* him?"

Cat concealed it behind her back. "No, I didn't shoot anyone. Go get some breakfast, sweetie, I don't want you to miss the bus."

Cat grabbed the canister, carried it up to her room, sat on the bed. She dialed Victor's number, released the clip.

"Hello?"

"It's me."

"Is something the matter?"

"Victor, someone broke into the apartment. Ellice went down there this morning, and found a window open."

"Did you call the police?"

"Of course I called the police. Nothing was taken, except ... except maybe a little food and heat. Victor, I was thinking it was that kid. Mark."

"Why would he go to your place?"

"I don't know. But he lifted the spare change from my ashtray, he could have checked the glove compartment and found my registration. He's thinking he wants to get away from Atlantic County maybe, the address sticks in his head, he checks the place out."

"If he takes the trouble to look you up, why doesn't he knock on the door?"

"I don't know, maybe he saw Ellice or the kids or—" *Or Dom and Kevin.* "I mean, he's fourteen, Victor, I don't expect him to have the aptitude of a hardened criminal."

"Cat, love, I'm afraid fourteen today isn't what it was when I was young. Are you and the children okay?"

"Yes, I'm getting Jane ready for school."

"And where will you be today?"

"I did have a lunch date ..."

"Cancel it."

Cat bit her lip. The resentment at being ordered around was lessened by the fact that she welcomed an excuse to get out of a meeting with Cusack. "Okay."


Victor got to the office early, found Adane waiting for him in his office. "What's up? Sit down."

"I'd like to stand, sir."

Victor looked at her. She looked a bit pale but otherwise her unflappable self. "Very well." He remained standing.

"I spoke with James Easter's receptionist, Miss DeTullio, by telephone. She confirmed that Easter parted amicably from

Renay Harris and Carmen Oliva, and she was certain he wouldn't have objected to her giving Miss Oliva a personal reference when she was job hunting."

Victor thanked her. "What else?"

"Mr. Raab called, said he'd like to talk to you about assigning a volunteer to the murders. I'm sorry, sir, he referred to them as the Seaside Slasher."

"Fed?"

Adane shook her head. "I believe it's Carlo Fortunati."

Victor stroked his lower lip with his thumb. Last week he would have welcomed Carlo's aid; now an uneasy instinct told him to decline. "What do you think, Adane?"

"I'm sure we could use the help, and the King—that is, Chief Fortunati—is a very knowledgeable man. And I think ..." She bit her lip, raised her chin, her blue eyes direct, unflinching. "I think it would be good for you to find someone who could pick up my share of the investigation, sir. I'd like to be removed from the case."

"I beg your pardon?"

"I would like to be removed from the case, sir, if I could be spared."

"What's the problem, Adane?"

"There's no problem, sir, I just think circumstances have arisen that might make it difficult for me to perform as well as the investigation deserves."

"What circumstances? Is it a health problem?"

"I ... really would rather not go into it."

"All right," Victor said, evenly. "Unfortunately, you can't be spared. I'm sorry, Adane, but you're to stay on it at least until there's a break, a suspect."

He saw a shade of sadness pass over her face, the trace of emotion startling. "Yes, sir," she said.

"You're dismissed. Please put me through to the Ocean City department."

"Yes, sir." Her voice was almost a whisper. She turned and left the office, closing the door.

Victor sat, shook his head. *What the hell?* The phone on his desk buzzed, he picked it up, got through to one of the officers who had gone to the scene of Cat's break-in. "We're canvassing the area, nothing's come up. That time of the morning, there's a lotta kids around headed to school. I think Mrs. Austen's right, just someone wants to get outta the cold."

Victor gave him a brief report and description of Mark.

"I'll check over the high school. They're supposed to wear ID now, but a lotta the kids're getting around it. And with thirteen hundred kids, one skinny fourteen-year-old tends to blend."

"He took some prescription medication. He may be using."

"Like I said, he'll blend right in."

Cat dropped Mats at preschool, returned to Ocean City, stopping at a used book store on Asbury Avenue, the island's half-dozen blocks of "downtown," and bought a copy of *CopWatch: Life on The Reel Streets.* There was a picture of Cusack on the back cover, leaning against some ivy-strewn railing, wearing a tweedy jacket over a work shirt over a turtleneck. Airbrushed to look closer to what he had looked like seventeen years ago.

When she got home, Carlo was sitting in her breakfast nook, his fist wrapped around a mug of coffee.

"Ellice told me what went down. Whaddaya think, it was that kid you brought over Dom's?"

Cat nodded, swung her shoulder bag onto the counter. "I called Victor. Where is Ellice?"

"Down checkin' out paint samples. You know what's going on with him?"

"With Victor?" Cat sat opposite him, looked at Carlo. There was something forlorn about him that weakened his bullish expression, something recent. It disturbed her.

"Raab said he needed help with this thing, he says anyone

wants to pitch in, as long as it don't cost, he'll take all the help he can get. So I make an offer, and it's thanks-but-no-thanks."

"Carlo, what are you talking about? Kurt Raab ought to thank God he's got an offer from someone like you, someone who'll take up some of the burden *and* some of the spotlight. You must have misunderstood."

"I don't think so." He polished off his coffee, squeezed out of the booth. "I don't know, maybe it's the way he pulled Testa in, he thinks there's gonna be some kinda conflict of interest, 'cause Annie and I known Isadore so long. So, you goin' to Lombardi's retirement dinner Friday with Victor?"

Cat felt a weight form in her chest, pressing down on her heart. "I guess so."

"Well, we'll see you there. I better go down, see if Ellice wants me to pick up that paint or anything." There was a defeated rhythm to his slow, heavy gait that tightened Cat's throat and brought tears to her eyes.

Ellice came in several minutes later. "I sent Carlo off to get a half dozen cans of Brandon's beige. I figure he picks it up, no one's gonna question his artistic orientation—honey, what's the matter?"

Cat was sitting at the kitchen table, sniffling.

"You and Carlo have words?"

Cat wiped her eyes on her sleeve. "Ellice, did you tell your brother about Freddy yet?"

"What, that we're gettin' married?"

Cat nodded.

"Honey, what brought this up?"

"You said he won't like it."

"No, I said he'd kidnap me and de-program me and have Freddy knocked off."

"Now I remember. Don't you feel awful, Ellice? Having to choose between family and the guy you want to marry?"

Ellice slid into the booth, patted Cat on the arm. "Is this really about me and Freddy?"

Cat shook her head.

Ellice's face relaxed in that exquisite serenity that Cat envied. How could she be so at ease with herself after everything she had endured with Ira? "Cat, I already made my choice. The man I want to be with, the one I know is gonna be good for me, that's been done. Freddy's just the incarnation of what I already worked out in my head and my heart. All I need now is the courage to follow through."

Cat recalled what Dom said about needing to be free in her head, her heart. "Yeah, well, maybe that's where I've got the problem. That courage thing."

"I think you got the courage thing down cold."

## CHAPTER NINETEEN

The retirement dinner for Captain Benedetto "Bennie the Beak" Lombardi had been the sort of affair that Cat and Chris Austen had deftly avoided. There had been social obligations, of course, during their marriage, but Chris had refused to allow his professional life to regulate their social one. "Why don't we ever do anything with any of your writer friends?" he had asked Cat, and she had replied, "I don't have any writer friends." Cops were clannish and writers were rogues.

Victor's ease surprised her. They hadn't spoken much for the past day and a half, and when they had it was impersonal, weighted with the volume of not-to-be-discussed topics accumulating between them. She expected him to be ill at ease, standing beside the woman who had bested Raab at the press conference, whose byline was under SERIAL MURDER INVESTIGATION LAUNCHED IN COUNTY, in the *Cape-Atlantic Chronicle*'s debut issue, and who was the kid sister of the Fortunati clan.

But it was she who tensed up when his polite "Hello" to Carlo and Annie was returned with uncharacteristic aloofness from her brother, when many of their mutual acquaintances drifted toward Carlo, who was holding court at the other end of the room, his massive form and bellowing laugh carrying to the corner where Victor and Cat quietly chatted with Detectives Long and Adane and Mary Grace Keller. And then there were the "Hellos" that segued into calculatedly offhand inquiries on how the *CopWatch* team was doing, and whether they were going to be looking for any tech help when they came into the area to shoot.

Cat hadn't the heart to tell them that she had backed out of the third day of the open call, canceled on lunch with their writer and never rescheduled their meeting; how at her follow-up interview with Sunny and Misti, she had watched while they discarded half the callbacks, often with comments that made Cat blush for the poor hopefuls, and that so far, the three days that produced "CopWatch Casts in AC" for the "Life Style!" page of the *Chronicle* had been the most tiresome assignment Ritchie had stuck her with, save for the interview with last year's Little Miss Jersey Shore, who had turned to her mother in the middle of their chat and told the woman that "this stinking crown is giving me a headache."

Cat spied Jackie Wing, who was poured into a red beaded sheath. They edged toward each other, Jackie keeping one hand on Stan's arm. Sunny and Misti had given Jackie's snapshots an envious nod, groaned over her tiny waist, snug jeans.

"Isn't this the weirdest party you've ever been to? Stan says we've gotta stay for the after-dinner speech, then we can cut out. Where's Ellice and Freddy?"

"They had premarital counseling class; they're running late. They'll probably bring Dom, he's supposed to say the benediction."

Sherrie winnowed through the crowd in a silver/blue strapless, Joey at her side. Women turned to sneak a look at him, and if he wasn't unconscious of the admiration, he was doing a good job of faking it. "I switched place cards so we can sit with you guys," Sherrie whispered to Cat. "We were with Vinnie and Lorraine and a couple public defenders and their wives, and you know what Vinnie thinks of the guys in the PD's office. I didn't want to get in the crossfire."

The call to dinner came just as Freddy and Ellice arrived.

Cat and Victor sat with them, Sherrie and Joey, Jackie and Stan and the Atlantic County Sheriff and his wife. More than once, Cat heard Carlo's resonant laughter and felt an odd sense of estrangement from her family.

There was the benediction, which caused a slight ripple during the introduction, for Dominic was absent, and Kevin Keller filled in. Cat detected, in his delivery, the strain of a sudden and unprepared understudy and she edged her bowed head toward Ellice and whispered, "Where's Dom?"

"Got called away just as we were leaving. Amen."

Dinner; the speech. An Atlantic county mayor highlighted "The Beak's" career: how he had broken three ribs and a femur in an altercation with the four-hundred-pound madam, Shamu Jackson; how his canine partner, appropriately named Randy, had abruptly abandoned pursuit of a fleeing mugger to scale a seven-foot fence and engage in an enthusiastic flirtation with an AKC registered, pedigreed, prize-winning standard poodle; how he had absent-mindedly inverted the numbers on an arrest warrant causing the TAC team to break into the home of a pregnant welfare mother who was able to raise her preemie comfortably on the half million dollar settlement the city was induced to pony up.

"I'm new at this. These are his career highlights?" Ellice whispered in Cat's ear.

"This is nothing. Freddy tell you why they call him The Beak?"

"I was thinking the nose."

Cat whispered again into Ellice's ear. Ellice gulped audibly and clapped her hand over her mouth. Victor and Freddy looked at them, at each other.

Then came the part Cat hated, The Farewell. She leaned over to Ellice again, "This is where he gets to the part about the little gals."

"... and expecially to my own wife Celestine and all the little gals who stand behind their boys in blue."

"Crowd applauds the little gals," Cat whispered.

The crowd applauded, politely.

Victor saw Cat's fists clenched in her lap, saw her bite her lip, imagined what she must be enduring, listening to the captain's phony sentimentality, the women who sat wet-eyed beside husbands who were still alive.

She rose, said, "Excuse me."

Victor got to his feet immediately, but she was already hurrying toward the back of the room. Her silver-white dress with its cowl neck and long sleeves made her shimmer like a ghost in the darkened room; the white roses pinned around her loose chignon glowed like a halo.

A figure emerged from the coffee shop/bar near the restrooms. Cat sensed it following her, turned.

Ted Cusack stood, smiling at her. His gaze was a leer. If Cat still believed she had fooled him, it was refuted by his "The roses look lovely. I'm so glad you wore them. Allegrezza."

Cat felt a chill steal over her ribs.

"I remembered how you admired the white rosebush outside the faculty office building."

He had known her from the first.

"As I'm sure you remembered how I hated being stood up."

There had been no card; she had thought the roses were from Victor. She grabbed at her hair, gave her chignon a vicious twist, flung the handful of crushed rose petals at his face.

"Charming gesture. But then you always did have a bit of temper, even—how long ago was it? Sixteen years? Seventeen? Spent entombed in domesticity. Was that satisfying, I wonder?"

He was blocking the route back to the banquet room.

"Get out of my way."

"Didn't have the courage to hear that drivel out? The little women and all? You were one of them and I hear you're flirting with the idea of becoming one again."

Cat clenched her jaw, as if the act would dam the flow of adrenaline. "I think we had better keep what limited contact we'll have on a professional standing."

"Now, now. Didn't April Steinmetz tell you you have to be nice to me? I can cut off your access to the production, you know. I do have a little pull, remember?"

"I have no recollections at all of your pull; I'll have to take your word that it's little," she spat back. She couldn't believe she said that, was so stunned by her boldness that she was taken off-guard by his response.

Cusack seized her shoulders and shoved her against the wall between the pay phones and pressed his mouth to hers. Cat tried twisting her head, realized that when she had freed her mouth, she couldn't scream. Wouldn't scream. He misinterpreted her silence and moved in again. Cat raised her right fist to her left shoulder, drove her right elbow into the hollow of Cusack's throat. He staggered back, making a hoarse choking sound, his face reddening with anger.

Seven-thousand five-hundred dollars in consulting fees from *CopWatch* flushed with one little pull, along with the three or four stories she would have gotten from hanging around the set. Cusack raised his hand and Cat backed into the ladies' room, shouldered the door, afraid he would push his way in after her. She heard him gasping angrily outside, heard fading footsteps dissolve in the noise from the bar.

Cat staggered into the room, faced herself in a mirror. *I look like a five dollar hooker on an off night.* That had been one of Joey's expressions. There was a rip in the shoulder seam of her dress, and her lipstick was smeared onto her cheek. Strands of hair fell loosely from the knot at the nape of her neck.

Ellice walked in, looked her over. "You look like a five-dollar hooker on a slow night."

"Off night. Did Victor send you?"

"He said to see if you were okay. I am not sure I'm seein' myself as one of the future little gals of America. An' whose idea were those Brussel sprouts? Sherrie and I dropped them into the water carafe, so drink with care."

"Chris hates—hated—these things. I don't know why I came."

"You see all the *CopWatch* people in the crowd? Those gals in the casting are here with cops. You got your film people who're wannabe cops and cops who are wannabe actors."

Cat stood straight, fluffed her bangs. "I wonder if I could get a piece out of that. I'll be looking for work."

"What went down here?"

"'Went down'? You see how it's catching?" Cat finger-combed her hair into loose waves that fell to her shoulders, grabbed a paper towel and wiped her lips. "Ted Cusack must be one of the wannabes. He was in the bar. Followed me and we had sort of a confrontation."

"Are you okay?"

"I'm better than he is."

There was a knock on the door; it opened an inch and Freddy whispered. "Hey, Ellice, you guys in there?"

"Yeah."

"Cat, too?"

"Freddy, what are you whispering for?" Cat asked.

"Whaddathey got cake in there or what?"

Ellice shot Cat a wry smile. She slipped her hand through the door. "Honey, give me your car keys. I'm gonna drive home with Cat and you can get a lift from Victor."

"What for? We came boy-girl-boy-girl, how come we gotta leave same sex?"

"'Cause Cat and I gotta talk."

"You live in the same house, you got all day to talk."

"Freddy."

There was a pause. "You sure you're okay, Cat?"

"I'm fine, Freddy."

Another pause. "What about dessert?"

"You get mine, Victor gets Cat's."

"Yeah, but what about dancing? I mean, look, I like Victor and everything, but I'd rather not take him for a spin if it's all the same to you."

"I suspect Victor feels the same way," Cat said.

"Okay. But somebody owes me. I am owed something for this."

Cat and Ellice retrieved their coats and stepped into the street. "Let's go to Bud-n-Lou's for a drink," Ellice suggested, climbing behind the wheel of Freddy's Cherokee. "We won't run into anyone there, they'll all be here."

"How do you know about Bud-n-Lou's?"

"A gal from premarital class works there, keeps tellin' me and Freddy to stop by. She's engaged to a cop, too. They skipped class tonight, I guess she had to work."

There was plenty of parking on Baltic. Ellice and Cat walked in together, saw a couple guys—plainclothes probably—sitting alone, saw Lou rubbing the bar down with a rag. "This ain't no girlfriends bar, ladies."

Cat smiled. "I'm Cat Austen," she said. "Cat Fortunati? Carlo's sister." Why hadn't anyone written a story on Bud-n-Lou's? He had rebuffed some Philly magazine reporter, but he might cooperate with her.

The creases sprang out on Lou's face. "The little one, the one they called Alley Cat?"

"That's me. And this is my girlfriend."

"Awww, cut it out."

Ellice slid into a bar stool. "Sheila working?"

"Nah, she's s'posed to go to some retirement shindig for Bennie the Beak with Gino."

"Gino Forschetti?" Cat asked. Carlo knew him.

"Yeah. Great guy. Looks ain't everything. Little on the scatterbrained side, he's in here a while ago, lookin' to see if Sheila was workin', she's prob'ly home coolin' her heels wonderin' why he's not pickin' her up. We got some money floatin': He's gonna keep her waitin' at the alter while he tries to remember what church they're supposed to tie the knot." Lou had a hearty laugh at the expense of poor Gino's forgetfulness. "What'll you ladies have?"

"Pepsi. Diet. And don't be stingy, baby," Cat did her Garbo and Lou laughed, a loud guffaw that raised the few lagging heads in the corners. He rummaged around in a small refrigerator, brought up a couple cans of Diet Pepsi. "I keep these around for the—"

"Girlfriends."

"Yeah." Lou shoveled ice into a tumbler, poured. "So, I hear you're with that guy over Major Crimes, one who took Sheila home the other night?"

"Oh?" Cat said.

Lou flushed. "Aw, he was just givin' her a lift. Lotta times one of the guys'll give her a lift onaccounta Gino's been workin' so much overtime, they're savin' for the house." He put the Pepsi in front of her. "Not like he's a regular; I know my regulars. Think he wannid to have a chat with one of the incoming."

"Incoming?"

"Street meat. Great looking, but a little on the small side. Me, I like an armful of woman. And brunette, whereas I like your redheads."

"Real long hair, wears a malachite cross?"

"A what cross?"

"Dark green stone."

"That's her. He's talkin' to her awhile, I'm thinkin' he's gonna bust her. Then he takes Sheila home, the brunette hooked up with some older guy." Lou shrugged. "I don't even like their comin' in here, but as long as money's just changin' hands for liquid refreshment, I keep it zipped. Now your pop," Lou grinned. "He was a great guy."

Cat raised her Pepsi to that.

"Honey, it's not what you think."

"He used to date a bartender, he told me that once. He practically admitted they had an affair."

"Well, it must have been a while ago," Ellice said. "She and Gino, they said they've been together over a year."

Ellice drove along Atlantic Avenue. She flipped the left turn signal.

"What are you doing?"

"Dominic's finale tonight was how we shouldn't let the sun go down on our anger and let the devil get a foothold. Ephesians, I think." She had turned down Delancy, parked in front of the three-story house where Victor rented a second floor. "This the place?"

Cat looked up, saw a light on in the living room.

"Honey, look. Ever since that trip got called off, you been treatin' it like a reprieve. Like another chance for you to back out. You been readin' break-up into everything that's happened: Victor against your career, Victor against your family, Victor against the memory of Chris—"

"I never said that."

Ellice looked at her. "You thought it, though. More than thought it, you've been storin' it up like something you can use to back off because Victor wants to get married and you— You don't know what you want."

"If something happened to split us up, it would be so hard on the kids—"

"Don't use them as an excuse. You don't want to get hurt again. Be honest. I mean, at least Victor was honest with you. He told you about his past."

"He was on his own for eight years. There were a couple women. I don't have a past."

"You never told him about Cusack, did you?"

"Did you tell Freddy about Ira?"

Ellice nodded.

Cat was surprised. "What'd he say?"

"You mean after the 'I'm gonna make lunchmeat outta his *cuglioni*' and so on and so forth?"

Cat looked at her and burst into laughter, tears collecting at the corners of her eyes. "Oh, God, I'm hearing that Oscar Meyer jingle in my head."

They started singing it.

A shimmer of light illuminated the Jeep's interior. Cat looked up at the porch, saw the door open on the second floor landing, saw Victor's silhouette outlined against the light.

Ellice let down the window, leaned across Cat, called, "Go ask Mrs. Cardenas can Victor come out and play."

Victor descended the steps. He had shed his coat and tie, his shirt sleeves were rolled above the elbow. "Sadly, I have no Mrs. Cardenas to report to." He leaned on the open car window. "Where have you ladies been?"

"Bud-n-Lou's," Cat said, watched for a shift in his countenance, saw none.

"Have you been drinking?"

"Does Pepsi count?"

"Would you like to come in?"

"I'm just dropping off Cat, I gotta jet."

Victor opened the passenger door, held out his hand. Cat shot Ellice a look over her shoulder that clearly said she intended to be liberal with the blame if this turned out to be as bad an idea as she suspected.

Victor helped her out of the car. "Are you all right to drive, Ellice? Do you want to come in and call Freddy?"

"No. You two didn't take to the dance floor, did you?"

"Our women run off to go bar hopping, I hardly think we can be held responsible for conduct unbecoming."

Ellice laughed.

"Lock your doors," Victor said, waited while Ellice rolled up the window, locked the doors, put the car in gear.

He held Cat's hand as they ascended the porch steps, glanced around at the street, saw a curtain whisked shut in Mrs. Ricci's front window. He closed the door. "Well," he commented, "I expect this will confirm Mrs. Ricci's opinion that Mrs. DiLorenzo should never have rented to what I believe she refers to as a 'Portorikkan' because we'll be carousing at all hours of the day and night and who knows what sort of people we'll bring around."

Cat slipped out of her coat. "What sort of people do you bring around?"

"Cat, love, what's the matter? Was it that speech?"

Cat sat on the sofa. "Do you have pictures of Marisol?"

"Yes. Put away."

"Did you think of her as your 'little gal'?"

Victor sat opposite her. "Lombardi's a patronizing halfwit. He was when I came onto the force and that's how he's going out. I suppose there's some comfort in the consistency of it all."

"Have you ever thought about what it will be like when you retire?"

"Will I be standing on some podium praising my little gal, you mean?" He rose, walked around the coffee table and sat beside her. "I hope you'll be with me, yes. But I'd prefer we skip the dinner, most particularly the Brussel sprouts, which Ellice and Sherrie had the ingenuity to deposit in the water carafe, hock the gold watch and take off to Fiji or Tonga, cavort naked on some tropical isle."

"Be serious."

"I've never been more so."

"It's not easy for a cop. Retiring. Six months from now, Lombardi will probably be in withdrawal, hanging around Bud-n-Lou's looking for what I believe is referred to as a contact high. Or making everyone around him crazy, puttering around in their lives. A year from now, his little Celestine will probably be ready to kill him."

"We're not talking about Lombardi, are we?"

"Why didn't you want Carlo's help? You've said yourself he's forgotten more than most cops soak up in a career."

"Cat, the investigation is taking a turn that involves people your brother has had a personal relationship with."

"Like Mr. Testa?"

Victor nodded, not looking at her, told himself it wasn't a complete lie. "And Annie works with Easter's wife."

"But it's okay for you and me to see each other?"

"Well, probably not, but I'm willing to make the sacrifice."

Cat moved away from him. "What if your work was the thing you had to sacrifice?"

Victor realized that there was something simmering beneath conversation, something he had failed to identify. He put an arm around her. "It would be difficult, I admit. But sometimes making the difficult choices tells us who we are, what we're made of."

"I don't know about that. I seem always to run away from the difficult choices."

"No, you don't," Victor whispered into her hair. "You just think about them a bit too cautiously. And then follow up by acting too wantonly."

Cat's glance slid toward his, primly.

"Did I say wantonly? Excuse me, I meant recklessly." He pressed his lips to her hair, inhaled the faint scent of roses. "What happened to the flowers, love?"

"I threw them away."

"I thought they looked pretty."

"I thought you sent them." She hesitated, gathered her courage. "I found out Ted Cusack sent them, and I threw them out."

"Cusack?" He probed short-term memory. "That writer from the TV show? The one who's been calling the unit, trying to get an interview?"

Cat nodded.

"What, was he trying to bribe you to get to me?"

She realized she could let him think that, it was plausible enough. *Can you trust him with the truth?* "It's more complicated than that ... Victor, did I ever tell you that I left college, before I married Chris?"

"Somebody mentioned it. Freddy said you went back later, after Jane was born."

Cat nodded. "The reason I left ... Victor, if I asked you to promise me something, would you?"

"Such as what?"

"That you won't, you know, overreact."

"Have I impressed you as someone who has a tendency to overreact?"

"No." It was what made him so imposing, really. No one could be that controlled unless there were some powerful passions to be contained. "But promise anyway."

"Cat, love, you're asking me to promise blindly?"

Cat grabbed his shirt front in both fists, pushed him against the arm of the couch.

Victor looked up at her in amused surprise, saw the earnestness, a trace of fear in her expression. "I promise."

"And you'll let me tell you the whole thing and you won't interrupt?"

"Yes."

Cat sat back on the couch, took a deep breath. "It was junior year. There was this course: Documentary Film Production. I was a Lit major, journalism minor— Ten students from those departments paired off with ten of the film majors and we had to write, produce, shoot and narrate a documentary short. The course was by professor's pleasure—two hundred kids applied every semester, twenty got in." She paused. "The professor was one of those charismatic 'older men,' the kind young girls get serious crushes on. Older at the time being mid-thirties, but I was only twenty. There were only twenty of us in the class—"

"You said that." Victor realized that there was a pressure developing in his chest, that suddenly, he was conscious of his breathing. "Go on, I'm listening."

"It started out as just chatting after class. You know, how he liked my writing and what were my plans and was I thinking about graduate school. And then we were meeting for coffee. I felt so grown up, you know? That stupid sense of sophistication that you only have when you're twenty? One afternoon, late, it was nearer evening really, he had asked me to come by his office, something about talking about a masters program he would be willing to recommend me for."

Victor didn't want to know. He didn't trust himself to keep his promise to her if he knew.

"Most everyone was gone, his secretary and, well, everyone. He offered me something to drink, something he had never done before, I started to get a bad feeling ... Victor, I can't tell you this if you're going to look like that."

His eyes were opaque with some dark emotion. When he said "Go on," he truly believed his voice sounded composed, but to Cat it was a growl.

"He'd locked the door. I was wearing this blouse. Red. A sort of satin. Wearing my favorite things for him, you see ... stupid." She shook her head. "Before I went off to school, Carlo took me aside and showed me a few things he thought I should know in case any of the boys—what did we say then, 'Got fresh'? And then Vinnie took me aside and showed me all of his tricks, and then Marco and so on. Except Dom. Dom told me not to forget to go to Mass." She realized that she was starting to ramble, clasped her hands together. "Anyway, I was so surprised that I don't think I did any of it right, but I think *he* was surprised that I fought at all. That's probably what got me out of there before ..."

"This professor tried to rape you in his office?"

Cat nodded.

"Did you file charges?"

Cat shook her head. "I didn't know what to do, and by the time I had decided, he'd had time to write the scenario. Infatuated, rejected coed versus a tenured professor. My counselor suggested perhaps I would be happier at another school, take a semester off at least. Pop's health was starting to fail around this time, I didn't want to do anything to add to that, so I just quit. I quit." Her voice choked on the last syllable. A tear slipped down her cheek. "It's so hard, sometimes, to do some of the things I have to do to get a story, to put up with Ritchie and all, but it's ... I'm so afraid of what Jane will become if she sees that her mother's a quitter. I mean, I see how she looks up to Ellice and ... and—"

"And every woman but her mother." Victor put his arm around her. "Kids go through that, don't they? Everyone adult is cooler than their own parents. I think Jane's lucky she's got you for her example." He took her hand in his, stroked her hair. "You didn't tell your family?"

"No. Only Freddy—not the guy's name or anything, and I left out a lot of the details—and I swore him to secrecy. Carlo would have killed him. Then Freddy introduced me to Chris and we started going together and you know, with time, perspective changes, gets distorted, and I wondered if maybe I did misinterpret everything. Except every time I thought that, I'd hear the sound of tearing satin. But with all this talk of false memory and recovered memory, who would take my word for it implicitly, when I was beginning to doubt it myself? And then I sort of got back into writing. Chris made me finish up my degree, turned my pantry into an office. Funny, how sometimes someone who loves you knows you better than you know yourself."

"You didn't tell your—Chris?"

She shook her head. "I always meant to."

"Always waiting for the right time. Well, I know what that's like. Why are you telling me now, love?"

"Do you believe me?"

"Of course I believe you."

"You don't think I've lost my mind or anything?"

Victor's mouth turned down in a reflective scowl; he stroked his chin, thoughtfully.

Cat elbowed him in the ribs.

"Ah, yes. Let's just say, the workings of your mind continue to intrigue me. How's that?"

"Remember what you promised?"

"I do."

"Cusack was the professor."

The warmth in his gaze cooled, froze; his glance taking in the small rip in the shoulder seam, the loose hair that had been pinned back. "What happened tonight?" he demanded.

"Nothing."

"What happened tonight?"

"He was at the restaurant. I don't know if he was at the dinner. There were some TV people there. Ellice said it was all wannabe cops and wannabe show people. He grabbed me when I was going into the ladies' room and we had words."

Victor fingered the rip in her sleeve. "Words?"

"He tried to get fresh and this time my memory worked just fine. I gave him a shot he won't forget and if you don't stop glaring at me, I'll give you a demonstration."

Victor's scowl relaxed. "No, thanks. So how's he going to write the scenario this time, what with you two working on the same project?"

"I think I'll probably be written out."

"You have a contract with them."

"They're a production company for a major television show and I'm a local nobody. That's more extreme than a professor versus a small-town coed. What makes you think they're going to fulfill they're obligation to me?"

"Because you have a deal?"

"Deal schmeal."

The phone rang. Victor ignored it. "Look, Delareto's not my favorite person, but if they try to back out of their deal, I think you should call him in on this."

"Shouldn't you pick up the phone?"

"Let the machine pick it up. If you have a contract—"

They heard Victor's cursory message, Adane's tentative, "I'm sorry, Lieutenant, it's Jean Adane. I'll try your beeper—"

Victor strode to the phone, picked up the receiver. "What is it, Adane?"

"I'm sorry to disturb you, sir. It appears to be—I haven't been to the scene—but it's a woman, and the officer on the scene informed me that it appears similar to the others."

"Call Rice and tell him to take point."

"Well, I—of course I would have done that, sir, but I

thought—well, I understood from the officer that the woman is the fiancée of a detective. One of your former partners. And so I thought you might want to take it. The victim's name is Sheila—"

"McConnell." Victor's voice was like death.

"She lives at—"

"I know her address. I'll be there in fifteen minutes." He hung up, turned to Cat. "Stay here. I have to go out."

"It's okay, Victor, I can take a cab."

"No."

"Victor what's wrong?"

"I don't want you getting into a cab."

"There's been another one, hasn't there?"

He was taking the 9mm from the holster slung over the coat rack, jamming it into his waistband, not looking at her. "Yes."

"Someone you know?"

He looked at her then. "Why do you say that?"

"I heard you tell Detective Adane you knew her address."

Victor laid his hand on her cheek. "Is your mother with the children?"

Cat nodded. "And Ellice will be home by now."

"Stay here until I come back. Lock the door when I leave." He kissed her briefly. Cat closed the door after him, locked it and went to the phone, dialed home.

Ellice answered. "I just got in, everything okay?"

"No. Victor just got called out. Are the kids okay?"

"They're sleeping. How late will you be?"

"I don't know. Another woman's been murdered. I got this feeling Victor knows her; I overheard him tell his detective he knew the address. Someone named McConnell."

"Sheila McConnell!"

Cat swallowed hard.

"Oh, God, Cat. They were going to get married in the spring. All she talked about was how she finally found such a great guy, the big church wedding they were gonna have. Oh God, poor Gino. Maybe you'd better call Dominic and tell him. Maybe he could get to Gino before ... oh, my God ..."

Cat told Ellice she had her key, not to wait up. She hung up and called the rectory; the phone rang, rang, rang, rang. At last she got Kevin, who said a muddled, "Hmmlo?"

"I'm sorry, Kevin, did I wake you?"

"I fell asleep over a book."

"Can I talk to Dominic?"

"He's not here."

"Are you sure?"

"I just passed his room. The door's open and the lamp on the night stand's on. Wherever he went tonight, he hasn't come in. No big deal."

"Didn't he tell you where he went?"

"Just asked if I could cover for him at the dinner. What's wrong, Cat?"

"Nothing, I ... I just wanted to ask him something. Nothing ..."

## CHAPTER TWENTY

*When you're young, you throw your mortality over your shoulder and run a race with time; and then one day the people around you start to die. You look over your shoulder to see if your mortality is catching up with you and when you turn around, the devil is staring you in the face.*

Victor's father had said that, sitting on a chair in their kitchen above the bodega, holding on his knee the letter that announced the death of his younger brother.

They were already there, Stan Rice and Phil Long muttering to each other in the hallway, uniforms milling about and the forensic people beginning their sweep of the apartment. Their inarticulate murmurings, the exchanges reduced to monosyllables, sounded to Victor like rumblings from an abyss, like the first tremors of a earthquake. Like the devil snickering in his face.

Stan looked up, ran his hand through his hair. "They sent someone for Gino; we didn't want him to hear it over the air."

Victor heard someone inside the apartment mutter, "Anyone want one last peek before we bag her?"

He stepped into the room, saw her slumped over the arm of the couch. She had been sitting on the small sofa, wearing a dark skirt and stockings, a white blouse that had gone crimson, the head slumped to one side, exposing the open pucker at her throat. Blood spackled the ceiling, blossomed on the wall opposite, soaked into the carpet. The auburn hair fell over her collar. As one of the crime scene people passed, a strand of it shivered and settled back on the immobile shoulder, and that whisper of motion knifed at Victor's heart. Nothing was evident to the others; the lieutenant was as grave and professional as ever, but when the ME said, "Looks a little old to be hookin', but the bone structure's pretty classy, she'll clean up real good," Victor turned and said, "Shut up."

Eyes flickered toward the lieutenant; they had heard worse, of course, but never from Cardenas, who was renowned, even ridiculed, for his propriety.

Victor ignored the glances, called Stan into the room. "Talk to me."

Stan shook his head. "Building manager, he says Sheila's real friendly, liked talkin' about work, about gettin' married. She told him she's goin' to the dinner tonight with Gino. This morning, around ten or so, he's on his way out to the store, he sees her comin' in dressed sorta like she is now. The super says Gino knocks on his door around seven tonight, he tells the super there's no answer at Sheila's apartment and he forgot did he tell her he was picking her up or to meet her over at the restaurant. The super says does Gino want him to let him in Sheila's place, onaccounta Gino's got his own key, but he left it home. You know how Gino is. Gino says no, he's gonna run over Bud-n-Lou's 'cause he forgot, maybe she was working an early shift, lost track of the time. They both been puttin' in a lotta hours, 'cause they're savin' up for a mortgage. We called Lou, he says Gino tells him he's gonna go over the restaurant, he thinks maybe Sheila went over without him. Meanwhile, the super? He hears her phone ringing, heard it ring a couple more times, when he goes out back to put out the trash, he sees her place is dark and he knows Sheila, she works nights, goes out, she always leaves a light on. So he's like, 'What the hell?', let himself in, the worst he can do is surprise her in the shower. Comes in, finds her like that." Stan dropped his voice. "You know, Lieutenant, I had my money on Easter. But Sheila?" He ran his hand over the salt-and-pepper waves of his hair. "Look, no offense to Gino, I heard she liked her men, but I don't think she took paying customers, you get my meaning?"

The stiletto twisted. "Yes."

"Besides, I'm pretty sure that was all over with. She was turning over a new leaf, she and Gino were gettin' married in a few months."

Turning over a new leaf. Carmen Oliva had been turning over a new leaf. So had Tammy Montgomery. So had Renay Harris. Even Estrella Murillo, who was no longer comfortable being paid off the books. Victor's eye roamed the apartment. Today's paper, mail on the table.

"She have the paper delivered?"

"No. Musta picked it up this morning when she went out."

"What time's the mail come?"

Stan yanked his notebook from his breast pocket. "Between ten-thirty and eleven-thirty, is what the super says."

"So whoever got to her did it after ten-thirty," Victor murmured. He turned to the ME. "Time of death, Doctor, can you estimate it?"

The ME shrugged. "Ten hours. Twelve." Shrugged again.

Victor turned back to Stan. "I want a team through this neighborhood. I want to know what kind of killer walks around in the middle of the day in a residential neighborhood with impunity."

"Lieutenant, this is blue collar. People work shifts, they go out, they come home. It's too damn cold for a stroll, nobody's on the street unless they got business—"

"This man's not invisible," Victor replied, shortly. He paused. *Don't lose your temper, you're in command here.* He saw that Stan was watching him expectantly, with a shade of bewilderment. "He's not invisible," Victor repeated, almost to himself. But perhaps he was. A ghost. Or, what was it Murillo's building manager had said to Cat? That Estrella Murillo would not open her door to anyone, that only the devil could have walked through. *You just don't know who to trust anymore,* Sheila had said. Sheila was a savvy woman, particularly cautious because Gino would have told her what he knew about the investigation, would have harangued her about keeping her door locked.

"No sign of forced entry." It wasn't a question.

"That's right, lieutenant."

"Find out the name of the carrier on this route, see if he remembers seeing anything."

"Okay."

"Anything missing?"

"Jewelry's there. And it doesn't look like she's been assaulted."

The paramedics were laying a plastic body bag on the floor, preparing to lay her inside. Victor held up one hand, looked at her again. Dark skirt, similar but not identical to what she had worn the night he had gone over to Bud-n-Lou's; the skirt was longer, the white blouse buttoned well above the cleavage. And, at ten in the morning, coming in from someplace, not going out.

Victor nodded, watched them lay her out, settle the dark skirt over the knees. There was a murmur down the hall, shouts and a scramble of footsteps. Victor turned and strode to the door but not before Gino Forschetti burst into the room. They had been too late, he had picked it up on the radio. Victor grabbed him, tried to shove him back, but Gino got a glimpse of her frozen face as the zipper was run up the body bag. And then Gino, burly, simian Gino, who had survived the undercover assignment with Victor, even taken a bullet for him, saved his life, threw his long arms around Victor's shoulders, cried out "Jesus Christ Victor, Jesus Christ!" and sobbed like a child.

Victor stood in the street for a long time after everyone left. It was a new and troubling experience for him, not knowing what to do. Knowing that the reason he hesitated was because of Cat; because of Cat he wanted to turn the investigation away from where it insidiously lead. He wanted to ignore the fact that it was three blocks to St. Agnes, that he could see the steeple clearly from the sidewalk outside Sheila's apartment. He stood trying to summon the courage to follow-up on what might be true. Knowing that if it was true, it would be the end of his relationship with Cat. Yet, not knowing would cast a shadow between them that would always be unresolved.

He drove to St. Agnes, parked in the lot and rang the rectory doorbell. He saw a light come on in the hallway through the glass, then in the kitchen, saw a dark figure approach the door. A pair of startled blue eyes peered through the glass and Kevin Keller opened the door. "Lieutenant, come in. What's wrong?"

Victor wiped his feet, stepped into the kitchen. "I need to talk to Dominic."

"He's not here. He got a call and left sometime after six. I don't know what came up. He told Maggie he wouldn't be back for dinner, told her to have me fill in for him at the banquet. Is something wrong with Cat?"

"Why do you ask?"

"She called here. Maybe an hour ago. Asked to talk to Dom, didn't say what she wanted, but she sounded upset." Kevin wore a long black robe that looked like a cassock, black slippers. Victor recalled Freddy's story about the turtle's burial, Kevin presiding in a borrowed robe. He followed Kevin into the kitchen. The room gleamed of Sister Maggie's fierce cleaning in the harsh overhead light.

"This is a professional call, isn't it?"

Victor nodded. "You know Sheila McConnell?"

Kevin hesitated. "Tall, redheaded? She's engaged to one of the parishioners. I think they come to Dominic's premarital counseling class."

"That's right. She was killed."

Kevin's mouth dropped open, closed. "An accident?" Then he closed his eyes, shook his head. "Of course it's not an accident, is it?"

"I'm afraid not. She was murdered."

"Her fiancé, Gino. Is there someone to stay with him?"

"Yes."

"Sheila McConnell," Kevin muttered.

"Can I ask you a few questions?"

The blue eyes looked startled. "I suppose ..."

"Gino was a parishioner. Was she?"

"They came to Mass together sometimes. She'd been raised a Catholic, I believe, sort of slipped away. I got the impression she was finding her way back."

Like Harris, like Montgomery, like Oliva. Even Murillo, in a manner of speaking.

"Was there something else, Lieutenant?"

"When was the last time you saw Miss McConnell?"

"Why ... now that you mention it, I believe I saw her leaving church this morning."

Victor was surprised. "What time are the weekday Masses?"

"Eight. Confessions before."

"Had she been coming to Mass, to confession, on a regular basis?"

Kevin shrugged. "You'd have to ask Dom or Greg. But I wouldn't be surprised. Like I said, she seemed to be turning over a new leaf. I'm not sure what was under the old one. Men, possibly; she looked the type."

*Turning over a new leaf.* Stan Rice had used the same phrase. "What type is that?" It was an effort to keep his voice neutral.

"I didn't mean to speak ill of her. I just meant ..." Kevin sighed. "Lieutenant, I've been everywhere in the world where sin's taken root, I've seen every type there is. I suspect Miss McConnell had a rather promiscuous past, though, again, she did seem to be coming back to the faith. And the newly converted, or reverted? Sometimes they're the most zealous. Dom calls them recovered Catholics."

"And Renay Harris, Tamara Montgomery, Carmen Oliva, Estrella Murillo, were they recovered Catholics, too?"

Kevin stared at him, too amazed at this speculation to respond. There was the sound of a car door slamming, a weary tread laboring toward the back door. Dominic appeared on the threshold. He looked up, his eyes tired, but not surprised, as if he expected to find Victor there. "They got in touch with you then," he sighed, sank into a chair.

Victor shot Kevin a glance. "Yes."

"Thanks for covering for me," he said to Kevin. "There's no change, he's still unconscious."

"He?" Victor said.

"They don't even have his last name yet. Mark Doe."

"You're saying the boy's been found?" Kevin said.

"You said they got in touch with you," Dominic said, looking from Kevin to Victor. "What are we talking about here?"

Kevin rose, put a hand on his shoulder. "Sheila McConnell was killed today."

Dominic looked past Kevin to Victor. "Like the others?"

Victor nodded. "Tell me about the boy."

"He's at the med center, intensive care. God only knows what he took."

"Who contacted you?"

"The police. They found my pills on him. Prescription had my name on it."

"Prescription for what?"

"Muscle relaxant." He turned to Kevin. "Maybe you'd better get dressed and go over Gino's."

"If you don't need me anymore, Lieutenant," Kevin said. Victor shook his head and Kevin excused himself, went upstairs to dress.

"I just heard her confession this morning." Dominic sighed. "Okay, Victor, it's the middle of the night, you're not here to make funeral arrangements."

"I've got five women dead, one killed in the last twenty-four hours and every one of them with a link to this church."

"Don't beat around the bush, just come out and ask me if I killed her."

"Did you?" *Cat's brother.*

Dominic shook his head, ruefully. "Well, that's blunt. Should I be putting in a call to Steve Delareto?"

Victor hesitated. *Cat's brother.* "It might be a good idea if you kept his number handy. And I'd appreciate it if you would provide me with a list of your congregation, church employees, and volunteers. Anyone who'd have access to your parishioners' addresses."

"I could ask you to supply me with a warrant."

"And I could ask to continue this discussion at the station." Victor rose. "But I think it would be best if we kept this as civil as possible for as long as possible."

He rose and headed for the door, stopped on the threshold. "Father, if the person who's killing these women should come to you in confession and disclose it, what would you do?"

"Do you mean would I go to the police?"

Victor nodded.

"No. The sacramental seal is inviolate."

"Even if there was a chance he would kill again?"

"Even so. I would try to counsel him to give himself up, of course." Dominic smiled, sadly. "Victor, we all sin, and sin again. I'm not so naive as to think that anyone who confesses to me is out of the life for good."

Out of the life. "Was Sheila out of the life? For good?"

"Victor."

"You have prostitutes coming to confess?"

"Of course."

"And receive absolution?"

"I can refuse absolution. But I believe ... I believe absolution can transform us. Sometimes, if you really believe that you've been forgiven, that's the best incentive to reform."

"Restoring someone to a state of grace transforms them? Go and sin no more?"

"It happens. Not often. But often enough for me to trust that it might happen one more time, and once after that."

Victor wondered if Sheila had confessed their nights together. "'I wonder men dare trust themselves with men,'" he murmured.

"'Methinks they should invite them without knives; Good for their meat and safer for their lives.' *Macbeth*, right?"

Right. *Present fears are worse than horrible imaginings.* "Goodnight, Father." Victor said.

"No, it's not, Victor. It's a miserable night."

Saturday morning slow-down did not account for the pall that had fallen over the prosecutor's units. Gino Forschetti was enormously popular.

Victor walked into the office, was not surprised to find Adane standing before his desk waiting for him. He and Freddy had left the dinner early, as had Adane's companion, and knew why she wanted to be removed from the case, though he didn't believe Freddy had made the connection.

Victor took off his coat, hung it on the rack, noticed that she had neatly inscribed Sheila McConnell's name on the list of victims. "Is that the ME's report?" he asked, nodding to the papers in her hand.

"No, sir. It's my resignation."

Victor looked at her. Sadness shaded Jean's blue-eyed gaze, and there was a touch of color on her smooth cheeks.

"Sit down, Jean."

Jean sat, folded her hands on her lap, her nail beds white with the pressure.

"You're not going to work for Delareto are you?"

"Oh no, sir!"

Victor crossed one leg over the other, folded his hands on his lap. "I saw that you decided to leave the dinner early. Those events can be a little hard to take."

Adane said nothing.

"I saw you in the parking lot getting into her car."

Adane sighed. "I've tried to clear my desk. I've already spoken to the hospital. The boy's condition hasn't changed. And Phil says he's willing to go over to St. Agnes and question the staff again and to work with Mr. Raab about getting a subpoena for their records—"

"How long have you and Mary Grace been together?"
Her eyes met his. "Ten years."

Victor was stunned. "I had no idea."

"Well, we never ... did anything to be completely open about the way things are with us. When we go to the movies, we're just girlfriends. A dinner like that, we wouldn't be taken for anything but a couple women sitting at the singles table."

"What about Mary Grace's family?"

"I don't think they communicate much. Most of them live out of the area, and she hasn't been particularly close to her brother and sister at the church. I think because she's sort of fallen away from the church; she doesn't go to Mass anymore. We met in college. It was her idea that I should go into law enforcement. I never really thought about it."

"Sometimes someone who loves you knows you better than you know yourself," Victor murmured.

Jean blinked. "Yes, exactly."

"And—if you don't mind my asking—your family?"

"Oh, I think they've always known. They've always been fine with it. I have two sisters, so they've always treated Mary Grace like just another one of their daughters."

Victor rubbed his chin, unconsciously. "Has there been a problem? Someone's said something to you that made you uncomfortable?"

"No, sir. It's just that, well, after questioning Mr. Testa and then Miss McConnell's murder ... I was home when the call came in and Mary Grace called her brother at the rectory; he told her you had informed him of Miss McConnell's death. I began to see that at some point our careers were bound to intersect in ways that might make it uncomfortable for our colleagues, or raise allegations of conflict of interest in the unit that might compromise an investigation. She talked about resigning from the prosecutor's office, but really it would be easier for me to find something else."

"So you're not resigning because of anything I've said, or anything that's been said to you?"

"No, sir."

"Because if anyone has said anything out of line, I hope you would bring it to me."

"No one's said anything, sir."

"Would you like a transfer?"

"Oh, no. I like—liked—working here."

Victor rose. "I wasn't very understanding when you asked to be removed from the case, was I?"

"Well ... no, sir."

"Then you should derive some satisfaction from the fact that I'm consistent." He tore the resignation in half and tossed it in the recyclable bin. "I suggest you go back to work."

"Sir—"

"Adane, you've been with this unit longer than any of us. Stan was assigned before I came on board and I recommended Phil. I've read the performance evaluations of everyone assigned here. Yours have been excellent. There's never been the slightest suggestion that anything in your personal life had a negative effect on your professional performance. And we've all taken Behavior One Oh One. What's the most reliable indicator of future behavior?"

"Past behavior," she replied, promptly.

Stan Rice appeared at the door, knocked on the jamb. "Sorry to interrupt, guys down Burglary are takin' up a collection for flowers, coffee can's on my desk if you wanna kick in."

"Come in, and ask Detective Long to come in, also."

Stan called Phil in, closed the door. "What's up?"

"The ME's report on Miss McConnell?"

"Same."

"Drug screen, too?"

"He thinks so, yeah."

"Adane wants to resign."

"What—!" Stan cried. "Jeannie, what's wrong?"

"Detective Adane believes that her relationship with Mary Grace Keller might raise allegations of a conflict of interest."

"Her wha— Her wha—" Stan sputtered.

"Jeannie, you can't quit!" Long protested. "I'm just gettin' up to speed on that online thing. I haven't got you through the alphabet!"

"Her wha— Her wha—"

"Lieutenant, they got this thing, computer assisted victim ID, Jeannie showed me how to hook up—"

"Link through," Jean corrected, meekly.

"Whatever. She quits, who's gonna take me through all that stuff? We're gonna have some twelve-year-old Rent-a-Geek in here showin' the boys in Arson how to download nudies and don't tell me it won't happen, I see what they got taped to their lockers."

"Am I the only one here surprised by any of this?" Stan exclaimed. Then, "I never saw anything taped to their lockers."

"They gotta take it down when there's a sexual harassment sweep," Long explained. "Try Friday afternoons."

Victor sank into his chair. "It would be gratifying if we could return to the subject at hand."

"You mean to tell me that Jeannie and Mary Grace Keller are ... you know ..."

"Shi— shoot, Jeannie, that's old news. I know that from way before I signed on here."

"So how come this is the first I'm hearin' about it," Stan argued. "I been around."

"You didn't wear a dress and troll the highways and byways," Long said. "We ladies hear things."

"So how come you didn't tell me?"

"'Cause it's none of your business. Jeannie wants to tell you her personal shi— stuff, she'll tell you."

"Jeez. Jeez." Stan ran his fingers through his curls. "Jeannie, I'm sorry. Look, all those times I said stuff, like I was coming on to you, I was only kidding around. Honest, I didn't mean anything by it, I didn't mean to hurt your feelings or anything. You know how I am."

"You didn't hurt my feelings, Stanley."

"So whaddaya gotta quit on us for? We're a great team

here. We're like that old show, *The Mod Squad*. You know, one black, I'm you're basic white guy, and one—"

"Blond," Jean concluded. "Stanley, you have to admit that the boundaries were always very clear. Investigations were turned over to the prosecutor's office, sometimes Mary would be assigned, but it's never overlapped before. Not like it's doing now with the apparent connection to St. Agnes. And Mary's brother and sister work there. It just occurred to me last night that those boundaries could become shaded."

"The hell! 'Scuse me, Jeannie. Holland-Johnson's an ADA and she's married to a judge, for cryin' out loud."

"An' on your *Star Trek*," Stan continued, "you got your earth folk, and you got your Vulcans and you got your guys with their heads all mashed up—"

"Klingons," Long interjected.

"Adane," Victor interrupted. "It would be ideal if we could hold our personal life apart, shelter it from the taint of what we do here. We all have something we want to protect from corruption, from compromise. Sometimes that's not possible, not entirely. When it's not possible, well, we continue to do the best we can. We may have to compromise that separation between the personal and the professional, but we don't have to compromise our conduct."

It occurred to him that there was something he could use for his Diversity Day talk next week, resolved to make a few notes. He paused, and they saw that he was speaking more personally than he had ever done. "And I would be very glad if we could cancel this subject entirely and have you go back to work." He dug into his pocket, drew out a twenty, handed it to Stan. "Put this in the can for me. Leave the ME's report and give me a few minutes to go over it, then we'll reassemble. You're dismissed."

The three left him alone and he picked up the report. *Star Trek*. Did television infect everything? *Mod Squad*. One black, one white, one blond. And Victor Calderone.

*Dios mio.*

# CHAPTER TWENTY-ONE

Cat had thrown her coat over her rumpled dress, run down to the cab before his honking roused Mrs. Ricci across the street. She peeked in her compact mirror, finger-combed her hair, rubbed her lips together. The cab driver checked her out via the rearview mirror, wondered, fleetingly, what a classy dame like her charged. "Lady, it ain't none of my business, you can tell me to butt out, but watch who you take on until they get this Seaside Slasher guy, okay? And I don't mean to be tellin' you your business, but make sure he wears a safe."

She had thanked him kindly for his advice, sat demurely during the drive to Ocean City; but later, when a dream replayed the encounter and she was Kate Auletta, Chick Dick, doing undercover call girl to lure the Seaside Slasher, she told the cabbie, "I don't like to play safe, you get me?" and shimmied the skirt of her silver-white dress well above her knees.

The phone cut off his reply, the throaty, "Did I wake you?" dissipated the image of the alter ego.

It was April Steinmetz. "Look," April began, "I got a call from Teddy who says he wants you off the shoot and outta the loop. Says there's enough on file about the Dudek case, we can package this without your input."

"I understand," Cat said, shutting her mind to the evaporating cash.

"What was it, he was lookin' to score a little input?"

"What?"

"I shoulda warned you, I guess, but I thought: You're a widow, got all these cops around you, Teddy's gonna mind his manners. Besides, he usually goes for the younger stuff, even if they're wearin' a price tag. Thing is, like I said, he an' Red go back to the day, he takes this to Red, you're yesterday, I can't do anything about it. Lemme see if I can grab Red's ear before Teddy gets to him, maybe I can do a lube. Oh, an' that church you told me about sounded terrif– I'll tell Red that you get dumped, your brother won't let us have the church. He's still enough of a Catholic to not wanna mess with a priest. And take my advice, Teddy crosses the border once again, you knock him back where."

Cat thanked April and said goodbye, rolled out of bed, listened, heard the muted thread of cartoon repartee filtering through the quiet. She padded downstairs, caught a whiff of basil/tomato, went into the den behind the staircase, saw Freddy sitting on the sofa flanked by Jane and Mats. There were breakfast sandwich wrappers from Dunkin' Donuts on the table in front of them, box juices. "I was sure there were only two kids in this household," she said, gave Jane and Mats forehead kisses.

"We wanted to let you and Ellice sleep. I'm gonna hang around wait for the guy's gonna replace the downstairs window screens. Are you feelin' okay?" He mouthed that last so as not to be overheard by Jane and Mats.

Cat nodded. "Freddy, I think you and Ellice are putting too much money into the apartment."

"Are you kiddin'? A little paint and maint for a place a block to the beach?"

"What smells so good?"

"Nonna's cookin'," Mats said. "She let me stir the pot."

"She's makin' sauce to take over Sherrie and Joe's. Like the kid can't get christened if we don't got a vat of sauce."

Cat grinned, went into the kitchen and found that "vat" was not that far off the mark. Mats could have fit in the pot Jennie was governing carefully. She had brought it along when she came to babysit the kids, slept over, figured she may as well get an early start on the food for Joey and Sherrie's christening party, and, though Jennie had raised her, none of Cat's pots were quite big enough.

"You're not goin' out running this morning?"

Cat shook her head, slumped into the booth. Freddy had brought in the paper, laid it on the table. The headline read, POPULAR BARTENDER SLASHER'S FIFTH VICTIM.

Cat scanned the story; the account was lurid, but brief; few facts, which Cat suspected was the result of a police lockdown.

"You want some coffee? It's made."

"No, thanks." Cat pushed herself up, went over to the refrigerator, got a Pepsi.

"You still feel sick? Freddy says you got sick at the dinner last night."

"I wasn't sick."

"It's none of my business."

Cat gave her a one-armed hug. "Since when is anything that goes on in this family none of your business?"

"You gonna be able to get this pot in your car?"

"Yeah. Do you have to go right away?"

"I gotta run by the church, make sure Isadore got the carpet vacuumed and put the church bulletins in the pews." She shook her head, turned off the heat under the pot. "That man hasn't been himself since Mary passed. Lemme tell you, she finally died, it was a blessing. I ever get like that, I can't do anything, can't talk, one of you's gonna have to shoot me."

"Mama, nobody's going to shoot you."

"You put me outta my misery. Don't let me hang around, tubes all here and there, all of you gettin' so worked up you gotta be put on drugs yourself so you can get a night's sleep. You get sick like Mary, everyone around you gets sick, nobody's good for nothing. Who wants to hang around five, six years waitin' to die? You're gonna die, you die an' get it over with, not be a burden on your family, get them all worked up and not eating right. You don't eat right, you know what happens?"

"You get sick?" Or was that the heart attack?

Or maybe you went crazy.

Cat closed her eyes and summoned the image of Isadore Testa; no matter how she tried to warp the image, it emerged weak, benign. She could not mold it into the semblance of a killer. "I'm going to get dressed, Mama. I'll drive you back home."

Cat got a quick shower, pulled her hair into a braid, blow-dried the bangs. She pulled on jeans, white turtleneck, a navy sweater, Wigwams.

The phone rang, setting off Cat's ESP. She picked up the receiver and said, "Hi, Ritchie. I guess you don't mind being shaken up on a Saturday this week."

"Whaddaya think? It's the fiancé? I heard she had her share. He flips out and slashes her throat."

"I don't think it's the boyfriend."

"Why not?"

"Then how would you account for the others?"

"Practice. He's workin' up to it. He knows the vics from church, picks out ones who live alone, does a couple to get his act down, throw the cops off the track, then he does the girlfriend."

Cat leaned with her back against the headboard, her knees bent. "Ritchie, where do you come up with this stuff?"

"I seen it on TV. This guy wants to kill his wife, so he kills a couple broads and then kills the wife exactly the same way and the cops think it's some whacked-out serial killer. But the guy goes overboard, kills another one, tryin' to keep the cops runnin' in circles, but he gets caught 'cause this one smart cop, the star? He figures its the husband all along, so he gets this gal cop who looks like the other vics to go undercover and get this guy to go after her and they nail him."

"So you're saying I should tail Gino?"

"I'm sayin' we should add him to the list. I got some problems with Easter. The old man's got that prior that—"

"What!"

"The old guy I was tellin' you was takin' sedatives? Works for St. Aggie's? He's got a prior."

"I don't believe that."

"Tryin' to pick up a hooker. Y'know how it is, every couple months or so, they do one of their equal-op sweeps."

Cat was stunned. Old Isadore Testa trying to pick up a prostitute? Isadore Testa was her *mother's* age. *God doesn't bring about a woman's death to harry us into righteousness.* Was that what Dominic had meant? That Mary Testa's illness and death was not God's way of punishing a wayward husband? Perhaps that was why Dominic had been so reluctant to tell her about those "personal questions" Victor had asked Isadore Testa.

"Only other suspect's the kid and he's out for the count."

"What are you talking about?"

"That kid you told me about. Mark what's-his-name? He OD'd and they brought him over the med center last night. I tell you, you gotta get one of these scanners."

"He's in the hospital?"

"Uh-huh. An' don't tell me he's just fifteen, plenty kids fifteen knock you off for a nickel."

"Fourteen," Cat said, softly. "Ritchie, I have to go."

"Yeah, well, you got any contacts over the med center, get the word on the kid. I heard they got a guard on him."

Cat took a sip of Pepsi. Kate Auletta would start working the phones; no, she would get on her computer and take to the keyboard and there would be a tight shot of the monitor as the clues were typed in and the name of the perpetrator was unveiled in a glowing readout and there would be a close-up of Kate's face, radiant with the computer's reflected light (green) and you'd know she had her killer, because you would just see it in her face.

Cat decided to work the phones. She called the hospital and was told that they were not permitted to release information on Mark Doe and referred her to the police department.

She called Isadore Testa's number; no answer. She dug up Easter's home number. The phone was answered by a child, who said politely, "May I ask who's calling?"

Cat heard Easter's fluid baritone said, "You go upstairs get dressed, honey, Daddy's gonna take us out for some pancakes." Then, "Mrs. Austen, I heard about that McConnell woman. How you gonna tie me to that one, you thought about it?"

Cat sighed. "I don't suppose there's any point in asking you where you were yesterday?"

"I was at my office from right after I dropped the kids at school to about four-thirty. You can ask the garage attendant, ask Gloria. Four-thirty, I picked my girls up at swim practice. I think you need to look a little harder, Mrs. A. Gutsy lady like you oughtta be able to handle it."

"I don't know where to look."

"Y'ever read mystery stories, Mrs. Austen? Not this new crap, the good ones? Was one by Poe, about this guy spends the whole time lookin' for some letter or something and you know where it is? It's right there tacked on the wall, he's making himself nuts, and all the time it's not even lost."

"*The Purloined Letter.*"

"Yeah, that's it."

"You're a connoisseur of classical mystery?"

"I read that stuff to my girls sometimes, spooky stories, kids today, they like that stuff. Now you, I'm thinkin' you're the type likes to peek at the ending."

"You have to know where the ending is to be able to take a peek at it," Cat observed.

"Uh-huh. But y'ever noticed in how many a those mystery stories the ending is right where the beginning was? You can't see to the end, maybe you gotta work your way back to where you came from."

Cat thanked him, wasn't sure for what, and hung up. Where the beginning was? Where *was* the beginning? The cops probably didn't even know that, but the beginning of her involvement had been at St. Agnes when she had run into Luz Molina, praying for Carmen Oliva.

And Luz Molina fit the description of the woman Victor had been talking to a few days before, at Bud-n-Lou's. Where Sheila McConnell worked. Cat shook her head. No, that wasn't significant, Lou had said Luz wasn't a regular, just someone hooking up with her date. *Hooked up with some older guy,* Lou had said. She had tucked Luz Molina's address away somewhere, hadn't she? If not, Luz had said she was in the book. And, since Cat was going into Atlantic City anyway, why not drop by and see if Luz would give her the name of the older guy she had hooked up with at Bud-n-Lou's?

In the den, Jane, Mats and Freddy sat motionless before the TV, as though they had frozen in time. The image had changed to a massive orange crocodile who was singing, *I want you to be my friend, Be my friend until the end!*

Cat looked at Mats' bobbing head, mesmerized gaze. "I'm taking Nonna home, anyone want to come along?"

Mats, bobbing back and forth, altered his rhythm to a shaking head, reverted to the lateral sway.

"When I come home—" She stared at them, planted herself in front of the television. "WHEN I COME HOME—"

"MomMMMMM!"

"I want to see you guys dressed for action. Nobody better still be sitting here in their PJs when I get back. You hear that, Freddy? *Freddy!*"

"Yeah, yeah, I'll get 'em dressed. Want me to drive Ma?"

"No, I'll do it, I want to run an errand."

Cat bundled her mother in the Maxima, wedging the pot on the floor of the back seat. She dropped the pot at her mother's house, then drove Jennie to St. Agnes. Cat walked her mother into the church. The nave was darkened; morning Mass had finished. Jennie threw her coat over the back of one of the pews. "I'm gonna get the things outta the janitor's closet. You don't have to stay, Dom or Kevin will gimme a ride home."

"Let me just go see if anyone's here." Cat left her mother rummaging through Isadore Testa's closet, walked the long corridor that connected the back of the church to the kitchen pantry. She heard someone in the kitchen, called, "Hello!"

"Come in." Maggie.

Cat stepped into the kitchen, found Maggie pulling on a shapeless black coat with buttons the size of silver dollars. "I hope I'm not interrupting. Is Dom around?"

"He's making hospital rounds. I think Kevin is visiting the shut-ins. I'm just going grocery shopping. You'd be surprised what three men can put away, Lent or no."

"Mama's in the church cleaning up."

Maggie understood. "The baby's christening's tomorrow, that's right. After the last Mass. Kevin said you're the godmother." She sighed, heavily. "You heard about that boy, I suppose. Mark."

Cat nodded. "I heard he's unconscious."

"I think Dom got to see him last night, then today, they wouldn't let him in." Maggie's harrumph encompassed the police and hospital bureaucracies.

"Why did they let him in last night?"

"They called him. Asked him to identify the boy." Maggie drew a pair of simple wool gloves from her pocket.

"Why Dominic?"

"They found his prescription bottle on the boy. Apparently the boy took it, though I don't think it's what he overdosed on. Probably tried to sell it. You know, boys like that, that brown prescription bottle's a dollar sign."

Cat nodded. "Ask Dominic to call me when he gets in, will you? It's nothing urgent." She went back to the nave, saw her mother urging a fifteen-year-old Eureka upright along the worn carpet in the aisle. Cat approached with the familiar unease, never knowing if she should still genuflect. "Mama, is there a phone book in your office?"

"Yeah, it's unlocked. Why? Whaddaya lookin' up?"

"What happened to 'it's none of my business'?"

Jennie chuckled, went back to her work. Cat went into the cramped office, found a fairly recent white pages in the bottom desk drawer, double-checked on Luz Molina's address, did her geography, which was becoming increasingly challenging in AC. But Luz had said she lived near Carmen Oliva, so her place couldn't be that far off New York Avenue.

Cat got into her car, drove down Tennessee, which ran parallel to New York, spotted a high-rise on Mediterranean just off Tennessee, with the building's address mounted above the entrance in numbers large enough to see that it was Luz Molina's address from a block and a half away. Which was good, Cat realized, since she was going to get no closer.

People were milling in front of the building and two black and whites, bumper to bumper, blocked off the intersection. A white NewsLine90 van was cruising toward the scene. Another white van, from the Medical Examiner's office, was parked on the sidewalk in front and Cat had the sickening sense that someone else had taken an interest in Luz Molina and beat her to the scene.

Cat parked in a nearby medical clinic's small lot, got out and locked her car. She approached, one eye on the lookout for Victor or anyone else she should avoid, the other scanning for someone who would tell her what was going on. She saw a tall blond in dark denims, a black pea jacket, black Kate Auletta boots.

"Hey, Karen."

"How'd you get a line on this one, Austen?"

"I was just coming from visiting family," Cat hedged. "Line on what?"

Friedlander nodded toward the building. "Detectives haven't arrived yet. I picked it up on the scanner. I've got a gut feeling Seaside Slasher Slaughters Sixth, though I'll come up with something classier for my lead."

"Anybody got a name?"

"She's on three, that much I found out, and I got the names of the tenants on three. Darnell, Kenney, Myers, Rivera, Molina, Catrambone, anything ring a bell?"

Cat swallowed. She said "No," felt guilty after Karen had been forthcoming with the little she knew and reconsidered. "Wait, I think I do recognize one of the names. There was a woman named Molina who was a friend of one of the victims. The Oliva woman. Who called it in?"

"Anonymous female, they're thinking it was called from that booth over there—" Karen tossed her mane toward an open booth across Tennessee. "Ritchie got you working this?"

"Well, I've sort of been working it on my own, and seeing what Ritchie will pick up."

"So I come up with something, you don't mind if I float it past him?"

Cat felt a twinge of resentment. "No, of course not," she lied.

"You don't know anyone else this Molina woman might be friendly with?"

*The brunette took off with some older guy.*

"Well ... I got the idea she was friendly for a living."

Friedlander laughed, and a couple heads turned toward them. Cat saw a cameraman from NewsLine90 approach.

"I've got to run," she said, and ran, praying the camera had not been running as well.

She got behind the wheel of her car, saw Luz Molina sashaying in front of the mirror the day of the open call. But what she heard was Ritchie's voice: *Tryin' to pick up a hooker.* Dominic's voice: *Victor started asking ... personal questions that I thought were a little out of line.* Cat tried again to cast Isadore Testa in a vicious shade and it was still hard, but for some reason, not nearly as hard as before.

## CHAPTER TWENTY-TWO

Stan Rice and a couple uniforms were shepherding curious tenants back to their apartments when Victor arrived. Raab was at the threshold of the Molina's door.

"He's getting sloppy, like he was with Harris," Rice muttered. "I don't get this guy. I don't get any of 'em, but I especially don't get this one. He's all over the map."

"Who's the victim?"

"Gal named Molina."

Victor looked at him. "Luz Molina?" he asked, slowly.

"You know her?"

"I spoke with her. She was acquainted with a couple of the victims. Is there another entrance to this place?"

"Service elevator, you can access it around back. They usually have a security guard down there can see if someone comes in the rear entrance."

"Nothing about this is usual. Talk to the guard, I want to know where he was and when. How many tenants on this floor?"

"Eight. Two married couples, the rest of them singles."

"Find the woman who called it in?"

"No. They'll dust the pay phone, but jeez ..."

Jeez, in this sense, translated to "Every mook between here and the Boards with two dimes to rub together used that phone once in a while."

Victor signed the clipboard a uniform offered him, approached Raab. The DA's thin face was deathly pale. There was no levity now, no tales of diversionary tactics at the synagogue. "This can't go on, Victor. I'm calling in anyone who'll give us a hand on this."

Victor said nothing, entered the small foyer. There was a closet to the right, mirrored sliding glass doors. He wedged past, careful not to let his sleeve brush the slick surface, possibly eradicate prints.

The living area was small, standard low-nap carpeting, department store drapes in solid beige. But the furniture was lipstick pink adorned with cushions of lime green satin, bright blue velour pillows. There was an all-white kitchenette, a vase of fading pink rosebuds on the counter. The abbreviated corridor that led to the bedroom had a closet on the left, bathroom on the right. Adane stood at the open bedroom door, talking to a criminalist in a wraparound smock. They edged aside and allowed Victor to pass.

Luz Molina lay face down on the bed, a sheet pulled to her shoulders. Victor saw a flowered satin robe thrown over a chair, flowered sheets drenched through with blood. A trail of it slid along one limp arm that hung over the side of the bed, a droplet of red congealed at the tip of the middle finger.

Victor asked for a flashlight. One of the blues handed his over. Victor drew on Latex gloves and swept the light over the floor of the room, the wall behind the bed. He approached the body and turned the beam on the dead woman's face. The half-closed eyes shone with eerie luminescence. He lifted the sheet with two fingers. The woman was nude, the sheets beneath her soaked, red-black. Victor lifted a lock of her hair to expose the throat, saw the small, deep cut over the carotid, below it a thin dark line circling the throat. He looked at the visible portion of face, the full lips parted about a half inch, the slight protuberance of blood-tipped tongue.

"Adane?" Victor nodded toward the victim's throat. "Ligature?"

"I want to know if this mark is recent." He turned his glance to the rumpled sheets, the upturned lamp.

Raab had stepped into the doorway. "Was it a mistake? Calling the press conference? Maybe made him panic, step up the agenda, flip out? McConnell and now this, one right after the other."

Sheila and Molina. Shrewd women. They should have been on their guard. Why hadn't they been? "No, it wasn't a mistake," Victor said, wasn't sure if he believed it. How could any of them know at this point what was going through this guy's mind?

The ME padded into the bedroom, paper booties on his feet. "Camera jockey's on his way up." His glance swept along the dead woman's form. "Looks like we may have some sexual contact here. Our guy's raisin' the stakes."

"Can you estimate a time of death?" Raab closed his eyes.

The ME prodded at the girl's upper arm, squinted at her face. "What, twelve hours? That's my guess right now, give or take. Means he did her and McConnell in the same day."

The photographer entered, shouldering a hand-held sixteen millimeter, a flashlight in the opposite hand.

"What the hell is that contraption?" demanded the ME.

"I'm just tryin' it out, see how it goes. I figure I come in, do a slow pan, I center it for my master shot—"

"*CopWatch* in the air and all of a sudden everyone's Cecil B. DeVille."

"DeMille. Plus I can do one continuous take, and you got instant playback, and—"

"I want standard black and whites on my desk tonight," Victor cut him off. "Doctor, was she strangled?"

"You see it, too? Ligature? And the blood dispersion's more like your Niagara Falls than your Old Faithful. She's not bled out, like the others, either."

"You mean this time he strangled her and then cut her?" Raab asked.

"Looks to be."

Victor spotted the handbag slung over the door handle, a beaded clutch among a jumble of cosmetics on the dresser. He poked through them carefully, came up with a wallet, about a hundred in small bills, a checkbook. When he opened the jewelry box a tiny ballerina popped up, twirled madly to the theme from *Love Story*. Earrings, pins, bangles, flashy but a few of good quality. He recalled Luz sitting tensely in the booth at Bud-n-Lou's, a large green crucifix dangling from her throat. He had seen it the day she emerged from St. Agnes, too. "Look around the sheets, under the pillows for a cross, dark green, jade, maybe malachite."

The criminalist looked up, nodded.

Victor peeled off his gloves, stuffed them in his pocket, nodded for Adane to follow him. In the small living room, the lab was dusting the tables, countertops for prints. "I saw this woman on two occasions: at St. Agnes the day Oliva was discovered and a couple days later at Bud-n-Lou's. She was wearing this green crucifix."

"A departure? He hasn't been taking tokens."

Victor nodded. "Check around for a notebook, diary, anything like that. She didn't have a pimp, worked solo. She'd have to schedule her appointments somehow."

"Yes, sir."

"I'll have Rice follow the post-mortem. Have him find out where James Easter and the church custodian, Testa, have been for the past twenty-four hours and tell Long to start showing Molina's picture around. He'll know where."

"Yes, sir."

He was about to continue his orders when his beeper went off. He heard the sound echoing from within the bedroom, saw Raab emerge, pluck his own beeping unit from his belt and the two of them looked at each other.

Isadore and Mary Testa had lived alone in a small rancher on Drexel, four blocks, Cat realized, from Carmen Oliva's apartment, and from Luz Molina's apartment. Six or seven from Murillo's place. A good, but not impossible walking distance from the inlet where they had fished up Montgomery, and from the abandoned tenement where they had found Renay Harris.

Had that been what Easter had meant by the purloined letter? That no one noticed an insignificant old man walking the streets?

The rancher was surrounded by a chain-link fence. There was a concrete walkway to the front step and something on either side that might have been a lawn in summer, plaster-of-Paris birdbath, the underside darkened with last summer's mildew.

Cat passed through the open gate, rang the front door bell, rang it again, heard its echo inside, heard silence. No footsteps, no television, no radio sounds. Perhaps he was taking a nap. Perhaps he was out. Or had a heart attack. Cat circled the uneven stubble of lawn, walked around back, mounted two concrete steps, knocked on the screen door. No response.

Cat opened the screen door and peered through the backdoor glass. She saw a kitchen counter wiped clean, narrow trestle table pushed against a wall. She leaned in, trying to shift her viewpoint to take in more of the kitchen. Her weight settled against the door and it opened a few inches.

Cat swallowed. The door hadn't even been closed all the way. She tried to remember what she had observed driving down the street, cars, vans, pedestrians who looked like they didn't belong. *Ladies, you're alone on unfamiliar turf is no time to go on automatic pilot*, Marco had instructed in Self-Defense for Women. *You're drivin' alone, you're walkin' alone, you pretend like behind every* (expletive deleted) *building, every* (expletive deleted) *rock, every* (expletive deleted) *tree is someone out to get you. Ninety-nine percent of the time, nobody's there, but you get that antenna up those ninety-nine, you're combat ready for number one hundred.*

Combat ready. Well, she'd held her own against a fourteen-year-old kid, she could handle a seventy-year-old man, couldn't she?

She stepped into the kitchen, looked around, kept the door open behind her. She said, "Mr. Testa?" Then realized it was a mistake, you do not signal your position to the enemy, Marco had said so. *Once those antenna start to vibrate, you get the heck out of Dodge.* Marco had not said heck.

There was a passage on her left that led to the dining room, segued into the living room, a second passage to her right that appeared to lead toward the bedroom, bathroom. Cat edged toward the center of the room, and then her nose took over and determined her course. She stepped into the small dining room, peered around the open passage to the living room, saw the large side window of the living room, the white sheers inside the window splattered crimson by a spray of such force that a large swatch of the gauzy fabric had adhered to the glass.

Cat froze, felt her abdomen go slack. She shut her eyes and took a tentative step toward the living room, readied herself to see what she knew she would see. He had killed again, this time in his own home, fled. She didn't want to know how this had played out; she didn't want her peek at his victim, but she peeked nonetheless.

The image, consciousness itself, flashed like the shutter on a camera, a forceful blow struck off her mastoid process, throwing her against a partition. She never remembered falling, and this time her eyes shut and stayed shut.

The hubris of eighteen-year-olds, they were all coasting on it, but it had been Danny Furina's idea, as all warped ideas tended to be. Still, the rest of them, on a graduation high, had followed suit: Cat, Freddy, Steve Delareto, Trina Morosco, Rose Cicciolini, Kevin Keller. They had piled into Danny's battered Buick, headed for the graduation party Cat's parents were hosting in a banquet room at Fortunati's, veered through the narrow inland streets of Atlantic City, honking the horn, waving their mortarboards out the window. Danny had pulled up before St. Agnes and declared he was going to get into the bell tower and carve their initials inside the steeple, at the top of the city. Kevin protested that it would be a sin to desecrate the church, but Danny had already dashed into the building, was jimmying the keyhole on the tower door with his pocket knife. The rest had followed, eager to see how far Danny would actually go, trailed him up the cylindrical staircase, their footsteps echoing in the narrow passage.

Over Kevin's pleas, Danny carved their initials into the wall of the stucco chamber, then glanced up and studied the short length of rope hanging from the clapper of one of the bells and declared his intention to "Pull a Quasimodo." "Danny, my dad's going to kill me if we don't get out of here," Kevin appealed, and Trina and Cat and Rose shrieked as Danny climbed the metal rungs protruding from the outer wall, leaped out and grabbed at the rope with both hands. He kicked his legs out, pushed off against the opposite wall, swung back. The sound was a disappointment, more of a "HBMMMM" than the "BONNNGGG" that Danny had anticipated. Then his grip gave way, he took the Lord's name in vain and plunged to the floor, which gave way in turn. He crashed through the ripened wood up to his hips.

The commotion roused Father Gregorio, who lumbered up the stairs, took one look at Danny planted hip deep in the tower floor and emitted a stream of expletives, several in English, but primarily in Spanish, astonishing the group, who had always opted for Father Greg in confession because of the gentleness of his remonstrances, those lightweight penances. Danny was yanked free and taken to the hospital where several painful splinters were wrestled from his gluteus maximus, a tetanus shot jabbed therein. The accomplices hung around outside the emergency room while Danny was being treated, every "YeooooWWW! *JE*sus!" setting off a surge of wicked mirth in Freddy and Steve, who didn't dare laugh aloud, but sat doubled over, pounding on the coffee table with their fists, while Kevin admonished them with "This isn't funny, guys." His sober reprimands only forced the laughter nearer the surface and the two boys stamped their feet on the floor, their faces crimson with suppressed glee.

Stamping their feet, pounding, pounding, but she couldn't hear Danny's cries anymore, they must have finished stitching him up, maybe sedated him, but Freddy and Steve were still pounding their feet on the floor, so hard that the floor shattered from the force and the people outside the waiting room started shouting, grabbed Cat by the throat as if to toss her out and she tried to tell them it wasn't her fault. Someone said "Put in a call to the DA's people and don't touch nothin'," and Cat was afraid that Danny had gotten them into serious trouble this time if they were calling in the DA. But there was no anger in the words, only urgency, and she heard a far-off voice say "Got a pulse here, I think she's just knocked out," and Cat realized that they had mistaken her for a patient, too.

She tried to tell them it was Danny who had been hurt, but she couldn't make her mouth move; it took a conscious effort to open her eyes, and she saw red, and she felt a rush of horror, realized that Danny must have been badly hurt if there was so much blood. She squinted, focused, realized she was horizontal, low, that there was scratchy nap under her cheek, that she was not in the emergency room.

Wheels rolled alongside her, eye level and Cat felt something collaring her throat, felt herself being turned over. Two men were standing above her, lifting her onto a gurney.

"Ma'am, just try to relax. Can you see me?"

"Yes."

"That your car out front?"

Someone in the background said, "Forensics on the way, homicide guys."

Cat was laid on the gurney. Someone slipped her arm out of her coat sleeve, wrapped a blood pressure cuff around her arm. Cat heard someone whisper, "Fortunati."

A uniform squatted down beside her and Cat's brain replayed the image that had flashed in her last second of consciousness and she asked, "Is he dead?" and the cop said, "Yes, ma'am."

## CHAPTER TWENTY-THREE

Cat heard tires squeal somewhere outside, voices near the front of the house. "The back door wasn't closed all the way. When I knocked it just opened." Then she heard "Where is she?" A trace of urgency accelerated the professional cadence; the uniform faded away and Victor appeared.

"Is she all right?"

"The collar's just a precaution."

"Victor ..."

"Don't say anything," he said. "Get her over to the med center, send an officer with her."

Cat groped for his sleeve. "Call Freddy, okay? Don't call Carlo. Tell them to call Freddy."

"All right." He looked up, "Okay, get her out of here."

He rose, saw a glance exchanged among the cops and the paramedics. They had heard the gossip, heard Cardenas had hooked up with Fortunati's sister, Chris Austen's widow. None of them believed it, none believed he would stand so calmly, giving orders, waving away the stretcher if he really cared for the woman. Except there was something, the merest trace of something in his fixed expression as he looked through the front window, watched her being lifted into the ambulance, saw the door shut, that hinted the rumors might not be very far from the truth after all.

But Victor was all professional when he turned to them, said, "All right, what have we got?"

The cop jerked his head toward a frayed, overstuffed chair against the living room wall where the victim sat. Testa had looked so diminished and insubstantial in life that death seemed to make no significant difference save for the deep gash in his throat, the lifeblood that had erupted from the severed artery. Victor examined the curtains (still moist), sized up the house. Living room, dining room, small kitchen, two bedrooms, bath; inexpensive furniture, a couple pictures on the wall, dime-store seascapes. Quiet neighborhood, stay-indoors weather.

Victor absently reached in his pocket for the Latex gloves he had worn at Molina's apartment, stopped. He borrowed a fresh pair from one of the uniforms, donned them as he headed down the corridor to the bedrooms. One had a double bed, made up, a plastic tub containing a few items of folded laundry, little in the way of ornamentation. The other room contained a single hospital bed perpendicular to the wall so that the occupant faced the back window, the small leaded-glass ornament tacked to the pane and the scrap of backyard beyond. There was a piece of equipment that looked like a some sort of ventilation machinery, sheathed in plastic, a small television.

Victor backed out, walked into the bathroom. Small and neat, 'fifties pink, with a bath mat hanging from the bar of the glass shower door. Medicine cabinet over the sink.

He slid open the medicine cabinet door with one gloved finger, saw an assortment of aspirin, toothpaste, disposable razors, shaving cream. He checked the wastebasket wedged under the sink, came up with a brown plastic prescription bottle. He lifted it out, checked the prescription. Diazepam. Five milligram tablets to be taken twice daily. Thirty pills, one refill. Empty. Victor checked the date. Nearly three weeks ago, which would mean he had finished the prescription recently, started on the refill. Unless he doubled up on the dosage. Unless he overdosed. Unless he used them on someone else.

Victor set the bottle on the sink. He walked into the kitchen. "There's prescription bottle for sedatives in the bathroom. Bag it, send it to the print lab. And see if you can turn up the refill."

The woman nodded, tersely. She didn't need Cardenas to tell her her job. Victor checked his watch, walked back into the living room where the photographer was angling around Testa's body, snapping away.

The ME hustled in the back door, pulled on paper booties. "Hey, guys, check your flies, NewsLine90 followed me over here. I did a flashy number so Raab could duck around Adriatic and cut through someone's backyard. And I'm not even on call this weekend, they're all up the Spectrum, some game or other. Y'ever been there? Three bucks for a candy bar." He patted his pockets, came up with a pair of Latex gloves. "What, our boy's crossin' the gender line, now? What'll they think of next?"

"What's the possibility the wounds could have been self-inflicted?" Victor asked.

The ME bent over the chair, squinted at the small, neat aperture in the man's throat. "Small, same kinda double-edged instrument. Don't see nothin' in his hands, on his lap. Look around the floor. Self-inflicted, you'd see the weapon. Plus, you'd see your starter cuts."

"Hesitation wounds," Victor interpreted.

"Yeah. Testing out your pain threshold. He's clean."

"What if he had taken something beforehand?"

"Got himself liquored up, you mean?"

"Or drugged. There's a prescription in the bathroom. Diazepam."

The ME shook his head, dubiously. "Couple of those, you're feelin' so good you forget why the hell you wannid to off yourself in the first place."

Victor nodded, somberly.

"Plus, why not just OD? Plus, I don't see a weapon. Anybody got some Lifesavers or anything?"

"Lieutenant, the DA's comin' through the back," one of the uniforms said.

"I'd like your report by tomorrow morning, Doctor."

"Tomorrow's Sunday."

"Tomorrow's Sunday for me, too. And for the killer and any other potential victims." He turned to the uniform. "Whose knocking on doors?"

"Two of ours. Neighborhood's pretty thin."

"Call Detective Long, get him the name of the victim's physician, the late wife's physician." Victor stepped out the kitchen door, saw Kurt Raab hustling across the back yard, was surprised to see Kevin Keller talking to one of the uniforms.

Raab approached Victor. "The victim was a suspect, wasn't he? Suicide?"

"It doesn't appear so."

"Guy's been killing women, young women. All of a sudden there's McConnell who was, and I mean this diplomatically, not in her twenties. Now this? He's takin' a detour from the game plan."

Victor's gaze roamed, impatiently. "The victim's or the killer's?"

"Whaddaya mean?"

The gaze returned to Raab. "Eliminate age and gender, the remaining factors are the same. No sign of forced entry. Nothing taken. No staging, no sign of a struggle. Again, a connection to the church. It's considerably closer to type than the Molina woman."

"Who found him?"

Victor hesitated. "Mrs. Austen. She said the back door was open. She walked in, someone hit her on the head."

Raab rubbed his forehead. "You still got that ticket to San Juan? I'll buy it off you, name your price." He looked over his shoulder, jerked his head toward Keller. "Who's that? He looks familiar."

"Deacon at the church. Keller."

"Mary Grace's brother? You know she asked for a leave? What's he doing here?"

"I'll go see." Victor approached Kevin.

"Lieutenant, is it true? Isadore's dead?"

Victor nodded. "Would you mind telling me what you're doing in the neighborhood?"

"I was making hospital rounds and I heard Cat was brought into the ER. I went down and hung around until Freddy came by. I think they were going to release her, but she still seemed pretty shaken up. Scared. She asked me if I'd pick up her car." He drew Cat's key ring out of his pocket. "I can take it, can't I?"

"I'll ask Raab. I believe it'll be all right." Victor nodded toward the house. "How well did you know him?"

"Isadore?" Kevin rubbed his brow with a shaking hand. "Forever. I mean, he and Mary had been going to St. Agnes even back when I was a kid. I'd been out of the country for so long, when I came back, settled in at St. Agnes, Mary was already bedridden. Dom and Greg were good about allowing him to work his schedule around her needs."

"It was generous of the church to keep him on."

Kevin shrugged. "Beth Easter's an intensive care nurse, she helped out a lot, recruited a few others who could tend Mary for a few hours here and there."

"Recruited them, you say? We're talking about Carmen Oliva? And Tamara Montgomery and Renay Harris."

"Yes," Kevin hesitated.

"You think Mrs. Easter was also the one who recruited them into the church?"

"I wouldn't be surprised."

"What about a woman named Murillo?"

"Don't know."

"Did you know her?"

"Yes. She came to Mass regularly. Spanish Mass."

"You speak Spanish?"

"*Si, un poco.* So do Dom, Monsignor Greg and at least a third of our congregation. I also speak a smattering of Portuguese, Italian, criollo and a word or two of Vietnamese. Look, Lieutenant, would it be possible for me to ... I mean, could I go in and say a prayer?"

"I'm sorry, I can't allow that. I'll see about getting Cat's car released." Victor walked back into the house. The ME's people were finishing, laying Testa out. The crime scene people were methodically extracting blood samples from the walls, taking snippets of curtain, carpet.

Phil Long rapped on the back door, stepped in. Victor looked past him to the backyard, saw Kevin standing on the lawn, his head bowed in prayer.

Cat lay in the cubicle waiting for Freddy to come for her. *Why didn't he kill me? Why did he leave me alive?*

Jackie Wing crept in. "I heard they brought you in here. Cat, you're so lucky. Stan says it looks like you walked in on this whacko, you could have been killed."

*But I wasn't.* "Jackie, what do they take for muscle pain?"

"Gee, I guess Ibuprofen, Tylenol. Why, you hurting?"

"What about something that would be prescription strength?"

"Flexeril? You don't wanna take it if you're gonna drive, though, you get kinda drowsy."

"Mellowed out?"

"Yeah."

"Jackie, you know anything about that kid they brought in last night, the overdose?"

Jackie shook her head. "Poor kid looks like he hasn't eaten in a month. I'm not on his duty."

"Who is, do you know?"

"Beth Easter, the day shift. I don't know if she's on today. Want me to find out?"

"No, that's okay."

Freddy got her signed out of the hospital, sat holding her hand in a waiting room while she gave a statement to a sympathetic cop named Moore, who told her to take care of herself, handed her a card. An incubus lodged inside Cat's skull, hammering to get free, causing her eyes to water, so she figured, what the heck, have her cry and get it over with.

Freddy reached over, patted her arm. "What were you doing over there, Cat?"

"I dropped Mama at St. Agnes and I was driving down Tennessee and I saw the barricade and heard this woman got killed? So I was just detouring around the neighborhood, and I passed Mr. Testa's house and, you know, I knew he hadn't been feeling well, and I thought I'd stop by."

"Don't talk to me like you talked to that cop in there."

"She went for it, didn't she?" Cat sniffed.

"Victor won't. What's the cover story for the kids?"

"I fell and bumped my head. That's all you have to tell them." Cat looked at the expanse of water as they crossed the narrow bridge. It glittered like hard glass.

"Why didn't he kill me, Freddy?" she whispered.

"I don't know. Jesus, Cat, I don't even wanna think about that." Freddy paused. "Maybe he heard something, maybe he was on the clock, maybe there was someplace he hadda be."

"But there was a chance I could recognize him."

"Did you?"

"No. But why was he willing to take that chance?"

"I don't know."

But Cat did. Knew what Easter meant by the purloined letter, knew why Victor didn't want Carlo on the case, knew why the killer of five women, of Testa, couldn't kill her.

Because he loved her. Like a brother.

## CHAPTER TWENTY-FOUR

Jane hung about her mother, wariness and fear mingled on her face, suspecting that something was up, something serious, like the time they had come to get her at school, taken her to the hospital, told her Mom had been shot.

But Mom was right there, not talking much, but she checked Jane's homework and they all had pizza and Mom didn't read them any of that stupid Dickens, either, but picked one of Jane's *American Girls* books.

Cat put them to bed and went to her room, pulled a robe over her flannel pajamas. She went to tuck Mats in and gave him a hasty private reading of *Fast Rolling Fire Trucks*, to mitigate the torment of having to put up with *American Girls*. There was a knock on the door and Ellice poked her head in. "How you feeling?"

Cat rapped her knuckles against her forehead. "My least vulnerable spot, apparently. Freddy gone?"

Ellice nodded. "He goes back onto four to twelve tomorrow. Vinnie called, wanted all the what and wherefore."

"No, Lorraine did. She's probably mad because she's not the one who got whacked on the head and sent to the hospital. She acts like my life is one huge romantic melodrama."

They heard the distant chime of the front doorbell. "I'll get it," Cat sighed.

"Watch who you open the door to."

Cat descended the stairs, each step sending a little jab of

pain behind her ear. She flipped on the porch light, squinted through the block glass, saw the blurred and disjointed figure of someone who was tall, black-garbed. A black-gloved hand held up something by the fingertip, something that glinted in the porch light. Kevin, with her car keys.

Cat wrestled open the front door, felt an icy shock of night wind, saw her Maxima parked in the driveway.

"Maggie got held up at a bridge opening; she'll be coming in a minute to pick me up," he explained.

"Well, then, come in, I was just going to put on some water for tea."

"Don't go to any trouble, Cat. How're you feeling?"

"I've been better. C'mon, some company will do me good."

They sat in the kitchen. Cat's inquisitive genes prodded her throbbing brain cells. She fixed a pot of Formosa Oolong, set two mugs on the table.

"I stopped by Jennie's, to make sure she's okay."

"Thanks." Cat propped her elbows on the table, dropped her head into her hands. "Kevin, if I asked you something, would you tell me without asking why I'm asking?"

Kevin sipped his tea. "Probably not, but ask anyway."

Cat smiled, was relieved that the muscles engaged didn't set off another pulse of pain. "Mr. Testa's back door was open. Unlocked. How would his door get unlocked? I don't think many people in AC leave they're doors unlocked anymore, not like when we were kids."

"No," Kevin hesitated. "But there were people who had a key."

"What people?"

"Well, he left one with the church. He worried that if something happened to him, Mary wouldn't be able to call for help."

"Was it kept where just anyone could get at it?"

"We kept it in the rectory, on a peg in the kitchen."

"Did any of you ever use it?"

"He was usually there when I went to visit. I think Maggie let herself in once, I really don't know."

"Dominic visit him?" Cat lowered her gaze, blew on her steaming tea.

"He visited, of course. He was Mary's priest."

"Kevin, don't you think it's odd that all the victims went to the same church?"

Kevin shrugged. "I guess. Of course, Sheila McConnell only started coming when she got engaged to Gino. And Tamara Montgomery wasn't really a parishioner; her home parish was in Vineland, somewhere."

"Well, yes, and I guess you could say that Estrella Murillo's was in Guatemala somewhere. But they attended Mass at St. Agnes."

"True."

"Did you know the Montgomery girl?"

"Is this for the paper or something?"

Cat gave him a Jennie shrug.

"Well, yes, I knew who she was. Saw her several days before her body was discovered, in fact. We had an Advent dinner at the church. Dominic tried very hard to bring more young people into the congregation; that age group, it's always a struggle."

"She used to work at Nothing Sacred. I don't get the segue from modeling lingerie to Advent pot luck."

Kevin stared at his mug. "I don't always see it myself. Don't trust it, either. I'm always waiting for them to revert." He smiled, disarmingly. "Don't print that."

There was a heavy tread on the back stairs, and Cat started. No one used her back stairs.

"Might be Maggie," Kevin said, rising. "Sit, I'll get the door."

Cat heard him open the back door, heard Maggie's deep voice, the resolute wiping of her feet on the rush mat.

"Can I get you some tea, Maggie?" she asked.

Maggie shook her head. "No, I have to get back. I didn't want to ring the bell, thought the kids might be asleep."

"Thanks, but go out the front, those back steps are wobbly." She walked Kevin and Maggie to the door. Kevin couldn't help saying, "You know, Dom would love to have you come to Mass before the christening tomorrow."

"I really admire a guy who has a goal and doesn't let up. Do they call you The Terminator behind your back?"

Kevin tucked his muffler inside his coat. "I don't know what they call me behind my back. You get some sleep, Cat."

She locked the door, turned out the porch light. The phone's ring set off another round of throbbing in her head. She didn't want to talk to Victor, not quite yet, but when she heard Marco's voice follow her brief message, she picked up the phone.

"Did I or did I not tell you, you keep your antenna up, you do not go in the house?"

"You said you don't go in the *car*."

"You don't go in the car *and* you don't go in the house."

"What about the alley? Do you get to go down the long dark alley?"

"This isn't funny, Cat. How's the head?"

"Fine."

"Everything else okay?"

"What do you mean by everything?"

"It's none of my business." He told her to get some sleep and hung up.

The phone rang.

Carlo. "So you okay or what?"

"What."

"They X-ray your head?"

"I'm fine."

"'Cause if they did, I hope you told 'em to put the lead over you. They don't do that, they could fry your organs."

"My organs are fine, thanks for asking."

"What kind of idiot stunt did you think you were pullin'?"

"Carlo, why is it when I do something it's my fault and when something happens *to* me, it's *still* my fault?"

"'Cause you don't got enough sense to stay away from where stuff's goin' down. So what's the deal with you gettin' canned by *CopWatch?*"

"I guess they decided they didn't need my input."

"Yeah, well get this: they gimme a call, asked me do I wanna be their law enforcement technical advisor."

Cat felt her fist gripping the receiver. Damn Ted Cusack. Manipulative creep. Trying to play with her head by seducing her family. He really was the perfect medium for the saga of someone as downright despicable as Jerry Dudek.

"I'm glad for you, Carlo. It will give you something—" *to keep you out of everyone's hair.* "They couldn't have picked a better person. They're lucky to have you."

"What the fuck are you talking about, lucky to have me! After they can my sister, I'm gonna go do any favors for *Cop* fucking *Watch?*"

"I thought you gave up the F-word for Lent."

"I gave up hoagies for Lent. So you gonna go to Mass tomorrow before the christening?"

"No, we're just coming for the baptism."

"Victor, too?"

Cat hesitated. Somehow he had found out *CopWatch* dumped his sister and Carlo had told them where to go. Victor had shut Carlo out of the investigation and it was Cat's turn to demonstrate who's side she was on. "I don't know," she waffled. "I'm coming with Freddy, Ellice and the kids, I think he's coming on his own. He's been tied up ..."

"Yeah, I heard. Things're gettin' too much for his people to handle. I hope Victor knows what he's doin'."

Cat hung up, turned out the downstairs lights, went back to her room. Ellice was watching the early Philadelphia news, saw a snippet about the Atlantic City murders, saw a few seconds' worth of Victor walking from Luz Molina's townhouse, while a reporter trotted after him.

Cat dropped onto the bed. "Carlo got a call from *CopWatch*, they wanted him to be a tech advisor. He turned them down."

"You're kidding."

Cat shook her head. "I think he did it because Ted called April and told her he wants me off the story, off the set, off the whole thing."

"Good for Carlo."

Cat rolled on her side. "Ellice, doesn't it bother you that you've gotta make a choice between your brother and Freddy?"

"Yes. But if it's the right choice, then I can live with it."

"You ever think that maybe your brother might like Freddy?"

"Honey, Freddy's white. No way Elon's gonna like me marrying white. To his way of thinking, you stick to your own."

Cat nodded. She had been coached to pick out a nice, white, Catholic, Italian boy, and Chris had been nice, white and a boy, three out of five. Yet, when Aunt Sofia and Uncle Condoloro arrived from Messina for the wedding, they had taken one look at him, drawn Cat aside and said, "Allegrezza, he's not Italian."

"No."

"But's he's a Catholic?" Zia Sofia had whispered, hopefully. Cat shook her head.

Zia Sofia's firmly set mouth, her silences only broken by conversation in her native tongue, lasted until the reception when Chris had taken her by the hand, drawn her onto the dance floor, waltzed her around the room, then escorted her back to her seat, kissed her hand and thanked her in rudimentary Italian. "A lot of my family didn't like Chris at first," Cat commented.

"But they liked him at last."

"It just seems like an awful choice to have to make."

Ellice looked at her with a serene smile. "I had a professor who said that 'first we make choices and then our choices make us.' My kids are gonna look less like my people than they would if I married a black man, and *fratelli* Fortunati may never come around completely, and there will always be those looks Freddy and I get when we go out. But then, Freddy's the one who loves me and trusts me and who's earned my trust. What choice? I wish they were all this easy."

*So do I*, Cat thought.

Cat stood beside Freddy, holding baby Gio in his christening gown, promising to renounce Satan in all his works, the promises hollow in her own ears. She repeated the responses that Dominic read to her, having forgotten the words, remembered how she had stood in Sherrie's place when Freddy and Chris's sister Charlotte had consented to be godparents to baby Mats.

Gio let out a squawk when the holy water was drizzled onto his forehead, and Cat could feel Sherrie tense behind her. Dominic performed the ritual smoothly, taking the baby from her as he pronounced him baptized in the name of Jesus Christ and kissed him under the chin. Baby Gio let out a squeal of delight that echoed through the church and his bevy of uncles, aunts and cousins laughed.

Dominic took the baby to the center of the alter to present him to his family as a child of God, and if the horror of two parishioners murdered in two days weighed on him, he never showed it. Cat glanced over her shoulder to the pew where Victor stood apart from her family, watching the ceremony, his expression courteous and unemotional. Ellice stood beside him, holding Mats by the hand, Jane stood on his other side; the rest of the family was stationed across the aisle.

Victor looked at her, thought she looked especially pretty in a wool crepe suit of deep purple, seemed perfectly calm after the ordeal of the day before, though once or twice he caught a small gesture, a deliberate straightening of the shoulders, a resolute lift of the chin that suggested the strain beneath her attempt at composure. He had lost her, he knew; he would never win out against that family of hers. Even Jennie would abandon him.

The ceremony concluded and Cat handed the baby over to Sherrie, she and Freddy standing on either side of the parents as Nancy snapped a few pictures. Out of the corner of her eye, Cat saw Kevin struggle with a frown; he did not approve of cameras in church. As soon as that was done, Mats hurried forward to reclaim his mother. "Gio made noise in church," he informed her. Cat had instructed her children on church etiquette. Mats' only exposure to church was his own christening, and Jane's memories of the few Masses she had attended had alloyed with other events that required her to be dressed up, to mind her manners and she came away with a sense of disappointment because she had thought she'd understood that Uncle Dom was going to dance.

Cat saw Victor nod Dominic to one side, saw him say a few words, heard Dominic reply "I have a half hour of confessions, people receiving communion at the McConnell Mass tomorrow, then we can talk."

Victor came up beside Cat, and if he felt the coldness emanating from her brothers, he never showed it. "Go with Freddy, Cat, I'm going to be delayed."

"I'll wait."

He shook his head, walked her out of the church. The Fortunatis were maneuvering their cars out of the lot, queuing into a caravan while Jennie and Sherrie fussed with the baby's blanket.

Cat pulled Mats' wool hat down over his ears. "Sweetie, you're going to go with Uncle Freddy to the bakery, okay? And I'm going to follow in a little bit."

Mats thought about it, decided he wanted to stay with his mother. "Are you gonna ride in the car with that baby?"

"No, I'm coming with Victor and Uncle Dom."

On the other hand, if he went to the bakery, there was a good chance Uncle Freddy would buy him a cookie. "Okay. But are you coming right over?"

"As soon as Uncle Dom can get changed."

Cat told Freddy she would be riding with Victor, that the kids wanted to go with him to pick up the cake. Freddy, always closest to Cat, said, "What's the matter?"

"Nothing. I just need to talk to Victor for a few minutes alone."

Freddy knew better, but also knew when to leave well enough alone. He bundled the kids in the back seat, promising to buy them a cookie and Cat waved them off.

A few people were wandering up the steps of the church, some she thought she recognized. Going to confession so that they could receive the sacrament at the Requiem Mass the next day.

Cat stepped into the vestibule, heard the wind rushing down the bell tower shaft, rattling the door; the sound was eerie and loud against the hush in the nave. She saw a few people kneeing in the rear pew, waiting to enter the confessional, saw Kevin Keller praying at the alter.

She tiptoed across the back of the nave, headed down the corridor toward the rectory, heard Victor's voice from the direction of the small church office. She moved closer, heard him say, "No, I think tomorrow will be soon enough, after the service. No, I don't think we're dealing with a flight risk." He looked up. He had been sitting at the desk, rose and said into the phone, "I'll call you back," hung up.

He looked at her. She looked so lovely in a suit of deep royal purple, her hair brushed loose, a little disordered by the wind. It had been too easy, falling in love with her, so easy that he had disarmed himself, pretended that he was invulnerable, certain no crisis could come that would sever them. And now it had. All trails wound toward one core, St. Agnes, and there was no denying that there was where the murderer of seven people would be found, just as there was no denying what would become of his relationship with Cat when the truth was exposed.

"Victor ..."

"What?"

"Were you in love with her? Sheila McConnell?"

"No. We had an affair, but I never loved her."

"It was one of those things that just happened?"

"No, Cat. That isn't one of the things that just happen. Tragedies, like Marisol's illness, that was something that just happens; it's not the same as something I chose to do. Sheila and I were lovers because we chose to be, and the worst part of it was that we didn't love each other, we never had any intention of committing to each other. I'm not going to let myself off the hook by saying it just happened."

"Do you want me to go to her funeral with you tomorrow?"

"No. You're supposed to come in to the bureau to make your statement, about the incident at Testa's residence."

"Victor—" she felt her voice choke up, swallowed, forced herself to look at him. "It isn't Dominic."

He walked around the desk and took her face in his hands. "I'm glad we didn't go to San Juan."

"I'm not." She arched her head up and brushed her lips against his.

"Why didn't you go with your family?"

"I'll wait for you. We'll go together."

"Love—"

His beeper went off and he snatched it from his belt, impatiently, checked the number. His dark brows raised.

"What is it?" Cat asked.

"The hospital. ICU extension." He went back to the phone, punched in the number. "This is Lieutenant Cardenas returning the call."

Cat watched him, scanned his face for some indication of what had occurred.

"All right. I'll be there immediately." He hung up, hesitated before he spoke. "The boy's awake. I can get a few minutes with him if I go right now. Can I drop you?"

"No. I'm going in the other direction. I'll see you later, won't I?"

He took her by the shoulders, kissed her, fervently as if it would be some time before they kissed again.

"Victor," she called after him as he left the office.

He turned.

She shook her head. "Nothing. I love you, that's all."

"I hope it's more than nothing," he replied, gravely. "I hope it's enough."

The boy in the bed watched the nurse with a feverish and wary gaze as the nurse offered him ice water, angling the straw toward his mouth. Her angel's smile disarmed him and he arched he head up, sipped tentatively, then more avidly, nearly draining the glass. The nurse's hands slipped under his head, adjusted his pillow; then she placed her palm on his forehead for a second as if offering a benediction, smiled.

"Can you beat it," muttered the uniform, stationed outside the room, watching through the shuttered glass. "She's Jimmy Easter's wife."

Victor watched her. She, too, moved with a fluid grace, but unlike Easter's animal agility, there was an ethereal quality to even her most mundane gestures that left Victor half expecting to see a halo glimmering above the prim braids that formed a tiara above her hair.

She left the room, closing the door gently. "Lieutenant Cardenas?" she smiled. The smile was slightly gap-toothed, the skin a pale brown, a scant shade darker than his own. There was a scattering of freckles across the bridge of her nose, a pleasing fullness to her mouth and the slightest cleft in her chin, barely more than a dimple.

"Mrs. Easter, how is your patient?"

"I think you will have to discuss the particulars with his

doctor, Lieutenant, but we believe he'll pull through. Through this crisis, at least. God only knows what the long term holds. I've explained to him that you're going to talk to him. It would be best if you could confine your questions to ones that wouldn't require more than a yes or no. He's very weak."

"I understand. I'd like to speak to you for a few minutes when I'm done, Mrs. Easter."

"I'll be at the nurse's station." She walked down the corridor, her rubber-soled shoes chirping ever so lightly on the polished linoleum. As they receded, a definitive click, click, click replaced them and he heard a familiar voice asking for information.

Victor walked into the room, saw the kid's sullen gaze turn on him. He saw the trace of fear behind it, erasing all bravado; he had skated on the edge without confronting the possibility that he might plummet into the pit.

Victor lifted a vinyl chair from the corner, placed it near the bed. The kid's thin fingers clutched at the blanket. An IV was taped to the back of his left hand.

Victor drew out his identification, his badge, showed it to the boy. "My name is Lieutenant Cardenas. You're Mark, is that right?"

He hesitated, then nodded.

"I want you to understand that you don't have to talk to me at all. Or, if you do talk to me, decide you don't want to continue, you can tell me to get out. Do you understand that?"

"Yeah." It was a whisper, the hoarseness of disuse.

The door opened and Lauren Robinson entered the room. She wore a deep burgundy suit with lipstick to match; some unhappy reptile had been skinned and tinted to outfit her with matching accessories, the briefcase and the combative light in her amber eyes suggested she was of the disposition to do the skinning herself.

Victor rose. "Mrs. Easter called you?"

"Of course."

"You're a fortunate young man," Victor said to the boy, as he offered the chair to Lauren. "Ms. Robinson is one of the best defense attorneys in the state."

"*One* of?" she inquired, raising one heavy brow. "Did the lieutenant tell you you don't have to talk to him?" she asked the boy.

Mark nodded, staring at the elegant woman who had come to act as his defender. Victor suspected the boy hadn't encountered many women as dazzling as Lauren Robinson.

"And there won't be any questions about my client's physical condition, or substances he may or may not have taken?"

"None," Victor agreed.

"Or about any illicit activities in which my client may or may not have engaged?"

"Fine."

"Or about anything he may or may not have had in his possession when he was found?"

"Lauren, it's been a rough winter, would you consider cutting some slack?"

"Slack is the thing I would be least inclined to cut. Anything else you'd like cut, I'm the woman to do it."

Victor was glad he wasn't a prosecutor; he'd hate to come up against her in court. "Look, let's start with mid-December, around the twelfth, thirteenth or fourteenth. Your client was in a unit on St. James Place—"

"I don't recall my client stating that he was ever inside any such property."

Victor's mustache mimicked his scowl. "Lauren, your client is a material witness to a homicide."

She looked at him, gravely. She had known Gino, too, known Sheila McConnell. "What is it you want to ask?"

Victor looked at the boy. "Did you see his face?"

The boy bit his lip.

"You did see his face, didn't you?"

The boy nodded, slowly.

"He didn't see you?"

"I don't think so."

"You saw him again? Recently?"

The boy squinted back tears, nodded.

Lauren slipped her hand onto the bed, under the boy's palm. His fingers closed tightly over hers.

"You saw him when Mrs. Austen brought you to St. Agnes."

Another nod.

Victor reached in his coat pocket, drew out a manila envelope. The pictures of Oliva's funeral were inside. He removed a close-up of Testa, held it up to the boy. The boy shook his head. He held up a picture of the pallbearers and again, the boy shook his head.

He took out the picture of Dominic standing at the gravesite, the mourners in the background, one hand held high over the coffin in that act of benediction.

The boy's eyes grew wide; then he shut them, tightly, nodded and turned his face away.

Lauren Robinson looked at the picture, and then up at Victor. He was not a demonstrative person; she had never seen him give in to temper or to passion, but she could not recall ever seeing his countenance so devoid of all emotion, abandoned even by the hope that emotion would return.

## CHAPTER TWENTY-FIVE

Cat had forgotten how to pray. Kneeling in the last pew of the church, she could get no further than "God. God, God, God." God, what? It was no use. *God, no, please don't let it be Chris, not Chris!* And a week after that *No, God, not my baby, not the baby, too!* How could she come back to Him again, begging *God, not my brother. Let it be anyone but my brother.*

The last person had completed her confession, moved toward the bank of votive candles and begun silently working through her prayers of penance. Cat rose and walked into the confessional, knelt, felt the darkness close in on her. The panel slid aside and there was only a dark mesh of screen separating the two of them, Dominic's silhouette on the other side.

"My child ..?" he prompted.

Cat hesitated. "I forgot the words."

There was a long pause. "Just say what's in your heart."

"I can't ... I can't read from my heart anymore. It's too dark. Or I'm too afraid. Is that a sin, being afraid?"

"In the book of John, it says that God is love and that there is no fear in love. That love drives out fear. That we can't be made perfect through fear, only through love."

"I don't think I've got a shot at perfection."

"Well, I suppose if fear keeps us from doing good—doing what's right—it's a sin. The world is full of things that provoke fear. Despair. It doesn't entitle us to give up."

"I've tried not to. You know I have."

"I know, dear."

"It's just that ... my past is starting to look like another life. I look at pictures of Chris and me and it's almost like it's someone else's life."

"You're not mourning anymore. You've accepted that he's gone and you've fallen in love with Victor."

Cat felt a tear slide toward the corner of her mouth, wiped at it with the back of her hand. "What if Victor wants to marry me?"

"Is there a reason why you shouldn't marry?"

"I'm afraid. Something could happen to separate us. Or could separate me from the family."

"Cat, you'll never be apart from your family." He leaned toward the screen so that Cat could almost see his features. "That's wishful thinking."

A laugh forced it's way past the sob. "But what if I ever had to choose between ... well, between Victor and one of— All of you? What if his work made me choose?"

"It's this particular case that's bothering you."

"So many of the, well, victims ..."

"Went to church here at St. Agnes," Dominic said. "Well, let's face it, Cat, we're a poor parish and the sort of people who make up most of the congregation are the sort of people who fall prey to what's out there. The punks who beat up Louie Cicciolini. Mrs. McAllister surprised a burglar and he fractured her skull. Even Kevin got mugged last year bringing the Sacrament to shut-ins."

"I didn't know that."

"Well, Kevin isn't a complainer. Not about anything suffered in the cause of the church, anyway. All the Kellers had to put up with growing up, none of them turned out to be whiners, come to think of it."

"And it seems that's all I *do* do."

"Do not. Growing up, we didn't call you the Alley Cat for nothing. You're one of the bravest people I know."

"I'm not. I'm scared all the time. Scared I'm screwing up with the kids, scared I won't be able to make it with my writing. Scared one day I'll answer the bell and see Carlo and Vinnie at the door again, with that look in their eyes."

"You want a guarantee that you'll never suffer again. You won't get it, not in this life."

"That's no comfort," Cat sniffled. "I though you priests were supposed to throw out some crumbs of comfort."

Dominic sighed. "Trying to live a life in Christ, prepare for the promise of eternity is not a comfortable existence. It requires some hard choices." He paused. "Do you love him, Cat?"

"I think I'm afraid to."

"But that wasn't the question, was it?"

Cat wiped her eyes again. "Are your confessions always this Socratic? No wonder they all line up for Monsignor Greg."

"They do not."

"Do so. Yes, I love him."

"And do you believe he would be a good husband and father?"

"Yes. And he's a Catholic, so there's that."

"Has he proposed?"

"I think he's waiting for the right time."

"And how will he know when that is?"

"Do you ever know when it's the right time?"

Dominic paused. "Living in faith ... well, it's not easy. Even after all this time. You think you're going to get to that exalted place, where it's gonna be easier to know what's the right thing to do, when's the right time. And you never get there. The rung always gets raised a little higher. All you do is maybe buy yourself a little breathing room, a little time to get stronger before you continue to rise. That plateau of perfection, where all doubt, all conflict is removed, that's not for this life. And the struggle is not what holds us down; it's the refusal to climb. Only God truly knows the right time. The rest of us just have to make the best of the time we're given.

And not to hold ourselves to the level where we can maintain control. Love is not about control."

"How come I'm looking for answers and all you do is sermonize?"

"I have to sermonize. It's in the job description, Homilies One Oh One."

"I thought you'd at least push the single blessedness."

"Yeah, well, celibacy's a pretty hard sell in this day and age. I'm thinking Victor's not gonna go for it. You want my advice, okay, I think you and Victor ought to spend some more time getting used to each other, getting used to the idea of what a commitment like marriage means, and if you want to be together, come check out my premarital group. Because marriage is the only right and honorable covenant between a man and a woman. How's that? Too preachy?"

"No, it's fine. I'd better go. Can you give me a lift to Joey's?"

"Why don't you ask Kevin to drive you over? I think Victor wants to wait. He wants to talk to me."

"Oh, you didn't hear. He had to run over to the hospital. He said Mark was able to talk."

"He's conscious? Thank God for that. I'll get changed and go over there."

"Are you going to pray for me now or something?"

"I pray for you every day, dear."

Cat placed her palm against the screen, felt the warm pressure of Dominic's palm in answer. Then she rose and left the chamber, raised her hand to wipe her eyes and saw reddish streaks of rouge, a trace of mascara she had wiped from her face. She could count on the fingers of that hand the number of days per year she wore rouge, eye makeup. *I can't even do that right.*

She went to the little closet under the stair and peered at herself in the small mirror over a sink. Not too bad. She turned on the spigot and yanked the last two paper towels from the dispenser, moistened them and rubbed the remaining rouge from her cheeks, rinsed them in the sink to re-use, ran her blotchy hands under the stream of water.

*Déjà vu* crept from the pit of her abdomen to her stomach, choked her as it tried to wedge itself through her throat. Cat swallowed hard. Stared at the faint red streaks running down the white porcelain, into the drain.

*This happened before.*

She closed her eyes, saw herself standing at this sink, rubbing rust from her hands under the water, rust she had gotten from the rotting chain coiled in the bell tower. Only she hadn't touched the chain. Kevin had startled her and she had slipped, clutched at the first thing in her grasp, the old black rain slicker hanging on a peg.

*I seen the coat. Black. Shiny. Maybe satin or something.*

Like rubber.

Coated with a something, invisible on the dark coat, something that had crusted into powder, come off on her hands.

Blood.

The purloined letter, the thing that had been hanging around so long it had slipped into the background, there and yet not there.

Cat peeked out of the closet, saw Dominic walking down the passage to the rectory. She scanned the cluttered shelves, found the key ring hanging on a peg underneath some spare overalls, the key ring Testa had handed over the day she had conned him into letting her into the bell tower.

She clutched the ring in her hand and moved swiftly to the bell tower door. The door was shuddering softly under the pressure of the wind spiraling down the stairway. Cat slipped the key into the padlock; she slipped into the stairway and closed the door behind her. The downdraft of air smelled slightly brackish, the marshy scent that it had picked up on its way across the bay. Her hair blew in her face, and she shook it free, turned her collar up, covering her throat.

It was the same. The boards criss-crossing the open floor, the coil of chain, the extension cord, the slicker hanging on the peg, the initials carved into the wall.

*What do you want to be when you grow up? What's your most cherished ambition? What's your dream?*

Billionaires and scientists, cops, lawyers and writers.

And to die in a state of grace.

He was unlocking his car when it hit him.

Cat had said she had brought Mark to the church, that Dominic had grudgingly agreed to take him in, fed him, given him a bed, called Maggie in to get him cleaned up, watch over him. He had seen Dom, talked to him, yet taken the food, stayed the night.

The following morning, he had thrown on the clothes Victor brought and fled. Because the person who had knocked on his door and handed him the bag was the person he had seen descending from Estrella Murillo's apartment. The person who had heard someone on the apartment stair and retreated to Murillo's apartment rather than confront and kill the intruder. Because the intruder wasn't part of the killer's agenda. Not part of the plan.

Victor strode back into the hospital, past the nurses' station and walked into the kid's room. The boy looked at him, startled, his eyes flashing with fear. Victor whipped out the picture, Dominic praying over Carmen Oliva's gravesite, tapped the figure standing at Dominic's shoulder. "This one? It was this one?"

And the kid rasped, "What did I tell you, man?"

She heard the footsteps scraping against the stone stairs of the passage, edged away from the door, keeping clear of the open shaft at the center of the floor, trisected with wood planks. She looked out the open archways. Too small to squeeze through and besides, it was at least fifty feet to the ground.

*Ladies, you do not give your back to the enemy unless you put him down and you can get free. Cornered, you wanna meet him head on.*

Cat pressed her back to the narrow masonry between the arches, felt the wind rush over her shoulder, blowing her hair in her eyes. She shook it free, raised her chin.

He stopped on the threshold and looked at her. Looked just like he had the night before when he had stood on her own threshold, when Ellice had said *Watch who you open the door to.*

*Come in, I was just putting on some water for tea. Letting the devil through the door was as simple as that.*

"Cat, what are you doing up here?" And the voice was familiar, the voice of a friend, and that's how the devil got close to you.

She pressed her palms behind her against the cold masonry. The night Danny had pulled his stunt their cries had roused Father Greg. Surely her screams would rouse someone now.

Had any of them screamed? Had any of them had time to scream in that last split second before the cut, before their life was released?

"Did you follow me up here, Kevin?"

"Yes, Cat."

"Because you wanted to know what I was doing up here? Or because you saw me come out of the confessional?"

"Because I saw that you had confessed."

"But I didn't." The emptiness in her voice surprised her. She thought she would have sounded strained, hysterical perhaps. "I wanted to talk to Dom, that's all, and he was in the confessional. I'm not justified, not reconciled, not restored to grace, not absolved of sin. So what do you do now? Kill me anyway?"

Kevin's blue eyes went blank as if concentrating on a math problem that wasn't all that difficult, just a bit more difficult than he had anticipated.

He took a step forward, one foot on the plank that cut a straight course between them; Cat kicked her foot forward, shoving her end of the plank toward the center of the floor, sent it plummeting into the darkness of the shaft. She kicked again, sending a second plank after it, opening the space between them.

"There are not enough of us, Cat." How reasonable his voice sounded, how normal. "Not nearly enough, and the ranks are diminishing. I thought I could do the most good working outside the priesthood, but you have no idea ... no idea what the world is made of."

"I don't want to know."

"Neither did I. But I found out. How evil it was."

"So you gave up?"

"No!" He sounded eager, as if he wanted very much for her to understand. "'Just as the Son of Man did not come to be served, but to serve, and to give his life as a ransom for many.' I forfeit heaven so that others may attain it. Those who were in the greatest danger of falling back into sin. And it didn't hurt," he assured he. He had begun to circle the perimeter of floor; Cat edged along the same course keeping the open space between them. He saw that if he continued, she would get to the door. He stopped, slipped one hand into the deep pocket of the slicker, drew out a small instrument that flashed silver, something short and sharp, like a letter-opener or a scalpel.

"Renay Harris fought," Cat said. Kate Auletta, TV sleuth, would probably have started him talking; Cat wasn't so sure about Kate anymore.

"We went to look over a house the neighborhood wanted to rehab. She was very enthusiastic about getting involved. That's how they are, you know, they come back to the church. They don't stay, though. I met up with her after confession, asked her to check out the house with me. Everyone in the neighborhood, they see me so often on my rounds, they don't think twice."

The purloined letter.

"A woman like that, she accepts the sacrament of penance, but she's bound to fall into sin again. Fall away from grace. And what's going to become of a woman like that if she should die before she can be reconciled to God?"

She and Freddy used to walk to confession Saturday afternoons, held hands and raced across the street lest they get hit by a car before they had confessed and gotten themselves back safe in a state of grace. One unconfessed sin tarnishing their immortal souls combined with one nut behind the wheel and it was hell and damnation for sure.

"But she didn't see things your way," Cat continued. "She fought you. So you decided to drug them. Make them more compliant."

"They didn't suffer."

"You took the pills from Isadore Testa, didn't you? And nobody thinks twice about inviting the parish deacon in for a cup of tea."

"They get so calm. And it's so quick, Cat, they don't see it coming. They don't have time to be afraid."

"And that's how it was with Estrella Murillo. And Tamara Montgomery? Sheila McConnell?"

"Estrella was working illegally. She had quit. She said she wanted to go home, but she wasn't a very resolute person. Tamara, well, a young attractive woman like that, she was already starting to talk about how much better the money was working at Nothing Sacred. Before long, she would have gone back to being a whore, so would Harris, so would Oliva." He paused. "It was most difficult with Tammy, because she wasn't living alone. We cleaned up together after a church dinner, shared a cup of tea. She was feeling a little lightheaded, so I offered to drive her home."

"And suggested a stroll in the fresh air to clear her head."

"Exactly. You always did have a good imagination, Cat."

"And why the interval between the Montgomery murder and Carmen Oliva?"

"I don't like to call it murder, Cat. I call it their release. And there wasn't an interval. It took a week for them to find Montgomery. Sometimes it takes longer."

Cat felt horror sweep through her, sapping her of her little reserve of strength. "Why did you choose those people?"

"I chose the ones who seemed weak in their faith. The ones who would have fallen back. If you want to save them, you have to catch them when they've been restored to grace, Cat. Catch them before they fall back."

"No one's unsalvageable," Cat echoed. "You just have to catch them at the right time."

"And for some people, that state doesn't last long." He sighed, heavily. "You start out thinking you can redeem the good. And then you see how much evil there is in the world, how ... how outnumbered you are, and you fight for each soul, and the devil fights back, and he's got the numbers on his side. And you see them restored to the faith for a moment, and you watch them slide back into the pit and it becomes some fiendish tug of war. There's only one way to win at that game."

"You cheat," Cat whispered. "You cheat the devil."

A pale smile flickered over Kevin's face. "You can't remove evil from the world. So you remove the world from evil."

"One sinner at a time."

"They weren't sinners when they died, Cat."

"That's right. They'd confessed. Been restored to grace. Reconciled." How could he stand there reciting this as calmly as if he were reciting the Mass schedule at St. Agnes? *In the name of the Father and of the Son and into the hole he goes.* "And Isadore Testa?"

"He'd been weak where women were concerned."

"You didn't lock their doors."

"What was the point? My work was done. I had no reason to prevent them from being discovered."

"And you didn't kill the boy at Murillo's apartment because he hadn't been redeemed." *God. God. God.* "And that's why you didn't kill me when I walked in on you at Isadore Testa's."

"I never damned anyone."

"And what about Luz Molina?"

"That woman they found Saturday morning? I didn't kill her. Why would I have killed her?"

"You're a liar." A sob cut off the last syllable. Cat swallowed, squeezed down the tears that were forming in her eyes. She had known Kevin since he was a kid. "It's over, Kevin."

"It can't be over, Cat. I have more work to do. Much more."

"It's over."

But he had stopped hearing her, was focused only now on what to do.

And then he decided, perhaps he had been calculating all along, stringing her along as she had him. He sprang. Leapt at her, spanning the ten feet of open space between them. Cat screamed, saw the flash of the instrument in his hand and instinctively crossed her arms, raised them to protect her face. She felt a weight fall against her, slam her against the wall. She felt her arm wrenched forward by the sleeve and opened her eyes, saw him falling back. She screamed his name, saw his head strike the wooden perimeter of the room, saw his outstretched arms; then he was swallowed by darkness. She screamed again, as she lost her balance and tumbled forward toward the blackness into which Kevin had vanished, twisted and grabbed at the rim of planks bordering the room.

She clung to the shelf of wood, hanging by her hands over the open shaft. She felt the rough edge of the wood cutting into her palms, looked over her shoulder, saw nothing but darkness below her, knew that it was a fifty-foot drop onto the hard earth of the crawl space below the church. She tried to wriggle herself up, inched her palm along the wood, felt her wrists straining under her weight. Her left shoe slipped off her foot; she didn't hear it hit bottom. The final surge of adrenaline coursed into her fingertips and she whispered, "God, God, God ..."

\*\*\*

Victor did not wait for Maggie to answer his knock, walked into the rectory kitchen. Maggie looked up from her cup of tea, startled. "Where's your brother?" Victor demanded.

Dominic came down the hall, donning a sport jacket over his dark shirt. "Victor, how's the boy—"

"Where's Kevin?"

Maggie rose from her chair, her flat blue eyes scanning Victor's face. "He was ..." she looked at Dominic. "He was in the church, I think."

Car doors slammed outside and a heavy, quick tread cut across the parking lot. A fist pounded at the back door and Dominic walked past Victor, pushed it open. Two uniforms stood on the threshold, spied Victor. "Lieutenant, we got two people out front."

"Keep an eye on the exits." He looked from Maggie to Dominic. "Anyone else in the church?"

Maggie began to shake her head. And that's when they heard Cat's screams.

She had worked her palms onto the wood, wriggled her rib cage onto the ledge. If she could swing one knee up she could roll onto the perimeter of flooring; if she tried and failed the effort might shift her weight, loosen her grip and she would fall into the void. She looked ahead of her, saw the curving metal rungs fixed into the wall. They had formed a rudimentary ladder, used to access the bells and the catwalk. They had not born human weight for many years. She watched with detachment as her fingers walked toward the loop of metal, saw them slip around it, almost as if they were not her own fingers. She inhaled, ready for the rung to pull away from the masonry. *I told Mats I would come right over Sherrie's, I promised him. I'm not leaving my kids without anyone. God, I'm trying. I'm trying to help myself. You're supposed to help me if I try to help myself.* She felt the sharp pressure of the ledge pressing into her breasts, swung her leg, the forward movement bringing the rung into reach. She let go of the floor with one hand, swiped at the rung. She felt her hand close over the cold metal, felt a vibration below her, pounding, and something that sounded like her name, with her last reserve of strength pulled herself upward and rolled onto the floor.

When Victor and Dominic burst into the room, she was lying on her back, the front of her suit covered with dust. Embedded in the stucco several feet above her was a sharp instrument, like a letter opener or a scalpel, planted in the wall.

"Don't move," Victor demanded. Cat turned her head, saw that his gun was drawn; he jammed it in his waistband and worked his way around the perimeter of the chamber.

"Cat, where's Kevin?" Dominic asked, looking at the space in the middle of the floor.

Cat said nothing, turned her head toward the wall and began to cry.

He wasn't dead, not when Dominic kicked in the crawl space panel and squirmed under the church ahead of the paramedics. Victor grabbed a flashlight from one of the uniforms and crawled in after him, swept the beam over the soft, cool sand beneath the church. There was a dark mound near the area of the church entrance and the two of them squirmed toward it.

"Nothing to anoint him with," Dominic muttered, coughing out sand. He grabbed a handful of the fine earth and pressed a cross onto Kevin's forehead. "Kevin ... Kevin ..."

Victor raised the light, saw the glow fading rapidly in Kevin's half-opened blue eyes.

"God, the Father of mercies, through the death and the resurrection of his Son—*Kevin!*—has reconciled the world to Himself and sent the Holy Spirit among us for the forgiveness of sins. I ... I absolve you from your sins in the name of the Father and of the Son and into— In the name of the Holy Spirit."

And Victor said, "Amen."

\*\*\*

They had put Cat in the kitchen. Monsignor Greg was somewhere with Maggie, calling Kevin's family and a couple uniforms stood at the door, shuffling their feet awkwardly, not knowing what to say.

Victor entered. Cat looked up, saw that the knees of his trousers were smeared with dirt. He held her shoe in his hand, knelt and helped her slip her foot into it. The act seemed to revive her. She stood, shakily. "I have to go to Joey's."

Victor stood. "Sit down, Cat."

"I have to get to Joey's. I told Mats I would be right there," Cat said thickly. She took a few steps forward, felt his body block her path. "I have to get to my children."

Victor turned to the uniforms. "Ask one of the medics to come in here if he could."

"I don't need a medic!" Cat's voice was shrill. "I need to get to my children. If you won't take me, I'll walk there!" Cat pushed at him, not seeing him, seeing only the door ten feet beyond that lead to the street.

Victor gripped her arms. "All right," he said, soothingly. "I'll get you there. But you don't want them to see you like this."

Victor called Raab, called Phil Long and told him to come take point, asked the police to leave them alone, pulled a chair next to Cat's and took her hand in his.

"He told me everything." She placed her trembling hands over her ears as if there were more horrible confessions to come, admissions she did not want to hear.

Victor disengaged her hands, held them tightly. "It's over, love."

"He told me ... He told me ..."

"Shhh."

"He sprang at me. I—"

"Don't say anything, love. It's over."

"What's going to happen?"

"The criminalists are on the way. Raab and Long will handle the scene. You'll get cleaned up so that you can go be with your family."

"Don't you want to know why he did it?"

Victor sighed, pressed her hand between his. "Even when I know the reason, I don't think I'll understand why." He thought of Sheila, the rest of them, killed for an obsession, a whim, a passion. What did it matter? The reason would not make them any less dead. "I'll leave the why up to the pop psychologists and the news junkies and the local talk shows. They'll keep it going, when they go into withdrawal, they'll go looking for another high. It's over, and you're alive and that's all that matters to me."

## CHAPTER TWENTY-SIX

Victor called Carlo and asked him to come by and get Cat. And when Carlo came, there was little that had to be said, no lengthy Q and A to run through. Carlo was a cop, knew what had to be done, trusted Victor and his people to take care of it. When they got Cat settled in the car, Carlo turned on Victor. "You thought it was Dom."

Victor nodded.

"It's why you didn't want me on the team. You thought it came to arresting my brother, I had a hand in putting him away, I couldn't take it, is that it?"

"That's right."

Carlo eyed him, remembered how he'd been regarded with anger and suspicion by a fourteen-year-old kid a quarter century ago, how he'd thought the shooting of that kid's father had ended any chance he might have had to stay straight. "I used to think about it sometimes," he said. "Worry maybe you'd go wrong, give your mom more grief. But you did all right, Victor." He turned to get into the car. "You're not attached, I'll introduce you to my sister."

"My mother has her heart set on a nice Latina from the neighborhood."

Carlo clapped him on the shoulder. "Tell her to lighten up."

In the rectory kitchen, Raab was lecturing the uniforms, who stood scuffling their shoes on Sister Maggie's pristine floor. Raab's voice was clear, unwavering. "There's been what appears to be an accident. The church deacon was in the steeple and he fell. Major Crimes will thoroughly investigate the particulars of this apparently accidental death, because I wouldn't want the media to have any unanswered questions regarding this apparently accidental death when I decide to release information to them. Are there any questions?"

The cops shook their heads.

"There will be no theories, suppositions or additional information leaked to the media. If anything other than the most cursory account of this apparently accidental death should find its way to the media, I will find the person responsible and I will see to it that that person has spent his or her last day in law enforcement. Are there any questions?"

The cops shook their heads.

"You're excused."

"Okay," he said to Victor, when they were alone, "here's how it plays: he had an accident. My investigators are going to look into that accident as they would investigate any suspicious death. I anticipate St. Agnes getting some heat from the city building inspector. I don't want any erroneous conclusions drawn, so I expect the investigation to be thorough. Take as much time as you need. I understand that as my investigators look into this suspicious death, they may come upon some evidence or testimony that points to the deacon as the killer of Harris, Murillo, all of them."

"We've got what I believe is the weapon," Victor said.

Raab nodded. "Well, we won't know that until the lab makes a thorough examination of the evidence. I don't believe we'll have any indication that Keller was responsible for these murders for at least— When would you say his funeral's gonna be?"

"Thursday or Friday, probably."

"Until at least the beginning of next week." Raab sighed. "I'm not mitigating what he's done. God knows. But there's people left behind deserve to be able to bury their dead without NewsLine90 in their face."

From somewhere else in the rectory came a low, rasping sob. Sister Maggie.

"They wanna salivate over this, they can hold their juice 'til he's in the ground."

Victor arrived Monday morning, felt the current of curiosity eddy in his wake. Stan was perched on Adane's desk, talking to her, looked up when Victor entered. "How's Cat?"

"She's fine, thank you. What's the word on the Keller autopsy?"

"Nothing yet. Testa's not finished and then he's got the Molina woman. Raab said to take them in order."

Victor nodded. "Adane, may I speak with you alone for a minute?" He walked into his office, closed the door after her. Adane was pale, faint crescents, pale blue underscoring her eyes. "Sit down, please."

Adane sat.

"How is Mary Grace?"

"She's as well as can be expected, sir. She'll be taking a leave from the prosecutor's office, of course."

"What about you, Adane, do you need a few days off?"

"No, sir. I'm fine. I'll be fine."

"If there's anything you need, I hope you'll ask."

"There's nothing, sir."

"I'll be attending Miss McConnell's funeral service this morning." He picked up the small stack of messages from his blotter. "I should be back by the time Mrs. Austen comes in to make her statement."

"Is that necessary, sir? I mean, in the light of what happened yesterday—"

Raab wants us to proceed as we would if the book were still open." He held up one of the pink sheets. "What's this one from Loeper's secretary? He want to see me?"

Adane bit her lip. "No, it's— I tried to put it off. I explained that you were attending a friend's funeral, and that we were in the middle of a very time-consuming investigation, but he got to Captain Loeper and Captain Loeper said you would see him."

"Who's 'him'?"

"That writer from *CopWatch*."

Victor paused. Might as well get it over with. "What time is he coming?"

"In about fifteen minutes," Adane said, apologetically. "I thought you might as well get it over with. I thought perhaps he might become overly curious or bothersome if we kept putting him off."

"You're right. Send him in when he gets here."

Cusack arrived on time, wearing charcoal slacks, a plaid jacket, olive-gray sweater. He carried a slick, black attaché case, sunglasses dangling from the index finger of his left hand, his right hand extended to Victor.

"Thank you, Adane," Victor said, ignoring the outstretched hand, waited until she left, closed the door before he sat.

"You have five minutes, Mr. Cusack."

Cusack looked awkwardly at his vacant hand, dropped his arm to his side. "I understand. After the rather dramatic mishap yesterday, I consider it good of you to see me at all. Of course, from a strictly promotional aspect, it can help the show enormously to use the site in the shoot."

Victor looked at his watch.

"Sorry, I'm know how limited your time is, and I heard you were attending the funeral of one of the victims this morning. Fascinating matter—from the perspective of someone in my field, that is." Cusack settled into a chair, glanced around the office. "I'm almost tempted to beg off the Dudek killing and follow up on these slasher murders. How is the investigation coming along, or would it be out of line for me to ask?"

"It would be out of line for me to respond."

"I hope, Lieutenant, you don't feel any animosity toward me because I had to go over your head to secure this interview. Captain Loeper felt quite strongly that your unit could use the positive PR an association with the television show could give. Tremendous advantage to the area."

"A murder investigation is not a television show. The ramifications last well beyond two hours, minus commercial breaks, and I don't believe that dramatizing an incident has any positive effect upon the community and could, in the matter of the Dudek investigation, possibly compromise the prosecution."

"Actually, Victor—may I call you Victor?"

"No."

Cusack stiffened, the crow's feet at the corners of his eyes freezing into hostile crescents. Victor saw a pair of small flesh-colored Band-Aids on his jawline. "Well ... I would like to go over your CV here and make sure I get the introduction accurate for your appearance on the show—"

"I beg your pardon?"

"You understand how *CopWatch* works, surely. The docudrama is first, then there's a half hour roundtable with a moderator and the principals. We usually have one of them lead the discussion with the actors who portrayed the people in the show. And of course, with your background, your presence in front of a camera, your work with the hate crimes—"

"I don't discuss that."

"Of course," he said, but his liquid inflection stated "Of course not, until I go to your superior." Still, there was a flicker of discomfort in his gaze that darted over Victor, trying to pinpoint the source of the lieutenant's hostility. "Believe me, I do understand how pressed you are for time." He scrambled for his attaché case, drew out a couple sheets of paper, handed them over the desk. "Here's a proposal for the sort of thing we have in mind, and the waiver. You could look it over when you have a few moments, there's no hurry. Filming won't begin for another four to five weeks at least, and the roundtable could be shot last. I'll give April Steinmetz, the line producer, your number—"

"Don't bother."

"Excuse me? I understood from Captain Loeper—"

"Captain Loeper asked me to see you. I've seen you."

The prim mouth went slack, mean. Victor imagined that mouth on Cat, those hands touching her, saw his loathing reflected in the visible shudder that passed through Cusack. Victor subdued his expression, rose. "I'll have Sergeant Rice show you out." He would not consign this creature to Adane.

"Lieutenant, I think you're making a mistake."

"We all make mistakes. We should try not to repeat them. Now, I'll have to ask you to excuse me."

Cusack rose, took a step back as though barring the door. "I'm not going to pretend I don't know what this is about. I don't know what lies the Fortunati woman told you, but I'm certain she conveniently forgot that it was she who made overtures to me."

"And Friday night? Was she the one who made overtures then?" His voice was barely audible.

*Tell me who put his hands on you!*

He had badgered it out of Remy, gone to the man's home, actually kicked in his door. He remembered the taste of the hatred, the white wall of fury that had clouded his vision. *You don't ever touch my sister again. You don't set your eyes on her again. You see her walking down the street, you turn and walk the other way.* It had amazed him to hear that the words sounded so dispassionate, that their composure reduced the man to a gelatinous state, cowering from the blow that never came. It was Victor's first lesson in control, the power of understatement.

"I think it would be best if you refrained from speaking Mrs. Austen's name again. And if you left immediately."

Cusack's brows arched in mock surprise. "Lieutenant, that almost sounds like a threat."

Victor's mouth relaxed in a thoughtful frown, considering the man's observation. "No, it was a suggestion. I believe it could be characterized as a threat if I said I would kill you unless you left immediately." The frown inverted. The smile began as a cordial arc and consolidated into something colder, deadlier without perceptible transition. He walked around the desk to open the door. "Now don't you think it would be a good idea if you got out of my office?"

Cusack clutched his briefcase to his chest as if shielding himself from a lethal thrust, hustled out the door.

Victor returned to his desk. The burst of laughter was so brief, so astonishing that a moment later, Victor's unit wasn't certain whether they actually heard it or not.

Depression corrupted her dreams, dragged her from her fitful sleep, but the scent that greeted her was the warm, rich aroma of cinnamon and coffee. She heard a murmur of voices and rolled out of bed, leaned over the worktable at her window and pushed the heavy drape aside and saw a line of cars parked along Morningside.

They were all here. She had made a superhuman effort, a truly Kate Aulettian display of self-command when Carlo had brought her to the christening party. Watching Cat fuss over Mats so he wouldn't be jealous of that baby, sitting for the family photos that Nancy shot, helping Sherrie serve the cake and coffee, they could not believe the terrible news that Carlo quietly circulated. They could not believe that through sheer will she could suppress her own horror and pain to keep from upsetting her children, from ruining baby Gio's christening party. They especially couldn't believe she would not need them to get through this crisis, of course she needed them, weren't they all family?

Cat shook her head, ruefully, but felt a weary smile tug at her mouth. Maybe if Kevin had had a family like hers ... no. No excuses, no mitigation. Cat pulled on her robe and padded down the stairs. Freddy, Ellice, Joey and Sherrie, Vinnie and Lorraine, were sitting at the dining room table picking at toast and coffee. Joey was dressed in a black suit and silver-black tie, an ice-blue shirt, Vinnie in charcoal-gray that matched his salt-and-pepper hair. Sheila McConnell's funeral, Cat realized.

More voices from the kitchen, Jane saying, "I can pack my *own* lunch, Uncle Carlo."

"That's not enough lunch for a growing girl."

"Cat," Freddy rose, went and put an arm around her. "We wanted to let you sleep some."

Cat felt a pulsing in her palm, saw that the splinters had left a pucker in her flesh.

Jennie came out with a coffee pot, began refilling cups. said, "You come get something to eat." Cat saw that her mother's eyes were red. "I just don't know. I guess I'm getting old. I just don't know anymore."

Mats came out from the kitchen, clutching a triangle of toast in his hand. "What don't you know, Nonna?"

Jennie wiped her eyes. "I don't know how come I got such good kids."

"Mom says she got us 'cause she kicked the other moms outta the way. Mom says when God was givin' out kids, she kicked the other moms outta the way and grabbed me an' Jane first."

Even Vinnie smiled at that. "Cat, you need me or the boys to do anything for you today?"

Cat shook her head, slumped in a chair.

Jane plopped her lunchbox on the table, put her arms around her mother's neck. Yesterday, she demanded to know what the adults were all whispering about and when they got home, Cat had taken her aside and told her that Uncle Kevin had had an accident and died, and Nonna was crying because she knew Uncle Kevin since he was a little boy.

"Did the paper say anything?" Cat asked.

Vinnie scowled. "Just the region section. Accident at the church, popular local pastor. But it looks like the building inspector'll come down on them, maybe make them tear down the steeple."

"Unless *CopWatch* comes through with some money," Lorraine suggested. She had finished a sweet roll; the prospect of a second and the subject of *CopWatch* put a light in her eye. "Tell them if they want to use the church, they're going to have to put up money for repairs."

Cat rose. "I have to get dressed. I'm going to drop Mats at preschool—"

"I'll do it, Babe," Carlo offered.

Cat shook her head. "Look, I guess it just hasn't hit me yet. It will, I know, but it hasn't yet. And I have to meet Steve in Northfield; I promised I'd make a statement about what happened at Mr. Testa's house. Let me get the important stuff out of the way before it does hit, okay? Let me try to see if I can act like this is just another day."

## CHAPTER TWENTY-SEVEN

Victor was putting his desk in order, preparing to leave for Sheila's funeral when Kurt Raab knocked on his door. Victor looked up.

Raab came in, closed the door, dropped into a chair in front of Victor's desk, his elbows on his knees, rested his face in his hands. "Victor, Victor, Victor, tell me on the day after we get our guy and he's the brother of one of my own ADAs and I gotta hold my breath for four days tryin' to hold off the press so his family can bury him in peace and I'm goin' nuts wondering if I should take Gino aside and tell him the truth, should I call the Montgomerys and tell them how it is and would they please not go runnin' to NewsLine90 until after Keller's in the ground, tell me when I got all this on my head, you did not threaten some hack TV writer works for the *CopWatch* episode they're gonna shoot down here."

Victor lifted an eyebrow.

Raab raised his head. "This guy Cusack gets me on my cellular, he's flipping out, he says you said you were gonna kill him if he didn't get outta your office. On the *cellular!* Where any bozo with a scanner can pick it up! I do not need some boob-tube bonehead tellin' the public a homicide cop's threatened to kill him."

"I didn't say I was going to kill him. I asked him to get out of my office. He said he found my tone to be threatening and I suggested a simple request that he vacate my office was not a threat, that it could only be construed to be a threat if I had told him to get out or else I would kill him." Victor paused. "And I think you would have to agree that if I had set out to kill him, he wouldn't have survived to file a complaint."

Raab looked at him. In math, they called it the unknown, and finding it was never hard for Kurt as long as he had all the rest of his data in order. Victor's file was a thorough as any of his investigators' and yet there always seemed to be about him some dark unknown that could not be set in type, deciphered. The trial following his undercover work had brought forth harrowing testimony; even Raab, who had handled the prosecution himself, had been shaken, yet impressed by Victor's composure as he sat on the witness stand hour after hour, day after day, nothing in the implacable voice, the immutable expression suggesting the dangerous opponent he had proven himself to be. "Look, Victor, I wanna be reasonable here. Just tell me what it is set you off. Help me out here."

Victor hesitated. "He insulted Mrs. Austen."

"Insulted how? She wanna file a complaint?"

"Not to my knowledge."

"Look. You partnered with Gino, you knew McConnell, you'd met Keller, this whole business has too many hooks in you. I think you should take a couple days off. Let things come back into focus."

"You suspending me?"

"Look, Cusack hasn't actually filed a complaint. Just maybe take a break."

Victor said nothing.

"A day. Go to McConnell's funeral and take the rest of the day. What's one day gonna matter?"

"All right. One day."

Cat arrived at the complex where the prosecutor's several bureaus were located, found Steve waiting for her at the side entrance. She felt the stares as they made their way to the second floor. Stan Rice caught sight of them, leapt from his chair. "Hey, Cat, how you doin', hon?"

"Stan, you know Steve. Am I late? I know some of you were going to Sheila's funeral."

"No, everything's fine, I can take your statement, that's no problem," Stan offered. "I don't think the lieutenant'd mind if we used his office."

"I thought Victor would be here."

"He's not coming back in today. Don't ask me why."

Stan began the questioning with a review of her discovery of Isadore Testa, Delareto watching with hawkish intensity, but not interrupting. Stan asked her to repeat a particular point once or twice, checked her responses against the report from the first officer. Cat observed that his questions were the right ones, that Stan's casual charm camouflaged considerable skill, and that people often made the error of underestimating him.

"Okay, now there's just a couple questions about, well, yesterday—"

"Mrs. Austen isn't answering any questions about what happened yesterday."

"Steve, I don't—"

"You wanna ask my client about what happened yesterday, you let me know what kinda questions you got in mind, I'll submit them to my client, and we'll see what we can set up."

Cat looked at him.

"Don't even think about it, Cat."

Stan shrugged. "No problem, counselor. That aspect of the investigation, we're in no hurry." That morning, when Raab had come by to talk to the lieutenant, he had told Stan, "Mrs. Austen, she'll have Delareto with her, he's gonna have her stonewall on the Keller business. She does, don't push it. She's probably still in shock, let her memory have a couple days to gel."

They were preparing to leave when the phone rang. Stan answered it, handed it to Cat. "Some guy asking to speak to you."

Cat took the receiver and said hello.

"Your charming mother told me you would be over Major Crimes this morning. Which means you won't have to come far to have brunch with me. And don't think of hanging up the phone, Allegrezza."

Cat's eyes darted from Stan to Steve. "Why not?"

"Because I'm sure you're curious to know why your paramour isn't in his office."

"There's a friend's funeral this morning."

"Well, there's that. But I'll bet he won't be back at all today. I suspect if he hasn't been suspended, he's been asked to take a cool-down day, at the very least. I'm at the Marinea Towers, room Two-Thirteen, I'll be waiting for your call." He hung up.

Cat handed the receiver back to Stan. "Why did Victor come in this morning, if he was going to take almost the whole day off?"

Stan shrugged. "He and Raab had a confab, when the lieut left, he said he was signing out for the day. You need to get in touch with him?"

Cat shook her head.

"What was the call about?" Steve walked her to her car.

"Just an interview. I've got several lines in the water right now."

"Cut bait," Steve said. "You need to go home and get some rest."

"You sound just like my family."

"I wish." Steve stopped her at her car. "Look, Cat. I keep thinking. Kevin. God. You told me one of those Colucci bastards was this slasher guy, maybe Trina Morosco's brother hell, even Danny, I'd buy it in a sec, but Kevin?"

"I'm trying not to think about it. It seems so ... disloyal to all his victims to feel anything for him at all, but it's not easy to forget. It's not easy to cut out all the things I was remembering about when we were kids."

"I'm gonna run over see how Mags is doin'. I heard Mary Grace is takin' a leave. You gonna be all right?"

"I'll be okay. I just have one errand to run, get some background for a piece I promised Ritchie."

Steve opened her car door. "The lieutenant or Raab have any problems with your statement, you tell them to call me."

"Why would they have a problem? I have nothing to hide."

"Don't lie to me, Gioconda, you hide plenty."

Cat kissed him on the cheek, got into her car and headed into Atlantic City, pulled over at a service station that had a pay phone, called the Marinea Towers and asked for room Two-Thirteen.

"I don't want to play games," Cat declared when Ted said "Hello." "And I'm pretty much immune to your threats."

"Threats? Interesting you should bring it up; I had a discussion with your lover this morning about that very subject. Threats of violence and how ugly an IA investigation could get for him if I filed a complaint."

"You're saying the lieutenant threatened you? I don't believe that."

"Really? Room service is actually quite good here. It's Two-Thirteen, remember. An hour? That should be time enough for you to check with your lover, validate my story."

"You can go to hell."

She got back into her car and drove into Atlantic City. Victor's car was parked in front of his apartment. He answered her knock, still wearing his black suit.

Victor drew her inside, shut the door, took her in his arms and kissed her. "How are you today, love? Did everything go all right at the bureau?"

"It went okay. I don't know how I am. I think it's going to take a couple days for me to figure it out and a much longer time to put it all in perspective. Mama's upset." She paused. "There was nothing in the paper, just an article in the regional section that reported it as an accident."

"It was an accident."

"Raab could be jeopardizing his career by not releasing any information to the press."

"What information? It's only good policy to complete the investigation and be sure of our facts before we release them to the public. That could take days, weeks. By then, you'll have a television crew in town and you've got the identity of the killer who died a month ago, versus filming a TV show right now. Wanna bet who wins the war of the headlines?"

"You'll never keep it from the press that long."

Victor's face set in determination. "But we can hold off at least until after Keller's funeral. His family did nothing wrong. They deserve to bury him in peace."

"Are you taking the day off?"

"Is that an invitation?"

Cat crossed her arms over her chest.

"I'm off for the rest of the day, yes."

"Then he wasn't just baiting me!"

"Who's baiting you over what?"

Cat pushed her hair behind her ear. "Ted Cusack. He told me you were in trouble because of something you said to him, and if I wanted to find out the details, he'd tell me in person."

"You're not going to meet him."

"Why not?"

"Love, that wasn't a question."

"What did you say to him?" Cat demanded.

Victor studied the stubborn pucker of her lips, leaned down to kiss her. She pushed him away. Victor sighed, resigned. "I don't recall my exact words. But I believe he inferred that if he didn't get out of my sight I was going to kill him."

"Why did you have to go and do something like that?"

"I didn't go and do it. He came to me. Loeper has been promoting cooperation between the real cops and TV cops, though I suspect that the distinction between the two is becoming decidedly shady in the public mind."

"Red Melendez is playing you on TV. That is, he's playing Victor Calderone."

Victor stroked his chin, thoughtfully. "Red Melendez. I think I saw him in some PSA recently. Doesn't he have a ponytail?"

"*And* an earring."

"Which ear?"

"*El derecho.*"

"Ah."

Cat's expression sobered, suddenly. She walked around the coffee table, dropped onto the couch. "Victor, why would you jeopardize your position just to intimidate Cusack? I never should have told you about what happened in college; that was seventeen years ago, it's over. Last night and this morning? As horrible as it was, I could pull myself together for the kids. I amazed myself, really. And if I could do that, then I can pull myself together enough to put up with some lecherous cop junkie for a couple weeks—"

Victor's glance fixed on hers. "What did you say?"

"I said ... I don't know what I said. What's wrong?"

"Nothing. I've heard that phrase used recently, that's all."

*I think he's some kinda cop junkie.* Luz Molina. Victor sat opposite Cat, took her hands in his. "Cat, I need you to tell me everything Kevin said to you when you were in the tower."

Cat hesitated. "Steve told me not to discuss it."

"All right. It's important for me to know, but if your attorney thinks—"

"No, I'll tell you. We have to trust each other, Victor."

"No, I don't want you to tell me everything, not just now. Delareto's right. But tell me this much: what did Keller say about Luz Molina?"

"Victor, it's so strange you would ask that. He denied killing her. And it seemed so odd. That he would deny it, you know? Except when you think about it, she doesn't really fit the profile of the other victims, does she? Kevin was obsessed with the notion that these people be pure of heart and soul when they died, and I don't see Luz Molina as a penitent."

"True. But then, Keller wasn't rational."

"But he was consistent," Cat argued, gravely.

Victor's mouth turned down in an appreciative frown. "'I have seen too much not to know that the impression of a woman may be more valuable than the conclusion of an analytical reasoner.' Sherlock Holmes."

"I'll bet Victor Calderone never quotes Holmes to Kate Auletta."

"That's the trouble with TV folk. No class, no imagination."

No imagination. Why would Kevin have denied killing Molina, what would have been the point, when he was so willing to admit to killing the others? Suppose Molina had been killed by someone else, what would a desperate killer do? He would probably attempt to mask the killing so that it would appear to be one of a series of crimes. Like the guy in Ritchie's TV drama.

And if Raab wasn't releasing the information about Kevin for several days, why not use those days to see if she could figure out some way to identify Molina's killer? There were two days until the *Chronicle*'s weekly deadline, and it would be something to occupy her thoughts, possibly get a head start on a lucrative story. If she knew where to start.

Start with people who knew Luz Molina. There were her neighbors in the apartment building, but they'd probably already been interviewed by the cops, and neighbors weren't always knowledgeable. After all, the Ufflander's had lived two doors down for ten years, and Cat had yet to see them at close range, exchange more than a casual wave. She didn't even know their first names, come to think of it, which was not unusual in a seasonal, sparsely populated neighborhood.

Who else had known Luz? Who had Luz known? Well, she had known Carmen Oliva and Tammy and Renay, known them from "back in the day" when they had all been in the

same profession, more or less. Carmen and Tammy and Renay
had been Easter's women. Maybe there were other Printemps
girls who knew her, swapped confidences with her.

And, too, Victor had exacted from Cat a promise that she
wouldn't go from his place to the Marinea Towers and Cat
had agreed, so since she was already in Atlantic City, what was
the harm in stopping by Printemps offices and asking to speak
to someone who'd known Luz Molina? The worse they could
do would be to throw her out.

Printemps Escorts was located in a newish building on
New York Avenue between Atlantic and Pacific. Cat pulled into
the ground-level garage, took an elevator to the second floor,
and was deposited in a deceptively shabby hallway, located the
simple door with only PRINTEMPS ESCORTS on the brass plate.
But the plate and the brass knob were polished and unmarred,
in an area where the onslaught of salt air corroded any brass
surface that wasn't subjected to meticulous buffing.

Cat rang the buzzer; the door buzzed in reply, clicked,
and she turned the handle. The Printemps sanctum was done
up in royal blue carpeting, walls papered in subtle ecru-on-
ecru stripes with a thread of deep blue running through,
blanched oak furnishings, lined draperies over sheers, over
shades that were pulled two-thirds shut.

Cat hadn't quite figured out how she was going to Kate
Auletta Easter into putting her in touch with Luz Molina's
pals. She decided to do the unKateable and opt for outright
honesty, when the course of her investigation made an unanticipated shift.

The MISS DETULLIO nameplate on the desk conveyed nothing; the face set off a tremor of recognition but it was the
walk, as the woman sashayed from a file cabinet to the desk
that pegged her: She was the woman from the open call, the
one who had shared makeup with her friend, Luz. Gloria.

*You're not doin' the trick, I'll book him elsewhere.*

"Gloria?"

"Yes?"

And when Cat had called Printemps that morning, trying to track down someone named Renay, it had been Gloria who had answered the phone.

"May I help you?" The eyebrows were high, smooth arcs that rose above the frontal bone. Skepticism yanked them almost to the hairline, but the eyes below were red-rimmed, the "Is there something I can do for you?" thick with suppressed emotion. The way her own voice had sounded yesterday. Sorrow, fear, for a friend who had gotten killed.

"I'm a friend of Luz Molina's."

"Who?"

*So that's how you want to play it?* "May I speak to Mr. Easter?" she asked.

"Mr. Easter doesn't see anyone without an appointment."

"You tell him Mrs. Austen is here. He'll make time."

"It might be better if you left a message."

"Fine. The message is his receptionist has been booking Printemps rejects. Did Luz Molina give you a kickback?"

Cat did not believe it was possible for those brows to get any higher without disappearing into the glistening waves altogether, but ascend they did. Gloria licked her lips, glanced over toward the door at the end of a short corridor. "Look, what is it you want?"

"Just a few answers. I saw you in the ladies room at the *CopWatch* casting call. You and Luz Molina were chummy."

The eyes flicked toward the door again, and she lowered her voice. "Okay, so what?"

"You call in the nine-one-one when you found her?"

"I don't know—"

"What I'm talking about? That's not original." She probably watched too much television. "Do you know who was roughing her up?"

"Jimmy does not allow his women to work the rough trade."

The office door opened and James Easter emerged with a stack of folders in his fist, his gleaming pate nearly brushing the door frame. "Well, hello there, Mrs. Austen. How's that brother of yours doin' today? Mrs. Easter's real upset about that accident over the church, said that deacon was a real upstanding man."

"My brother says in the book of John it states 'judge not according to appearance,'" Cat replied, gravely.

"Like just 'cause he's wearin' a dress, that don't make him a priest."

Cat realized that what she knew was confined to a very small circle, that as far as the public was concerned, there was still a killer at large. Easter had probably suspected Dominic all along, suspected him still.

"That might be one example. Another might be— Well, let's take Miss DeTullio here. A model of efficiency and loyalty. Who would have thought she would launch a thriving enterprise right under your nose, accommodating clientele with certain predilections that Printemps declines to gratify."

"You wanna run that by me in English?"

"You don't let your women get roughed up; someone wants to play rough, Gloria here puts him together with a willing companion."

"You been running bookings from my office, Gloria?"

"Look," Gloria asserted. "I never took business from you, I just worked out something with some girls who weren't your type, put them together with guys Printemps was turning away."

"And one of the girls was Luz Molina," Cat added.

Easter looked puzzled.

"They found her murdered in her apartment two days ago. She was a friend of Gloria's."

Gloria gulped. "Luz, she could always take care of herself."

"Don' look like it," Easter growled. "Who'd you sic on this gal Luz, Gloria?"

Gloria eyed Cat in sullen resignation. "Eddy. No, Teddy. Teddy Something. I don't know, it's always 'please-call-me-Teddy.' Real educated type. He was strictly cash and Luz, she was willing, so I don't know where he lived, but last week I ran past him over the Towers. Maybe he's got something to do with that TV show."

Cat rummaged in her bag, pulled out the *CopWatch* paperback. She showed Gloria the photo in back.

"Yeah. That's Teddy."

Adane got back to Victor an hour after he called. "You were right, Lieutenant, they're not the same blood type. Mr. Keller's blood type was A, the man who had sexual relations with Miss Molina was O. And another thing, the times of death, Mr. Testa's and Miss Molina's, are very close. Of course, these things cannot be fixed precisely, but they're close enough so that the ME thinks it would have been difficult for the same person to have committed both crimes. Logistically speaking."

"Thanks Adane."

"There's one thing more, Lieutenant. The criminalists didn't find any records or diaries in Miss Molina's apartment, and we're still checking on the phone numbers, but, well, there were flowers. Pink rosebuds in Miss Molina's apartment? So I thought I would just try contacting some local florists. And Rima's on Atlantic Avenue, they remember a man who bought pink rosebuds a few times in the recent past, most recently last week. The only reason the florist recalls it is because the man had been in again Friday and bought white rosebuds, paid for those with a credit card and had them delivered. The pink ones, he always paid cash and took them himself. The salesgirl remembered him because he kissed her hand when he paid her. She said even if she didn't remember his face, she would certainly remember the voice. She said it sounded like he swallowed motor oil. But of course, she has the credit receipt from when he bought the white roses."

"Edward Cusack."

"Yes, sir."

Victor was glad that Cat had decided not to meet him.

## CHAPTER TWENTY-EIGHT

Cat had told Victor she was not going over to the Marinea Towers. Of course, Cat reasoned, as she drove along narrow Pacific Avenue, she hadn't said she wasn't *ever* going over there, just that she wasn't going *right* over there. And since she had stopped at Printemps first, she hadn't exactly fibbed. Besides, she had given Easter an hour to have a heart-to-heart with Gloria and then contact the police. Or else. Cat had absolutely no idea what "or else" implied, but it seemed like a Kate Auletta thing to say. "And," she told Easter, "Gloria had better be intact when the cops come to question her."

"Looky here, I never raised a hand to a woman in my life, and I'm not about to start with the hired help," Easter had grumbled. Cat believed him. There was a pretense to his grumbling, and a glimmer of respect for Gloria's enterprising nature that she suspected might actually work to the girl's advantage.

On TV, women did the dumb things: They walked down ominous alleyways; they ran into dark rooms when something went thump; they hung around and said things like "Who's there?" when they should be beating feet. And they always had to confront the killer instead of just dialing nine-one-one and going home, getting some of the laundry done, starting dinner, reading to the kids. But Kate Auletta did take-out, had the quaint launderer, did not have kids, so she was at her leisure to do the dumb stuff, which somehow always worked out for her. And Cat decided, what the heck, *CopWatch* was cutting her loose, why not be Kate Auletta one last time be-

cause there was nothing she wanted more than to see Ted
Cusack's face when she tricked him into revealing he had
killed Luz Molina.

His suite was a comfortable sitting room, separate bedroom. He had left the bedroom door open, keeping the bed
in view. There was a table with a bottle of champagne chilling
in a hotel ice bucket and a pair of tulip-shaped glasses.

Cat had checked out the scene thoroughly. She had said a
conspicuous "Hello" to the girl at the reception desk, asked
for Ted Cusack's room number. Two-Thirteen was directly
across from the elevator; the fire alarm box and the stairs
were twenty yards to the left. Escape route brain-mapped, Cat
allowed Cusack to take her coat, said yes, she would like some
champagne and covertly unlocked the deadbolt that he had
locked when he turned to pour.

Cusack rose, smiled. "Allegrezza. I wasn't sure you were
coming."

Cat forced down her loathing. *By the time this thing is over,
they'll be giving me the damn Oscar.* No, what was that thing they
gave for TV, the Emmy. "If I want to work with *Copwatch* we
have to work together," Cat said, flatly. "It doesn't matter
whether I like it or not; if I want to get my consulting fee, and
a few features out of the shoot, I have to play by your rules."
*The bloody Emmy!*

"I thought you'd come around."

He was wearing the same outfit on the book jacket, or
similar at least. Tweedy jacket with honest-to-God suede elbow patches. All he needed was a pipe, perhaps a snifter of
brandy. He guided her toward a table in the corner and Cat
sat across from him, amazed at her coolness. *I can do anything,* she thought suddenly. *I'm not afraid of him anymore.* "So
tell me why you're filing a complaint against Lieutenant
Cardenas?"

"He threatened me." He clinked his champagne glass
against hers.

The sound recalled the Valentine's Day dinner at Carolina's. A lifetime ago. "I don't believe that."

"You ought to. You provoked it."

"*I* did!"

"Quite the macho stereotype, isn't he? Protecting his woman and all that. Red's going to have a field day, playing him."

"If you stereotype him, it'll be because you haven't done your homework. Or because TV doesn't scrape beneath the superficial."

"It's the audience that's superficial, dear. I'm just accommodating."

There was a knock on the door. Cusack excused himself and admitted the waiter, who pushed in a wheeled cart bearing two silver-domed platters, dinner service. Cat made a point of saying "Good afternoon."

"I'll take that." Cusack slipped the man a few bills, closed the door after him. Cat listened, heard the click of the lock. The dead bolt. *Damn.*

"What did he threaten to do?"

"He said he'd kill me, actually."

"You're a liar. Why didn't you file a complaint?"

Cusack placed a napkin and silverwear in front of him. How she would have loved this when she was twenty! Would have thought she was perfectly capable of handling him.

"I still may. Unless I can be persuaded not to." He lifted the lids on the platters, set them aside, sat.

Cat's fingers closed tightly against her glass, and she kept her arm from flinging it into his face with effort.

Cusack smiled. An easy, even inviting smile. "Still the small town Catholic girl, are we? That played when you were twenty, Allegrezza. I'm not sure you can pull it off now."

Cat swallowed. *Don't back down.* She leaned forward on her elbows, stared straight into his eyes. "Don't discount what I can pull off unless it's something you're sure you're not going to need."

He started. The alcohol flush rose, against which contrasted the pale rectangle of a Bandaid that peeked from the rim of the turtleneck. "You can threaten, too, Allegrezza. Not quite as ominous as the lieutenant, but quite bold enough. Odd, I am not seeing the two of you together. So tell me, what might I come up with that would persuade me to forget the Lieutenant's insulting behavior?"

"I can't think of anything you might come up with." And it hit her, like a physical blow: He doesn't matter. Nothing he had done had hurt her permanently. Maybe she wasn't Kate Auletta, maybe she wasn't even as savvy as Karen Friedlander, but she was doing all right, with every expectation that she would do better. *You lost your wife,* she had said to Victor some months ago. *You never lost yourself.* And Cat realized she hadn't lost herself, not really. Perhaps Cusack had robbed her of a part of herself, perhaps, in the anguish of losing Chris, she had misplaced a part of what she had always been. And now it had turned up.

She wasn't afraid of him.

Cusack misconstrued the silence, interpreted it as a change of heart and reached into his breast pocket to draw out a slender white box. Cat thought again of Valentine's Day, how close she and Victor had been to escape.

"I don't want anything from you."

"But I've gone to the trouble of picking out something that I especially thought you'd like. Do open it. Think of how little an effort is required to keep your dear lieutenant from charges of police misconduct."

Cat knew it would never come to that. Still, she thought it best to play along. She opened the box, and felt a swift constriction in her throat as if her heart had actually risen to choke out her scream.

He hadn't even had the sense to get a different chain for it, left it on the black silk cord tied in a bow. Cat laid it on the placemat in front of her, put her shaking hands on her lap.

Carlo had told her about such things. Killers who took some trinket from the victim, a necklace, earrings, a bracelet and actually presented it to a wife, girlfriend. Cat had not believed him, thought it was more wild cop lore, nine-parts falsehood, but her other brothers had insisted it was God's truth, and even her mother had advised "A man gives you jewelry, ask to see the receipt."

Cat cleared her throat. "Where ... where did you get it?"

"I beg your pardon?"

*This is what you get for doing the dumb thing.* She looked at the fiber of the cord, wondered if Luz had been wearing it when she died, if it held some trace of her.

"I ... in case I wanted to get a ... a chain for it or something."

"I hardly expected you to be so speechless, Allegrezza. Put it on."

Cat saw Luz shimmying up the church aisle, the green cross swinging between her breasts. *I can't. I can't.*

Cat had sat with Sunny and Misti when they went over the files, picked out the callbacks. They had looked over Luz's Polaroid, placed her in the Yes pile. Cat had seen it, seen the picture of Luz in her short skirt and wraparound blouse, the green cross perched on her cleavage.

Raab had said no, Victor was not to question Cusack. "Send Rice to do it. He's so laid back, fools people into thinking he's none too bright."

Victor agreed, reluctantly, hung up and his phone rang almost immediately. "Tell me you have not been suspended."

"Sorry to disappoint you, Lauren, no. Just taking a sanity day."

"Listen, dear, my client, Mr. Easter, relayed some information to me. I called your office and they said you'd left. I'm not interrupting anything, am I?"

"No."

"Well, I just thought Mrs. Austen might have dropped by after she spoke to James. I have to tell you, I do admire her ingenuity."

"When did she talk to Easter?"

"About an hour ago. She deduced, God knows how, that James' receptionist has been operating a little business on the side. James' employees have rather high standards in matters of civility and Gloria has been privately arranging to accommodate clients who are not inclined to be—"

"Civil. So the secretary's been booking Easter's turn-downs. She call in the nine-one-one on Molina?"

"Well, of course I'm not going to speak for her on that score, or to allow her to speak at all, without representation."

"Did Easter's receptionist tell Mrs. Austen who Molina'd been keeping company with?"

"You understand that Miss DeTullio kept everything cash and first name, but she thought he was someone affiliated with television. I believe she said his name was Ted."

"Why don't you put it on?"

Cat swallowed. "It doesn't go with what I'm wearing." She placed the white box into the pocket of her jacket, zipped it in.

"Aren't you going to thank me at least?"

"Thank you," Cat whispered.

Cusack picked up his fork, his knife, began to eat. "I heard there was a nasty accident at that church yesterday. I'm not going to say I'm sorry, I didn't even know the man, and it certainly will give the place some cachet as a location. We never did get together and look over the place, did we? Shall we plan on doing that this week?"

Nasty accident. Nothing could mitigate the enormity of Kevin's crime, but the fact that Ted had attempted to disguise his own crime, pass off Luz Molina as one of Kevin's victims sickened her.

"What's the point? I'm off the show."

"My dear, I thought the purpose of this meeting was to reach a little accord. A sort of détente. Besides, if Atlantic City offers this much in the way of drama, *CopWatch* may want to do more than one shoot here. Why, in just this past weekend, there were three more murders, weren't there? And the police no further to identifying the killer?"

Cat looked at her plate. Steamed salmon, string beans, rice with some flecks of red and green. "I believe the police think at least one of them may be the work of a copycat."

"What, the old man?" Cusack shrugged. He ate European fashion, keeping his knife in his right hand. "Probably a burglar, the old man surprised him, the crook's seen the reports in the paper, uses the same MO. That's the trouble with criminals, you know. Police, too. No imagination." Cusack put the knife down, took a sip of his champagne.

"I've heard the same said of television people."

"Really? And we all think we're so very clever."

"'The Devil whoops as he whooped of old: It's clever, but is it Art?'" Cat whispered.

"Kipling," Cusack smiled. "Very good."

*Wait until his hands are engaged. Until he's holding his fork and—well, just his fork. Then run. Leave your coat. Run. Don't wait for the elevator. Can't leave your coat, the necklace is in there, it's evidence.* Cat casually slipped her arms into her sleeves.

"Are you cold? Take a sip of that champagne."

*As soon as you hit the hall, start screaming.*

He smoothed his napkin on his lap, picked up his fork, reached for his knife.

Cat slid her palms under the table and with a sudden surge, threw herself upright, shoving the table and its contents onto him. She sprang for the door, right hand on the deadbolt, snapped it open, had her left hand on the doorknob lock when his elbow hit her cheek, slamming her head against the wall. Her knees buckled, and she braced her hand against the wall, sensed something descending around her neck. Instinctively, she slapped the back of one hand to her throat to break the hold of the belt that Cusack had looped, thrown over her neck. She felt it pulled tight, felt the metal belt loops imbedding themselves into her hand, felt her windpipe constricting.

She groped with her free hand, grabbed the back of his right hand, closing her fingers over his thumb, rotated outward, hard. Cusack cried out in pain, shook his wrist. Cat pulled at the belt encircling her throat, yanked it free. Cusack slammed his fist against the side of her head and Cat felt the floor lurch upward and whack her, hard.

Victor pulled up behind the two black and whites, saw Stan Rice's Camaro swerve into the lot, jerk to a halt.

"Look, Lieutenant, Raab said I should take care of this, everything's cool, why don't you—"

Victor's gaze panned the lot, froze on Cat's Maxima.

"Come with me," he said, strode into the lobby.

A young woman with shiny, blue-black hair stood over a monitor at the registration desk. Victor approached, his shield held aloft. "Get me Security," he demanded.

She raised a receiver to her ear, her mouth agape.

"Cusack." Victor spelled it. "What room?"

She punched a few buttons on the keyboard. "Two-Thirteen, sir."

"Get a security guard up there with a pass key."

Victor didn't wait for a reply, sprinted toward the stairwell, Stan and the uniforms in his wake.

Cat began to get up, stopped. *You gotta be careful kicking from your upright position*, Marco had instructed. *'Cause you don't wanna give him anything he can grab onto, and you don't wanna lose your balance. But in your ground defense*—he had curled on the floor in a fetal position, fists clenched to his breast—*you will go for the outside of the thigh, whatcha call your common peroneal nerve*— He snapped his leg straight. *Then you*

*will go for the back of the knee, which will put him down. And then,
ladies, you do not hang around to do a tap dance on his face, you get
your keester outta Dodge. Of course, he should drop a knife, a sharp
implement within your reach, you maybe wanna hamstring him, but
of course, being a police officer, you did not hear that from me.*

Cat curled on the floor fetal tight; Cusack leaned toward
her and she made her move, lifting her bent leg and snapping
her leg straight, shooting her heel into what Marco referred to
as his lucky charms.

Cusack's face looked like it was about to explode. Cat
struggled to her knees and hip-butted him aside, groped again
for the door lock, gave it a twist. She felt herself grabbed by
the hair, dragged toward the center of the room.

She threw her hands behind her head, gripped Cusack's
wrist with both hands and dropped her weight, yanking him
off balance, then shoved her weight against him. They fell to
the floor and Cat rolled on top of him. She did not get out of
Dodge. Instead, she planted her keester on his chest and began
a tap dance on his face with her fists. She felt his hands seize
her throat and wedged her arms between his, snapped them
outward to break his grip and began pounding his face and
chest, hand-over-hand, the rage taking hold, until she could not
feel the pressure of the blows on her fists, could not see the
purpling face beneath her, just pounded, pounded, pounded.

She did not hear "Police!" Did not hear the door crash
open. Did not hear "Cat!" Did not hear Stan stifle a laugh.
When someone grabbed her around the waist, she continued
to swing wildly, until her waist was released and her flailing
wrists were seized, and she was half-pulled, half-lifted away
from Cusack. She saw two men in uniform lift Cusack by the
arms, set him on his feet. Cat broke free and lunged, slamming her fist toward Cusack's exposed chin; the blow was
intercepted and she was dragged into the hallway, blocked
from making another lunge. "Cat, Cat, it's all right. It's okay."

Victor's voice was calm, soothing.

"... kill him. I'll kill him ..." Victor held her by the shoulders, looked back into the room where the uniforms were placing Cusack in handcuffs, one of them reciting Miranda from a three-by-five card.

Victor brushed her hair away from her face. There was a darkening under her jaw, a thick weal of something that had imbedded itself around her throat, and she saw the light of amusement in his eye fade rapidly, the gaze go opaque with fury. "Stay here, love."

He walked into the room. "Sergeant, please take Mrs. Austen downstairs and stay with her until I come." He turned to the uniforms. "You can leave him in my custody. I'll bring him in."

There was a heartbeat of silence, then Stan spoke up, his voice unsteady, "Can't do it, Lieutenant."

The uniforms wavered, not knowing whether they should intervene.

"It will be all right, Sergeant. I'll take very good care of Mr. Cusack."

Cusack was hyperventilating, a bead of blood forming at the corner of his mouth, one eyelid threatening to swell.

"I can't do it, I can't. Sorry, Lieutenant." Stan stood with his fists clenched, holding his ground though he might catch hell for it later.

The silence was brief, but it set Cusack quivering. At last Victor said, "Yes, you're quite right, Sergeant. Take him in," he said to the officers. "Someone from the DA's office will meet you at the department. I'm off duty, actually, so Sergeant Rice will handle the paperwork. I'll file my report in the morning."

He stood beside Cat, shielding her while the cops walked Cusack into the elevator. Then he took her back into the room, closed the door on the onlookers who were poking their heads into the hallway.

Victor looked at the food scattered over the floor, the champagne bottle leaking the last of its contents onto the carpet, the overturned table and chairs.

Cat thought she would feel some glee, some spiteful gratification at the thought of Ted Cusack going to prison for a long time. But she felt no emotion, nothing except the beginnings of pain nudging aside the waning fury; she realized that everything that was starting to hurt was going to hurt worse. She fumbled in her jacket and handed the jeweler's box to Victor. "Ted gave me this, a gift he said. It was the same one Luz Molina wore. The casting people have a snapshot of her wearing it."

She did not say *We've nailed that sucker*, though the words passed through her head; *CopWatch* would have followed up the close-up of the green crucifix with a shot of Kate and Victor eyeing each other with a your-place-or-mine? in their eyes. Or, maybe Kate would simply do a "Nice working with you," saunter off and you'd have the shot of Victor giving her that look, half admiration, half lust, and then you'd have to tune in next week to see if they got it on. Something titillating. Kate Auletta would not have cradled her cheek and whimpered, "My face is going to swell up like a balloon."

## CHAPTER TWENTY-NINE

Raab shrugged. "Guy who drew the case, Levine? He says Cusack will plead to involuntary manslaughter. He says he and Molina were engaged in some erotic something or other, you'll excuse me if I don't go into detail here, I think you get my drift, and she's asphyxiated and he panics and decides to cut her so it'll look like our killer." Raab paused. "Looks like the ME's gonna back up that scenario. I'm not seein' premeditation here." And with a swift glance around the office so that his secretary wouldn't hear "Tell me, when you went in, she was really on top of the guy, pounding the stuffing outta him?"

And Victor said, "No comment."

Except for the shift from toast and coffee cake to three or four varieties of pasta, the scene at Cat's house that evening was pretty much the same as it had been when she left to drop Mats at preschool. That, and the fact that her face had swollen on the one side, which was going to make eating difficult, consonants tricky.

Cat retreated to her room, took a quick shower and pulled on her gray caftan, plopped on the bed. She heard the sound of Mats' footsteps, her door opened a bit.

"Mom, I drawed you something in school."

"Well, come and show me, baby."

Mats came in clutching a paper, Jane on his heels with

two outfits on hangers over her arm. "Mom, I don't know which one to *wear* tomorrow? What's everyone *doing* over here? And what happened to your *face?*"

Cat studied Mats picture. "Who's that?"

"Baby Gio."

"Is he in a cage?"

Mats giggled.

Cat looked up at Jane. "I like the red-and-black sweater and the black pants. I bumped my head, that's all."

"*Again?*"

Again. "Bumped my head" had served her when she had passed out the night of the Dudek murder, after the tussle with Mark, when she had come home from the scene of Mr. Testa's murder, when she had arrived at Sherrie's yesterday looking like she had been worked over. She was going to have to come up with a new cover story, and thought, what the heck, give the truth a shot.

"Well," she said, propping Mats on the bed next to her. "Today? I was working on a story—undercover ... I was working on this story undercover, and I got a clue that this guy was a killer. He killed a woman in Atlantic City."

Jane slipped onto the bed, curled her thin legs under her.

"And so I went over to where he was staying to see if I could trap him into telling me whether or not he was the killer."

"Did he have a gun?" Mats asked. A gun would have made the story more dramatic.

"Not exactly. He had a—" Fork and knife and his belt. "No. And he sort of admitted he was the killer without intending to. He sort of gave me a secret clue."

"The *murder* weapon?" Jane demanded.

"Not exactly."

"What was it?"

"A necklace."

"A *diamond* necklace?"

Cat sighed. "Not exactly. But it was evidence. And when I got it and was trying to escape, he grabbed me and we fought."

"Karate?" Mats entreated, hopefully.

"Not exactly."

"And he *socked* you in the jaw," Jane concluded.

"Not exactly. He hit me and I sort of stumbled and bumped my face against the wall. And I got mad," Cat raised herself on her knees, drew her hands into fists. "And I elbowed him like that"—she wriggled her elbow between Mats' ribs—"and I knocked him down, and I punched him, and I punched him—" Cat jabbed at the air. Jane and Mats were rapt, wide-eyed. "And I punched him so hard I couldn't even feel my hands anymore, and by the time the cops came, it took *four* of them to pull me off him. And if you think my face looks funny, you should see the other guy."

"Is that true?" Jane demanded.

"Every word. Ask Victor, he was there."

Jane threw her arms around Cat's neck. "Mom, when I grow up, I wanna be *just like you.*"

Which is what every mother wants to hear.

They were assembled around Cat's dining room table when Cat came down; Carlo gave her a tap on the head, muttered "What'd I tell you. Nothin' but mush in there," but for the most part they skirted around the topic of Kevin's death, Cusack's arrest. Cat had been through enough. Jane interpreted their tentative conduct as intimidation, thought her uncles were afraid if they said the wrong thing Mom was going to beat them up.

Cat spooned soup tentatively while the rest of them worked on Jennie's *lasagna Siciliana*. Carlo sopped up sauce with a hunk of bread. "You know that kid, the one over ICU, they found his dad. Guy's a loser. Dope dealer. Mom's gone. Where's a kid like that gonna wind up? Prob'ly go into foster care. I don't know, these kids who got nobody gives a damn about them. Kids like that, what they need is someone to set 'em straight." Carlo pushed the hunk of bread around his plate, looking at no one in particular; Annie's eyebrows lifted in a sort of resigned shrug.

Cat got up and went around the table, poked Carlo's girth in the vicinity of his oversized heart. "What'd I tell you," she muttered, the consonants laboring past the swelling in her jaw. "Nothing but mush."

Later, after they had left, after Cat had put the kids to bed, Victor came by, found her lying on the living room sofa with an ice pack under her swollen cheek, a book in her hand.

"What are you reading, love?"

Cat looked up with a grave smile. "Wilkie Collins. *Blind Love*. Listen to this: 'Are there, infinitely varying with each individual, inbred forces of Good and Evil in all of us deep down below the reach of mortal encouragement and mortal repression—hidden Good and hidden Evil, but alike at the mercy of the liberating opportunity and the sufficient temptation?'"

Victor nodded. "Most of what I see reinforces the idea that the best predictor of what we are, will be, is what we've been. Cusack was what he had been when you knew him seventeen years ago. And I suspect, when those closest to him have the courage to examine the past, Kevin's acts can be put in that perspective, too."

"And after years of losing out to the devil, he found himself faced with unconquerable temptation and a liberating opportunity?"

"I spoke to Mark again; we put him with the state police artist and he gave a very accurate description of Keller. And we found Testa's prescription in the pocket of that raincoat. That, the murder weapon, the trace blood on the coat, I think we'll have enough to close the book, even without your statement. Cusack's signed a confession, so Raab gets to file away two big cases without bringing anyone to trial. Of course,"

Victor paused, "when the papers run Cusack's arrest in the Molina murder tomorrow they'll probably assume he's the killer in all the other cases, until Raab gets around to setting them straight. And even then, you can have all the blood and fiber and eyewitness testimony in the world and some people will still believe what they want to believe, if it makes for a better story. And if you changed your testimony ...""

Cat sat upright. "What, you mean lie? Not reveal what Kevin told me?"

Victor shrugged.

"Let the media cast Cusack as a serial killer?"

"You're not responsible for what the media might do."

"But I'm responsible for what I do. I hate Ted Cusack. But I'm not going to lie to exonerate Kevin, or to implicate Ted in something he didn't do."

"Kate Auletta would," Victor observed. "She'd probably figure that she owed it to a childhood friend to keep quiet about what he'd confessed to her, figure Cusack was a likely serial assailant, that he had murdered some poor callgirl, anyway. And years before, Cusack lied about her, now Kate gets her payback. Think of what a nice ironic twist it would give to the end of a screenplay."

"Kate Auletta makes me sick."

"Do you be lookin' at people when they be *day*id?"

The faintest ripple passed over Victor's impassive features. He presented an intimidating figure, in his black suit and tie, the black mustache arched in a permanent scowl, his impenetrable dark eyes. "Yes," he replied.

"Do they be gross?"

Twenty-four pairs of avid nine-year-old eyes were fixed on him. Victor interpreted the discreet cough from Jane's teacher to mean that this was probably not the moment to elaborate on the diverse appearances of the hundreds of corpses he had viewed in his career on the force.

"Most of the time, they look like they're asleep," Victor lied, diplomatically.

"Do you ever be shot?"

"Yes." He glanced at Jane. She was in heaven.

"Is it like on *Cop*Watch?"

"No. There's not much about police work that's like what you see on television. Most of the time, police work is somewhat"—he caught a flash on panic in Jane's eye and jettisoned "boring" in favor of "time-consuming." "On television, they solve an entire case in an hour. In real life, it can take days, weeks, months. Sometimes they aren't solved at all. Sometimes the police aren't the ones who finally solve them, either."

Jane beamed, knowingly.

A girl with a ponytail perched high on the left side of her head raised her hand. "How do you know which are the bad guys?"

"You don't know. Not by looking at them. Sometimes people who look strange or different are perfectly good and sometimes people who appear to be good do bad things. You don't go by what people look like, you go by what you observe. Evidence. Things that are left around the crime scene that might—" He hesitated, wondered if "indicate" was in the fourth grade vocabulary. "They might tell you who committed the crime. You talk to people who knew the victims, you look at what they did during a day, sometimes go back and examine what they did in the past. And you try to figure out who might have wanted to commit the crime and who would have had the opportunity."

"On *CopWatch*, they say think like the bad guys."

"Sometimes it helps."

"But if you think like he thinks and his thoughts get in your head, how come it don't make you start doing bad stuff, too?"

Victor paused. "It's not the bad thoughts that make you do bad things. You always have a choice, whether to do something bad or something good. To do something or to keep from doing something doesn't have a lot to do with what you're thinking, really, it has to do with whether you decide to act on what you're thinking. Like sometimes, you might want to hit someone or say a bad word, but stop yourself. Maybe you're afraid you'll be punished or you just decide it would be wrong; either way, you had a choice, right?"

The little boy nodded, awestruck at this concept of self-control.

"And in the end, that's what it comes down to," Victor said, praying he could bring this thing to a close, wondering if he had come out ahead of Cardozo's Cakery on points. "It's not what you look like, it's not what you think in your head, it's what you do. We all look different, think different thoughts"—*should have said, Have* diverse *thoughts*—"but in the end, all that matters is how we behave."

They were silent. There, he'd skated across the issue of differences, even thrown in a smattering of morality. At least they looked impressed. "Are there any more questions?"

The girl with the ponytail raised her hand again. "Lieutenant Cardenas, are you *married?*"

There was no trace of despair in Dominic's service, no waning of conviction, though it had been preceded by a funeral each day that week. Cat had gone to Luz Molina's service the day before, smiled as Dominic mesmerized the mélange of professional sisters who showed up, suspected that more than one of them would take him up on his promise of salvation; that for each life Kevin had taken away, one had been drawn back to the faith.

Cat was surprised to see that Victor was not the only member of his unit to attend Kevin's funeral, for Detective Adane was there, too, standing next to Kevin's sister, Mary Grace. The Kellers had all come back, stood beside the open grave stoically as Dominic pronounced the final benediction. The old crowd was there, too: Danny Furina, looking dapper in a dark overcoat, costly suit; Rose Cicciolini, pregnant for the fifth time; Steve Delareto, calm and dignified; Trina Morosco, who had restored Kevin's battered form to wholeness. Owen Johnson, a judge married to an ADA, who had passed on presiding over the Cusack arraignment because of his acquaintance with Mrs. Austen, declined, too, because what Cat had done to Cusack was too reminiscent of the time she had ambushed and beat up Tony Colucci when Tony called Owen a nigger; Louie Cicciolini, his head bandaged, one arm in a sling, leaning on his mother; and the Colucci twin who was not currently incarcerated. James and Elizabeth Easter.

Victor gave his arm to Jennie, who was weeping openly, weeping for little Kevin, the stray who came in from the cold of the Keller home for a glimmer of warmth at the Fortunati table. And then Dominic concluded, "In the name of the Father and of the Son—"

Cat looked up and her eyes met Freddy's and she saw, reflected, the spasm of giddiness—*and into the hole he goes*—and she held her breath, looked down at the ground until the sensation passed.

Afterward, Cat was maneuvered away from the crowd by the Easters and Easter introduced Cat to his wife. "I expect I owe you an apology, Mrs. A., what I was thinkin' about your brother."

Cat hesitated, didn't know what she should say.

"Hey, look, I got the picture. I don't get it, but I got it, you know what I mean?"

"Yes. I know what you mean."

"C'mon, Betsy, let's get you out of the cold."

"In a minute. I'd like to say something to Mrs. Austen. And I think you need to go have a word with Father Dominic, ask his forgiveness for what you've been thinking, James."

To Cat's amazement, Easter replied with a meek, "Yes, Betsy," strode off to where Dominic was talking to a couple of the Kellers.

"Jackie Wing speaks highly of you, Mrs. Austen. I'm glad to meet you at last."

"I wish the circumstances were better."

Beth looked toward the gravesite, an ethereal calmness in her eyes. "I blame myself, you know. I brought them into the congregation, you see. I met Renay when she was in the hospital. Tammy came to visit her. Carmen was a friend of hers. Estrella Murillo's boss serviced the medical suite around the corner from where I work. Sometimes when people are looking for something, a word at the right time turns them in another direction." She looked toward her husband who was standing beside the limo, waiting. "Now, I don't know if I did right ..."

"I think we can all blame ourselves for something, give in to that 'I should have done this, I should have done that.' Sometimes we have to forgive God, which really means to forgive ourselves, because God doesn't require our forgiveness."

"That's very wise, Mrs. Austen."

"Cat. Everyone just calls me Cat. Why does he call you Betsy?"

"That's what they called me when I was a girl. That's when we met, you know. I was nine. I told my mother I was going to marry him." Beth smiled. "And I got on with my education while he got all that running around out of his system and when he was ready to settle in, there I was. And don't you just know, he still thinks getting married was all his idea. I know he's a sinner, but so are we all. And I think if I just do like I did, just wait him out, sooner or later, he'll come into the faith."

"And think it's all his own idea?"

Beth nodded toward her husband who was having an earnest conversation with Dominic, smiled.

Victor walked Jennie to her car. She had insisted on opening her home to the mourners, because the Kellers were all from out of town except for Maggie, who lived in the convent, and Mary Grace. "And you know," she muttered to Victor, "Maggie told me she lives way out by Hamilton township. And I figure the way her and that lady detective work long hours, which one of 'em's gonna have time to do any cooking?"

Victor looked down at her.

"Don't look at me like I don't know what's what. I know plenty. You follow after the boys; I'll wait around for Cat 'til she's ready to come. Annie an' Nancy, they'll get the food started."

Victor looked up, saw Cat talking to Beth Easter.

"No, you go, I'll give her a lift."

"Let her have a little time to herself. She and Kevin, they grew up together."

"Jennie—" he gave her a discreet wink. "Don't talk to me like I don't know what's what. I know plenty."

Victor waited until there was no one left but the two of them, save for the groundskeepers who began laying earth on the coffin. He got the sheaf of white narcissi from the trunk of his car, handed them to her.

"It's today, isn't it? I thought maybe you hadn't had time to pick up any flowers. Is it near here?"

Cat looked at him. "Across the drive, under those two maples."

"We can walk it, then."

"Victor, I can always come by later."

"We're here now."

"Why don't you go on with the family?"

"I'll wait for you. Then we'll go together."